With its memorable characters, rich atmosphere, and shrewd plot, *Without Blood* is a welcome addition to Montreal noir.

— Kathy Reichs, author of the Temperance Brennan Bones series

With a strong Montreal setting and a twisty, dual-strand plot that keeps you guessing, Martin Michaud's *Without Blood* is the real thing.

— Peter Robinson, author of the Inspector Banks series

Atmospheric and compelling, *Without Blood* is a spine-chilling read with an intensely memorable cast.

— Ausma Zehanat Khan, author of *A Deadly Divide*

Praise for the Victor Lessard Thriller *Never Forget*

Never Forget will leave you bloodless, and I mean that in the nicest possible way.

— Alan Bradley, author of the Flavia de Luce series

A raucous crime thriller.   — *Publishers Weekly*

[An] immersive thriller full of darkness, loathing, and vengeance.
— *Montreal Review of Books*

A fine crime novel featuring a cast of well-delineated characters and a plot that demands the reader's undivided attention.
— *Booklist*

Never Forget is a crackerjack read. Michaud artfully constructs the world of the Montreal police and a broad cast of characters while keeping his eye steady on ways to ratchet up the tension at every turn.

— *Quill & Quire*

Martin Michaud is a master at twisty storytelling and compelling atmosphere. This kept me on the edge of my seat from start to finish. I can't wait to read Lessard's next case!

— Catherine McKenzie, author of *I'll Never Tell*

Michaud is at his best recalling ... fraught times through the cooler lens of our present day. It's great to see Canadian history used to such good effect in a story that resonates as well today as when it happened.

— Margaret Cannon, *Globe and Mail*

A VICTOR LESSARD THRILLER

MARTIN MICHAUD

THE DEVIL'S CHOIR

Victor Lessard Thrillers

Without Blood
The Devil's Choir
Never Forget

MARTIN MICHAUD

THE DEVIL'S CHOIR

A VICTOR LESSARD THRILLER

Translated by Arthur Holden

DUNDURN
PRESS

Publisher: Scott Fraser | Editor: Shannon Whibbs
Cover designer: Sophie Paas-Lang
Cover image: istock.com/Instants
Printer: Marquis Book Printing Inc.

Library and Archives Canada Cataloguing in Publication

Title: The devil's choir / Martin Michaud ; translated by Arthur Holden.
Other titles: Chorale du diable. English
Names: Michaud, Martin, 1970- author. | Holden, Arthur, 1959- translator.
Description: Series statement: A Victor Lessard thriller ; 3 | Translation of: La chorale du diable.
Identifiers: Canadiana (print) 20210168129 | Canadiana (ebook) 20210168218 |
   ISBN 9781459742703 (softcover) | ISBN 9781459742710 (PDF) | ISBN 9781459742727 (EPUB)
Classification: LCC PS8626.I21173 C4613 2021 | DDC C843/.6—dc23

We acknowledge the support of the Canada Council for the Arts and the Ontario Arts Council for our publishing program. We also acknowledge the financial support of the Government of Ontario, through the Ontario Book Publishing Tax Credit and Ontario Creates, and the Government of Canada.

Care has been taken to trace the ownership of copyright material used in this book. The author and the publisher welcome any information enabling them to rectify any references or credits in subsequent editions.

The publisher is not responsible for websites or their content unless they are owned by the publisher.

Printed and bound in Canada.

Dundurn Press
1382 Queen Street East
Toronto, Ontario, Canada M4L 1C9
dundurn.com, @dundurnpress 𝕐 𝐟 ◉

To Geneviève

To my family

And to those who are dear to me,
who struggle against illness in silence, courageously,
without ever surrendering to self-pity

Be sober, be vigilant;
because your adversary the devil,
as a roaring lion, walketh about,
seeking whom he may devour.

— Saint Peter

Fanaticism is a plague
which, from time to time,
produces seeds capable of infesting the earth.

— Denis Diderot

The bayonet plunges into a swamp of entrails.

Dulled at first, the pain takes a moment to arrive. The blood glides over his skin.

Clutching the handle, young Carbonneau stares at his abdomen as though it were an oddity, and suddenly understands the meaning of what he's just done.

Seppuku.

The boy who probed his thoughts is observing him closely. The other one, the Asian, is keeping his distance. Young Carbonneau's screams bounce off the bedroom walls and wash over the astronauts on the wallpaper.

How could he have let himself be talked into this?

Val-d'Or
April 1985

The seven-year-old boy watches through the window as the wind shakes the trees' high branches. Ice crystals whirl in the air, settling on the ground in a carpet of frost.

He puts on his duffle coat and woollen toque, then slips his sheet music into his knapsack. As he goes down the stairs to the main door, he glances toward the nave. It's almost empty. Only a few worshippers are still kneeling there. Among them is a woman in a fur coat who seems to be praying fervently.

Her lips are moving in silence.

He can't hear her. He doesn't know her. But he does know that she's asking God to forgive her sins and watch over her husband, who is gravely ill. He also knows that the husband will die in the next few hours.

The Mass was magnificent, as it is every Sunday. The sermon was stirring.

He loves singing in the choir.

Despite his young age, he's learned all the pieces with ease. The parish priest, who directs choir rehearsals, is always choosing him to sing the solos.

He's about to leave the building when someone calls out.

"Just a minute, my boy. I'd like you to meet someone."

He doesn't need to look to know who the speaker is: he recognizes the priest's voice.

Without a word, the boy follows him to the sacristy.

Another man in a cassock is waiting for them.

The priest says the man's name, but the boy pays no attention to such details.

He looks into the eyes of the new arrival, as he does whenever he meets someone for the first time.

In this case, he sees nothing.

The conversation drags on. The boy is tired. He wants to go home.

He isn't scared that his mother might worry — if she were still alive, she'd be blind drunk by now, sprawled at the bar in one of the many watering holes on 3rd Avenue — but the man in the cassock isn't letting up. He peppers the boy with questions.

At last, the interview ends.

The priest gives him some candies in a kraft paper bag.

Despite the lash of the cold air, the boy strides without haste toward the youth centre where he lives.

At the window, the man in the cassock watches him walk away through the snow.

He's the one.

So much weight on such frail shoulders.

Montreal
May 12th, 2008

"Death is worth living through."

I heard that sentence a few hours ago. Take it from me, a statement like that makes you freeze. It encrusts itself on your consciousness.

The man who spoke those words has vanished. Lucky for him. If I got my hands on him, I'd show no mercy. For starters, I'd pistol-whip him in the mouth, knocking his teeth out. Then, with the barrel of my Glock tickling the back of his throat, I'd coldly squeeze the trigger.

As I watched his brains splatter the walls and his dark soul slip out through the window, I'd say in a casual voice:

"Death is worth living through."

Thus endeth the lesson.

I'm awake again.

I know exactly what's happening. I can see the ambulance attendants working feverishly. They've pulled out all the stops: IV tube, catheter, oxygen mask. There's already something cadaverous about my pallor.

I can't speak.

In medical jargon, I'm in a state of shock.

That's how one of the attendants described me as he talked to someone on the phone.

The ambulance is racing through the night, siren howling, headlight beams stippled by the rain.

The rain …

For seven days, Montreal's been caught in a ceaseless downpour. Tempers are frayed. Everyone feels sticky.

When will it end?

My leg is in bad shape.

I can see a twisted bone poking through mangled flesh.

The attendants have managed to stop the bleeding, but the short one tells his partner that the leg may have to be amputated. They think I can't hear. They think I'm out cold. I've just closed my eyes to cope with the searing pain.

I'll need all my strength later on.

And nobody's going to amputate my leg. I'll kill the first guy who tries.

Got it?

I can't feel anything anymore.

Not the pain, not my body, not the sting of ammonia hanging in the air.

I open my eyes. Blood has soaked through the dressing on my leg.

That can't be good.

Does a person know when he's going to die?

Do the body's restraints fall away little by little as the spirit slides into the reaper's endless embrace?

The ambulance attendants look at me.

"We're losing him," the short one says.

I can feel my heart slowing down.

"Hang on, Lessard," the tall one says. "We're almost at the hospital."

I know, I know …

You're probably wondering how I ended up in this mess.

It all started seven days ago. In the rain.

THE EXODUS OF THE FLIES

*Feats of valour. Legends are born: the garrulous flies
come and go in the mouths of the dead.*
— Claude-Michel Cluny

1

Montreal
A week earlier, May 5th

Simone Fortin rests her head on Victor Lessard's shoulder.

Lessard is holding his umbrella at an angle, trying to shield her against the torrential rain. After a moment, he lowers the umbrella and lets it fall to the ground.

It's hopeless. They're soaked.

The detective sergeant's arm is draped over the young woman's shoulders. He pulls her close. She's holding on to his waist.

Simone is crying. So is Lessard.

Though the rain hides his tears, he's making no effort to conceal them.

A few weeks after the actual anniversary, they're marking the sad occasion once again.

They're at Notre-Dame-des-Neiges Cemetery, where, for a moment, time stands still, allowing Simone Fortin to recall the friend who was like a sister to her, and letting Victor Lessard remember a passion that was snuffed out after its first brief spark.

Ariane Bélanger was only thirty when she died, cut down in her prime by the stroke of a crazed killer's knife.

From the cemetery, they walk arm in arm along Côte-des-Neiges Road toward the café where Lessard talked to Ariane for the first time.

Simone breaks the silence as she looks at Lessard appreciatively. He's wearing designer jeans, a black T-shirt, a well-tailored jacket, and a pair of running shoes.

"You look great, Victor. I can't get over how much weight you've lost!"

Taken aback by the compliment, Lessard reddens and growls something unintelligible. Simone is right. He's lost nearly forty pounds since the last time they saw each other.

They step into the café.

Apart from a couple of freelancers lingering over their coffee as they take advantage of the free Wi-Fi, the place is almost empty. The waitress, a barrel-chested woman with a head like a shrimp, comes to take their order.

"I'll have a decaf double lungo with a little hot milk," Lessard says.

Simone gives him an impressed glance.

"How can you possibly remember all that? I'd like a regular coffee, please. Black."

Lessard shifts in his chair.

He wonders how the young woman can seem so lighthearted when he feels so numbed by his emotions. Every time they get together, the ghost of Ariane Bélanger hovers over them, and Lessard is pulled back into the nightmarish events that led to the tragic deaths of Ariane and Constable Nguyen. He and Simone have never discussed the subject. He supposes she's just more resilient than he is.

"How are things at the hospital?" he asks, to break the ice. "Still doing emergency work in Trois-Pistoles?"

"Yes. But I'm also completing a specialization in gastroenterology."

"That's gotta be a barrel of laughs," he says disgustedly. "Spending all your time poking around in people's shi— I mean ... you get the idea."

Simone certainly does get the idea, and she can't help chuckling.

"There's more to it than colonoscopies, Victor. It's a fascinating field. There have been some great advances lately."

"Yeah, well, it's still gross. How's Laurent?"

"Terrific. He's at the hotel with Mathilde."

Though he hasn't seen Mathilde in a while, Lessard has fond memories of Ariane's young daughter, whom Simone adopted after Ariane's death. Simone occasionally emails him pictures of the child. And he always sends Mathilde a present for her birthday.

"Are you and Laurent an item yet?"

"I wouldn't say we are, but I wouldn't say we aren't. We're happy. We support each other."

"Has he fallen off the wagon?"

"No. It's tough, sometimes, but he always gets through. What about you, Victor? How's it going? How are things with Véronique?"

Lessard's expression darkens.

This is the question he's been fearing, but he won't try to dodge it. He's about to launch into his answer when his cellphone rings. He sighs.

"Sorry, Simone ... Hello? ... Now? ... No, I was just having a cup of coffee ... hang on." He takes out his notebook. "Okay, forty-one thirty-nine Bessborough. Got it."

The cop rises wearily from his chair.

"I have to go. Sorry."

Simone needs no explanation.

"We're in town for a few more days before heading back. If you have any free time, it would be lovely to go out for dinner with Laurent and Mathilde."

He leans down to kiss her cheek.

"I'll call you. I promise. Give Mathilde a hug for me."

He walks back to his parked Corolla.

I'm like an oncologist. I offer people hope without knowing whether I'll actually keep my word.

Death seems to be part of his karma today.

First there was the visit to Ariane's grave, and now this call from Nadja Fernandez. Without going into details, she's just let him know that they have a homicide on their hands. The investigation team is waiting for him at the scene.

His rust-eaten car is speeding through the rain when he sees Véronique Poirier's name on his caller ID.

He picks up at the last moment.

"Yes?"

"It's me," Véronique says. "Is this a bad time?"

"No, but I can't talk for long. Something urgent has come up."

"Okay ... Listen, we've been over this more than once ..." Véronique hesitates, but her tone is calm and detached.

Too detached, Lessard thinks.

"You need to come and get your stuff, Victor."

He closes his eyes.

For weeks now he's been putting the moment off, hoping that Véronique would change her mind — telling himself that she might start missing him, that she might realize they can't live without each other.

He and Véronique shared a carnal passion, a sensuous interlude during which he felt like he was being reborn. Since their break-up, he's been wishing he'd never met her. Yet the relationship did have some positive effects: it prompted Lessard to adopt a healthier lifestyle (he now drinks decaf, eats mostly vegetarian, and goes to the gym three times a week); to take an interest in art (Véronique is a painter); and to experience unrestrained eroticism (apart from Ariane, he'd only had a single sexual partner, his ex-wife, whom he'd been with since his teens). Véronique also introduced him to trendy boutiques. He now knows where to buy clothes and how to dress with taste.

The problem was that, being unfamiliar with the rules of dating, he was no good at respecting boundaries. He didn't know when to call, when not to call, when to show interest, and when to keep his distance.

It's clear, in retrospect, that the relationship went sour when Lessard started spending most of his free time at Véronique's con-do instead of at his place. One evening, he showed up at her door, wearing a smile and holding a box filled with his belongings. He explained that he'd lent his apartment to his son Martin for a few months. Véronique's welcome was icy. Lessard had jumped without a parachute. The resulting free fall ended with a brutal impact that brought him perilously close to hitting the bottle again.

"You seem so cold, Véronique, so distant ..."

"I'm not cold, Victor. I'm just not in love with you anymore."

"Were you ever?" he asks softly. "You and I weren't a real couple. I'll tell you one thing: I'll never love for two again."

Cold silence greets this remark.

"Come and get your things when you can."

. . .

After crossing the security perimeter established by Constable Thibodeau at the intersection of Terrebonne Street and Bessborough Avenue, Lessard parks his Corolla in front of 4139 Bessborough. It's a single-family home, clad in white aluminum siding. Lessard is familiar with the neighbourhood. His daughter Charlotte's best friend used to attend the school at the end of the street.

Several patrol cars and four ambulances have pulled up haphazardly nearby, their emergency lights flashing. The mobile command post — or MCP — is parked thirty metres south of the house.

Tanguay has brought out the heavy artillery, Lessard thinks.

As he walks, he notices a recycling bin in the driveway and a garbage bag at the curb.

Several uniformed cops are standing in a circle on the neighbouring lawn, smoking and talking as they wait for orders. Lessard nods to them as he goes by. He's known most of them for years.

Fernandez emerges from the house and greets him on the porch. She answers the question before he can ask.

"Domestic murder-suicide. They're all dead — father, mother, three kids."

"The father did it?"

"Sure seems that way."

Lessard feels like an arrow has just pierced his heart. A distant memory comes back.

He knows he's breaking the rules.

He's supposed to go straight back to the house.

But Marie is finally letting him walk her home.

She's so beautiful in her sundress.

His brother Raymond haunts him with a silent reproach.

"You okay, Victor?"

Lessard snaps back to reality. He nods and blinks.

MARTIN MICHAUD

"Hunting rifle?" he asks in a weak voice.

"No. He killed them with an axe. I'm warning you, it's not pretty. Total bloodbath."

"Who found them?" Lessard asks.

"The cleaning lady. She's at the MCP with Macha Garneau."

"Did you question her?"

"She saw nothing. Knows nothing."

"Any note? Any kind of message?"

"Not for the moment."

"Who's in the house?"

"Just Doug Adams and his assistant, looking for prints, and the blood-spatter specialist. I've asked Sirois and Pearson to question the neighbours. Tanguay's at the MCP. He wants to see you when you're done here."

The detective sergeant makes a face. He and Commander Tanguay have been on bad terms since he got back from his leave, following the investigation during which he met Simone Fortin.

Nothing new there. Lessard and Tanguay had already been at daggers drawn.

"Sorry, Nadja. Where's Berger?"

"Oh, right. I forgot to tell you. He's come and gone. He doesn't know whether he'll have time to do all five autopsies himself."

Lessard is barely listening.

He takes a deep breath and puts his hands in his pockets so that Fernandez won't see that they're shaking. He has no desire to go inside. No desire to be carried back thirty years to his own father's murderous rampage.

But what choice does he have?

"You sure you're okay, Victor?"

Fernandez is looking at him with a puzzled expression. He makes an effort to smile.

"I'm fine. Let's do this."

"One more thing before you go in. Something weird."

"What?"

"Flies. The house is full of them."

2

A cloud of flies weaves through Lessard's field of vision.

As he bats away the insects, he's puzzled.

When Fernandez mentioned that the house was full of flies, he expected to see them buzzing in the air. And yes, they're everywhere. But most of them are dead.

On the light parquet floor, under the living-room drapes, across the pale leather armchairs, the flies form a polymorphous carpet, stretching out like a path in front of him.

With Fernandez at his heels, he advances slowly into the kitchen.

His gaze follows the winding trail of dead insects along the floor.

There are hundreds of them. Thousands. A broom is leaning against the counter. Someone has swept the bugs into a pile and pushed them next to the refrigerator.

Probably Adams's assistant, Lessard thinks.

He glances around the kitchen.

One detail immediately catches his attention: there are droplets of blood on the white wall behind the kitchen island. Having tried drip painting with Véronique, he can't help thinking of an artwork. A canvas by Jackson Pollock comes into his mind — he forgets the title.

Doug Adams, the crime scene technician, is crouched near the island, holding his camera. Its clicking shatters the silence.

Like the moon, the kitchen island has a side that can't be seen. Lessard knows a body is lying there.

"Hey, Doug."

"Hello, Victor," Adams says, without looking up from his work.

"What's with the flies? How come they're dead?"

"I sprayed the place. I wouldn't have been able to work otherwise. Don't worry, the crime scene isn't compromised."

Lessard steps closer, then recoils.

A cry of surprise catches in his throat.

Wearing nothing but briefs, a man is lying on the ceramic tiles. His eyes are rolled back and his mouth is open. His cheeks are smeared with dried blood. The handle of a kitchen knife projects from the left side of his throat, just above the carotid artery; its point is sticking out the other side. The man's chest and abdomen are covered with a complex pattern of lacerations and punctures of various depths, fringed with yellowish discolorations. There's a gaping wound in the left shoulder, through which severed muscles and tendons protrude.

The flaccid belly hangs to one side.

Blood is everywhere, spattered on the walls, streaked by fingers onto the surface of the island, and, surrounding the head and shoulders, in a pool whose shape recalls the contours of the African continent. Flies are lying in the crimson lake. Lessard has no words to express his horror.

Near the corpse's bare feet, Adams is taking pictures of a bloody object.

"What's that?" Lessard asks.

"His tongue."

Nausea overwhelms him. He vomits into the sink.

Walking unsteadily, he goes from bedroom to bedroom with Fernandez.

In the first room, there are two little girls, aged five and seven, lying in their beds — two sweet-faced angels obliterated by an unimaginably violent attack.

Pinned to the wall is a drawing of a big red heart.

You're the best daddy in the world. Love you forever.

Lessard tries to swallow, but his throat has gone dry.

In the second bedroom, they find an eighteen-month-old boy stretched out in his crib.

The wallpaper is patterned with brightly coloured cats.

Lessard winds up the musical mobile over the bed. Its melody is sinister.

"You okay, Victor?"

In the master bedroom, they come upon the naked body of a slender blond woman who was probably quite pretty when she was alive. Her face is now a death mask. She's covered in purplish wounds from her waist to her face. The lower body is intact.

Shaken, Lessard averts his gaze.

That's when he first sees him, from behind, at the end of the hallway.

Pale, with legs as thin as toothpicks, the boy is wearing shorts and a striped tank top that's too big for him.

"Who's he?"

Fernandez turns and looks in the direction Lessard is pointing.

"Who?"

"There was a boy in the hallway."

"That's not possible, Vic," she says, her voice wavering slightly. "They're all dead."

An axe is lying on a white chest of drawers, now covered in red. Lessard puts his face in his hands.

"Victor?"

I hear you, Fernandez. I hear you. But what can I say?

That I'm okay, when nothing is okay?

That I have what it takes to be professional, to overcome the disgust, to subdue the revulsion and nausea making me want to run away as fast as my legs will carry me?

That I wish I were anywhere else? That I wish I'd never seen these things, which will stay with me forever?

That I have to fight back the urge to gouge my own eyes out, to draw a black veil over all this death?

What do you want me to say, Fernandez? What's left to say when a father desecrates life, killing his own children and the woman who bore them?

That I wish I could beat his corpse until nothing remains but a shapeless pulp?

No. You expect me to stay in control and issue appropriate instructions.
You expect me to be reassuring, like a well-trained dog.
No one at the station knows the truth about me, Nadja.
No one but Tanguay.

July 23rd, 1976.
The day that will haunt me for the rest of my life.
Olympic fever was at its height in Montreal.
My younger brother Raymond had pleaded with me to come home with
him after day camp. He was scared of Dad. We were all scared of Dad.
Because Dad hit us often, and hard.
For more than three weeks, I'd been asking Marie Bisson for permission to walk her home after camp — and she'd been refusing. That
day, at lunchtime, I'd slipped her a note under the table. Not that I
was holding out any hope. Really, I'd just written the note out of habit,
convinced that, as always, she'd stick it in her lunchbox, the graveyard
of my ambitions.
I had hung my head, defeated by the certainty that I would never be
worthy of the noble feelings that I longed for.
A nudge from the kid beside me heralded the good news: Marie had
sent back the slip of paper.
On it, at great length, she'd written YES.
The brevity of the message didn't bother me. That "yes" opened a
window onto a whole world of possibilities, offering a view of the infinite promise that lay in her eyes.

Marie didn't say a word during the entire walk.
But when we were out of sight of the building, she slipped her hand
into mine. Then, a block before her house, she kissed me on the mouth.
A quick, sharp kiss, delivered with surgical precision before she fled,
calling over her shoulder:
"See you tomorrow, Victor Lessard."
I was well aware that when I got home, Dad would reward me for
my lateness with several well-aimed whacks, but my spirits were high

enough to carry me beyond the weight of his knuckles and the welts
that his signet ring would leave on my flesh.

As I stepped into the house, I heard the music.

Mick Jagger was singing that season's hit, "Fool to Cry," on the stereo
that my father had bought the previous month. Mom had dared to sug-
gest at the time that, since he'd lost his job, the expenditure might not be
a good idea. The next morning, her left eye resembled an overripe plum.

"Mom? Raymond?"

I dropped my knapsack onto the kitchen floor and opened the refriger-
ator. I took a big bite out of an apple. There was a house rule — which I
resented — against eating anything but fruit or vegetables before dinner.

As I entered the living room, I stopped chewing.

My mother was sprawled on the couch in her flowery dress.

Like Rimbaud's sleeper in the valley, she had two red holes in her
right side.

She was holding my four-year-old brother, Guy, who had taken
a bullet to the forehead. Raymond was lying face down on the floor
in front of her. One bullet had gone through his throat. Another had
lodged in his heart.

Raymond, oh, Raymond.

Even now, I sometimes catch myself imagining that you're there. I
ask myself what you might think in a given situation.

If only you were still alive.

In a fit of madness, my father had come into the living room, where my
mother was watching TV with my brothers, and opened fire.

Brutal, violent, ugly.

Death.

I found him stretched out on the bed.

The bullet had entered under his chin and exited through the top
of his skull.

The wound was bubbling — which meant he was still breathing.

And that is how, on the day that Nadia Comăneci won her third gold medal and became the queen of the Montreal Olympics, death robbed me of the people I loved more than my own life.

The rain is bouncing off his cheeks as he takes a nervous drag on his cigarette.

Lessard lets the smoke fill his lungs, then blows it out furiously.

Puff by puff, the tobacco burns away. He flicks the glowing butt to the far end of the yard, near the shed, and paces back and forth along a path laid out by his imagination.

Fernandez comes up behind him.

She hesitates, then gently rests a hand on his shoulder.

Lessard steps away. He doesn't want her to see his distress. Above all, he doesn't want to answer the thousand questions that lie behind her gaze.

At his request, Fernandez goes off to assemble the investigation team in the mobile command post. Alone in the yard, he lights another cigarette.

The tobacco is steadying him.

As he's about to go back inside, he becomes aware of being watched.

Within seconds, he spots the observer: a boy aged five or six, at the window of a neighbouring house.

Lessard waves to him.

The boy returns his wave sadly.

Inside the MCP, Lessard learns that Commander Tanguay has been called away on urgent business. Lessard doesn't know where his superior officer went, but he's relieved that he doesn't have to deal with him.

Not now.

Detectives Pearson and Sirois, along with Constable Macha Garneau, are standing near the coffee machine. Pearson fills some recyclable cups and hands them out. Fernandez joins the group.

Lessard, meanwhile, reluctantly pours himself a cup of hot water. Since getting back from his leave, he's been taking medication for his gastric reflux. He allows himself a single decaf every morning, and he considers his daylong abstinence thereafter to be a heroic struggle against temptation.

The smell of coffee fills the room, its aroma tickling his nostrils, whispering its seductive urgings in his ear, but he shakes his head. One decaf every morning — that's it!

"Let's get started, Pearson."

The young detective leafs through his notes and clears his throat.

"The man's name was John Cook. He was thirty-nine years old and worked as a production supervisor at Royal Tobacco. His wife, Elizabeth Munson, thirty-one, was a sales clerk in a clothing store. They'd been married ten years. The children's names were —"

"Skip that part," Lessard says sharply.

There's a brief, tense silence. Fernandez places a discreet hand on the detective sergeant's forearm.

Calm down, Victor.

Cautiously, Pearson resumes. "So, the million-dollar question: Did Cook act alone, or was it a suicide pact? Thus far, we haven't found any kind of note that might explain his actions."

"Looks to me like quadruple murder, followed by a suicide," Sirois says. "Judging from the violence of the crime scene, Cook went haywire."

"I agree," Fernandez says. "Even if she was suicidal, a woman wouldn't kill her own children in such a gruesome —"

"Yeah, we get it," Lessard says coldly, cutting her off. "Go on, Pearson."

There's another awkward pause. Pearson and Fernandez exchange surprised frowns, their gazes engaging in a silent dialogue:

What's with Lessard?

No idea. Let it go.

"I did a background check," Pearson resumes. "Neither of them had a criminal record. No substance abuse or gambling problems.

They moved into the neighbourhood three months ago. Their mortgage was manageable, and bank statements suggest that while they weren't rich, they weren't in any financial trouble."

"Relatives?"

"Cook was an only child. His parents are both dead. Munson has a sister living in Australia. Her father walked out on the family when she was born, but I spoke to her mother, who lives off-island, in Repentigny."

"And?"

"She's devastated. Baffled. She and her daughter talked almost every day. There were family get-togethers on weekends. The mother says they were a happy, loving couple. They'd just booked a family trip to Disney World in August."

Lessard closes his eyes.

That last detail affects him terribly.

But he manages to ask, "Does she think it's possible that her daughter was having an affair?"

"I wondered the same thing, but she said no. They talked yesterday, and Munson mentioned how glad she was that the family had finally settled into their new house. She said she loved the area, the neighbours, et cetera."

"Speaking of the neighbours, what do they have to say?"

Looking over his notes, Sirois picks up where Pearson left off:

"'A close-knit, devout family'; 'really good people'; 'I often saw him playing in the yard with his kids'; 'you never imagine something like this might happen next door'; 'he always said hello on the street'; 'they were always smiling'; 'the kids seemed happy' ..." Sirois looks down at the litany of praise in his notebook. "I've got pages of this stuff. Want me to go on?"

"No, that's fine. Did I hear you say they were devout?"

"Yeah, that came from a woman who lives across the street."

"So they went to Mass every Sunday? Or were they in some weird cult or religious group?"

"Good question. I'm guessing if they'd been members of a cult, the neighbour would have said something, or at least dropped a few hints."

"Try to find out more."

"Right. I'll get on it."

Lessard is suddenly overcome by fatigue. So far they have nothing that might explain the crime. Despite his efforts not to prejudge the case, the detective sergeant is inclined to agree with the general view that Cook spun out of control. In cases like this, it's often the father who's responsible. If so, they need to understand his motives.

If Cook didn't leave a note, if he gave no hint as to his reasons, they may never know exactly what happened. The annals of the law are full of cases like this — stories of seemingly normal human beings who harboured unsuspected darkness in their souls.

"On paper, they're just regular folks," says Macha Garneau, who's been silent until now.

Lessard hasn't worked with Garneau before. He looks her over. She's a slim, strong-featured young cop.

"Has Adams found anything unusual?" he asks.

"Nothing yet," Fernandez says. "Apart from the flies."

The flies. He'd completely forgotten about them.

"It's unusual to have this many flies around the bodies so soon, isn't it?" he says to Fernandez.

"According to Berger, when a corpse is lying in the open air, the first Diptera will arrive within an hour of death, sometimes even within minutes."

"Diptera?"

"Flies," Fernandez says.

"Okay. But what about a corpse that's lying indoors?"

"That depends. If the place is sealed, the infestation will start later, between eighteen and twenty-four hours after death, sometimes more. If there are open windows, it'll happen faster."

"Were there any open windows here?"

"Yes."

"Without a screen?"

"Yes, but according to Berger, that still doesn't explain the presence of so many flies so early in the decomposition process."

"I understand. Has he come up with an approximate time of death?"

"Yes, around two o'clock this morning."

Frankly, at this point in the investigation, Lessard isn't very concerned about the flies.

"Okay. Pearson, Sirois, as soon as the bodies are taken away, I want you to go over the house with a fine-toothed comb. Garneau will help you. I don't need to tell you what you're looking for — a note, an email, anything that'll help us figure out whether Cook acted alone or with his wife's help. If you don't find anything in the house, search the shed in the yard."

Pearson nods.

"I'll also go back across the street," Sirois says, "and ask the neighbour what she meant by 'very devout.'"

"Perfect," Lessard says. "We'll meet back here for an update in two hours. Call me if you find anything. Same goes for Adams and Berger. Come on, Nadja."

She straightens up, surprised.

"Where are we going?"

"Royal Tobacco."

There's something soothing about the noise of the rain on the leaves.

But as their footsteps click along the pavement, Lessard is barking at himself in silence. *Get a grip! Lock up the family history in a mental drawer and don't think about it. Not now.*

With a gallantry worthy of Humphrey Bogart, Lessard opens the passenger door and steps aside to let Fernandez get into the Corolla.

"Are you sure you're okay, Vic?" she asks as she climbs aboard.

"Sure, why do you ask?" he says, pretending not to understand the question.

"No reason. You just seem a little on edge."

As soon as he turns the key in the ignition, ear-splitting music fills the car. He thrusts out a hand to turn down the volume.

Too late.

Fernandez, a music lover, has recognized the first chords of "Rebellion."

"Arcade Fire?" she says, with a small smile. "I'm impressed, Victor. I figured you for a seventies progressive rock guy."

A uniformed cop lifts the yellow police tape, and the Corolla rolls out.

Lessard avoids her gaze. His cheeks have turned red.

"Whatever," he says. "It's one of Martin's CDs."

Having Fernandez in the car is intimidating. The nearness of her body unsettles him.

"It's terrific that your son is introducing you to good music. Arcade Fire is a great band."

"No question, but I'm more of a Stars fan," he says, focusing on the road to keep his nervousness at bay. "They're amazing in concert. Martin helped record their last album."

"You've seen them in concert?"

"Yes. With Charlotte and Martin. At their age, it's not easy to find stuff we can do together. I don't want them to feel like seeing me is a chore — you know, the three of us just sitting around with nothing to say. So the deal is, if they can come up with an activity that interests them, I'll buy the tickets. We went to check out a hypnotist a couple of weeks ago. I've forgotten the guy's name. But mostly, we go to concerts — Stars, Arcade Fire, The Dears, Malajube ... next on the list is Karkwa. You like them?"

"Love 'em! How are your kids, anyway? It's been a while since I saw them."

Lessard loves his children, but sometimes he wishes he'd never had kids. Since he and Marie separated, his relationship with his offspring has had its share of ups and downs. The passage through adolescence hasn't been entirely smooth.

But a wave of nostalgia hits him.

It's already been two years since we got back from our trip out west.

It was a fun trip, despite a few challenging moments. One evening, returning from a hike in the Rockies, Lessard discovered that their tent, whose pegs weren't properly secured, had blown out into the middle of a lake. Later, in Vancouver's Chinatown, he had his wallet stolen.

Since the wallet contained his ID and police badge, he had to call Station 11 to notify his colleagues. This earned him a ribbing from Pearson and Sirois, who sent along numerous mocking text messages. As a result, Lessard decided to turn off his cellphone for a few days.

And that was when Marie called to find out how the kids were doing. Lessard didn't need to listen to all nine of his ex-wife's panic-stricken messages to realize that he'd screwed up yet again.

She didn't go thermonuclear in the end. But it was a close-run thing.

"Victor?" Fernandez says.

The gentle voice of his colleague pulls Lessard out of his reverie.

"Yeah. Sorry. They're doing great."

An inner voice rebukes him.

Get real. You don't think they're doing great at all. Your sixteen-year-old daughter is seeing a guy who's twenty-two, looks thirty-four, and has the mental capacity of a geranium. Your son barely made it through high school. Sure, he's working as a sound engineer these days, but he still smokes pot every time you turn your back. And there isn't anything you can do about it. He's legally an adult, and he's convinced that he knows what's best for him.

"Do you still have them every second week?"

"Not really. Martin's living with me these days. I mostly see Charlotte on weekends."

The truth is, you've never done what it would take to make shared custody work.

Lessard parks the car in front of Royal Tobacco's offices on Saint-Antoine Street. The building, constructed of metal, brick, and glass, stands out in the shabby architectural landscape of Saint-Henri.

While Fernandez goes inside to talk to the security guards, Lessard has a quick smoke on the sidewalk. He's never really thought about it before, but now, examining his pack of cigarettes, he realizes that he's smoking a Royal Tobacco brand.

Three kilometres to the east, the office towers of downtown Montreal are outlined against the sky.

. . .

An unsmiling secretary with her hair in a severe bun leads them through a maze of corridors to a conference room with a view of Atwater Avenue and the old Forum. The former home of the Montreal Canadiens has been converted into a multiplex cinema. Once a shrine for hockey fans, the building now resembles a low-budget spaceship.

Lessard thinks nostalgically about the Forum, where he so often watched the Canadiens terrorize their opponents, with undoubted assistance from the ghosts of past Canadiens greats like Howie Morenz, Georges Vézina, and Newsy Lalonde. He recalls being thrilled as he watched the idols of his youth: Guy Lafleur, Serge Savard, and Ken Dryden. Later on, it was Patrick Roy's turn to electrify him during the championship runs of 1986 and 1993. When he thinks of Roy, shirtless, skinny as a schoolboy, holding his first cup aloft on Saint-Catherine Street during the Stanley Cup parade, the memory still gives him goosebumps.

Like other Montrealers, Lessard is still a fan of the legendary hockey club, but he can't deny that the years since that last cup victory have seemed like a long, painful drought.

He'll be glad when the ghosts of the Forum finally start working their magic at the Bell Centre.

"Coffee?" the surly secretary asks.

"I'll take a cup of hot water, please," Lessard says.

"We only have coffee."

"How about decaf?"

The secretary shakes her head.

He hesitates. An inner voice whispers:

One little cup … why not?

"Nothing for me."

The secretary sighs. Then, irritably, to Fernandez: "How about you?"

"I don't want anything, thanks," Fernandez says.

"Fine. Mr. Dubois will be with you in a few minutes.

She leaves, slamming the door so hard that a painting on the wall tilts off its axis.

"Wow," Fernandez says, taken aback. "Someone got up on the wrong side of the bed."

A man in a grey suit comes in. He's trim and well-groomed, with a moustache that makes him look like an old-fashioned dandy.

"Gérard Dubois, executive vice-president and head of operations."

Handshakes are exchanged, introductions are made. Dubois gives the cops his business card.

"Please excuse my assistant's lack of manners. Cécile is a little rough around the edges, but effective as hell. Your coming by has forced her to rearrange my schedule."

"We're used to it," Lessard says. "Do you know why we're here?"

"No idea. Something to do with cigarette smuggling?"

"I'd better fill you in."

Lessard tells him about the carnage on Bessborough Avenue. Dubois's composure evaporates. He's visibly shocked.

"I can't believe it. This is awful …"

"Are you surprised?"

"Yes," Dubois says. His gaze is vacant, abstracted. "I've known John for fifteen years. Everyone liked him."

"What did he do here?"

"Production supervisor, quality control. His team makes sure that our various brands meet manufacturing standards."

"Did he report directly to you?"

"No, to a manager. But we talked often."

"Was he a good employee?"

"One of the best. Conscientious, hard-working, devoted. He had an excellent sense of humour."

"So he wasn't a depressive person?"

"I imagine he had his problems like everyone else, but John was positive and energetic."

Lessard frowns. Often, the image that people project in public is radically at odds with the anguish and darkness of their private lives.

"Did you spend time with him outside the office?"

"At cocktail parties, and occasionally at corporate family events."

"Did you ever meet his wife?"

"Yes, a few times."

"What was she like?"

"Radiant, pretty, bright. They were a great couple."

"And the kids?"

"What can I tell you? They were like any other kids."

"So you can't think of anything that might explain what happened?"

"Not a thing."

"Who was his best friend at work?" Fernandez asks. "The person he felt closest to, the person he confided in."

"That would be Pierre Deschênes. They started out here at the same time. Two very different men. I never understood why John liked him so much."

"Is he here today?" she asks.

"Deschênes? Most likely. He works in production, at the plant across the street."

"Can we talk to him?"

"Sure."

"But first," Lessard says, "would you show us Cook's office?"

They walk through a fresh maze of corridors with beige walls, dark carpeting, glass-partitioned offices. Heads turn in the cubicles, casting curious glances at the two visitors.

Dubois stops in front of a door.

"This is it."

A clean, tidy office. Carefully stacked papers. On a corkboard, photos of Elizabeth Munson and the children, in better days.

The space is smaller than Lessard expected.

We'll be stepping on each other's toes.

"Is it okay if my colleague looks around?"

"Of course."

"See what you can turn up, Nadja. I'll go across the street and speak to Pierre Deschênes."

Gérard Dubois offers to accompany him, but Lessard would rather be alone when he questions Deschênes. Experience has taught him that some people behave differently when others are around. That's a particular risk in this case. Lessard wants Deschênes to feel at ease, unintimidated by the presence of a superior.

Following the directions that Dubois has given him, the detective sergeant shows his badge to a security guard in the plant's reception area. Then he steps into the production facility.

He pauses for a few seconds and watches, fascinated, through a large bay window as thousands of white cylinders move along the rails of a conveyor. The security guard escorting him is about to step around a corner at the end of the hallway. But the guard is thickset and slow-moving. Lessard catches up without difficulty.

Accompanied by the guard, the cop enters a fluorescent-lit warehouse. Employees on electric forklifts are silently moving crates of cigarettes around the space.

Two men are talking. Seeing that one of them is smoking, Lessard has an urge to take out his own pack.

"That's him," the security guard says, pointing at an immense man with tattoo-covered arms.

They're within ten metres of the two men when the guard says, "Hey, Pierre, there's a police detective here to see you."

There's a pause, then suddenly Deschênes is running for all he's worth toward the far end of the warehouse.

As soon as he realizes what's going on, Lessard takes off after the fleeing man.

Without breaking stride, he unholsters his pistol.

3

Deschênes moves well for a man his size, and he knows the place.

He enters a narrow aisle of floor-to-ceiling shelves stacked with wooden crates. Lessard, who's faster than Deschênes, is gradually closing the gap separating them. Without turning, Deschênes reaches out and, with a sharp movement, overturns a pile of crates bound together by metal clasps. He knocks them to the floor as effortlessly as if they were light packets of clothing.

The crates shatter on the floor. Cigarette cartons spill out into Lessard's path. Running too fast to dodge the obstacles, he trips over a carton and falls headlong on the cement floor. As he goes down, his forehead strikes the corner of a crate.

Swearing, the detective sergeant jumps to his feet and resumes the chase. By now Deschênes has reached the far end of the warehouse. Still running, Lessard uses a sleeve to wipe away the blood above his eye.

He sees a rectangle of light in the wall: Deschênes has opened a door and is heading outside. Lessard reaches the doorway in a few strides and sees Deschênes fleeing across the parking lot.

Though he has no intention of carrying out his threat, he yells menacingly: "Stop, Deschênes! Stop or I'll shoot!"

Deschênes starts to zigzag like a deflating balloon. He hesitates, casting a quick glance over his shoulder.

He sees Lessard twenty-five metres behind him, running like a madman, forehead bleeding, pointing a gun in his direction.

Deschênes continues to run, telling himself he can't be caught, he's opened up too much of a lead. But there's a flicker of doubt in his mind.

Insidious doubt.

Is the cop a good shot? Can he hit him at this distance?

The voice of reason gets louder and louder in Deschênes's head. A bullet is a lot faster than his running shoes. Better to give himself up than get shot in the back.

Deschênes slows his pace. His lungs are on fire. He finally stops altogether, resting his palms on his thighs as he catches his breath.

Lessard arrives within seconds, still pointing his weapon. He covers the last ten metres at a walk.

Deschênes faces him.

Locking eyes, the two men size each other up. They're both wheezing.

"On your knees, hands on top of your head," Lessard says in a hard voice. "No sudden moves."

Deschênes obeys, clenching his teeth.

Fernandez closes the door behind her.

She sits down in John Cook's chair and looks around the office for a moment, absorbing the atmosphere in which the man who just massacred his family used to spend most of his time. She knows from long experience that it doesn't always take much to unhinge a person. A loving, compassionate human being can suddenly be transformed into a ruthless, bloodthirsty animal. Consequently, Fernandez isn't expecting to make any earth-shaking discoveries in John Cook's office. If the man didn't leave a message explaining his actions at the scene of the crime, it would be startling to find anything here. But no stone should be left unturned. She browses over files. She opens drawers. Her fingers leaf through neat stacks of paper on the desk. She feels like a voyeur. She hates invading a dead man's private space, even if that man was a criminal of the most despicable kind.

Dubois has instructed John Cook's assistant to give Fernandez the dead man's computer password. She now examines emails, checks files, opens documents. Dubois didn't hesitate for a second before authorizing her to search the workspace.

The longer she searches, the more certain she becomes that her intuition is right: there's nothing in this office. No hidden secret.

Fernandez also becomes disconcertingly convinced that John Cook was a meticulous, organized, highly intelligent man. One only has to look at his agenda and read his emails to see it. The man expressed himself clearly, concisely, and with ease.

Which is troubling.

It's more comforting to believe that all murderers are insane, incapable of leading normal lives. But she knows that's not true.

She leans back in the chair.

Photos of Elizabeth Munson and the couple's children stand on the desk. Broad smiles, happy faces.

Nadja Fernandez's composure cracks. She puts her face in her hands and sobs.

When her cellphone rings a few minutes later, she collects herself.

The rain is whispering as it falls.

Lessard is soaked once again, but the water is reviving him. The chase has taken a toll. His legs are wobbly. Deschênes's hands are now cuffed behind his back. His co-worker and the security guard have come out in a panic, but the detective sergeant has sent them back inside with strict orders not to mention the incident to the other employees. He's under no illusions: in five minutes, the whole plant will know what happened, and the parking lot will be full of gawkers. He leads Deschênes behind the building, away from prying eyes.

"What got into you? Why did you run?"

"Go fuck yourself."

"Drop the tough-guy routine, Deschênes. You're going to have to talk. You can start by telling me what you did time for."

Deschênes stiffens and glares at Lessard. The cop's intuitive shot in the dark has hit home.

"Hang on," Lessard says. "Let me guess. Assault? Possession of narcotics?"

"Did my probation officer send you? Jesus Christ, are you really gonna get in my face 'cause I missed last night's curfew? It was the first time it's happened!"

"Shut up, Deschênes. Answer my question."

"I did three years for trafficking. But that was twenty years ago, goddamn it!"

"And lately?"

"DWI," Deschênes says, hanging his head. "On the third arrest, my car was stuck in a snowbank. My girlfriend was driving, I swear! The fucking cops didn't believe me. Neither did the judge."

"And?"

"And what?"

"Did you do time?"

"Two months to be served on weekends, plus a year's probation with a ten o'clock curfew."

"You missed it last night?"

"Yeah, but it's never happened before!"

"Where were you?"

"I went shopping downtown after work. I walked home afterward, lost track of time."

"You walked home in the rain?"

"I like walking in the rain."

"Where do you live?"

"Saint-Joseph and Papineau."

"Did you go shopping alone?"

"Yeah."

"What did you buy?"

For the first time Deschênes looks surprised.

"Nothing. I was looking for a birthday present for my girlfriend, but I didn't find anything. Why do you want to know about —"

"Did you buy any food?"

"A burger in the food court at the Eaton Centre."

"How did you pay for it?"

"Cash. What does this have to do with —"

"I'm asking the questions. What did you do when you got home?"

"Watched some TV, then went to bed."

"Alone?"

Deschênes lets out an irritated sigh. "Yes, alone."

"Did you speak to anyone on the phone?"

"No ... oh, that bitch. I'll bet she called at ten on the nose, just to fuck with me!"

"Did you send any emails?"

"To who? I don't have a computer."

"Where were you at two in the morning ... sleeping?"

"Yeah."

"Alone?"

"I went to bed alone, so yeah, I was sleeping alone."

"Tell me about your friend John Cook."

Surprise gives way to puzzlement on Deschênes's features.

"What's John got to do with it?"

"Did he know you were on probation?"

"John knows my past better than anyone."

"Had you seen him recently?"

"We had lunch in the cafeteria a couple of times last week."

"How did he seem —"

"Fuck this! What's going on?" Deschênes is looking anxious.

"Shut up. I'm asking the questions."

Deschênes's eyes narrow. His mouth is contorted by the hatred he feels for the police.

Fernandez's arrival has a brief calming effect.

Lessard called to let her know where they were, but it took her a couple of minutes to find the location.

"Is this Pierre Deschênes?" she asks.

"In the flesh," Lessard says. "He tried to get away."

"Why?"

"That's what we need to figure out."

She notices the trickle of blood on Lessard's brow.

"What's with your eye?"

"It's fine. We're taking him in."

"What the fuck?" Deschênes exclaims. "Why?"

Lessard thrusts a finger at Deschênes, from whose shirt collar a tuft of hair emerges like a sprig of flowers.

"Because as far as we can tell, John Cook murdered his wife and kids last night, then killed himself. When I showed up to ask a few questions, strange coincidence, you ran like hell. Oh, and you have no alibi."

The stunned look on Deschênes's face seems genuine. Either he's a brilliant actor, or he's hearing the news for the first time.

"Hold still, Victor," Fernandez says. "This'll just take a second."

Bending over him, she disinfects his wound with an alcohol pad from the first aid kit in the Corolla. While Deschênes, still hand-cuffed, waits quietly in the back seat, she places a Band-Aid over Lessard's brow, giving him a cockeyed, dangerous look — a little like Jake Gittes, the private detective played by Jack Nicholson in *Chinatown*.

Lessard swallows nervously.

Fernandez's open collar and heady perfume are affecting him.

Even though it's against standard procedure, Lessard uses the Corolla to transport Deschênes back to Station 11.

As soon as they arrive, the detective sergeant darkens. He tells Fernandez to place Deschênes in an interrogation room.

"You want to question him right away?" she asks.

"No. Let's let him stew for a while. Have Garneau take off the cuffs and turn up the heat in the room."

"What if he wants to call a lawyer?"

"He won't — that's not his style. Tell Garneau to watch him through the one-way mirror. Nobody's to go in."

"You think he had something to do with the killings?"

Fernandez is frustrated. She believes Lessard is handling this the wrong way, but she's reluctant to say so.

"He seemed genuinely surprised when you told him about Cook," she says cautiously.

"I'm not jumping to conclusions, but I have my doubts. The prison system is crawling with con artists who look plenty surprised when you start asking them questions. If Cook talked about his plans and that scumbag Deschênes did nothing to stop him, then he's got blood on his hands."

Lessard's voice has risen.

"He'd need to have clearly understood Cook's intentions and ignored them," Fernandez says calmly. "It's like when there's a suicide. Family members often fail to recognize the distress signals until after the fact."

The cruel face of Lessard's father appears before his eyes.

"We'll see."

His voice is suddenly harsh; he's on the verge of losing his temper. "I'm going back to the crime scene," he growls. "I want to talk to Adams."

"Victor ... did you notice that Deschênes was crying in the car?"

"What's your problem, Nadja? If you think I'm wrong, say so!"

Fernandez reddens. *This isn't like Lessard. He's not usually so emotional.*

"Aren't you being kind of hard on the guy? It's a fair guess that he just learned his best friend slaughtered his wife and kids before killing himself. And if Tanguay finds out you're holding him without questioning, he's going to hit the roof."

"Whatever! I don't give a shit! I'm going back to the crime scene."

Lessard's fury shocks Fernandez.

He's never behaved like this before.

Adams speaks in the flat voice of a man who's seen it all.

No, he can't say whether Berger's started the autopsy. Yes, he knows what he's doing, but his analysis isn't complete yet. Can he share his initial impressions? Sure, why not?

He thinks Cook killed the little boy first. One axe blow, two at most. After that? The girls. For them, too, a few blows would have sufficed. Adams believes that in both cases, the first blow was to the head with the back of the axe. The wife died last. How does he know? There were blond hairs in some of her wounds. Only the two little girls had blond hair. The strands must have adhered to the axe before

Cook struck his wife. Were the bodies moved? Not in the case of the children. Blood spatter on the walls around the beds confirmed as much. Adams's hunch? Cook probably attacked them in their sleep. Unless he drugged them first. Fingerprints? That will take more time. His preliminary report should be ready in a few days. The wife? No, he doesn't think she died in the suggestive pose in which she was found. Was her body moved or simply repositioned? He can't say. He'll have to do further tests before knowing the answer. The tongue? Adams thinks Cook cut it out with the kitchen knife before stabbing himself in the throat. And what about the flies? He has no idea, but one thing he can say with certainty is that those flies didn't swing the axe ...

I can't stay in this place one minute longer.

My head is spinning. I'm having trouble breathing. The walls are wobbling. I can feel myself being sucked into the corpses' eyes. Their empty gazes will be seared into my memory until the day I die.

Doug Adams's weary explanations are making me sick to my stomach. He's talking about axe blows that shattered children's skulls and snuffed out their lives.

How can he be so calm in this horrific situation? Am I the only one who's taking this so hard?

Is it because of my past?

And what about Fernandez? What does she feel in the deepest recesses of her heart?

Apart from my own father, I don't know what kind of malignant vermin could find it in himself to kill his own children. But I do know that after that darkness enters your heart, it never leaves. It turns you into a shadow of what you once were. It forces you to your knees, makes you crawl along the endless paths of despair.

Fernandez has just walked in.

She turns to look at me. Her gaze seems to be torn between compassion and reproach. She's beautiful in this light. A little knot forms in the pit of my stomach whenever she comes near.

Forgive me, Nadja ...

I never should have spoken to you the way I did earlier. I wish I could explain why I'm so quick to flare up. I wish I could tell you about my past. But I don't have the strength or the courage.

And that voice I just heard ...

Even if my brain refuses to admit it, even if I keep hoping until the very last second that I'm mistaken, I know who it is.

One of my worst failings is the persistent belief that if I close my eyes and wish very hard, life's misfortunes will slide over my shoulders like a soft breeze and disappear in a puff of enchantment.

Does that mean I'm prone to magical thinking?

Whatever it means, the voice I wish I hadn't heard is coming closer.

Commander Tanguay.

"Ah, Lessard. It's about time. Where on earth were you?"

"Fernandez and I went to question Cook's co-workers," Lessard says, his jaw clenching.

"And?"

Fernandez comes over. "Nothing significant," she says.

The commander is watching Lessard's face.

"Too bad," he says. "I spoke to headquarters. We won't be holding a press conference. For the moment, our PR person will release a simple statement confirming that there's been a domestic murder-suicide. Does that work for you, Lessard?"

Tanguay doesn't want a reply. The detective sergeant nods.

"Perfect. Then you can wrap the whole thing up in a hurry. I don't need any flights of brilliance, Lessard. Either the man acted alone, or it was a suicide pact. I want your report on my desk tomorrow."

"Yes, Commander."

"By the way, Lessard ..." There's a moment's silence. Tanguay takes a step back toward him. "I'm sure this business brings back painful memories. Don't let personal history affect your judgment."

That fucking son of a bitch! How dare he?

Before the infuriated Lessard can think of a response, Tanguay turns on his heel and goes out the door.

Fernandez has heard every word.

She looks at Lessard, her brows raised in puzzlement.

In answer to her unspoken question, Lessard mumbles a vague explanation about having been involved in a similar case a long time ago. Which isn't strictly a lie, but it leaves Fernandez with the impression that the murder-suicide in question was the subject of a past investigation, rather than something that happened in the heart of his own family.

He storms into the hallway without waiting to see how Fernandez reacts.

After barking orders to Pearson and Sirois, who are at work on the second floor, and exchanging a few words with Adams, Lessard steps out for a smoke, leaving the puzzled Fernandez by herself.

Outside, he fills his lungs with fresh air. The house emanates something unclean, something foul. Its tainted atmosphere makes him dizzy; its morbid aspect oppresses him. He wouldn't be able to explain why, but when he's inside that house, he feels watched, ill at ease, like a stranger in a hostile land.

"Motherfucker," he murmurs, thinking of Tanguay.

He lets the raindrops strike his forehead and roll down his face, gathering in beads on his chin. Little by little, his pulse slows down.

Easy, Lessard. Easy.

The rainstorm intensifies. Suddenly, all the water in the world seems to be pouring down on him. He needs to take shelter, but there's no way he's going back into that house.

The shed.

Hoping it's not locked, he sprints to the far end of the yard.

The handle turns. The door swings open. He steps inside and presses the light switch.

The rain is rapping on the windows as the match flame ignites his cigarette.

He leaves a voice mail for his son, who's living in Lessard's apartment, which isn't big enough for the two of them.

"Hey, Martin. I'll be home late tonight. You can heat up the pizza that's in the freezer."

A glance around the shed reveals that the Cooks led a classic middle-class Montreal existence. Lessard sees a wheelbarrow, some rakes, shovels, and bags of soil stacked in one corner. Paint cans and a variety of brushes are lying on metal shelves. High-tech bicycles are hanging from hooks in the rafters. A golf bag and a set of hockey equipment are leaning against a stacked cord of wood that covers one wall from floor to ceiling.

As he looks out the window, the detective sergeant shakes his head.

What got into you, Cook? What got into you?

Suddenly, his eyes widen.

The boy is there, standing in the driveway that runs up the side of the house. His shorts and his striped tank top are dry.

What's he doing? Is he looking in Lessard's direction?

It's impossible to see his face through the rain and the branches that rise like a wall between them.

Overcoming an irrational dread, Lessard opens the door and puts his head out.

"Hey, kid!"

The boy runs off toward the street.

"Kid!"

The rain is drumming on the roof.

Lessard finally calms down and thinks.

He has no choice. He needs to go back into the house and take charge of operations.

Just as he's about to turn off the light, he sees a tiny irregularity in the alignment of the logs in the stack of wood — a gap that seems to have been deliberately created. Without thinking, Lessard reaches in with one hand and pulls out a piece of paper that was stuck between two logs.

He unrolls it and, in astonishment, reads a brief handwritten note:

It's not me, Viviane.

4

It's a modest apartment in the Rosemont district, a tiny three-room place on the top floor of a building that's seen better days. It consists of a bedroom, a bathroom without a bath, and an area that does multiple duty as living room, dining room, and kitchen.

Like the rest of the apartment, the bedroom is disordered, ugly, and badly decorated, with drab, beige-painted walls.

The bed is unmade.

Atop immaculately white sheets, an amber-skinned girl is writhing. She's naked.

With her left hand, she strokes her ample breasts. With her right, she caresses her pubic area. The room is hot; droplets of sweat are visible on her forehead and chest.

At various locations throughout the Americas, Europe, and Asia, men are paying to watch her masturbate.

An HD camera on a metal tripod is catching every one of her movements. Within reach is a remote control that enables her to activate and control the camera.

The girl looks at the lens and presses the zoom button.

She fondles herself and shudders suggestively.

On the website where users access her feed, she calls herself Jennifer. Her real name is Laila François.

Laila is of Haitian origin. She's seventeen years old, though she looks twenty-five, with abundant curly brown hair and a flawless complexion.

Laila has been performing webcam pornography for eighteen months now. It was her friend Mélanie Fleury who turned her on to it.

Mélanie was working as a high-end escort until her pimp, Nigel Williams, decided to diversify his range of services by going high-tech and adding webcam porn to his menu. That was when Mélanie decided to quit the world's oldest profession and specialize in virtual sex — an easy, simple, and, above all, safe way to make good money without working too hard.

Mélanie first met Laila at Émilie-Gamelin Park, next to the Berri-UQAM metro station, an area known as a hot spot for the local narcotics trade. Ten years older than Laila, hardened to the ways of the street, Mélanie instantly noticed the teenager among the park's colourful array of gangsters, dealers, junkies, mental cases, homeless people, and office employees from Place Dupuis across the street.

Mélanie isn't a saint or a social worker, but as soon as she laid eyes on Laila, she knew she was going to help the girl.

Why her? Why not someone else? Why at that moment?

Remembering her first days on the streets when she arrived in Montreal, remembering how she met Nigel and came under his authority, Mélanie may have feared, as she looked at Laila's angelic face, that she wouldn't be lucky enough to meet the right kind of people.

That evening, Mélanie approached Laila and, without too much difficulty, persuaded her to come and pay a visit to Monsieur Antoine's trailer, which made the rounds of downtown Montreal and the surrounding districts, providing street kids with hot dogs, warm clothes, personal care items, and groceries.

Was it the hopeful look on Monsieur Antoine's face that made up Mélanie's mind?

Whatever the reason, she brought Laila back to her apartment and let her sleep on a spare mattress.

"Just for a few nights," she was careful to say.

But the few nights turned into several days, the weeks turned into months, and, over time, the two young women forged a deep bond that went beyond friendship.

. . .

During the first few weeks, Mélanie was able to conceal Laila's existence from Nigel, and to keep the teenager in the dark about the true nature of her own activities. Meanwhile, Laila rapidly became a helpful presence in the apartment, enthusiastically taking care of shopping, cooking, and household chores.

Then the inevitable happened.

Laila learned that Mélanie was working as an escort, just as Mélanie was making the transition to webcam porn. Not at all scandalized, Laila was curious to know more about the work, and expressed a desire to start doing it, as well. At first, Mélanie was adamantly opposed. But Laila kept asking, and Mélanie reluctantly agreed to introduce her to Nigel.

After a few months, Laila had accumulated enough money to rent her own place in Mélanie's building.

Since then, the two women have been performing highly lucrative erotic duos several times a week.

Laila has never talked to Mélanie about her past, nor about how she ended up on the streets.

And Mélanie has never asked.

But she can tell that Laila is a runaway.

Did she flee from her past?

From a bad home?

From someone violent?

Yes, Laila ran away.

That much is certain.

Laila is stretched out on the bed, smoking a joint.

She enjoys the sweet sensation of the thick cotton sheets against her naked skin, and the smoke rolling on her tongue. With Mélanie's support and some costly therapy, she's succeeded in overcoming her dependence on hard drugs. But cannabis is a tenacious habit — a habit she's resolved to break in the near future.

The session has ended. The webcam has been turned off and her day at the "office" is done. Later on, this evening, she'll give herself over to her true passion: she'll try to finish the melody of a song she's working on. She has a lovely voice. She writes her own lyrics, and she's taking guitar lessons.

Laila's dream is to pursue a music career.

Why not?

After all, Montreal has become a hub for independent music, especially since Arcade Fire became a worldwide sensation.

There's a knock at the door.

"It's open!"

A young man with flaxen hair slips noiselessly into the apartment. He's wet from the rain, carrying grocery bags.

"Put the bags on the table," Laila calls out. "I'm in the bedroom."

He comes into the room and gives Laila a look that makes her shiver.

"Hi, David."

"Hello, Laila," the delivery man says timidly.

Electrified by his presence, Laila moves her hands down to her groin, where they resume their silent ballet.

"Come closer, David."

Laila met David at the convenience store where he works.

She was immediately charmed by his kindness, his intelligence, and his almost pathological shyness. Little by little, watching him come and go, she got into the habit of talking to him.

Early on, she made several attempts to entice him to ask her out, but he failed to pick up on her clues. So she started ordering cigarettes and various other items for delivery, as a way of seeing him more often.

The ruse was repeated on several occasions, until she proposed that they go for a walk together — which, unexpectedly, became a habit.

Time slows down when he's around.

They often walk for hours, sometimes as far as Monsieur Antoine's trailer. But David is always too shy to go inside with her.

He's a good listener, and he's unusually open-minded, which Laila appreciates more than anything. So much so that she's talked to him about something she never discussed with anyone before: the reasons why she ran away from home.

Laila is frustrated.

Over the last few weeks, she's tried repeatedly to seduce David.

She started out subtly, letting the strap of her camisole slip off her shoulder, revealing the curve of her breast. Then she arranged matters so that he'd find her lightly dressed when he came into the apartment.

When the young delivery man still didn't react, she went even further, seeing to it that he caught her in the middle of a webcam session.

She's convinced that David is interested in her, but whenever the opportunity for physical intimacy arises, he becomes unreadable, shy, bereft of initiative.

Today, she talked suggestively while looking him straight in the eye.

He didn't look away; she could sense that he wasn't immune to her attractions. She imagined that inwardly he was burning with desire to touch her — but, as usual, he did nothing.

A few days ago, she took the bold step of asking whether he preferred men. He simply replied that he found her very beautiful. When she tried to kiss him, his expression darkened and, with an apology, he hurried out.

Laila is probably going about it the wrong way. But offering up her body is the only way she knows how to seduce men. It may not be infallible, but it's yielded good results up until now.

She hopes he'll eventually succumb and touch her.

Is she obsessed with him because he declines her advances and shows an interest in something other than her ass?

That would certainly be a first in her life ...

Laila's cellphone rings.

She recognizes the number on the caller ID, but she lets the call go to voice mail.

Terror flickers in her eyes.

5

As excited as a hyperactive child on a sugar high, Lessard goes into the house with the slip of paper in his hand. He looks around for Fernandez, eager to share his discovery with her.

He doesn't see her, but he can hear her voice in conversation with Commander Tanguay in the next room.

Shit.

He makes a face and stuffs the paper into his pocket. There's no way he's going to trust Tanguay with this information — not yet, anyway. Taking care to avoid being noticed, he waits for a few moments, hoping Fernandez will free herself, allowing him to pull her aside. But the conversation drags on.

Since the house gives him the creeps, and since he can't stand being anywhere near his boss, Lessard decides to hurry back to Station 11 and question Pierre Deschênes.

Going out discreetly through the back door, he briefly considers walking back to the station, but, faced with the ongoing downpour, he gets into his car instead.

The rain oppresses him.

Will it ever end?

Driving along Terrebonne Street, Lessard can't help thinking about the possible implications of his discovery. He pulls out his notebook and pats his pockets, trying to locate his pen.

Where did he put it?

He opens the glove compartment and reaches in with one hand, searching for a pencil. As he does so, his eyes leave the road. The car swerves dangerously toward the sidewalk.

He swears and straightens out with a tug on the steering wheel.

Unable to find anything to write with, he makes a mental effort to get his thoughts in order.

Was John Cook the author of the message? To know for sure, Lessard will have to locate documents that Cook wrote out by hand and compare them to the note.

Is the message related to the murders, or has the slip of paper been in the shed for some time now? It's possible, for instance, that Cook and Munson organized a treasure hunt for their children, and the message has no connection to the case.

What does the message mean? Suppose Cook isn't the killer, as the note suggests. The slip of paper proves, at the very least, that he knew what was about to happen. In that case, why did he seek to exonerate himself in the eyes of a third party, rather than alert the police and prevent the carnage? Is it possible that he was threatened in some way, leaving him unable to contact the police?

Who is Viviane? A relative? A friend? A mistress?

If Cook didn't commit the murders, who did? Deschênes? Someone else?

Macha Garneau is busy doing paperwork when Lessard walks in. Soaked to the skin, he shakes his head, sending drops of water flying in all directions. She gives him a bright smile.

"Still raining?"

"Yep," Lessard says, unbuttoning his jacket. "How's our guest doing? Has he asked for a lawyer?"

The detective sergeant is unable to resist a glance at the youthful cop's physique, which her uniform shows off to excellent advantage. Constable Garneau is a well-built young woman whose attractions have made her the subject of quietly appreciative conversations among the male officers of Station 11.

"He hasn't said a word since he got here. Hasn't moved, apart from taking off his sweater, because of the heat."

"So he's bare-chested?"

"No, he's in his undershirt."

"Okay. Open the door. I'm going to talk to him."

"Sure thing."

"Oh, and turn down the thermostat."

Lessard walks straight to the empty chair and sits down facing Deschênes, who's staring at the wall, seemingly oblivious of the cop's presence.

Lessard gets straight to the point. "You've had time to think things over, Deschênes. Do you have anything to say?"

A long minute crawls by. Deschênes turns and looks at Lessard.

"I've said all there is to say about being late for my curfew."

His voice is calm. Clearly, the time he's spent waiting has led him to understand that the best way to get released is to co-operate.

"At this point," he adds, "I'd say you're the one who needs to do some talking. What happened to John?"

"I'm asking the questions here, Deschênes. What kind of guy was your friend Cook?"

"Tell me one thing, first. That stuff you said in the car — is it true?" Deschênes sounds like a broken man.

Lessard lowers his guard. He knows Deschênes will answer his questions even if the two men don't play their assigned roles — himself as the hard-nosed cop, Deschênes as the badass.

"I'm afraid so."

"I had nothing to do with it." A tear rolls down Deschênes's rough face.

"We'll see about that," Lessard says. "Does the news surprise you?"

"John would never have done something like this."

Lessard thinks about the slip of paper he found in the shed.

"How do you know?"

"John was a steady guy, positive, upbeat. He loved life."

This isn't the first time Lessard has heard warm words of praise for people who committed terrible acts.

"He didn't lose his temper now and then? Didn't turn violent?"

"Never. Not John."

"You seem convinced that he didn't do it. Did he have enemies that you know of?"

Deschênes slumps, as though reality were suddenly catching up to him, despite his refusal to believe it.

"No," he murmurs.

"Was he more depressed than usual, lately? More anxious?"

"Not really. He seemed excited about the new house."

"And during the past year, was there ever a time when he struck you as different? Changed?"

Deschênes seems to be genuinely searching his memory.

"It's easy to say after the fact … but maybe he was a little stressed out these last few months, what with buying the new house and moving in."

"Can you tell me more?"

"It was just a vague impression. He seemed more tense, maybe more nervous than usual."

"Enough to strike you as out of the ordinary?"

"No, I'm just mentioning it because you asked. There's a lot to think about when you're moving."

"Did you bring it up with Cook?"

"Of course not. We all have our moods."

"Where did they live previously?"

"In Rosemont."

"Why did they move?"

"I think their house was too small. It only had two bedrooms."

"When was the move? Do you remember?"

"A couple of months ago, I think."

Lessard writes in his notebook:

Look into move.

"When I questioned you this morning, you said Cook knew your past better than anyone. What did you mean?"

"Just that. When I was arrested, John was the first one I called. He was one of the only decent people I knew. Afterward, when my driver's licence got suspended, he put in a good word for me with company management."

"Did you and he spend your off-hours together?"

"Not really. We were hired by Royal Tobacco at the same time, and we worked in the same department for several years. Then John got promoted and went across the street. We were always close at work, but that's as far as it went. I met his wife and kids a few times on special occasions. That's it."

"Did you notice anything unusual about them?"

"Not really. His wife was beautiful. They seemed happy."

"Did he talk to you about his private life?"

"Not a lot. Now and then he'd tell me that one of the kids was sick. Stuff like that."

"He was your best friend at work, the guy you called when you were arrested — but he didn't talk to you about his private life? Are you that tight with all your friends, Deschênes?"

"I'm from Pointe-Saint-Charles. I used to hang out with the wrong kind of people, but I've cut all those connections since I got a grip on my life. John was an educated guy, respectful, a good sounding board. I could talk to him when I was tempted to fall off the wagon. He always gave me wise advice. He was the one who showed me the way."

It occurs to Lessard that he doesn't have a whole lot of friends, either, and he knows almost nothing about the private lives of his fellow cops, despite the fact that he sees them every day.

"The way? You mean God?"

"Yes. It was John who introduced me to the teachings of Jesus Christ."

"Was he very religious?"

"He went to Mass every Sunday."

"Was he in a cult?"

"I know what you're thinking, but no. He was just a regular practising Catholic."

"Apart from your problems and God, what did you talk about?"

"Hockey. We were both Habs fans, so we'd discuss trades, or whether some player was getting paid too much, or the coach should be fired, or how the team looked during their last game ... you get the idea. Actually, that's what we spent most of our time talking about."

"Anything else?"

"Fishing, now and then."

"Did you ever go fishing together?"

"Yeah, for trout, a number of years ago, on a company outing. But John stopped after his kids were born."

"Why?"

"He said Elizabeth didn't like it when he was away."

"Did she strike you as jealous? Possessive?"

"I don't think so. I imagine she was just anxious, worried that something might happen to John. A wife thing, if you ask me. Are we almost finished? I need to go to the bathroom."

"A couple more minutes, and we're done. Do you know anyone named Viviane?"

Deschênes searches his memory for a few seconds, then answers unhesitatingly.

"No."

"Did John know a Viviane?"

"I don't think so."

"Could she be a co-worker, a cousin, a neighbour?"

Deschênes seems genuinely puzzled.

"Not a co-worker, that's for sure. If there was a Viviane at Royal Tobacco, I'd know. As for the rest of it, I'd say no, not to my knowledge."

"Was he having an affair?"

Deschênes reacts. He's visibly surprised.

"John? We never talked about that kind of thing, but I don't think so."

"Would he have told you if he was having one?"

"Not necessarily. He wasn't a boastful guy, and he was smart enough to know that the best way to keep people from finding out is not to talk."

"Why did you run when you saw me?" Lessard asks, looking Deschênes in the eye.

"I did it without thinking," the man says, looking ashamed. "You're not like the rest of them, but man, I hate the fucking police. Always getting in my face over stupid shit, just because I have a record ..."

Lessard feels sympathy for Deschênes. Though he isn't yet altogether convinced, he has a feeling the guy's telling the truth.

"You can open up now, Garneau," he says, pressing the intercom button.

He looks at Deschênes. "Go on home. All I ask is that you respect your curfew and not leave town — in case I have more questions." He hands over his business card. "If you remember anything else about Cook, don't hesitate to call."

The two men are on their feet, looking at each other without animosity. A mutual respect has grown between them during the interrogation. Deschênes turns and walks toward the door, putting on his sweater.

He stops in the doorway and looks back.

"I hope you catch whoever did this to John and his family."

It's after 8:00 p.m. when Lessard comes out of the interrogation room. He hasn't eaten since breakfast, and his clothes are still damp.

He considers returning to the crime scene on Bessborough Avenue, but he's so tired that there's only one thing he wants: to go home, have a bite to eat, take a hot bath, and get a few hours' sleep.

Sitting at his desk, he calls Fernandez's cell number.

"I questioned Deschênes," he says.

"I know. I spoke to Garneau a little while ago, while you were with him. What have you got?"

"I just let him go. The guy panicked because he'd missed his curfew. He hates cops. I'm pretty sure he had nothing to do with the killings."

Fernandez smiles, but refrains from saying she told him so.

"How are things on your end?" Lessard asks.

"Tanguay left at five, like the good civil servant that he is. He asked me to remind you that he's expecting your report tomorrow, without fail. I gave Pearson and Sirois permission to go home fifteen minutes ago. They didn't find anything — at any rate, no suicide note, no email, nothing like that. Doug and his assistant will be at it until late tonight. I went to the clothing store where Elizabeth Munson worked. Nothing there, either. All her co-workers are shocked, no one can understand. She seemed to be in love with John Cook, and when I asked whether she might have had a lover, the reaction was unanimous: she really wasn't that kind of person. So that's where it stands. We're looking at a domestic murder-suicide, but we don't know what's behind it. In any case, whether we come up with a motive or not, we can't take our time with this thing, or we'll end up with Tanguay on our backs."

"Speaking of which —"

Fernandez cuts him off. "Oh, I almost forgot. Berger called. He wants you to go see him in the morning. He'll be able to give you the preliminary autopsy report."

"Perfect. Meanwhile, I may have found a —"

Lessard hears a voice in the background.

"Hang on, Victor ..."

He catches snippets of conversation, but he can't make out what's going on.

"I'm going to have to call you back. Adams needs me for a few minutes. His assistant has gone out for a bite to eat."

"Sure. No problem."

"Was there something you wanted to discuss? Should I call you back?"

Lessard checks his watch. He considers inviting Fernandez out for dinner to talk about the case, but decides against it. They've often had meals together during past investigations, but he never had to worry that she might suspect ulterior motives.

So why is he hesitating today? Could it have something to do with the knot that forms in the pit of his stomach every time he sees her?

By now he's convinced himself that it makes no difference whether he mentions his discovery to Fernandez tonight or in the morning.

"No, we'll talk tomorrow. I'm going home soon. You should do the same."

"I'll be on my way as soon as Doug's assistant gets back. See you tomorrow."

"Good night, Nadja."

Lessard spends a good minute staring at his phone in a haze of exhaustion.

He walks slowly along the hallway, waving at Constable Garneau as he goes by.

He doesn't even have the energy to appreciate her looks.

He parks the car in front of his apartment on Oxford Avenue.

He lifts his gaze skyward and contemplates the rain, which is falling in chaotic sheets. As he turns the key in the front door, he's struck by an odour that he knows all too well.

He's smoking pot again.

Apart from a flickering glow in one corner, the room is pitch-dark.

A candle?

He hears laughter, a woman's voice.

"Martin?"

He presses the light switch and stares in amazement.

His son, two girls he vaguely recalls having seen before, and another boy — a boy he doesn't recognize — are stark naked in the middle of *his* living room. The remnants of a large white candle are guttering out on a low table.

To top it off, Martin's the one holding the joint.

An indescribable commotion ensues, as everyone struggles desperately to cover up. Hiding his erection with both hands, the boy jumps around as though he were walking barefoot on burning sand; the panic-stricken girls dart all over the room, grabbing at the same bra, emitting little shrieks.

Apart from calmly putting on his briefs, Martin remains motionless.

The chaos continues for another few moments, after which the three junior nudists leave the apartment, half-clothed, mumbling apologies as they go. Unfazed by everything that's just transpired around him, Lessard's son takes an occasional puff while looking at his father.

"What the hell was going on here, Martin?"

"Three guesses," the young man retorts.

"Hey! This isn't a motel!"

Martin's face flushes with anger. He throws on his clothes.

"Go on, say it! You'd rather we got up to this stuff somewhere else.... You were supposed to be home late tonight!"

"What the hell's wrong with you? Why do you always have to go overboard? One girl at a time isn't enough?"

"Don't lose your shit, man. It's just a foursome, no big deal. I'm having a little fun, same as you did at my age —"

"I'll lose my shit if want to! And put out that goddamn joint!" Lessard grabs the burning stub from his son's fingers and crushes it under his heel.

"You're one to talk," Martin says. "Like getting behind the wheel after a dozen beers is so much better than smoking a blunt with a couple of friends!"

The reference to Lessard's alcoholism and former bad habits couldn't be clearer.

Martin grabs his jacket and marches toward the door. Lessard tries to prevent him, but the young man shoves him aside.

"Where are you going?"

"Anywhere but here."

"Martin! Get serious —"

"I *am* serious. By the way, your sister called."

The door slams.

6

There is another world, but it lies within this one.

— Paul Éluard

Montreal
May 6th

Having showered and shaved, Lessard arrives early at the mobile command post, hoping to speak to Fernandez.

He wants to tell her about yesterday's discovery before getting an update from the rest of the team. He's decided not to share the information with the other detectives until he hears Fernandez's thoughts on the matter. Does this slip of paper justify widening the investigation? It's not that Lessard distrusts Pearson and Sirois. Quite the contrary. But he knows from experience that the more people he lets in on the secret, the harder it will be to keep Commander Tanguay from finding out about Cook's note.

And he definitely wants to keep Tanguay from finding out.

The commander has already practically closed the case, having announced to the media that it's a domestic murder-suicide. So, before raising doubts about whether Cook is the killer — and thus undermining the boss's credibility — Lessard wants to be sure that he's got something solid. Otherwise, he knows very well what will happen: Tanguay will dismiss the idea out of hand.

For that matter, Lessard himself isn't convinced that the note proves much. The implications are serious. If Cook didn't commit the murders before killing himself, then this isn't just a domestic crime. Rather, Lessard and his team are looking at a quintuple murder disguised as an act of family violence.

Which means there's a killer at large.

That's not a trivial claim, and it's certainly not one that Lessard wants to make to his boss in an offhand way.

But the real reason for his hesitation is much simpler: he wonders whether he's imagining things, whether he's trying to transform this domestic murder-suicide into a different kind of crime, seeking to sublimate his past, refusing to believe that Cook could have been driven by the same murderous madness that drove Lessard's own father to perpetrate a massacre.

He's pouring himself a cup of hot water, lost in thought, when Pearson speaks.

"Victor, Fernandez just left a message on my voice mail. She says we should start without her. She's running late."

"Late? That's not like her. Did she say why?"

"Huh …? Oh, no," Pearson says, absorbed in typing an email into his BlackBerry.

Lessard and the investigation team review the various pieces of information that have been gathered: Depositions from friends, relatives, neighbours, and co-workers are examined with care. The cleaning lady's brief account is noted. Sirois, having spoken to the neighbour across the street, confirms what the detective sergeant heard from Deschênes — that Cook and Munson were religious, but they didn't belong to a cult. Lessard tells the other cops what Cook's boss and Deschênes both said: that Cook had shown no signs of depression. Lessard also notes that, according to Deschênes, the move into the new house seems to have had an adverse effect on Cook's state of mind. Pearson observes that the month preceding his own most recent move was the worst period in his whole life. Even so, Lessard wants the team to get further information from Munson's mother. Did Cook's behavior change during the weeks before and after the move?

The meeting is wrapping up. Lessard can now go to Berger's office.

A glance outside makes his heart sink. Rain is pounding the cars in the driveway.

"Okay. Let's keep digging for a few more hours. But unless something unexpected turns up in the autopsy or in Adams's report, we'll close the case by the end of the day, whether or not we find a suicide note or something else that explains the crime."

The other cops nod.

Suddenly, Lessard feels ill at ease. He's just evoked the possibility that something unexpected may turn up, yet he's hiding the fact that he found a note in the shed.

"Let's not forget the flies," Sirois says.

Garneau and Pearson exchange skeptical looks. They see the multitude of insects as nothing more than an inexplicable coincidence, the kind of anomaly that inevitably crops up now and then, out of pure happenstance.

To be honest, Lessard hasn't had a moment to consider the matter.

"Good point. I'll discuss it with Berger. Any news from Fernandez?" he asks, gathering his papers.

"No," Pearson says.

"Okay. I'm outa here. When she arrives, have her call me."

Lessard finds Berger in his office at the Forensic Science and Legal Medicine Laboratory on Parthenais Street.

The room is small and windowless.

Stacks of papers are lying on the desk and floor in an elaborate lattice, giving the impression that the removal of a single document might throw the whole structure off balance.

A shelf on the wall holds knives, machetes, handguns, and various other items that Berger has accumulated from the many investigations he's worked on. The piece that Lessard finds most fascinating is the goalie mask that was used by a rapist who briefly terrorized the city of Laval — a mask that recalls the one used by Jason in the *Friday the 13th* series of cult horror films.

"How's it going, Jacob?"

"Badly," Berger grumbles. "I'm completely worn out. I was up all night working on the couple's autopsies. I haven't gotten around to the children yet. I'm going to lie down for a few hours, then get back to work this afternoon."

The medical examiner can be a prima donna sometimes, and his haughty attitude gets on Lessard's nerves, but over time, the cop has come to like Berger and, above all, to trust his judgment, which has shown itself to be reliable.

"You're going to do the three children's autopsies by yourself?"

Berger sighs. "No choice. Cloutier's at a seminar in Rhode Island." He rolls his eyes irritably. "I left two voice mails. She's unreachable. Want a cup of coffee?"

"No, thanks. I've stopped drinking the stuff."

"You have?" Berger asks, surprised.

"I still have a decaf every morning. I'm taking pills for my reflux."

"Really? No more Pepto-Bismol?"

"That's right," Lessard says, laughing, "No more Pepto-Bismol. I do miss the taste, though," he adds, without a trace of irony.

"You're aware that reflux sufferers shouldn't drink decaf, either?"

"Yeah, but it's the only pleasure I have left. What have you come up with so far, Jacob? Any surprises?"

"Not really. I can confirm that the man started out by inflicting a number of shallow cuts on his own torso, as though he were trying to commit *hara-kiri* and hadn't yet worked up the nerve. Next, he cut out his tongue. And finally, he drove the knife into his throat. That's what killed him. The blade sliced right through an artery. Hemorrhaging was massive."

"Was he intoxicated?"

"Either that or highly motivated."

"How did he manage to cut out his tongue? Seems to me that grabbing a tongue would be as tricky as catching a bar of soap in the bathtub — slippery, hard to keep in place."

"He used a dishtowel to hold on to it."

Lessard shakes his head, incredulous. "I see. Anything else?"

"It's the injury to the shoulder that bothers me."

An image flashes in front of Lessard's eyes. He remembers the open wound on John Cook's shoulder, exposing nerves and tendons.

"I've tried to re-create the injury with the axe that was found at the crime scene, but I can't do it."

"Why not?"

"Judging from the angle, it's hard to see how that wound was self-inflicted."

"Are you saying it's impossible?"

"Not impossible, but unlikely."

"Who else could have inflicted it?" Lessard asks.

"His wife," Berger says. "She might have managed to wrestle the axe out of his hands and tried to defend herself with it."

"His wife? That would support the theory of a single killer, as opposed to a suicide pact. Are her prints on the murder weapon?"

"I just spoke to Adams. His report is preliminary, but it seems like they are."

"Alternatively," Lessard muses, "she might have participated in the killings at first, then changed her mind partway through and turned the weapon against Cook. It wouldn't be the first time that's happened."

"Both theories are valid," Berger says.

There's a moment of silence, then Lessard says, "She was found on her bed, but according to Adams, she was moved."

"I think so, too."

"Could she have been drugged?"

"Possibly. I won't have toxicology results for a few days."

"If so, Cook would have carried her to the bed after drugging and killing her."

Lessard pulls out his notebook and scribbles briefly.

"What did she die of, Jacob?"

"Five or six of the axe blows were fatal. I estimate that she received fifteen in all."

Lessard shudders. The darkness of the human soul chills him.

"Anything else?"

"Nothing, except that I found semen in Elizabeth Munson's vagina. I checked: it's her husband's."

"So they had sex before —"

"Yeah. Pretty strange."

"Unless he raped her."

"I found no signs that would indicate rape, but yes, that's a possibility."

There's a low hum. Berger unclips his pager from his belt.

"What do you know? It's Cloutier, calling me back. Give me five minutes, Victor. I need to talk to her."

"No problem. I'm done here, anyway. One last question, Jacob. The flies — can you explain why there were so many of them?"

"It's pretty strange, but unfortunately, Lewis, our forensic ento-mologist, is at the same conference as Cloutier. I have a friend who works as an entomologist at the Insectarium. Lewis collaborates with her now and then, when particularly tricky questions come up. She did her Ph.D. on the taxonomy of Diptera. She's one of the only fly specialists in Quebec. As soon as I have a minute, I'll call her."

"Don't trouble yourself," Lessard says. "You've got enough on your plate. Give me her contact info, and I'll take care of it."

Lessard takes the Ville-Marie Expressway back to Notre-Dame-de-Grâce, getting off at the Saint-Jacques exit.

His stomach is rumbling.

No surprise there. He hasn't eaten yet. Among the healthy habits he acquired during his relationship with Véronique is his practice of eating a breakfast of fruit juice and whole grain cereal topped with plain yogourt.

This morning, though, he wasn't hungry. He hadn't slept well after the argument with his son.

Thinking back on the situation, Lessard realizes that he was more surprised than angry.

Martin never came home last night, and he turned off his cell-phone. Lessard has tried to reach him twice. Not that he's overly worried. They've been down this road before.

Before returning to the crime scene, he decides to go have a bite at the Old Orchard Pub on Monkland Avenue, where he occasionally has breakfast. He orders his usual meal from his usual waitress: an egg, tomato, and lettuce sandwich. Suppressing the urge to wash down the meal with a nice cold Guinness, he orders a decaf. As she always does, the waitress informs him that he'll have to wait a few minutes while they make a pot.

For crying out loud, is he the only idiot in the world who drinks decaf?

Lessard opens the car door.

Since the weather forecast calls for several days of rain, he takes out the old yellow slicker that he used to wear on fishing trips.

Actually, he's only gone fishing twice in his life.

He quickly realized that what drew him to the pastime wasn't actually catching fish; it was the idea of being in harmony with nature and leading a healthy wilderness lifestyle. But in the end, the whine of dive-bombing mosquitoes; the lake that was supposed to be "teeming with trout" yet failed to produce so much as a nibble; the rising at dawn to "get a good start" when all his body craved was sleep — in short, everything that actually had to do with fishing — held little attraction for him.

He wanders from room to room in the house on Bessborough Avenue. In the kitchen, he encounters Adams's assistant, who's packing up his equipment.

After going by with a polite nod, Lessard turns to ask the guy if he's seen Fernandez, but he's already left.

Apart from the traces of blood on the walls and floors, there's nothing to suggest that a murder was committed here.

In John Cook's office, Lessard opens the drawers and examines their contents. He takes several volumes off the bookshelf and shakes them, hoping a piece of paper might slip from their pages; he leafs through the folders in a file cabinet. On a shelf, he finds documents that have been annotated by hand. The notes were surely made by Cook, since the documents concern Royal Tobacco. To Lessard's eye, the handwriting resembles that on the message he found in the shed. He slips the papers into a pocket of his raincoat, telling himself that he'll compare the writing later, in a more comfortable setting. He goes on searching a little while longer, pausing to look at an old photo album. He even takes a framed picture off the wall to see what's behind it.

Pearson and Sirois have already gone over everything, but you never know ...

Now that he thinks about it — where are those two?

Lessard had expected to run into one of them, but the house is clearly empty.

As he turns to leave the room, he bumps into a vase containing water and bamboo stalks, which is perched on a corner of the desk. The vase teeters for a moment, hanging precariously at the edge of the work surface. Lessard tries to catch it, and almost succeeds, before it slips from his grasp. But the cop's clumsy fingers have slowed the vase's descent. It lands on the floor without breaking.

Lessard puts back the bamboo stalks and steps into the hallway, grumbling, to find something to wipe up the water. In the laundry room, he opens a cabinet and takes a towel off a pile.

As he's about to reclose the cabinet, he notices two VHS cassettes on the bottom shelf.

Strange place to leave videocassettes.

Deciding to screen them at his place rather than in the noisy environment of the police station, he pockets the cassettes. Will he be able to reconnect his old VHS player?

Martin would know how to do it in an instant.

Where is that kid, anyway?

Lessard loiters on the upper floor of the house after cleaning up his mess. Even though the bedrooms are deserted and the beds are empty, images suddenly begin to swirl through his mind: the bodies of Elizabeth Munson and her children mingle with those of his mother and brothers in a macabre dance.

The walls close in around him like a vise. A lake of blood begins to seethe beyond the windows.

Then he hears something behind him. A familiar voice murmurs in his ear.

"You abandoned me, Victor."

He spins around.

The boy in the striped tank top is standing in front of him.

Lessard refuses to believe what he's seeing. He shakes his head to dispel the vision. A panicky fear seizes him, the kind of terror that makes a child ask his parents to check for monsters under the bed and in the closet.

How long does he go on yelling?

He can't say.

A hand on his shoulder brings him back to reality.

"Are you okay, Victor? I was in the basement. You gave me a scare."

White as a sheet, Lessard takes a few seconds to regain his composure.

"I'm fine, Doug. Just a little stressed out. Sorry."

Before he even saw the boy's face, Lessard knew the identity of the scrawny kid in the striped tank top who's been crossing his path since yesterday. More than thirty years after hearing it for the last time, he recognized his brother's voice instantly.

The wounds and dried blood are still visible on his throat and chest.

Raymond.

She's put on a raincoat and rubber boots.

Recalling the child she was, just a few short years ago, she takes mischievous delight in jumping into puddles, watching the muddy water splash her thighs and snake back down her calves.

Laila loves rain the way a person might love springtime, or the smell of coffee, or a country walk. Her wet hair sticks to her face, a stray lock rising and falling to the smooth rhythm of her gait.

As she had expected, Monsieur Antoine's trailer is standing at the intersection of Berri Street and De Maisonneuve Boulevard. Two squeegee kids are smoking near the door.

Inside, a couple of goths with a German Shepherd on a leash are talking to a volunteer. A young, hollow-eyed girl, her face riddled with acne, is sunk in a corner. A little farther off, another volunteer is distributing syringes to three homeless youths who reek of urine.

Laila goes to the back of the trailer, where Monsieur Antoine is sitting on the same rickety, uncomfortable chair that he's occupied for so many years. The old man is reading to Felix, who's sitting on his lap.

Felix's mother, a heroin-addicted, HIV-positive prostitute, used to be an occasional visitor to the trailer. From the age of four, Felix would accompany her to seedy hotel rooms, where she turned tricks for disgusting men. An exceptionally intelligent child, Felix started keeping a diary during the long periods he spent alone in bathrooms, waiting for his mother.

By the age of seven, he was working the streets himself. One day, Monsieur Antoine found the little boy standing in front of the trailer holding all his worldly possessions: a few balled-up sweaters in a paper bag. Felix's mother had apparently left for Vancouver, leaving her son behind — surely the greatest favour she could have done him.

Monsieur Antoine immediately offered to become Felix's foster parent. After some back-and-forth with the youth protection authorities, the child was entrusted to him.

Felix, who's small for his age, hasn't uttered a word since he was brutally assaulted some time ago. When spoken to, he responds through gestures or mouth noises, or simply scribbles a few words on a little chalkboard or in his diary, which he carries with him everywhere.

"Look who's here, Felix."

A shy smile lights up the boy's face. He likes Laila.

"Hi, Monsieur Antoine. Hello there, Felix!"

The elderly man stands up. He's a little more bent and stiff than the last time Laila saw him.

"What a pleasure to see you, sweetie."

Laila hands him a canvas bag filled with items intended for street kids.

"I've brought some clothes that I don't wear anymore, and a few toiletries. I also have something for you, Felix."

She extracts a second-hand book from her pocket and gives it to the boy, whose eyes widen.

"Oh," Monsieur Antoine says. "*The Old Man and the Sea*, by Ernest Hemingway. A very serious book, Felix." He looks at the girl. "Have you read it, Laila?"

"Yes. It's beautiful. And very sad."

She thinks she sees a tear on Monsieur Antoine's cheek. But she isn't sure.

Felix steps close and gives her a hug.

The child is sitting in a corner, poring over the Hemingway novel. He's entirely immersed in it as Monsieur Antoine and Laila sip tea.

"Do you plan to keep doing that video stuff?" Monsieur Antoine asks.

"I don't know. For now, the money's good. I can do it at home, and it's easy."

"Have you considered going back to school?"

"I've thought about it. But not yet."

The old man lifts his head and looks into her eyes.

"You're not using again, are you, Laila?"

"No. I'm totally done with that."

"You don't seem too sure," he says doubtfully.

Laila isn't about to admit that she still allows herself an occasional joint.

"I'm telling you, Monsieur Antoine, the therapy really helped. Trust me, all that stuff is behind me."

"I'm glad to hear it, sweetie. I had to ask — better that than to sit here worrying about you. But there's something else I want to talk about."

"Yes?" Laila says nervously, wondering what's coming.

"I know how much you care about your work with the support group."

Some time ago, Monsieur Antoine (whose full name is Antoine Chambord), knowing Laila's past, put her in charge of a support group for drug-addicted street kids. He had some initial reservations because of her young age.

But after some thought, he decided that assigning the task to her would kill two birds with one stone: on the one hand, the young addicts who came to the trailer would benefit from Laila's experience, and on the other, the responsibility would help her to stay off drugs herself.

That was the hope, at least.

But last week, after a meeting, he found Laila sitting alone, in tears. One of the kids in the group had killed himself two days previously. The last thing Chambord wants is for Laila to get so caught up helping others that she neglects her own needs and falls back into her old habits.

"Yes," she says, "I love it. It's a major responsibility."

"That's what I'd like to talk about. I don't want you feeling overwhelmed, or putting too much pressure on yourself. You don't have to be perfect. You don't have to save anyone."

Laila can see where this is going.

"I get the message, Monsieur Antoine."

"Good. If ever there's a problem, Laila, come and see me. I'm always here for you."

"I know. Thank you."

Chambord smiles and asks in a lighter voice:

"How's Mélanie these days?"

"Just great. She says hi, by the way. And you, Monsieur Antoine? How are you keeping?"

"Oh, you know …"

Laila is sitting next to Felix, with her back to the wall.

"Can I see what's in your diary, Felix?"

The boy looks at her in silence.

"My bad. Forget I asked. How about drawing a picture for me?"

Laila gives Monsieur Antoine a peck on the cheek.

"Gotta go."

"Are you sure you're all right, sweetie? You seem anxious."

The girl hesitates. He's offering her a chance to talk. All she has to do is take it. Monsieur Antoine is wise, and he's an excellent listener. Most importantly, he doesn't judge her.

She's about to confide in him when a hand tugs at the hem of her raincoat.

"Oh, Felix, what a beautiful drawing!"

She crouches down and takes the boy in her arms.

"It was nice of you to come by, Laila. If you ever need anything, just say the word."

"Sure thing. Take care, Monsieur Antoine. 'Bye, Felix."

The boy watches Laila walk away in the rain.

Dear stupid diary,

Monsieur Antoine is sad because he's old, and he's old because he's sad. I guess I'm too young to understand, but I saw him crying when Laila gave me the book. I read the back cover. It talked about an unlucky old fisherman who wants to catch a big swordfish so he can save his honour as a man. Monsieur Antoine still has his honour as a man, but he's been fighting a big swordfish of his own for a long time now.

I think he's very tired.

A few days ago, he told me that I'll live to be a hundred, while his own years have nearly run out. On my chalkboard, I wrote, "Maybe I can share my years with you, because you've taken care of me and haven't made me work."

When he read what I'd written, Monsieur Antoine pretended there was something in his eye. Let me tell you, stupid diary, it really bugs me when words make people cry. You know how onions bring tears to your eyes? Sometimes words do the same thing. When that happens, I don't know where to look or what to do with my hands.

I remember the day Monsieur Antoine gave me my first card.

That's what Monsieur Antoine does. He laughs and makes jokes and watches you with his crinkly eyes, but if you do something he's told you not to — bam! He'll give you a card that's yellower than his teeth.

And then you need to be careful, because after the yellow card comes the red card. I'll tell you all about the red card later if you're interested, but just so you know, the red card is bad news.

When Laila came by a little while ago, I could see from Monsieur Antoine's face that something was wrong. He was looking at Laila with a stern face, the way he'd have looked if he'd given her a red card.

- - - - - - - - - - - - - - - - - -

Laila is walking back to her apartment, oblivious of the rain. She cuts through an alley near Charlemagne Street.

She's thinking about David, whom she wishes she could seduce. She's thinking about Monsieur Antoine, to whom she wanted to open up about her past — but Felix chose that moment to show her his drawing. Which was probably for the best.

Above all, she's thinking about HIM.

It's inevitable. Every passing day brings back memories of that living nightmare, that dark tide of misery that keeps rising in her, despite her best attempts to submerge it in an ocean of forgetfulness.

Jagged lightning ignites the sky.

At that moment, a hand covers Laila's mouth and an arm goes around her throat, pulling her backward.

She has no time to react or cry out.

8

In the yard, the clatter of the rain on the shed's roof reassures him. The cold raindrops invigorate him. Little by little, the colour returns to his cheeks.

His hand is still trembling as he brings the cigarette uncertainly to his mouth, but he calms down as the nicotine invades his lungs and takes effect on his central nervous system.

When it happened, the apparition seemed so real that he lost his grip. He panicked.

Now he finds himself laughing.

It's nervous laughter — but at least it's laughter.

Lessard doesn't waste time wondering what this incredible apparition means. His denial is absolute. He hasn't just seen a ghost or anything like that. There's a perfectly logical explanation: this case has forced him to confront the trauma of his past. In his extreme sensitivity, he's fallen prey to hallucinations.

End of story.

What does worry him, though, is the possibility that this episode could have an impact on the investigation, if the higher-ups find out.

As long as Adams doesn't tell everyone that he found me wailing like a terrified baby.

Once again, Lessard becomes aware of something behind him — a gaze focused on his back.

This time, it's not Raymond. He knows who it is. The little boy he saw yesterday is back at his window, wearing his sad expression. The boy waves.

Suddenly, Lessard has an idea.

He knocks at the door of the neighbouring house.

The mother is Moroccan, or perhaps Algerian. She wears a hijab and barely speaks any English or French. Is she the boy's mother? His babysitter? Lessard isn't sure. Whatever she is, she lets him in when she sees his badge.

Using a mix of sign language, sound effects, and a hodge-podge of French and English, he manages to make her understand that he'd like to talk to the boy.

She leads him upstairs.

Lessard doesn't pay much attention to the elaborate décor. The woman leads him into a child's bedroom, painted in bright blue tones and overflowing with toys and stuffed animals. On one wall, he sees a computer-printed banner.

WELCOME HOME, FAIZAN!

The boy is sitting at a low table. He stops drawing and looks up curiously at the detective sergeant.

He's small and chubby, with dark hair and skin, and very black eyes. On the left side of his skull, there's a scar shaped like an inverted U, which starts at his ear and arcs around to the back of his head. The sutures are still visible.

"Hey there, young man. Do you speak English? Français?"

"I speak both," the boy says, without an accent.

Lessard points to a chair facing the child. "May I sit down?"

The chair squeaks under the cop's weight, but doesn't give way. He's a foot off the floor, with his knees grazing his chin.

"My name is Victor. I'm a policeman."

The boy looks at him.

"What's your name?"

"Faizan."

"How old are you, Faizan?"

"Seven."

"Is this lady your mom?"

Lessard turns to the woman, who's sitting on the bed. She gives him a shy smile.

"Yes."

"What happened to your head, Faizan?"

"I had a tumour taken out."

"Oh." There's an awkward silence. "I … uh … are you feeling better now?"

"Yes. I don't sleep very well, because of the medication, and also because of my scar. It hurts when I move my head. But the swelling has almost gone away. I looked like a big pumpkin right after the operation."

"The scar will heal soon, Faizan. When your hair grows back, you won't even be able to see it."

"I know. I had a tumour taken out once before."

Lessard swallows.

Jesus. He's just a kid.

"You know what, Faizan? I'm betting this one's the last."

"I hope so. I want to go back to school and see my friends."

The mother looks at her son with love and pride.

"Say, Faizan, I noticed that you stand at the window quite a bit."

"Yes. I can't go outside, so I like to look out and imagine."

"Do you imagine all the things you'll do when you're well again?"

"Yes."

"That's great. Hey, Faizan, do you know the man who lives next door? Mr. Cook?"

"Yes. He has a daughter my age. Her name is Erin. She's funny."

"Did your mom explain to you why there are police officers at Mr. Cook's house right now?"

The woman's fluency is clearly greater than Lessard thought, because the moment he mentions the neighbour, she's on her feet, gesturing to him.

He raises a hand to calm her fears.

"No, she didn't tell me," the boy says.

"The house where Mr. Cook and Erin live was broken into, and we're trying to find the thieves who broke in. Do you understand, Faizan?"

"Yes."

"That's why I've come to see you. I'd like to know whether you saw anything strange at Mr. Cook's house."

Faizan answers without hesitation.

"Flies."

Shoved up against a brick wall where no one can see her, Laila feels a blade grazing the soft flesh under her right eye socket, while a hand squeezes her throat.

"Why don't you pick up when I call, bitch?"

The pressure on her carotid artery eases off for an instant. She coughs and gulps for air. Her assailant's foul breath fills her nostrils.

Razor.

Small and ginger-haired — the kind of scumbag who'd sell his mother for a bag of chips — Razor is a crazy motherfucker who deals drugs for the Red Blood Spillers. He's known for his expertise with an old-fashioned straight razor. And Laila owes him money.

She regrets not taking his call while she was with David. She might have avoided what's about to happen.

"You have the cash?"

Her lower lip trembling, Laila shakes her head. Razor hits the wall beside her face with the flat of his hand.

"When?"

"S … soon."

"Better be real soon, bitch."

He forces Laila into a crouch in the alley.

Lessard feels the hair stand up on his head.

"Flies? Tell me what you saw, Faizan."

"There were lots of flies at Mr. Cook's house. A big black cloud of them."

The cop has noticed a box of crayons on a shelf. He makes up his mind to ask Faizan to draw the cloud of flies later on.

"When was this? In the daytime? In the evening? At night?"

"At night."

"At night? Are you sure?"

The boy points to an alarm clock on the night table, its digits glowing.

"It was dark. There was a one and two zeroes on the clock. I learned to tell time at school. It was one o'clock in the morning."

"That's great, Faizan! You weren't asleep at that hour?"

"No. I woke up because of my scar. It was hurting."

"Where were the flies, Faizan?"

"In the kitchen window."

"Were the lights on in Mr. Cook's kitchen?"

"Yes."

"Did you see anything else?"

"I saw you in the yard. And a lady, too."

Faizan describes Fernandez in detail.

"That's right, I work with her. She's my friend. Her name is Nadja, and she's very nice. But let's get back to the night when you saw the flies, okay?"

"Okay."

"Did you see anyone in the yard that night?"

"Yes. A man came outside."

"Was it Mr. Cook?"

"No, it wasn't him. It was another man. He was wearing a long black robe, with a white square on his neck."

Lessard ponders for a moment, puzzled.

"You mean, like a cassock?"

"What's a cassock?"

"Don't worry about that." Lessard stands up and fetches the crayons. "Can you draw the man for me?"

He watches over the boy's shoulder as he draws.

A priest?

"Are you sure you're not making a mistake, Faizan? Did the man really have a collar like a priest?"

"He looked like my drawing."

"What colour was his skin?"

"Same as yours."

"White. Okay. And this man, this priest, did he go near the garden shed?"

Lessard is thinking of the message he found. Maybe someone wanted to create the impression that Cook had put it there.

"No."

"What was the priest doing in the yard, Faizan?"

"He was holding an axe in his hand."

9

Earth's fanatics make too frequently heaven's saints.
— Elizabeth Barrett Browning

Saint Joseph's Oratory

Father Aldéric Dorion no longer celebrates Mass in the regular way.

Though his advanced age and the state of his health aren't obstacles to the proper observance of the rite, the priest has grown openly weary of it. Churches are empty and parishioners are losing their faith; he prefers to be in direct contact with those who still believe.

Receiving the confessions of the faithful and, above all, offering aid to the poorest residents of the Côte-des-Neiges community are the sole activities to which he intends to devote his energy during the years he has left.

Today, he dons his clerical robe and departs from his usual practice as a favour to an ailing colleague. Though he's a little rusty, he gets through the Mass without too much trouble. He's wrapping up his homily when he sees two men — one wearing a cassock, the other imposingly large — walk slowly through the nave and settle into a pew twenty rows from the altar.

He can't help shuddering when he sees them.

Fear knots his stomach.

Father Dorion's office is in the presbytery that adjoins the basilica. He ushers in his two visitors with a trembling hand.

"Do you know why I'm here, Aldéric?" the man in the cassock asks, after they're seated.

"I'm sorry, Noah. I must decline to hear your confession. Even at my age, I want to protect my ears from filth."

"Very funny," the man in the cassock says, and makes a show of applauding.

Noah approaches until his face is a few centimetres from Dorion's. The two clerics look at each other with hostility. The large man keeps his distance.

"We've lost him. Tell me where he is, Aldéric."

"I have no idea. And you must leave him alone!"

"Mr. Moreno can be very persuasive," Noah says, referring to his huge companion. "Even with the most stubborn individuals. If I were you, Aldéric, I wouldn't make things difficult. Pain isn't a healthy option at your age."

De la Cathédrale Street, downtown Montreal
A few hours later

Occupying the top floor of the building, the office of Cardinal Charles Millot, Archbishop of Montreal, is tastefully decorated, without ostentatious luxury.

The large bay windows offer an exceptional view of the downtown skyline and Mount Royal.

François Cordeau, the cardinal's young assistant, has just brought in tea and cookies. His Eminence shoves the tray away with the back of his hand. Millot's multiple chins are quivering indignantly.

The man in the cassock, who has provoked the cardinal's fury, listens impassively to his diatribe.

"I refuse to believe that the *Propaganda Fide* endorses your actions!"

Red-faced, the cardinal breaks out in a fit of coughing.

"But it has," Noah says. "I've been given a mandate, and I intend to carry it out, despite the risks it entails."

"You're talking about the bloodbath on Bessborough Avenue as though you were a money manager discussing an asset portfolio. Human lives were lost!"

"I know very well what was lost and, need I add, so do those who sent me."

The reference to the operation's sponsors infuriates Millot even further. *How can Rome have agreed to this madness?*

"Have you thought about the repercussions if these events were to become public? The global media would have a field day!"

"All necessary steps have been taken to make sure that doesn't happen," Noah says.

"If I may, Your Eminence," François Cordeau interjects, "there's always the chance of a leak. Someone on the inside could very well let something slip."

Noah gives the young man a threatening look.

"Very few people know about this," he says, in a tone of thinly concealed warning. "It would be regrettable if anyone betrayed our trust."

Millot stands up, wearing a severe expression.

The cardinal would like to go on upbraiding Noah, but he needs to make inquiries among his contacts in Rome before venturing any further. Political alliances are volatile in the shadowy corridors of the Vatican.

"We'll continue this conversation later, Noah. Now, you must excuse us. François and I have an urgent matter to deal with."

The man in the cassock turns and leaves without a backward glance.

Noah goes into his bedroom and bolts the door.

He stretches out on the comfortless bed, brushing the coarse wool blanket with the back of his hand.

He belongs to the *Milites Christi*, or Soldiers of Christ — a secret, radical branch of the *Propaganda Fide*, the Vatican organization devoted to promoting Catholicism in non-Catholic countries.

He's also a high-ranking officer in the Vatican intelligence service, the *Servizio Informazioni del Vaticano*, or SIV.

Although the Vatican doesn't officially acknowledge its existence, the SIV has clerical and lay operatives on every continent,
with unlimited finances and ultrasophisticated communications
systems. Its electronic interception centre, known as the Circle, is
one of the most effective in Europe.

Despite his high rank, Noah has asked the cardinal to make sure
he's housed in accommodations reserved for low-level staff. He leads a
rigorous, ascetic existence marked by physical and material privations.

This austerity does not, however, prevent him from taking whatever measures are necessary to ensure the success of his mission. No
expense is too great if it's in the service of Christ.

The SIV agent opens a metal briefcase, takes out a satellite phone
equipped with an anti-eavesdropping device, and presses the auto-
dial button. The call doesn't go directly to its destination. A complex
network of connections winds through different countries, minim-
izing the risk that the conversation will be heard by inquisitive third
parties.

Numerous clicks come down the line.

Only after thirty seconds does he hear ringing.

In the Vatican City, a man picks up on the fourth ring.

"Hello, Noah."

"The Soldiers of Christ are at your service."

The urgent matter that the cardinal referred to is now lying on his
bed. François Cordeau is stroking the folds of fat on Millot's milk-
white belly.

"Ah, François," Millot says, "dear young François, you have such
magical fingers."

"I thought it was my mouth that was magical, Your Eminence."

"Your mouth, your fingers, all of you is divine," Millot purrs,
tousling his protégé's hair. "And don't call me 'Your Eminence.' Not
when we're alone."

Cordeau smiles. He likes it when Charles showers him with praise.

It makes him happy to be singled out for the cardinal's special
attentions.

He owes everything to Millot.

It was Millot who rescued him from the street, back when he was a twelve-year-old boy blowing greedy pedophiles for a few bucks a pop. And it was Millot who made it possible for him to study philosophy, and later to obtain a Ph.D. in theology. The young man doesn't share the cardinal's unrelenting spiritual fervour, but he keeps his skepticism to himself, putting on a show of enthusiasm whenever called upon to express his faith.

"If you can spare me for a few hours, Charles, I think I'll go to the gym."

"Of course. I'll take a nap. *Mens sana in corpore sano.* Take good care of that magnificent body, François. It's a gift from God."

Cordeau gets dressed and deposits a kiss on Millot's mouth — a graceful butterfly alighting on a scaly thornbush.

Before leaving, Cordeau adjusts his hair in the mirror.

"Look at you," the cardinal says. "Look how handsome you are."

The remark makes him smile.

His reflection in the mirror gazes at Millot, as though to say, *Not bad for a Verdun kid who bounced from one foster home to another after his worthless mother had the good sense to die with a needle in her arm.*

While the cardinal and his assistant are engaged in their lustful activities, the SIV agent reflects on his conversation with Millot.

The cardinal won't be a problem. The SIV agent has the necessary resources to keep him at bay.

The same can't be said of François Cordeau, who belongs to the new generation of seminarians, ambitious and opportunistic, with finely honed political skills.

Cordeau is a potential threat. Noah will have to deal with him.

After praying in silence, the SIV agent turns off the light and lies down for a short nap. At the threshold of sleep, in a semiconscious state, he sees a succession of fleeting images.

Screams, the seething of a red sea, blood rebounding off skin and flying in all directions, panicked eyes struggling to focus on the walls, more screams, departing souls reflected in the metal of the axe blade, the smell of fear crawling on the floor, the frenzy of violence, the cloud of flies somersaulting like a squadron of death, yet more screams, mutilated bodies, mangled organs, a shapeless mass of flesh and bone and cartilage, madness, carnage, chaos, a river of blood, an infinity of broken screams.

Then silence.

In the end: only death.

10

The water is overflowing onto the sidewalks. Montreal hasn't seen a deluge like this in a long time.

Through the holes in the sewers' manhole covers, foul yellowish water wells up — muddy sock juice, filthy and malodorous.

"Nadja, it's Victor. I need to talk to you right away. Call me as soon as you get this message."

He pockets his cellphone, grumbling, and searches for the keys to his apartment.

His running shoes and the bottoms of his pants are soaked.

He looks at his watch: almost noon.

As a rule, Fernandez is unfailingly reliable.

What are you up to?

Sitting in front of the TV set in his underwear, Lessard wipes the beads of sweat from his forehead. It took him more than twenty profanity-laced minutes to connect all the necessary wires and get the VCR working.

Claiming that they never used the device anymore, Martin wanted to throw it away after his father bought a new flat-screen TV and Blu-ray/DVD player. But Lessard objected and stored the old machine in a cabinet, reluctant to write off his collection of VHS cassettes.

Now he tries without success to insert one of the cassettes that he found in John Cook's home. He realizes that there's already a cassette in the player. He ejects it and looks at the label, which is marked in his handwriting, in blue ink.

MUHAMMAD ALI VS. GEORGE FOREMAN.

Kinshasa, October 1974.

That legendary fight, which he's watched at least a hundred times, saw Ali triumph over the hulking boxer whom America considered to be unbeatable.

A fight that pitted one man against a nation.

Lessard inserts the first cassette.

After ten seconds of blackness, he sees images of a mountainous countryside.

The sky is cloudy. A cottony fog has fallen over a forest of conifers.

The scene seems to have been captured by a handheld camera.

A long, panning shot reveals a lake at the foot of the slope.

The camera zooms and the image blurs for a few seconds before a log cabin appears, overlooking the lake.

The air seems cool. It must be autumn.

The only sound is the wind in the background.

Cut.

Next comes a shaky shot of a man's boots tramping along the hillside. The camera must have been turned on inadvertently while its operator was walking toward the lake.

Cut.

The next shot shows the interior of a cabin. Most likely the one that was shot in the previous sequence.

A woman can be seen from behind, washing dishes.

"Hi, baby," says a man's voice.

Looking younger than in the photos Lessard saw, Elizabeth Munson turns, smiling. She puts an index finger to her lips.

"Shhh."

She beckons to the invisible man — John Cook, no doubt — indicating that he should follow her. The camera moves through a succession of hallways. The image is choppy, alternating between darkness and light. The camera finally settles on something, but it's too dark for Lessard to make out what he's seeing.

"Wait, John," Elizabeth Munson murmurs.

The light in the room gradually becomes brighter.

A baby is sleeping peacefully in a bassinet.

"Hey there, Erin Cook," the man says. "Sleep tight, my love."

Cut. New image.

This time, Cook is shooting what seems to be a small dinner party. Elizabeth serves pasta to a scruffy guy in his twenties. A young woman — his girlfriend? — is feeding the Cooks' baby, who is sitting in a high chair.

Everyone is talking at once, and Lessard has trouble making out what's being said. The atmosphere is joyful: people are laughing, glasses are being raised. Suddenly, the lights dim, and everyone starts to sing the world's most familiar song: "Happy Birthday."

Elizabeth Munson comes forward with a chocolate cake and walks toward her little girl. Sitting atop the cake is a single candle, which Elizabeth inserted in front of the camera a few seconds previously.

Okay, so they rented a cottage in the Laurentians and invited friends — the godparents? — to celebrate their daughter's first birthday.

An old videocassette containing scenes from the early years of a marriage … not exactly headline news.

Lessard hits the fast-forward button, telling himself this is a waste of time. Images of the dinner flash by.

A little farther on, he resumes watching at regular speed.

The action is now taking place in a different setting — an apartment or a house.

The Cooks' former home in Rosemont?

Looking relaxed, John Cook smiles for the camera. Sitting at a melamine table, pen in hand, he's about to write something.

The camera comes closer and zooms in to reveal that he's scribbling on a greeting card.

Elizabeth Munson steps into frame. There's a cast on her arm. She kisses John's neck as he finishes writing.

A moment later, he hands her the pen.

Elizabeth leans down and, using her free hand, starts writing smoothly while John holds the card in place for her.

Judging from their appearance, this scene took place at around the same time as the one in the cabin.

Cut. A few seconds of nothing.

The next sequence takes place outdoors, in the backyard of a brick house. A group of twenty or so people are talking in low, conspiratorial voices around a table on which platters of sandwiches, salads, and beverages have been laid out.

A buffet?

An older woman runs into frame, gesturing broadly for everyone to be quiet.

"He's coming!"

It takes Lessard a couple of seconds to understand, but he realizes that he isn't watching a secret gathering of an obscure cult when he hears the group yell "Surprise!" at the man who has just walked into the frame, slack-jawed with astonishment.

Another birthday.

Lessard presses the fast-forward button once again.

There's a succession of similar sequences — one family gathering after another. Lessard has a similar cassette lying somewhere in the recesses of a closet: Uncle Fatso talking to Aunt What's-her-name, who's wearing so much makeup that keeping her eyes open must be a strain; Great-grandma, with wiry hairs sticking out of her chin, tucking a tissue into the sleeve of her cardigan after noisily blowing her nose over her plate; and Cousin X shrieking like a banshee as he chases Cousin Y up a hallway, while Cousin Z gets pulled aside for a scolding because he won't share his toys.

Lessard is about to give up and rewind the cassette when the image suddenly cuts out. What he sees next stops him cold.

Looking straight at the camera with a lascivious expression, Elizabeth Munson lifts her camisole and reveals her breasts, two white orbs, swollen with milk, whose puffy tips she kneads as she murmurs obscenities.

Droplets of milk run over her purple nipples.

Her profane vocabulary startles Lessard, who thought he'd heard everything possible from Véronique's mouth.

"Come here, John. Come here, baby, I've got something sweet and tasty for you."

Lessard swallows.

The young woman seems transfigured. Her maternal warmth has given way to unrestrained fetishism; her entire being radiates a burning, perverted sexuality.

A hand advances into the frame and seizes her breasts. A finger traces circles in the trickle of milk.

The image shudders, blurs, and disappears.

The screen is dark for a brief moment.

The next shot unsettles Lessard — who's seen his share of unsettling things.

The Cooks are stretched out on the bed.

Elizabeth Munson is simultaneously masturbating and breast-feeding her husband while uttering a stream of obscenities.

Lessard pauses the cassette and goes to the kitchen to pour himself a glass of water, which he drains at a single gulp.

He can't help murmuring, "Fuck!"

In a spiritless state, he fast-forwards through the remainder of the two cassettes, feeling sickened and disoriented. He finds nothing, zilch, nada, apart from a couple of hours of frenzied sexuality in which the Cooks seem bent on establishing some kind of Kama Sutra record — with a few family scenes from Erin's first months of life interspersed among the images of torrid fornication. The suckling-masturbation sessions are so frequent that, after a while, they become repetitive. The dichotomy between these depraved sequences and Erin's innocent gurgling nauseates him.

At one point, Lessard sees a calendar in the background. He rewinds and plays back the segment, but, unable to make out the print on the calendar, he can't date the recording.

A little further on, something about an uneventful outing with a stroller snags his attention — but he can't figure out what it is. Replaying the sequence several times yields nothing.

He ejects the second cassette, puts it back in its box, and goes to the bathroom.

While urinating, he notices that Martin's toiletries, which normally lie on a shelf beside the sink, are gone. He opens the hall closet and sees that his son's clothes have disappeared, too. Martin must have come back in Lessard's absence and cleared out his belongings.

On the kitchen table, Lessard sees a Post-it that he hadn't noticed when he came in.

YOUR NOT MY BOSS.

He sighs.

No, but at least I can spell.

Lessard opens a can of tuna, sprinkles it with pepper, and eats it with a fork, right out of the can.

To his surprise, his call is answered on the second ring, while he's still chewing.

"Elaine Segato."

He swallows hastily.

"Hello, my name is Victor Lessard ... uh ..." He runs his tongue over his teeth, trying to dislodge a piece of food. "... I work for the Montreal Police. Jacob Berger gave me your name."

"Hi."

"Jacob says you're an entomologist, Ms. Segato."

"Yes, I am. Call me Elaine."

The voice on the phone is open and direct. Clearly not a stuffy person.

"Okay, Elaine. Listen, I need your expertise for an investigation I'm working on. Can you give me an hour of your time?"

"Now, over the phone?"

"No, a meeting in person would be preferable. Do you live in Montreal?"

"Yes, in the Plateau. Does tomorrow morning work for you? I have an appointment at eleven, but we could meet for breakfast beforehand. How about Café El Dorado? Do you know the place?"

"Sure, that's great. Shall we say eight o'clock?"

"Whoa," Elaine says, laughing. "You cops are early risers. Eight o'clock is the crack of dawn for me. Let's make it nine, okay?"

"Okay. How will we recognize each other?"

Elaine laughs again. "Just look for the most crunchy-granola woman in the place. That'll be me."

"Great. Thanks, Elaine."

"No problem. Bye."

Lessard stays in the living room for a moment, straightening up some papers and various items. Then he returns to the kitchen, finishes the tuna, and distractedly eats a banana.

Since he began to take reflux medication, he's closely monitored what he puts in his mouth, scrupulously following the advice of his nutritionist.

No more orange juice, tomatoes, citrus fruit, chocolate, or fatty foods. He hasn't touched alcohol in several years now — which helps explain why his AA attendance has fallen off. He only goes to a few meetings each year.

Now all he has to do is quit smoking, and he'll have no vices at all.

But that won't be easy. Tobacco is his dark side, his psychological crutch. He suspects it serves the same purpose as antidepressants.

He grabs his pack and lights one up before fumbling at the buttons of his cellphone with his big, clumsy fingers.

"Hey, it's Lessard. Have you spoken to Fernandez?"

"Not yet," Pearson replies.

"What do you mean, not yet? This is a murder investigation, not a Club Med getaway!"

"I know, Victor. I'm surprised myself."

"Do you have her home number?"

"No, but I can ask Garneau for it."

"Keep trying to reach her, Chris. I really need to talk to her."

"By the way, I just saw Tanguay. He said the same thing about you."

"Not now. Tell him you haven't been able to reach me."

"Already done."

"Thanks. Have you come up with anything new?"

"Nothing."

"How about Sirois?"

"Nope."

"I was at the house on Bessborough Avenue a little while ago. I didn't see you two."

"We weren't getting anywhere, so I suggested to Sirois that we go back to the station and get a head start on the report. That's what you'd have wanted us to do, right?"

"Perfect. Thanks, Chris. I have a few more things to check up on, then I'll be there."

He ends the call.

Lessard is starting to get seriously worried about Fernandez's absence.

Since he lost two of his men a few years ago, while he was with the Major Crimes Unit, he's often found himself fearing the worst. Whenever an unusual situation arises, he quickly veers into paranoia.

Officers Picard and Gosselin were cold-bloodedly tortured and killed before his eyes by members of the Red Blood Spillers, a murderous street gang responsible for the spread of terror and death throughout Montreal North. Four thugs, jacked on crystal meth, caught Lessard and his men by surprise and disarmed them during what was supposed to be a routine surveillance operation.

With his hands manacled behind his back in his own handcuffs, and the barrel of a Beretta jammed into his mouth, Lessard was forced to watch as Picard's eyes were destroyed by acid before his skull was beaten in with a baseball bat.

Gosselin's death was slow and agonizing. One of the thugs brutally amputated his leg, cutting it off above the knee with a handsaw, while two others held the cop down.

Lessard was marked for death, too.

He owes his life to the courage and coolness of his partner at the time, his former best friend, Jacinthe Taillon.

Taillon, affectionately nicknamed "Tiny" by her fellow cops, was out getting coffee when the killers stormed the apartment in the abandoned building where Lessard and his team had been staked out for days. Alerted by Gosselin's screams, Taillon went to the unit's unmarked car for weapons. Appearing out of nowhere, she made quick work of the attackers with a 12-gauge pump-action shotgun.

The man pressing his pistol into Lessard's mouth had his hand literally blown off by a point-blank volley of buckshot.

Taillon finished the job ruthlessly, using her Glock to put a bullet in each of the four thugs' foreheads.

Shuddering like a goat with its throat cut, Gosselin bled to death in Lessard's arms just as the ambulance arrived.

Two stupid, useless, gratuitous deaths, whose only justification was the Red Blood Spillers' desire to establish themselves as a force to be reckoned with in the merciless gang war for control of Montreal's narcotics trade.

They were making a statement.

And every day for months afterward, Lessard was haunted by memories of his own helplessness. Even if he'd tried to do something that night, he'd have gotten nowhere. He would simply have died with the others.

But that, ultimately, was the trouble. He did nothing.

And he'll regret it for the rest of his days.

He was officially reprimanded by headquarters for "failure to take the necessary security precautions, given the nature of the operation." Which was just a lot of hot air: he hadn't made any mistakes. He knew it. The whole force knew it. Even headquarters knew it. But someone had to take the fall. Someone had to serve as a scapegoat so that the system could continue to function. Lessard didn't object — you can't fight city hall. He bowed his head and accepted the burden of blame. Rather than rat out Taillon, he lied about the origin of the four bullets that had finished off the gangsters. He never knew whether Taillon was grateful. She couldn't forgive him for the deaths of the two officers. The truth is, she hasn't spoken to him since.

Be that as it may, he felt obligated to lie and cover for her. It was his duty in the midst of this colossal mess.

In the wake of these events came the five Ds: demotion, depression, divorce, degradation … and drinking.

A lot of drinking.

The terrified faces of Picard and Gosselin, their inhuman, blood-curdling screams still come back regularly to haunt Lessard's nights. The images of the two cops' lifeless bodies have joined those of his murdered mother and brothers in his gallery of ghosts. More recently, the dead faces of Constable Nguyen and Ariane have been added to the gallery.

Lessard stirs himself to chase away these dark thoughts.

He looks at his watch and checks his voice mail.

No new messages.

Has something happened to Fernandez? If so, he'll never forgive himself.

"Nadja, it's Victor again. What's up with you? I'm worried. Call me."

As he steps into the shower, he makes up his mind. If Fernandez doesn't get in touch in the next hour, he'll head over to her apartment and find out what's going on. Drop by drop, the hot water imparts a soothing warmth to his skin, carrying him to a place where his misdeeds dissolve into a damp mist.

Taking the last towel from the shelf (he needs to think about doing his laundry), he gives himself a quick rubdown — neglecting his back, as usual — dries his hair, administers a few swipes of deodorant to each armpit, and brushes his teeth.

As he's putting on his underwear, he remembers that he left his cellphone in the living room.

Has Fernandez called?

When he walks into the room, his heart stops.

Fear gnaws at him once again.

His brother Raymond is sitting on the couch, his gaze filled with reproach, blue veins snaking under the diaphanous skin of his face.

"You let me down, Victor Lessard."

Frozen, incapable of taking a single step, the cop rubs his eyes to make the apparition go away.

"And now you've forgotten me, Victor."

He refuses to believe his eyes and ears. Even so, he shakes his head and murmurs, "No."

"And now you've forgotten me, Victor."

Lessard knows it's just his imagination. Yet the ghost is so real …

"Leave me alone," he says, to his own surprise.

"You should have come home with me, Victor."

"Leave me alone, Raymond. Get out of here!"

"You let me down, Victor. It's all your fault."

"Leave me alone, Raymond!" he shouts. "Get out of here!"

He closes his eyes.

This case is pushing me past my limits. My mind is playing tricks on me.

When he opens his eyes, the vision is gone.

Lessard drinks another glass of water and goes back into the bedroom, disoriented.

He retrieves an old shoebox from under the bed and sits on the quilt, disturbing the perfectly balanced pillows and piled-up cushions. That arrangement can be traced back to the early days of Lessard's relationship with Véronique, before everything went wrong, before Martin came to live at his place and he went to live at Véronique's. It was in those early days that Lessard had to endure the embarrassment of showing Véronique his apartment, which lacked even the rudimentary elegance of a one-room student flat. After walking in for the first time, she walked right back out in disgust and took Lessard to Ikea. A few thousand dollars later, he had a new hide-a-bed in the living room; a matched set of cushions, sheets, and quilt for the bedroom; blinds over the windows; new pots and pans in the kitchen — in short, everything necessary to give the impression of being a grown-up.

The trouble was, when Véronique wasn't there and he slept alone in the apartment, he couldn't manage to make the bed correctly — a fact she never failed to remark upon. So, to avoid the problem, he had gotten into the habit of spending his nights on the old La-Z-Boy that he had rescued *in extremis* from the garbage, over Véronique's protests, despite the stuffing that was leaking through the gaps in the faux leather.

He hasn't slept in his bed since the breakup.

Lessard sifts through the box's contents for a moment, then lays the yellowed newspaper clippings, all of them from 1976, on the quilt.

He looks grimly at the headlines:

HORROR IN HOCHELAGA-MAISONNEUVE
MAN KILLS WIFE, CHILDREN, THEN SELF
TWELVE-YEAR-OLD MIRACULOUSLY ESCAPES FAMILY
CARNAGE

Tears roll down Lessard's cheeks, spilling onto his thighs.

In a fury, he sweeps everything off the bed. The clippings flutter to the floor. When he's calm again, he picks up a more recent article. It's an *In Memoriam* item from the obituary page, dated 2001, containing a black-and-white photo, the last one ever taken of Raymond. Snapped two weeks before the fateful day, it shows him in the shorts and striped tank top that he was wearing the day he died.

After 25 years,
I haven't forgotten.
Your brother,
Victor

His cellphone rings.

The call startles him out of his reverie and wrests him from the grasp of his inner demons.

Fernandez?

He answers without looking at the caller ID.

"Lessard? It's Tanguay. When can I expect that report?"

"We're working on it, Commander," he says in a slightly husky voice. "But to tell you the truth, even if we're at it all evening, the report won't be ready by the end of the day. Everyone is tired —"

"Okay, Lessard. Spare me the sob story. Tomorrow, without fail."

"Yes, sir."

"I have your word?"

"Yes."

My word? My ass!

Driving through Côte-St-Luc to get to Fernandez's place, Lessard thinks about the videocassettes.

As far as he's concerned, the sex scenes are anecdotal. They don't change the underlying situation. The fact that the couple enjoyed kinky sex and recorded their activities doesn't help advance the investigation. At most, one could suppose that the couple's sexuality, occupying such an important role in their daily life, might have become an object of contention, leading to conflict. But the opposite interpretation is also possible: the bond of their eroticism was so strong that it would be hard to imagine their sexuality precipitating intense discord, leading to the savagery that wiped them off the face of the earth.

Lessard turns on his windshield wipers.

More rain.

Numerous memories flood into his mind at the same time.

For a second, he feels like something might emerge, but the impression is too vague for him to find the connecting thread.

He parks the car in front of Fernandez's building. She still isn't answering her phone, and she hasn't called back.

As he raises his hand to knock on the door, he sees that it's ajar. He unholsters his pistol and advances cautiously into the kitchen.

His pulse accelerates.

He listens, on the alert for any suspicious noise.

"Fernandez? Fernandez!"

A voice behind him makes him jump.

"Hey, Victor … whoa, what's going on? Put that thing away."

Fernandez, who was outside, steps into the apartment. Her hair is unkempt. She's wearing a tight camisole and leggings.

"What the …" Lessard stammers. "The door was open …"

Fernandez looks at him with an amused expression.

"I just took out the garbage. I was about to do the same with the recycling."

"What's going on, Nadja? I was worried about you. I've been trying to reach you for hours."

"I know. I just took my messages. Listen, everything's fine, it's just —"

That's all Lessard needs to hear. His worries evaporated the instant he realized that Fernandez was in no danger. After too many hours without his trusted confidante, the floodgates open.

"Hang on! I really need to talk to you about the case. I've come up with some new information. I think I have enough to convince Tanguay to back off while we dig deeper into this thing."

"Victor, I —"

"Let me finish. In the Cooks' yard, I happened to see a little boy in the window of a neighbouring house, and he —"

"What's up, baby?"

A man appears in the hallway. Wearing only his underwear, he's in his midthirties, olive-skinned, well-built. A good-looking guy.

Lessard glares at Fernandez.

"I didn't realize you were busy ..."

Fernandez reddens.

"Victor, I'd like you to meet Miguel Serrano Fuentes. Miguel, this is Victor Lessard, my mentor and friend."

Miguel's features light up.

"It's a pleasure, Victor," he says, with a Spanish accent. "Ferdie's told me a lot about you." He extends a hand, which remains suspended in the air.

Lessard scowls and mutters something incoherent. Fernandez kneads her fingers, visibly ill at ease.

"And here I was, worried sick about you!" Lessard says caustically. "Well, this is just great! Call me when you're ready to do a little work ... *Ferdie*."

He storms out, then turns and leans back through the doorway.

"Oh, I almost forgot. Have fun in bed ... *Ferdie*."

Fernandez stares after him, dumbfounded.

11

Laila brushes her teeth until her gums bleed. Razor is a disgusting, sadistic pig, but at least he didn't cut her face.

Her hands have stopped shaking.

She sheds a few tears of rage — but what's done is done.

As always in her moments of despair, a consolatory mantra goes through her mind.

I'll die at a hundred, in Milan.

Mélanie Fleury comes in without knocking and whirls into the centre of the room.

"Wassup?"

"Ugh ..."

Laila tells her friend what just happened. Mélanie unleashes a torrent of expletives, then takes Laila in her arms. After Laila assures her that she's fine, Mélanie goes into action mode, offering to call their pimp, Nigel, so that he can deal with the problem.

"No," Laila says, "Nigel will be pissed 'cause I bought heroin from someone other than him."

"You're one of his girls. He'll back you up. But why'd you get the stuff from Razor? What were you thinking?"

"I was an idiot. It all started a couple of months ago. I was jonesing one night, and I couldn't get through to Nigel. Blythe gave me Razor's number. At first he was nice. He let me buy on credit. So I went back for more. Then the threats started. Today was the first time he forced me to go down on him."

"How much do you owe?"

"Two thousand. I've already given him five hundred. I just finished paying off the fortune I owed for rehab."

Mélanie makes a face.

"Why didn't you listen to me? I told you not to touch that stuff!"

Laila hangs her head.

"I know."

"I can lend you five hundred. That should keep him quiet for a while."

"Thanks. You're the best."

"Still, you should go see Nigel. Maybe he can front you the rest. He's not a psycho like Razor."

"You're right. I will."

"And promise me something …"

"What?"

"Next time you have a problem, come and talk to me instead of hiding your head in the sand, pretending everything'll be okay."

The reference to Laila's secret is clear.

Laila's eyes mist over.

"I promise."

Mélanie takes her friend in her arms. They kiss, their tongues entwining.

"Okay," Mélanie says. "You ready?"

"Yeah. Let's do it."

The two young women undress in the bedroom. Mélanie gets on the bed, while Laila turns on the camera.

Their duo is one of the most popular on the website where their sessions are streamed. Users can communicate their requests to the two young women through an instant messaging system. Their comments appear on a screen hanging on the wall.

"Three, two, one … action!" Laila says playfully, then joins Mélanie on the bed.

Laila (alias Jennifer) kisses Mélanie (alias Cindy) on the throat, while Cindy fondles Jennifer's breasts. Within seconds, comments fill the screen.

COX44: Nice! Grab those big titties, Cindy.

MASTER_BATOR: Go down on her, Cindy.

VINCEINROMA: Yeah, I wanna see your tongue on her, baby.

Laila stretches out with her legs apart, so that her crotch is clearly visible to the camera. Mélanie kisses her inner thighs and works her way up to her groin.

JETERSON: U got the hottest bod I seen in a while, Jen.

HORNY_PRIEST: I saw you yesterday, Laila. On Berri Street.

MADMAX: Yeah, nice.

From the corner of her eye, Mélanie is following the comments on the screen. She gives Laila a startled look.

"Did you see that?" she whispers. "One of them just mentioned your name."

"Don't stop," Laila says. "I'll explain later."

COX44: Good job, Cindy. Give it to her.

HORNY_PRIEST: You were wearing a yellow raincoat, Laila.

COX44: Yeah! Way to go, girls!

JETERSON: Do a 69. Please:-)

HORNY_PRIEST: YOU'RE BEAUUUUTIFUL, LAAAAAAIIIILLLLLLAAA.

François Cordeau parks the black Lexus on Saint-André Street, pays the parking meter with his credit card, and walks to the Nautilus Plus in the Gay Village. The gym's broad glass façade looks out over Saint-Catherine Street East.

Cordeau loves to spend time in the festive, colourful, stylish environment of the Village.

Having travelled all over the world, he's concluded that Montreal is one of the best places on earth for gay men to live and express themselves freely. During his youth, he marched in several Pride parades, but in his current job, he can no longer be so open about his orientation.

In the locker room, he removes his jeans and shirt, puts on his gym clothes, and quickly slips into his running shoes. He doesn't want to be late for his personal-training appointment with Jerome.

A last glance in the mirror satisfies him: he looks more like an educated, fashionable young professional than a seminarian.

Emerging from the locker room, he makes his way past the workout machines, searching for Jerome. Before he even has time to realize that Jerome isn't in the gym, he sees a huge man in a Nautilus Plus track suit coming toward him. Cordeau quivers: the man is breathtakingly handsome.

"François?" the stranger asks, with a smile that would melt an iceberg.

"Yes?"

"I'm Vincenzo." The man extends a hand. "Jerome is off sick today. I'm filling in for him. I hope that's not a problem."

Cordeau can't believe his luck. Jerome is attractive, but Vincenzo is *hot* — nothing less than a demigod.

"It's a pleasure," Cordeau says, taking the extended hand. "No, that's not a problem at all."

The session is over.

Another day, another dollar.

Laila and Mélanie are having a cigarette in the kitchen. Smoke hangs in the harsh glow of the neon ceiling light. Laila has put on a T-shirt.

Mélanie takes a drag. "So who was the guy messaging you by your real name? A friend?"

"I don't know. He sent a couple of messages earlier in the week, while I was doing a solo show."

"Could be some kind of weirdo. Did you mention it to Nigel?"

"No. You think I should?"

"Yeah. Aren't you worried?"

"Not really. He didn't say anything offensive or scary. I figure it's someone I know, who's too shy to come forward openly."

"Like David, maybe?"

"David would never do anything like that."

"You're always sticking up for him. You love the guy."

"As if!"

"Come on, Laila, admit it. You've got a thing for him."

The teenage girl squirms on her chair.

"Okay, fine, I like him. But it's never gonna work between us."

"Why not?"

"He's too shy. Too strange."

"Strange how?"

"No matter what I do to turn him on, he won't touch me."

"Aha! That's why you're so interested. Finally, a guy who can resist you!"

"Whatever."

Laila tosses a matchbook at her friend, who's moaning, "Oh, David, yes, yeeesss, make me come!"

"You're such an idiot!"

They dissolve in laughter — musical laughter, from the soul, the kind of laughter that only simple minds and free spirits are capable of.

Before going up the metal staircase, François Cordeau has a moment of doubt.

Should he back out?

No. Charles Millot will never find out.

And even if he did, Charles has never insisted on an exclusive relationship.

Cordeau doesn't want to disappoint him. He has real feelings for Charles. But, to quote a well-known politician with whom he had a brief affair in another life, "Love and sex are separate provinces."

Vincenzo leads him up the stairs and unlocks the door of his loft on Amherst Street, a stone's throw from the gym.

What a gorgeous ass.

The interior is white, spare, ultramodern.

Three Le Corbusier armchairs and an Eames lounge chair — an icon of 1960s design — are the main furnishings in the space.

"How about a drink?" Vincenzo says, heading for the kitchen. Cordeau hears a tinkle of glass.

"Scotch on the rocks?" Vincenzo calls out.

"With pleasure," Cordeau says from the window, where he's admiring the view. "Nice place!"

"Thanks," Vincenzo says, handing him a glass. "The bedroom's in the back. Go make yourself comfortable. I'll be right there."

Cordeau does as he's told.

The bedroom is in keeping with the rest of the place: white bed, black wood floor, minimalist décor.

In the ensuite bathroom, the young man watches himself undress in the mirror. He flexes his muscles and smiles with satisfaction.

Wearing only his briefs, he takes a gulp of Scotch and drifts through the room.

No photos. No personal items. The furnishings are very fashionable, very sober.

His cellphone vibrates on the chest of drawers where he left it.

On the caller ID, Cordeau sees that Virginie Tousignant, a reporter friend, is returning his call. He and Millot use Tousignant's services when they want a piece of information to appear in the newspapers on an unattributed basis. This time, Cordeau has taken the initiative without consulting Millot. He believes that, in order to protect their interests, it's going to be necessary to leak some information about the events on Bessborough Avenue. He wants to give Virginie advance warning.

When Vincenzo arrives, he dims the lights and turns on a sound system that Cordeau hadn't noticed.

"I love Portishead," Cordeau says, as the first notes of "Wandering Star" fill the room. He sees that Vincenzo has no glass. "You're not drinking?"

"No, I went a little overboard this weekend," Vincenzo says with a sly wink, and adds, "Lie down. I'll be back in a second." He runs an index finger down the back of Cordeau's neck, making him quiver.

Vincenzo disappears into the bathroom. Cordeau pulls back the bedspread and stretches out on his back. Lowering his briefs, he starts to masturbate.

When Vincenzo reappears, bare-chested, Cordeau's erection hardens.

Vincenzo Moreno straddles Cordeau and caresses his balls gently with his left hand. In his right, he's holding a thin metal rod about thirty centimetres long, with a barbed end.

"What's that?" Cordeau asks, trembling with pleasure.

"You'll see."

Vincenzo shuts his eyes, as though trying to concentrate.

Cordeau smiles. *What is he doing?*

With a sharp, practised motion, Vincenzo thrusts the rod into the centre of Cordeau's heart.

Cordeau doesn't even have time to be afraid. The internal hemorrhage is overwhelming. Death is instantaneous.

Moreno closes the dead man's eyes, crosses himself, and says a prayer in Italian, kneeling beside the bed. Then he gets to work.

He needs to dispose of Cordeau's body.

12

Montreal
May 7th

Lessard wakes up. He slept fully clothed in the old armchair and had dreams of wives wearing diapers, women with abortionists' faces, darkness, and acrobatic birds skimming the treetops.

In the bathroom, he pops two acetaminophen tablets, along with his twice-a-day reflux pill, his every-morning blood pressure tablet, and an Omega-3 gelcap, which he's heard prevents mood swings. He washes the whole thing down with a gulp of water from the toothpaste-stained bathroom glass.

The sight he sees in the mirror isn't pretty: he's deathly pale, wearing the nasty expression that he gets on bad days, topped by an unchanging nimbus of grey hair.

He trudges to the bedroom and puts on a T-shirt that doesn't fit his slimmed-down body, but only realizes his error when he passes the hall mirror. With a sigh, he turns back.

Crappy way to start the day, he thinks, searching for a fresh shirt in the cracked chest of drawers.

Why did he react so emotionally yesterday?

Has he always taken it for granted that Fernandez would be available for him? Why, suddenly, should it pain him so much that she's seeing someone?

Unless he misread her, she was showing signs of interest before the relationship with Véronique hit him out of the blue. Since the breakup, he's the one who's been drawn to Fernandez — as proven by that persistent knot in the pit of his stomach. But day after day, shyness and fear of rejection have made him postpone taking the initiative.

Has he waited too long? Is Fernandez now in a serious relationship? Has fate decided, once again, to smack him in the face?

Alone in the oppressive silence of his kitchen, Lessard drinks a cup of hot water. He can feel himself slowly sinking. The darkness is swallowing him up. The shadows are opening their arms to him once again. Sobbing without reason, his mind lost in a sightless fog, his thoughts encased in verdigris, his memories lying in the dust, he feels like he's living at the margins of the world, a universe buried within another universe.

He knows the signs.

He doesn't want to relapse into depression.

What did he do after leaving Fernandez's place?

His recollections are vague.

After driving around at random, without any conscious destination, he went for an aimless walk. He remembers being on Saint-Catherine Street, seeing a TV screen, and stopping on the sidewalk to watch an NHL playoff game.

For the first time all morning, he checks his cellphone.

Fernandez has left three messages since yesterday. He knows he needs to apologize, but he doesn't have the heart for it right now.

He puts it off.

An old memory comes back to him, from the period before Charlotte was born.

It's a beautiful autumn day. Marie is sleeping. He and Martin get dressed without making a sound. He takes the little boy in his arms and carries him down the stairs. They head over to the park, where they fly a red kite in an azure sky. He remembers the smile on Martin's lips, the genuine joy in his eyes; and he regrets having gotten so caught up in life's continual whirl that he failed to understand how precious such moments are — gems snatched from the fabric of time.

His sobs rend the silence.

He finds a strip of antidepressants in the medicine cabinet, checks the expiry date, and tells himself that at worst, the pills simply won't work. In any case, he knows it takes at least six weeks of steady dosage before the benefits kick in. He's also banking on a placebo effect. A gulp of water washes the white capsule down his throat, adding it to the drug cocktail already in his stomach, where he hopes the right kind of chemical reactions will ensue.

Lessard approaches the tiled façade of Café El Dorado.

Making an effort to put some semblance of a smile on his face, he walks into the café and looks around. He sees a long banquette covered in worn leather, and tables lined up along the purple walls.

Elaine Segato told him to look for "the most crunchy-granola woman in the place."

What does that mean, exactly?

He sees a mother with two preschool-age children, a group of girls excitedly discussing their latest Facebook status, and other assorted strangers munching on their daily bread. Lessard's gaze finally comes to rest at the back of the room, where a tall woman is sitting near the bar. She isn't wearing any makeup and has elaborately braided hair. She's wearing a baggy African-themed dress and red shoes.

Are the shoes a coquettish style choice or a political statement?

Lessard walks up shyly, exercising as much caution as if he were approaching a squirrel to offer it peanuts. The woman is motionless, absorbed in a book he doesn't recognize — *One Hundred Years of Solitude*, by Gabriel García-Márquez.

She's motionless … and beautiful.

Amidst the wild hair and colourful getup, Lessard sees the loveliest features he's laid eyes on in some time. Is this the most crunchy-granola woman in the place?

Time to find out.

"Elaine?"

He's transfixed by the emerald eyes that look up and direct a piercing, magnetic gaze at him. Suddenly, he's reduced to the essence of a man, a mammal in the wild, an animal formed by millions of years of evolution — yet whose reptile brain retains its dominance.

"Victor? Hi."

They shake hands. There's some initial awkwardness. Lessard orders a decaf from the waitress. Elaine does likewise. They engage in small talk: "Yes, I live in the neighbourhood ... I ride my bike to the Insectarium, winter and summer ... I met Jacob through friends. We were briefly an item, many moons ago." And so on and so forth. A few shared laughs. Little by little, confidence grows, nerves abate, real communication begins.

Ah, human beings!

Elaine has a crystalline laugh that makes the glassware resonate all around them. After a few minutes, Lessard reluctantly ends the small talk and starts describing, in broad strokes, the investigation in progress.

"When you called," Elaine says, "I thought you needed help establishing chronology. But I spoke to Jacob this morning. He's already determined the time of death through thermometer readings."

From previous collaborations with Lewis, Lessard knows that forensic entomology generally focuses on flies and other insect species that successively feed on decomposing corpses. These feeding behaviours make it possible to establish a precise time of death. Lessard remembers hearing Lewis explain that eight successive waves of insects follow each other over a period of several years.

"Yes," he says. "The deaths happened around two in the morning. What I'm interested in finding out is why there were so many flies, and, specifically, why they were present so soon after death."

Having taken care to prepare Elaine for what she's about to see, Lessard shows her several photographic prints that he requested from Adams. There are wide shots and close-ups of flies buzzing in the air and lying dead on the floor. Elaine Segato doesn't flinch at the sight of the bloody images. She doesn't seem like the faint-hearted type.

"You're right," she says without hesitation, "there really are a lot of flies. It almost seems like an infestation."

"I was told that it usually takes about eighteen to twenty-four hours before flies show up. Is that right?"

"In a hermetically sealed room, yes, it can take up to twenty-four hours, sometimes more. But it can also happen faster. All it takes is an open window, or even some smaller openings. You know, houses are never completely sealed. In the open air, it occurs within minutes or an hour. If there's already a dead animal nearby, it can be very quick."

"In our case, there was an open window. Could that explain the quantity of flies?"

Elaine Segato smiles as though he were a naïve child.

"Not really. Let me give you a brief overview. Don't worry, it isn't too complicated."

"Okay," Lessard says without enthusiasm.

"The flies that appear on dead bodies during the twenty-four-hour period immediately following death are ultraspecialized. They've evolved to be attracted by the odour of decomposition, even at a distance of several kilometres. Why? Because in order to grow their eggs, female flies need the protein they derive from sucking up the fluids that form on dead flesh. By the same token, they lay their eggs on the corpse so that their offspring will have enough food to thrive. I say 'eggs,' but in certain species, the eggs develop inside the female's uterus and are laid in the form of tiny maggots. Are you following?"

"So far, so good."

"In the presence of a freshly dead corpse, you'll generally encounter Calliphoridae first. Certain fly species within that family are among the earliest to arrive at the buffet. You know the ones — they're the flies that have a metallic blue or green appearance. At the same time, you may also find Sarcophagidae. They're a little larger, grey in colour, with lines on their backs. They're also known as 'flesh flies.'" Elaine points out the two species in one of the close-up photos that Lessard handed her. "Sarcophagidae usually show up after Calliphoridae, but, as I just said, that's not a hard-and-fast rule. For your information, Sarcophagidae give birth to maggots, not eggs."

"Okay," Lessard says, less than thrilled by the distinction.

"Everybody thinks flies are a nuisance, but they help clean up the environment. The feeding maggots, with their pincer mouths, tunnel into the body, making conditions more favourable for bacteria. The body decomposes faster if flies are present." Elaine laughs and adds, "Having said all that, I won't dwell on the subject. You may get the impression that I'm a fly fanatic."

Lessard likes this woman. She's bright and funny, and she's lifting his spirits.

"There are some differences between the species, but to keep things simple, let's just say that after the eggs hatch, there are three larval stages, each with a precise duration — which is very useful in establishing chronology. During these stages, the larvae eat nonstop. After that, they leave the corpse and change into pupas, which are the equivalent of chrysalids among butterflies. Everything clear so far?"

"Crystal clear," Lessard says, scribbling in his notebook.

"Okay. This is where things get interesting. In the case of Calliphoridae, depending on the temperature, the transition from egg to pupa can take anywhere from a hundred and fifty to two hundred and sixty-six hours. That is, between six and eleven days. Then the larva leaves the body and goes away. An adult fly will emerge from the pupa seven to fourteen days later."

"Which means a fly will develop over a total period of thirteen to twenty-five days."

"Well done, young man! You get a gold star."

Lessard smiles. He's having fun with this woman.

Elaine continues: "Obviously, we're looking at approximate figures. Depending on the temperature, development can be faster. But now you understand why I said earlier that the open window didn't change anything. There were too many adult flies in the house. For them to come from eggs laid on the corpses, the victims would have had to be dead for a much longer time, not just a matter of hours."

"So what's the explanation? Could someone have caught them and brought them to the house?"

"I suppose anything is possible, but it would take a hell of a lot of patience to catch that many flies. Otherwise it would be necessary to raise the larvae, keep them until maturity, and then transport them to the location. But there's another, much simpler hypothesis."

"Which is?"

"There may already have been another body in the house, or near-by, that the flies had been feeding on for some time. It wouldn't have to be a human body. I saw a similar case in an old abandoned church, where there were numerous dead bats. With plenty of food to keep them going, the flies multiplied to the point of infestation."

"How long do flies live?" Lessard asks, still writing in his notebook.

"You mean their lifespan?"

"Yes."

"It depends on the species, of course, but generally speaking, flies have a lifespan of twenty to thirty days."

Suddenly, Elaine's big green eyes fill with tears and she takes Lessard's hand.

"I don't know how you can do your job, Victor. What happened to that woman and her children was horrible."

Lessard frowns. The idea of going through the house again hardly fills him with joy.

Is it possible that a body is hidden there?

Not another death!

Lessard leaves Café El Dorado and drives away from the Plateau Mont-Royal to go meet Fernandez at the Shäika Café on Sherbrooke street, in Notre-Dame-de-Grâce. For someone who's sworn off caffeine, this morning is a real test of willpower.

He's deliberately avoiding Station 11. First of all, he doesn't want anyone listening in on his conversation with Fernandez. Second, knowing that part of the discussion will be about personal matters, Lessard is more comfortable talking in private, especially since Tanguay, who's out for his scalp, is liable to turn up at any moment.

Fernandez is seated at a window that looks out on the old Cinema V building, the only neo-Egyptian structure in Montreal. The cinema closed its doors in 1992 and has basically been derelict ever since. Lessard knows about the place because he briefly sat on the board of a nonprofit organization that's raising funds to convert the building into a cultural centre. But efforts to get financial backing from the federal and provincial governments have so far been unsuccessful, and the project is going nowhere. Lessard had to resign from the board when his drinking problem began.

Fernandez gives him a wave and a smile, which reassures him somewhat. He was convinced that his offensive behaviour yesterday had alienated her.

"Hey, Nadja."

"Hey."

"I'm sorry about yesterday. I don't know what got into me. Do you forgive me?"

She smiles again. "Of course I forgive you. But you didn't give me time to explain. Miguel showed up unexpectedly. That's why —"

"Nadja, you don't have to explain anything. You're entitled to your private life. I haven't been myself lately."

For a moment, Fernandez studies his face. She wants to tell him that Miguel is her ex-boyfriend, and that it's over between them. But she decides not to. Without realizing it, Lessard has blown a golden opportunity. All he needed to do was let her talk.

"What's going on, Victor?" Fernandez asks, breaking the silence. "Is this case getting to you?"

For the fiftieth time since the day began, Lessard feels his eyes unaccountably filling with tears.

"That's part of it. Listen, there are two things that don't add up. I questioned a little boy who lives next door to the Cook home."

He recounts his visit to Faizan's house, and describes the boy's illness.

"The pain keeps him awake. He says he was looking out the window on the night of the murders, and he saw a priest holding an axe in the backyard."

"A priest? Cook was dressed up as a priest?"

"No. According to the boy, it wasn't Cook. And there's more. The kid says he saw a swarm of flies through the kitchen window."

"You believe him?"

"Yes. How could he have known about the flies?"

"How old is he?"

"Seven."

"And you say he had an operation on his brain ..."

"I know what you're thinking, but I'm certain that he didn't make this up. He's always at the window because he can't go out. He described you in detail, even though you spent less time in the yard than I did."

Fernandez seems puzzled.

"You have your doubts," Lessard says. "I understand. But there's something else."

He takes the note out of his pocket.

"I found this in the Cooks' shed."

Fernandez studies the slip of paper longer than necessary.

"You think Cook wrote this?"

"I compared the handwriting with some reports written by Cook that I found in the house."

"And?"

"I'm not an expert, but I think it's his writing."

"So this note has you thinking that Cook didn't commit the murders?"

"Between that and the boy's account, I'd say there's at least room for doubt."

"He could have left it behind simply to cover his tracks. Who knows? Maybe he wanted to restore his reputation posthumously. The other possibility is that the note has nothing to do with the crime."

"Do you think I'm imagining connections that don't exist?"

"I didn't say that. The boy's story intrigues me. I'd like to go back and talk to him. The note, on its own, strikes me as pretty thin. If there were a link with the crimes, why would he have hidden it in an almost inaccessible place in the shed?"

"I don't know. I just don't know anymore ..."

Lessard takes his head in his hands. This case is beyond him. He thinks of the drawing pinned to the wall in the girls' bedroom.

You're the best daddy in the world. Love you forever.

A terrible sadness suddenly comes over him.

"Are you ashamed to tell her about me, Victor?"

Raymond is standing behind Fernandez. The light glints off the hole in his throat.

Desperately, Lessard struggles to regain his composure, to hold back his tears.

"What's the matter? What's happening to you, Victor? You haven't been yourself for a while, now. Talk to me."

It's clear to Fernandez that something's wrong with her fellow cop. She saw it in his reaction to the bodies, in his irritable outbursts, and in his angry departure from her place yesterday. Not to mention his reaction to Tanguay's comment, which she didn't understand, but which clearly had a powerful effect. She knows Lessard well enough to see that something buried deep within him is tormenting him, dragging him down.

"You're ashamed! You're ashamed! You've abandoned me, Victor!"

It's more than he can bear. His brother's voice pushes him over the edge.

"I'm not ashamed!" he shouts, glaring at Raymond. "Leave me alone!"

Conversation stops in the café. Heads turn.

"Ashamed of what, Victor?!"

He can't keep it together anymore. He puts his face in his hands and weeps. Fernandez draws close and takes his arm.

They leave the café as the other customers watch in embarrassment.

Some things are better left unsaid, but at this point, Lessard no longer cares whether Nadja judges him, or whether everyone at the station learns his story. The moment they get into the Corolla, the words pour from him. His anguish flows out in an uninterrupted stream.

For a moment, he considers telling her about his hallucinations — but he decides against it.

Afterward, when Lessard's tears have dried, when Fernandez has listened in horror to his account of finding the mutilated bodies of his mother and brothers, the desolate silence enfolds them.

Returning to the crime scene, Lessard asks Adams to check whether there's another body in the house. The answer comes back in a hurry: no, there isn't. Lessard goes over the surrounding area with the digital camera that he always keeps in his car. He photographs the dead animals that he finds within a five-hundred-metre radius of the house. He discovers nothing noteworthy, apart from two squirrel corpses and a dead cat.

He'll have to speak to Elaine Segato again and get her opinion.

Lessard meets the investigation team for an update.

In the mobile command post, where he, Sirois, Pearson, Garneau, and Fernandez are crowded around the little polypropylene table, the atmosphere is tense. Though they don't know he's been crying, the other cops can see that Lessard's eyes are swollen, his features drawn, and his state of mind far from normal — yet they have no idea why.

Fernandez suggested that they postpone the meeting. Lessard refused, making her promise not to mention the note found in the shed or the information provided by Faizan until after they've had a chance to question the boy a second time. Despite her reluctance, Fernandez finally gave in, not wanting to upset Lessard in his fragile state.

The cops review the case once again. Garneau is given the job of keeping minutes. No one has come up with anything new. The team goes over the draft report that Pearson and Sirois have drawn up. Lessard has very little to add; he feels they've done a good job. Still, he suggests a few adjustments, which Garneau duly notes. He watches over her shoulder as she writes. Holding the pen in her left hand, she forms the letters with the precision of a schoolgirl inaugurating a new notebook on the first day of class.

One of the scenes he saw on the Cooks' videocassettes comes back to him: the one in which Elizabeth signs a card with her arm in a cast. A thought skitters through his mind — an idea, troubled and unclear, that he can't quite pin down.

Why has that vision come back to him? It fades away before he can glean anything from it.

The meeting is almost over. The moment he was dreading has come.

"After we make these changes, Victor," Pearson asks, "will we be good to go? Can we submit the report to Tanguay?"

The detective sergeant freezes, speechless. Suddenly, he doesn't know what to say.

"Victor?"

Fernandez is about to intervene.

"It's a very good report, guys," Lessard finally says. "Let me know when Garneau types up a clean copy. I'd like to look over it one last time before handing it in to Tanguay."

The front door of the house is opened by a shy, deferential girl of about ten. A woman Lessard doesn't recognize comes forward from the kitchen. He holds up a gift that he purchased at Kidlink, on Monkland Avenue.

"Hello, ma'am. This is for Faizan. Can we talk to him for a minute?"

The woman's expression is hard and inaccessible. There are purple rings under her eyes, and tears are rolling down her plump cheeks.

She starts talking in a language Lessard doesn't understand.

Fernandez steps forward, takes the woman's hand, and replies to her in the same language, whose stresses and tonalities are indecipherable to Lessard. After a short while, Fernandez turns back to Lessard, who's been standing there in silence.

"This is Faizan's aunt. She's babysitting his sister. Faizan's parents are with him at the hospital. He was having trouble breathing."

The news hits Lessard like a gut punch. He puts his head in his hands and struggles not to cry.

"How is he?"

"He's in intensive care, under sedation. His condition is serious, but he should pull through."

He drives a fist into his palm.

"Poor little guy."

Without thinking, he tears a page out of his notebook and scribbles:

Hang in there, Faizan! You're the bravest boy I know!

He signs his name and slips the note under the ribbon that's tied around the gift.

"Please give this to Faizan when he's feeling better. Good luck, ma'am."

Fernandez interprets his words for the woman's benefit.

They give her a solemn wave and walk down the driveway.

The two cops step into the backyard of the Cook house.

Despite the rain, Lessard has insisted on showing Fernandez that Faizan, looking down from his bedroom, would have had a clear view of the entire area.

His cigarette is so damp, he can barely smoke it.

"What was that language?" he asks, breaking the silence in which they've spent the last few minutes.

"Arabic."

"I knew you spoke Spanish, but not Arabic."

"There are a lot of things you don't know about me, Victor."

He gives her a searching look.

Was that a hint?

When she smiles, the mist gives her face a lustrous quality, and her white teeth create a splash of brightness in the midst of her olive complexion — a halo of incandescence. Lessard has a sudden urge to step close, take her in his arms, look deeply into her eyes and kiss her until the sun starts shining over Montreal again, and …

Get real, Lessard. Not gonna happen.

"Do you think I'm imagining things, Nadja? Seriously. Tell me."

"I'm not saying you're wrong, Victor. The facts you've uncovered raise some doubts. But it would be natural for you to be influenced by your past — to be desperately eager to prove that this is something other than a domestic murder-suicide."

He knows she's right, that the trauma buried deep within him is like an insidious creature gripping him by the guts, impossible to expel.

"Do you believe that's what's happening?"

"I don't know. Have you considered going for professional help?"

"Not really. Do you think I'm losing it? Going crazy?"

He's a hair's breadth from telling her about his hallucinations.

"Not at all. But the fact remains that what happened in your youth left a wound, which this investigation has reopened. This isn't good for you, Victor. You should take some time off, let me finish up the investigation with Pearson and Sirois."

Lessard stiffens.

"Not a chance!"

"At least go home and get a few hours' rest. In the meantime, since talking to Faizan is impossible, I'll see what I can find out about this Viviane. And I'll smooth things over with Tanguay if he starts to flip out."

Lessard sighs and nods. After a moment, he says, "Okay, Nadja. You win."

She brushes his cheek with her hand.

He closes his eyes to make the moment last.

On the way home, driving like an old lady, he can't stop himself from wondering whether his troubles are coded into his genes. Was his father a chronic depressive, like him — a chronic depressive who lapsed into paranoid psychosis? Or was he just a first-class bastard who also happened to be a bloodthirsty killer?

Stopping at the local convenience store, Lessard buys a carton of milk, a loaf of sliced bread, and a lottery ticket.

He usually resists the temptation, but the jackpot is thirty-four million dollars this week, and the clerk asked if he wanted a ticket. On his way out of the store, Lessard sees a display rack full of greeting cards. It reminds him of a scene in one of the Cook videos, but he can't figure out why.

He starts to daydream. What would he do with thirty-four million dollars?

After a moment's thought, the answer comes to him: he'd give Tanguay a round-the-world trip. By boat. A very slow boat.

He's still smiling at the thought as he fiddles with the front door lock of his apartment.

A glance around the place confirms that nothing has changed while he was gone.

No news from Martin, nor any indication that he was here.

Lessard spreads peanut butter on a slice of bread and drinks the milk straight from the carton.

He completely forgot to call Elaine Segato! He writes an *E* in ballpoint on the back of his hand as a reminder to follow up with her later.

After a long shower, he stretches out on the La-Z-Boy and immediately falls asleep. No dreams trouble his sleep — at least, none that he can remember when he wakes up with a start.

He trudges to the living room and puts one of the videocassettes in the tape player. This greeting card thing is still nagging at him. He wants to get to the bottom of it.

He scrolls through the footage in fast-forward. Not finding the sequence he's looking for, he rewinds and scrolls through the images a second time. He switches cassettes and rewinds the tape to the very beginning. After searching for ten minutes, he finally locates the scene that's on his mind.

Elizabeth Munson, with her arm in a cast, is signing a greeting card with ease, using her left hand.

She's left-handed.

Hurriedly, he calls Jacob Berger.

Was the wound in Cook's shoulder inflicted by someone right-handed?

If so, then Elizabeth Munson wasn't the person who struck the blow.

13

Chinatown

The alley is so dark and menacing that even rats avoid it. Two men dressed in black are standing in front of a metal door. Noah steps toward the combination lock and prepares to enter the code that Moreno, using his very persuasive methods, obtained from an old acquaintance.

"Keep an eye out," Noah says in Italian to his henchman, who is under orders to watch the alley. "If anything moves, let me know. Whatever happens, I want no gunfire."

"Understood, *Padre*."

There's a click. The lock opens.

Noah opens the door and descends a staircase without hesitation, barely noticing the concrete walls. The hallway is illuminated by the wavering glow of a naked bulb encased in a metal cage. As expected, he comes to a second door.

He punches in the second combination that was given to him, under extreme duress, by the man who had initially refused to part with it: Father Aldéric Dorion.

Noah steps into a long hallway.

He stops for a moment, giving his eyes a chance to adjust to the near-total darkness. After a few seconds, he makes out a white halo at the end of the hallway, against which he can see a silhouette. He's perfectly calm. Hearing a faint rasp along the floor, he knows someone is approaching.

"You have an appointment?" a cold, cavernous voice asks.

"No."

Noah guesses, more than he sees, the bulk of the questioner, who remains hidden in shadow.

"Do you have an invitation?" the voice asks.

"Are you Chan Lok Wan?" Noah asks in reply.

"There are no names here. No one enters without an appointment or an invitation."

"I knew the codes."

"That's not good enough."

A hand shoots forward, grabs Noah by the throat, and squeezes hard enough to asphyxiate him.

An iron grip.

"In fifteen seconds," the voice says, "you will be dead."

Noah doesn't doubt the truth of that statement, but he's undeterred.

"I was sent here by a mutual friend," he says, showing no trace of emotion.

"I have no friends."

The grip tightens.

"In ten seconds, you die."

"My friend's name is Aldéric Dorion."

The grip loosens instantly.

"You remember my friend?" Noah asks.

"Yes. I remember him."

"Then you know who I'm looking for."

"Follow me."

Cardinal Charles Millot is sunk in a comfortable armchair, listening to music. The rain is creating picturesque patterns on the bay windows of his office.

Millot has every reason to be savouring this moment, congratulating himself on the outcome of his efforts today. He dealt successfully with a complicated problem.

But anyone even slightly acquainted with His Eminence would remark, seeing him from behind, that his shoulders are more hunched than usual, that his head is drooping at an unaccustomed angle for this appearance-conscious man, and — when his ringed hand seizes the bottle from the table beside him and raises it to his lips — that gulping liquor from the bottle is hardly his usual style.

Stepping around to see the cardinal's face, the observer would notice that Millot's eyes are moist. Becoming more attentive to ambient sounds, the observer would now realize that the room is filled with the sad, solemn strains of Chopin's Funeral March.

Finally, bending down, the observer would see, lying at Millot's feet, a kraft paper envelope that the cardinal unsealed an hour ago, whose contents are the source of his unhappiness.

Inside the envelope, Millot found an address printed on a white card, along with the Holy Grail pendant that he gave François Cordeau for his thirtieth birthday. The envelope also contained a printout of Cordeau's cellphone log, with two calls highlighted in yellow: one outgoing, one incoming, involving the same number. A search revealed the number to be a cellphone belonging to Virginie Tousignant, the reporter with whom François had occasional dealings in the past — always, of course, at the cardinal's behest.

Millot didn't have to ponder long to understand the message that had been sent to him — and it was, unmistakably, a message. Shortly afterward, he ordered a trusted operative, Bournival, the archdiocese's head of security, to go to the address on the card and have a look around. As expected, Bournival found Cordeau's body in a disused warehouse in the city's east end, encased in a plastic body bag of the sort used by the morgue.

The corpse bore no marks of violence apart from a little puncture wound over the heart, on which blood had coagulated in the shape of a flower bud.

Nor did the cardinal need a signature to know who had sent the message. Noah, the SIV agent, was demonstrating that there was a price to be paid for crossing him, and for crossing his employers.

Ah, poor François!

Millot feels terribly guilty for not having managed to protect him, for having failed to give him sufficient warning. François was too ambitious, too unfamiliar with the Vatican's internal warfare, to realize, while he was still alive, just what they were dealing with. God rest his soul. When François called Tousignant, he signed his own death warrant.

What did he hope to gain from this suicidal initiative?

Why didn't he say anything to Millot?

The cardinal will never know.

He takes several swigs from the Scotch bottle.

Noah has delivered the body to him so that he can give François a proper funeral. Millot appreciates this mark of respect, despite the boundless hatred that he now feels for his tormentor.

Millot has already been in touch with his press secretary, a skilled, competent man.

The press secretary is, at this very moment, clearing away obstacles. A police investigation into the murder is obviously out of the question. Officially, François Cordeau will have died of a ruptured aneurysm. The fact that he had no parents or other relatives will facilitate the cover-up operation in which the cardinal and his inner circle must now engage.

Having tested the waters in Rome, he knows that there's nothing he can do, at least in the short term, to avenge the murder of his lover. Noah has too many powerful allies.

But the cardinal will be watching.

If the SIV agent puts a foot wrong, Millot will make him pay.

Noah follows Chan Lok Wan up the hallway.

Every five metres, they walk past a padded door. Here and there, a cry can be heard, or a sob, or moans, muffled by the padding.

Chan Lok Wan arrives at a double door at the end of the hallway. He opens one of the doors and signals for Noah to enter. The interior is lit by nothing more than the diffuse glow of four screens attached to the walls. Two desks have been placed so that individuals who occupy them can observe the screens. A woman in a goth outfit, who must be in her early fifties, is seated at one of the desks. Her eyes alternate between the screens and a magazine lying on her lap.

"Get out," the man says.

The woman obeys without a word, closing the door behind her.

Noah looks at his host: Asian, midthirties, with hard features and a cold, impenetrable gaze.

The SIV agent looks at the screens.

On one of them, he sees a naked man chained to a wall. On another, a woman is on her hands and knees, locked in a cage barely big enough to hold her.

"Those people are in the cells?" Noah asks, pointing at the screens.

"Nothing gets by you."

"Dorion spoke to me about your establishment. I must say, I'm impressed. You give people what we can no longer offer because we fear that the tide of public opinion might turn against us: you give them the chance to expiate their sins."

"In some cases, yes," Wan says. "But most of our customers aren't religious. They just come to be cleansed of their wrongdoings, according to their own moral code."

"I understand entirely. Are many of them sexual deviants?"

"Yes, but those who come here do so exclusively to receive penance. We systematically refuse requests from fetishists who want to play out their fantasies."

"Who decides on the punishments?"

"Entry is voluntary. They give me a list. I carry it out."

"You're an executioner."

"If you like. I prefer to see myself as an instrument of their conscience."

"What if the punishments go too far?"

"I have final say."

"What about injuries?"

"No one gets seriously hurt," Wan says. "I know what I'm doing. For superficial wounds, like cuts inflicted by the whip, my assistant is a registered nurse. That's part of our service."

The two men look at each other for a moment.

Wan breaks the silence. "What do you want?"

"He needs my help."

"Then he'll get in touch with you."

"You know how these things go. It's often when our need is greatest that we isolate ourselves."

The large man looks searchingly at Noah, trying to read his soul, but sees only emptiness.

"Does he come here often?" the SIV agent asks.

"That depends on what phase he's in. When he's particularly tormented, it's several times a week. At other times, he can be gone for months."

"Has he been here lately?"

"No … not lately."

The hesitation is slight, but Noah knows Wan has just lied. The two men gaze at each other in silence.

"What punishment does he usually ask for?"

"The whip. One hundred strokes. What do you really want from him?"

"I want what's best. If he comes back, call me at this number."

Noah gives Chan Lok Wan a white card with a telephone number. The card is identical to the one Charles Millot had the misfortune to receive earlier.

The large man gives a card of his own to Noah.

"Don't come back without an appointment."

Noah signals to Moreno, who pulls up next to him in the car.

He gets into the passenger seat.

"Well?"

"The Asian lied to me. He was here. Have your brother watch the place, in case he comes back. Tell him to stay out of sight. The alley is probably full of cameras."

"Understood, *Padre.*"

Noah's cellphone vibrates.

"Hello? … No, not yet. But don't worry, we'll find him."

Chan Lok Wan watches on his surveillance monitor as the car drives away.

He didn't want to help the SIV agent, and only answered his questions so as not to raise suspicions.

Was Noah fooled?

Regardless of the answer to that question, the card that Wan took from Noah goes into the wastebasket. So does the DVD that Wan received from Father Dorion.

He knows there's nothing he can do for the old man.

14

They're in the main laboratory, a ceramic-tiled space with drains in the floor and stainless-steel work surfaces that get hosed off after each autopsy.

Every square centimetre is illuminated by powerful neon lights.

Lessard is wearing a surgical mask over his face because he can't endure the smell of putrefaction that emanates from cadavers, or the noxious fumes that waft forth when organs are sectioned, viscera are sliced, and stomachs and intestines are drained of their contents. He can't stand the ghastly sounds that accompany a medical examiner's daily routine. The noise of the saw used to open cranial cavities is particularly awful, and has been known to make him faint. And then there are the sights: he'll never get used to looking at swollen bodies, at limp white flesh, at shattered skulls, at mouths distended in grotesque grins.

Lessard leans against the side of the autopsy table: his legs are weak, and he's feeling queasy.

"Of course, I should have checked," Berger says apologetically, unzipping the bag that contains John Cook's corpse, "but five autopsies in a row is far too much work for a single person."

Lessard looks away.

Death has reduced the body to a decrepit state.

Berger bends over the shoulder wound and takes out instruments that Lessard — though this isn't his first visit to an autopsy room — has never seen before. After a few minutes' work, the medical examiner puts away the instruments and recloses the bag. Then he places the body back in the freezer from which he retrieved it.

"From the angle, I'll admit that the wound in Cook's shoulder was probably inflicted by someone right-handed."

"Elizabeth Munson was left-handed," Lessard says. "I saw home video footage of her signing a card. Her right arm was in a cast, but she had no trouble writing with her left hand. If Cook couldn't have inflicted the wound himself, and it wasn't Munson, either, then ..."

"I know where you're going with this, but it doesn't mean anything. First of all, she may have been ambidextrous. Second, many people develop motor skills that allow them to use their dominant hand for some tasks and their non-dominant hand for others. This phenomenon is known as cross-dominance. For instance, you might see a person who writes with his left hand and throws with his right. Are you a golf fan? Phil Mickelson is naturally right-handed, but he hits the ball from the left side. Maybe that was the case with Elizabeth Munson — she was naturally left-handed, but she developed a skill for hitting from the right."

Lessard shakes his head. He's not ready to give up.

"It's still more likely that a naturally right-handed person did this, isn't it?" he asks, as though trying to convince himself.

"One thing seems clear to me, Victor. Cook killed his wife and his three children. Apart from the shoulder wound, the available facts make it reasonable to conclude that he used the knife or the axe to inflict all the other injuries found on his body. That includes cutting out his own tongue and driving the knife through his throat. The only unknown variable, I'll grant you, is the shoulder wound. It was caused by the axe, but we'll probably never know with certainty how it happened. Given that Elizabeth Munson's fingerprints are on the axe handle, I think it's reasonable to conclude that she struck the blow. If she didn't, who did? Was it self-defence? Did she initially participate in the murders and then change her mind? Had they agreed that she would kill him first, and she couldn't do it? When it comes to answering these questions, your guess is as good as mine."

"'Reasonable to conclude'? You sound like a lawyer, Jacob. And you're forgetting one possibility. A third person may have been present."

Berger shakes his head, frowning.

"Okay, that's theoretically possible. But considering everything I've just told you, I think it's unlikely that someone other than Elizabeth Munson inflicted the wound to her husband's shoulder. Otherwise, what are you thinking? That Cook may have had outside help?"

"Something along those lines. I don't know anymore."

Maybe Fernandez is right. My past is affecting me.

Lessard leaves Berger's office and walks through the Gay Village to clear his head.

It's raining.

For a change.

He can see the traffic already becoming congested on the Jacques Cartier Bridge. The suburban hordes are fleeing the city. His Oxford Avenue apartment, which lacks a deck or a yard, costs him a fortune in rent. He knows very well that for that kind of money, he could buy himself a nice suburban home with a lawn, a pool, and all the other amenities that make life happy for *Homo sapiens*.

Ah, the joys of ownership.

Take Pearson, for example. He lives in the South Shore suburb of Saint-Lambert, where he's hosted a number of barbecues that Lessard attended with the rest of the team. Pearson has it all: a pool, a garden, a vast lawn (which requires vast mowing) — yet he complains ceaselessly about how his weekends are devoted to maintenance work on his little kingdom, rather than to playing with his kids and enjoying life.

Clearly, it's a question of priorities.

Not that Lessard was always playing with his own kids when he had the chance — that's a separate issue — but when he imagines what it would be like to spend two hours a day in traffic; to watch the guy next door, clad in nothing but his underwear, washing both his cars every Saturday morning; to eat meals on the patio amidst a permanent cacophony of lawn mowers — when Lessard imagines all those things, he knows he's made the right choice.

Montreal is dirty, ugly, disorganized.

And he loves it.

The Gay Village, Chinatown, Little Italy, Old Montreal, the pretty girls rollerblading along the Lachine Canal, the people from all cultures and backgrounds, the architecture that is at once cosmopolitan, jarring, and unique, the litter in the streets, the whorehouses, the filth, the smog, the sweat, the spit on the sidewalks, the hobos, the crazies, the preachers, the dirtbags — it all adds up to a microcosm of the wider world.

It comforts him.

He hates the featureless sameness of suburban life, which has neither the effervescence of the city nor the charm of the country.

The country, on the other hand, he loves. What is his dream? What would he do with that damn $34 million in lottery winnings, apart from putting Tanguay on a slow boat to nowhere?

He'd buy a cabin in the woods where he could take refuge and live like a hermit when he was feeling low. Not a luxurious lakeside cottage. No, just a rustic, solid, simple cabin with a wood stove for heating and a big screened-in porch, because, paradoxically, he hates mosquitoes as much as mosquitoes love him. And, surrounding him on all sides, the forest would encircle him with its fragrant limbs.

The only detail missing from that fantasy is a woman with whom to share the lazy hours as they drift by. But in his search for that special someone, Lessard wouldn't need to scour the earth.

Fernandez is right there. She's always been right there.

The trouble is, it's taken him years to see what was staring him in the face all along. And now he's too much of a coward to go to her place, push Miguel out the door, and shower her with loving kisses.

As Lessard walks past Priape, a sex shop in the Gay Village, he sees the distant outline of the Radio-Canada building, whose construction led to the razing of an entire working-class neighbourhood — the "Faubourg à m'lasse" — and caused the displacement of thousands of residents. His adoptive father, whose boyhood home had been torn down, was still speaking bitterly of the event on his deathbed.

Lessard continues along Saint-Catherine Street, resisting the urge to stop for some crispy noodles at the Restaurant EstAsie. He wonders, as he walks, when Saint-Catherine will get its annual conversion into a summertime pedestrian mall.

Late May? Early June?

His cellphone rings. He sees Tanguay's name on the caller ID.

Here comes trouble …

"What's taking so long, Lessard? I want you in the conference room at Station 11, with your report, in one hour. Cook went haywire and killed his wife and children. The case is a no-brainer. It's the kind of thing that happens several times a year in Quebec."

"There are elements of the fact pattern that don't make sense, Commander."

"If you're talking about the shoulder wound, I spoke to Berger. It's not important."

Why did he speak to Berger?

"There's more to it than that, sir. I'm looking into two other details —"

"One hour, Lessard. With the report."

He feels like walking away from the whole thing.

Seeing a steeple, he trudges toward the Church of St. Peter the Apostle, at the corner of René-Lévesque Boulevard and De la Visitation Street.

Like every other church in Quebec, it's empty.

Lessard is no longer a believer. Even so, he likes to spend a few contemplative moments in a house of worship, now and then.

"People should pray, but they don't anymore," his mentor, Ted Rutherford, once said to him. Lessard knows that he ought to pay the old guy a visit before he gives up the ghost.

He walks to the front of the church and kneels before a yellowed statue of the Virgin Mary.

He's barely settled into his place when he hears a noise to his right. A boy is sitting with his back to him. Lessard doesn't need to see the boy's features: he knows who it is.

Raymond.

He puts his face in his hands.

It can't be! What's happening to him?
I'm worn out. It's just fatigue.
Let them come for him. He's not leaving this church!

Pasquale Moreno pulls the car over.

He really needs to get one of those gizmos that you stick in your ear so that you can talk while you drive. He takes the message that his brother Vincenzo left him a few minutes ago.

Since he doesn't have a pen and paper, and since his memory often plays tricks on him, he keeps repeating aloud the address on De la Gauchetière Street that Vincenzo has told him to watch, until he can safely note it as an unsent text message in his cellphone.

Once this is done, he guns the engine and does a U-turn, tires squealing.

He has just enough time to go home and kiss Maria and the kids before taking up his observation post. He'll also take the opportunity to pick up the notebook and blood pressure gauge that he carries with him everywhere, but that he neglected to bring with him this morning as he was hurrying out the door.

Lessard finally calms down. He stops in to see Fernandez, whose office, though overflowing with papers, is a model of tidiness compared to his own. Fernandez is speaking on the phone. As he waits for her to finish, he removes a stack of files from the visitor's chair and sits down facing the desk.

"Did you find a link between Cook and Viviane?"

"Victor, I combed through John Cook's past. I talked to Elizabeth Munson's mother, to the neighbours, and to the human resources people at Royal Tobacco. Nobody knows anyone named Viviane. I found no trace of a person by that name."

He shifts on the chair as he tells her about his discussion with Berger.

"And what do you think?" Fernandez asks.

"I think there may have been a third person present when the crimes were committed, Nadja. Another adult."

"You just finished telling me that Berger believes Cook killed his wife and children with his own hands. Then he committed suicide. The only unknown, if there is one, is the shoulder wound. How can you go from that to thinking there was someone else present?"

"Berger's explanation doesn't convince me. What about Faizan? And the note?"

"I don't know, Victor. Are you really so sure that someone else was there?"

"Yes. It was someone they trusted enough to let into the house, late at night. They were very religious, Nadja. They would have trusted a priest. Or someone disguised as a priest."

"We have nothing to support that hypothesis."

"Something's not right. I can feel it."

"There you go. You've always been rational, Victor. You've always avoided relying on gut feelings. That's what makes you a good cop. I'm sorry ... it's not that I don't believe you. But I think you're reading too much into details that simply aren't important. Berger is categorical. Cook killed his wife and children, then himself. We have what we need to close the case. Yet you won't let it go. You're bent on prolonging the investigation."

"You think it's because of my past, don't you?"

"I think you need to get help. You need to rest."

"Maybe." He looks at his watch. "Tanguay's expecting me. I've got a bad feeling about this."

"I already talked to him. And I wanted to tell you —"

"You talked to him? When? About what?"

"He stopped by an hour ago and —"

Lessard becomes aware of someone behind him.

Tanguay marches into the room, looking as obnoxious as ever.

"Ah, Lessard, here you are. I've been waiting for you in the conference room. Let's go."

The conference room.

It's a minimally furnished space with a large naked window that looks out over the parking lot, which is drab and lifeless at this hour.

There's nothing on the table, apart from a telephone, a notepad and a ballpoint pen. A fly is buzzing around Lessard. With his nerves on edge, he shoos the insect away impatiently. Tanguay is relaxed, smiling, affable. The detective sergeant thinks to himself:

This is fishy.

"I won't beat around the bush, Lessard. You and I have never been the best of friends. But I'm still responsible for you, and I have a duty to do what's in your best interest."

Lessard says nothing.

"Victor ..."

Lessard reacts. Tanguay has never called him by his first name before.

"... some of your colleagues are concerned about you. They've come to me to express their worries." Tanguay is speaking calmly. There's no ill will in his words.

"I don't know what you're talking about, Commander. And tell me, who's been complaining about my behaviour?"

"That's not what this is about. No one's been complaining about your behaviour. But it doesn't take a mind reader to know that you've been in rough shape lately. Which is understandable, considering the investigation you're working on, and your own personal history."

Lessard turns red. He jumps to his feet and points an accusing finger at Tanguay.

"You had no right to talk about my past in front of Fernandez! None!"

The paper-thin walls tremble.

"Calm down, Lessard. In light of, shall we say, the 'rivalry' that exists between us, I allowed myself to make that comment. And I'll admit, it was entirely inappropriate. I would never have done it if I'd known how sensitive you were on the subject."

"Easy to say after the fact. It was a cheap shot, completely uncalled for!"

Lessard is spluttering, furious, beside himself. A thick vein is standing out on his neck.

He kicks a chair, which tumbles across the room with a metallic clatter. Tanguay doesn't flinch. He remains ramrod straight on his chair.

Sirois's head appears in the doorway. Tanguay waves him away.

"I apologize, Victor."

Lessard glares at his superior.

"Please. Sit down."

Lessard paces behind the table, then finally accedes to Tanguay's request and seats himself. He takes a deep breath before speaking.

"I thought we were here to discuss the Cook case, Commander. I'm not ready to submit my report. There are some new elements that I want to discuss with you."

"I'm already aware of those elements, Lessard. Fernandez mentioned them to me a few minutes ago. As far as I'm concerned, the investigation is closed. There's no more Cook case, except in your head."

The news hits Lessard like a knife through the heart. He could have endured betrayal from anyone else on the team, but not Fernandez!

"We need to get to the bottom of this," he says, refusing to back down. "We need to question Faizan again when he gets out of the hospital, and we need to keep looking for a link between John Cook and someone named Viviane. Then there's the strange business of the flies that were buzzing —"

"You're the one who's buzzing, Lessard! It's time you had a talk with Barber. I've made an appointment for you to meet him two days from now. I want you to undergo a psychological evaluation."

Tanguay's words smack him in the face. The sky disintegrates, collapsing onto his head, pinning him to the floor.

"What? Are you suspending me, Commander?"

"Nobody said anything about suspension, Lessard. You'll keep your badge, your weapon, and all your privileges. I just want you to take some time off. Time to rest. And I want you to get professional help."

Speechless incomprehension is written on the detective sergeant's face.

Or is it deep distress?

. . .

Fernandez is waiting for him outside, leaning against the driver door of the Corolla. Locks of rain-soaked hair have fallen into her eyes.

Lessard has no wish to talk to her, but she blocks his path.

"Thanks, Nadja. Going to Tanguay to screw me over — that was real classy!"

Now it's Fernandez's turn to lose her temper. Her face turns red and her voice goes up an octave.

"What the hell are you talking about? Nobody went to Tanguay to screw you over. He walked in an hour ago and grilled the team, threatening us all with disciplinary measures if you didn't file your report. From the answers he got, he realized that everyone in the station thinks you haven't been yourself, lately, and that we're worried about you."

"You also told him about the note I found and the information I got from Faizan, after you'd promised to keep that stuff to yourself. That was a low blow, Nadja."

"What was I supposed to do? I took a chance, Victor. He was already planning to put you on leave. I figured if I told him why you were holding back on the report, he might understand. But his decision had already been made."

"Son of a bitch," Lessard snarls in bitter fury.

"I'm sorry, Victor. I know you're mad. But everyone here was trying to look out for you."

Lessard's rage evaporates. Fernandez is radiant in her anger. Suddenly, he wants to take her in his arms and kiss her.

"I'm the one who should apologize," he says. "I'm not mad at you, Nadja. I know you did what you thought was right. But believe me, staying at home and twiddling my thumbs is the worst thing for me. I'm thinking I should appeal Tanguay's decision. I'll file a grievance with the union."

"There's no way that'll do you any good. We both know you need to take a step back and get some help, Victor. Come on. Admit it."

"Okay. Maybe I am on the verge of a breakdown. But that has nothing to do with my thoughts about this investigation. Something doesn't fit here."

"I'm not saying you're wrong. Only that you need to take a break."

"Do me a favour, Nadja."

"Victor —"

"Just one. Please. Look through the databases and see if you can find any old cases that are similar to the murders on Bessborough Avenue."

"Go home, Victor. That's the best thing you can do."

"As a favour to me. It'll only take a few hours."

"You're a pigheaded pain in the ass, Victor Lessard! Don't you ever take no for an answer?"

15

Mélanie's birthday is coming up, and Laila still hasn't found the right gift. At the moment, Laila is at the Archambault music store on Berri Street. She's been seated at a listening station for several long minutes now.

She realizes that her ideas are totally unoriginal.

The fact is, she has no clue what she should buy.

She started off in the book section, but Mélanie isn't much of a reader. Then she looked through boxed sets of TV series, but nothing really spoke to her — and in any case, boxed sets are outside her budget. Laila has promised to come to the birthday party that Mélanie's friend Quentin is throwing for her. Laila's never met Quentin, even though he's a Facebook friend, but she has her doubts about the party. Quentin's profile doesn't indicate a whole lot of intelligence or subtlety. Even so, Laila will put in an appearance to make her friend happy, then slip away if things get boring.

When it comes to music, Mélanie goes her own way.

Most people would be delighted to receive the latest Coldplay or Black Eyed Peas album. But Mélanie's eclectic tastes encompass Radiohead, Nine Inch Nails, Nirvana, Jeff Buckley, Mogwai, Richard Desjardins, Amy Winehouse, Metallica, Charles Trenet, Miles Davis, Johann Sebastian Bach, and Harmonium. Laila pored over the racks by herself, searching for something special, then enlisted the aid of a clerk. She wants to surprise Mélanie by introducing her to something new, something she hasn't heard before — a band or a solo artist whose existence she hadn't been aware of, or, at the very least, a title that doesn't yet appear on her iTunes playlist.

After several failed attempts and a few false hopes, Laila thinks she may finally have found what she's looking for.

In her headphones, the closing notes of a song called "Glósóli," by Icelandic band Sigur Rós, have just faded away. The lead singer's falsetto soars over the first section of the piece, until the wild brute force of the band bursts out in the hypnotic buildup of the song's final third.

It's a blend of post-rock, progressive, and minimalist music: exactly the kind of thing Mélanie might enjoy.

Laila nods her thanks to the clerk who helped her, then heads for the checkout. It's almost closing time.

The pouring rain soothes her.

Unlike most people, Laila doesn't speed up when she's walking in the rain. On the contrary, she slows down, letting the drops run gently down her cheeks, soak her hair, caress her smooth skin. She's listening to Pink, her idol and constant inspiration, with the volume on her iPod cranked to the max. Her entire being is filled with euphoria, a sensation of extreme fulfillment, as though everything she wanted to accomplish were suddenly within reach.

Because Laila has a plan …

As soon as she finishes paying off Razor and Mélanie, she'll save up to cover the cost of making a demo. She wants to record four of her songs and put them on MySpace, as many emerging groups do these days. In Monsieur Antoine's trailer, she's met a few musicians who might accompany her, and even a guy who could record the sessions without charging too much.

Laila crosses Saint-Catherine Street and heads for the metro entrance across from the music store. As she advances along the sidewalk, a dozen young men are arguing in front of the entrance. Voices are raised, insults are hurled, and the conflict turns into a brawl.

Desperate junkies who can't get credit? Dealers battling over contested territory?

Laila has no interest in finding out. The last thing she needs is to get stuck in the middle of a fight. For a moment, she considers cutting through Émilie-Gamelin Park, but the area isn't very safe at this hour. She decides to go up Berri Street, almost skipping as she walks happily along, savouring fantasies of spectacular stage shows and triumphant concerts in foreign cities.

Delighted that she's finally found a birthday gift for her friend, Laila takes out her cellphone and starts to send Mélanie a text: Soooo happy! Got you a perfect pres

She lifts her head momentarily. She's about to cross De Maisonneuve Boulevard and enter the bus terminal, from which she can gain underground access to the metro.

Suddenly, from out of nowhere, a speeding white van comes to a stop directly in front of her, blocking her way. She can't see the driver's face through the tinted window.

Great. Another maniac.

But it would take a lot more than that to dampen Laila's cheerful frame of mind. She starts to go around the back of the vehicle. As she lowers her gaze to finish her text message, the van's side door flies open. Hands grab her and drag her violently inside.

Under the sudden assault, Laila drops her phone, which falls to the sidewalk.

Before she can cry out or struggle, she feels a hot sensation on the back of her neck.

As the van roars away, Laila is lying on the floor, unconscious, bound and gagged, with a black hood pulled over her head.

THE RELATIVE
POWER OF
ABSOLUTE SILENCE

The colour white sounds like silence: the sound of nothing before every beginning.

— Vasily Kandinsky

The eternal silence of these infinite spaces fills me with dread.

— Blaise Pascal

Montreal
May 16th

It's good to be able to open my eyes and not feel like the lids are concrete blocks. After days of delirium, of morphine highs, of dreams
filled with shadows and dark woods; after two days of having tubes
inserted into every vein in my body, of painful infusions and therm-
ometers under the tongue; after the indignity of having a catheter
stuck up my dick and a twentysomething nurse's aide wiping my
ass — after everything I've been through, I'm a lot better. Thanks
for asking.

Just don't go thinking I'm in perfect health.

Even so, things could be worse.

Much worse.

The surgeon who operated on my leg came by this morning: a big
toothy dimwit, more interested in making sure his Rolex was perfectly adjusted to his wrist than in showing the least concern for
bedside manner.

"Your leg is in bad shape, Detective Lessard. We did our best to
reconnect the nerve endings, to reattach the muscles, tendons, and
ligaments. Only time will tell whether it heals properly. And then
there's the risk of infection. Even in a best-case scenario, you'll certainly have some loss of function. If the pain is too great, we may,
at some point, have to consider amputation. You know, science has

made great advances. You'd probably find it easier to get around on a prosthetic leg than on the injured one. Give yourself six months to weigh your options."

Weigh my options?!

How'd you like it if your Rolex were hanging off an artificial arm, jackass?

Shortly after that, two guys from Internal Affairs came by.

Lachaîne and Masse.

A couple of keeners with no recent experience in the field, but who still have a lot of pull on the force, making them scary as hell for the detective team — two muckrakers who don't give a shit about anything but their career paths and the next rung up the ladder.

They questioned me at length about the events of the last eight days. I'll admit that, seen from outside, my behaviour, combined with the number of dead bodies I left in my wake, might raise some questions at headquarters.

I know they're the ones who'll have to clean up the mess I made. They're the ones who'll have to mop up the blood. But let me ask you this: Would any of those pencil-pushers have volunteered to take my place?

What's that I hear?

Nothing. Absolute silence.

No one would have stepped up to do the dirty work.

So, if you ask me, it's only fair that they should handle the public relations operation that's gotten underway since the smoking Glock fell from my hand.

You'll point out that I was supposed to be on sick leave.

True.

But that doesn't justify the grilling I got from Beavis and Butt-Head. I told them as little as possible, without ever soft-pedalling or hiding the truth.

Anyway, I know in my heart that I did the right thing.

The pursuit of justice?

Damn right.

It's sad to say, but justice is too often a costume party — and nobody told the innocent folks to bring a disguise.

I asked to see Fernandez, but they said no.

I know why. I can see what they're planning. They've got me isolated in a room, and they're controlling who visits me. I'm absolutely certain that Fernandez and I will be questioned separately. They'll try to get us to turn on each other. They'll look for gaps or, better yet, contradictions in our accounts. I have total confidence in Nadja. She won't let those two clowns run circles around her.

I ring for the nurse.

"Yes, Mr. Lessard?"

"I'm in pain."

"That's to be expected. You're due for your next dose of morphine. I'll come back and give it to you in a few minutes."

"Thanks."

"No problem. There's a young woman here to see you. Can I let her in?"

Nadja?

"Yes!"

"Come on in, miss."

A familiar face appears in the doorway. One of the few faces I'm actually happy to see.

"Hi, Victor. I got your text."

"Hey, Simone."

16

Montreal
Eight days earlier, May 8th–9th
Montreal Police
Major Crimes Unit

Man: I just saw a girl get thrown into an Econoline van.

911 Operator: Do you know the person?

Man: No.

911 Operator: Where did this happen?

Man: In front of the Berri bus station.

911 Operator: Can you give me the precise location?

Man: It was on De Maisonneuve, at the corner of Berri.

911 Operator: Okay. What did you see, exactly?

Man: A white Econoline pulled up in front of the girl. The
   side door opened. Somebody grabbed her and pulled her
   inside.

911 Operator: Did she struggle? Call for help?

Man: She didn't have time.

911 Operator: Did you see the assailant?

Man: No. It was raining too hard, and the van had tinted
   windows. The whole thing took, like, fifteen seconds,
   tops.

911 Operator: What happened after that?

Man: The Econoline ripped outa there.

911 Operator: Did you get the licence number?

Man: No. I was on the wrong side of the street.

911 Operator: Can you describe the victim?

Man: Black girl. Good-looking.

911 Operator: Height, weight, age?

Man: How should I know? Tall, slim, maybe twenty. Why
   don't you people do your fuckin' job? Send a car over.
   I've got her cellphone.

911 Operator: You have her cell number?

Man: No! I've got her phone. She dropped it. I'll leave it
   under a bench in the park. In a brown bag.

911 Operator: I'm sending a patrol car now. You can give
   the phone to the officers. What's your name, sir? … Sir?

Detective Sergeant Gilles Lemaire of the Montreal Police Major Crimes Unit stops the playback.

"Want to hear it again?"

"No need," says a woman's voice, loud and authoritative.

Lemaire is a small, slight man with an almost feminine demeanour, which has earned him a fair amount of ribbing from his fellow cops. One of them eventually hit on the perfect nickname for him, a nickname that has stuck ever since: the Gnome. One of the unit's most likeable and effective investigators, Lemaire is the father of seven children, all born of the same mother. Being as diminutive as their dad, the children are naturally known on the detective team as the "Seven Dwarfs."

A matter of genetics, no doubt.

"From the sound of the voice," Lemaire says, as he smooths the always-impeccable lapels of his suit jacket, "and considering the fact that he didn't want to stick around until the patrol car arrived, I'd say our witness was either a dealer or a homeless person."

"At any rate, someone who dislikes cops," the woman declares. "A street kid, probably. We should pay a visit to Antoine Chambord's trailer."

"Monsieur Antoine?"

"Yeah. He knows just about every kid who hangs out in that part of town. He may be able to give us some leads, or help us identify the caller."

. . .

The anonymous call came in to the 911 switchboard shortly after 9:00 p.m. on May 7th, and provoked a full-scale response. The patrol officers dispatched to the scene quickly located Laila's phone. After contacting her cellular provider, the police obtained her name and address. An hour later, the Major Crimes Unit was called in, and two detectives were sent to her place. When no one came to the door, they took the necessary measures to enter the apartment. Thirty minutes later, they had Laila's health insurance card, which she kept in the top drawer of a chest, as well as several fashion photos that she'd taken in the hope of landing a contract with a modelling agency. Using these items, an AMBER alert was immediately issued.

"Turn on the TV," the woman says. "Let's see how it comes out in the media."

Lemaire gets up and fetches the remote control. The conference room is much too big for two people, but it's the only space in the office that has a TV. Lemaire turns on the television and changes the channel to Radio-Canada.

"The alert should air in the next two minutes," he says, looking at his watch.

"We still haven't found the girl's parents?"

"No, but now that we have her health insurance card, that should simplify matters. I've got someone following up with the health authorities right now."

"What about the chick whose number we found in the phone?" the woman asks. "Have we reached her?"

"Mélanie Fleury? Not yet. The IT guy should be here shortly. As soon as we know what's in Laila François's computer, it'll be easier to trace her contacts."

"And to find out what she was doing with a professional-grade HD camera and fifteen thousand dollars' worth of computer equipment. I have a feeling there's a connection …"

"So do I," Lemaire says. "Hey, the alert's coming on."

"Turn up the volume."

Julie Roy, one of Radio-Canada's news anchors, appears on the screen. Holding a hand to her ear, she seems to be unsure for a moment whether she's on the air. After a barely perceptible hesitation, she begins:

"We interrupt our regular programming to bring you this special news bulletin. Montreal Police have issued an AMBER alert for seventeen-year-old Laila François, who was abducted last night at the corner of Berri Street and De Maisonneuve Boulevard in Montreal. Laila François is a Black female, measuring five feet four inches and weighing one hundred and twenty-one pounds. Police are searching for a white Econoline van with tinted windows. Anyone with information relating to this case is asked to call 911 immediately."

Lemaire turns off the TV.

"All the other TV networks, French and English, are putting out the same bulletin," he says. "Radio stations, too. The Transport Department's roadside panels are flashing a message that we've given them. I also spoke to Moreau at the motor vehicle office. Every available patroller is on the road, participating in the search."

"Nice work, Gilles. I'm going to pay a visit to Chambord's trailer. I want to question the guy who witnessed the kidnapping. Call me as soon as you locate the parents, or the chick, I keep forgetting her name —"

"Mélanie Fleury."

"Right. Fleury."

"No problem, Jacinthe," Lemaire says. "I'll keep you posted."

Taillon hoists herself from the chair that was sagging under her weight.

She and Lemaire have been partners for a few years now, ever since Victor Lessard was removed from the Major Crimes Unit.

17

Everything in life is a matter of perspective.

The apartment, which he usually finds too small, suddenly seems vaster than a football field. Time, which he's always been desperately short of, now seems to be widening, blurring, as though each second were merging with its successor, distorting the temporal flow.

When he got up this morning, Lessard puttered around for a while, his mind blank. He spent a little time surfing the web, then set about cleaning the kitchen. He restored some semblance of order to the countertop, which had been cluttered with unwashed pots, piled with crusty dishes, and stained by ancient leftovers. Now he's ready to complete the cleanup by sponging down the counter and sweeping up the prehistoric dust bunnies on the floor — but he abruptly sets that work aside when he becomes aware of the CDs lying randomly all over the apartment.

He spends several minutes putting some discs back in their cases, removing others from cases in which they've been wrongly placed, setting aside orphan discs whose cases he can't locate, and stacking unidentified CDs in a separate pile. When he comes across *The Eraser*, the solo album by Thom Yorke that he once gave to Véronique as a gift, his energy level crashes. Abandoning the unsorted discs on the living-room floor, he pulls a kitchen chair over to the window.

He smokes a few cigarettes, watching the rain fall.

Passing cars kick up high rooster tails of spray.

The downward spiral is irreversible. It's dragging him into the depths of an insidious black sea. He isn't praying for a miracle. He just wants to get his balance back, to find his footing in the border zone between all-consuming bleakness and transient depression.

But at this point, there's no turning back. He just needs to hold his breath and hope he makes it to the surface. The bleakest alternative of all crosses his mind …

Could that be the solution?

"It would be the easy way out," a voice says behind him.

Without reacting, as though resigned to his presence, Lessard sees Raymond sitting on the couch. His will to struggle is gone.

The investigation was tearing him apart, but at least it kept his mind busy.

And it gave him an excuse to spend time with Fernandez.

The vibration of his cellphone on the kitchen counter brings him back to reality.

"Hey, bro, it's Valérie."

Damn it.

He never returned his sister's call.

"Hey, Valérie. I apologize, Martin told me you called, but it slipped my mind."

"No problem. I just wanted to catch up. It's been ages."

"Yeah."

"How's it going?"

"I'm okay. You?" His voice rings false in his ears.

"Doing fine. How are the kids?"

He realizes that he has no idea.

"Just great. Yours?"

"Margaret's in the middle of college finals, and Soon-Yi's about to finish first grade. Her language skills have really improved."

A few years ago, after failing to conceive a second child, Lessard's sister adopted a little girl from Vietnam.

He's barely listening.

"That's terrific. How's Paul?"

"Paul?" There's a surprised pause. "I imagine he's okay. Still with that student of his. Why are you asking about Paul, Victor? We've been separated for two years now."

Lessard snaps out of autopilot.

"No, sorry, I was just wondering."

"Victor, are you sure you're okay?"

He's near tears again. He stifles a sob.

"If you really want to know, Val, I'm not even slightly okay. I've been put on sick leave. I may be having another breakdown."

"Oh my god! Do you want to talk about it? What's going on?"

"I was investigating a domestic murder-suicide. I think it got to me."

"I wish I were there to give you a hug. Do you want me to come over? I'll call a sitter. I can be at your place in an hour."

"No, it's all right. Really."

"Oh, Victor, after what you went through, anyone would have cracked."

"Have I ever told you about my brother Raymond?"

"Maybe once or twice. But when Mom and Dad adopted you, you were sixteen and I was ten. Your pesky little sister wasn't exactly the first person you wanted to come to with your deepest secrets." This makes Lessard smile — miraculously. "Mom only told me much later about what had happened to you. What your father had done. But she never went into detail. As I remember, your brother Raymond was the closest to you in age, right?"

"Right."

"Why are you talking about him? Have you been thinking about him lately?"

"I should have gone home with him that afternoon, after day camp," Lessard says, turning toward the couch where his brother is seated, listening intently.

"Victor, you're beating yourself up for no reason. It's been over thirty years. You need to let go of the guilt and forgive yourself for not having been there. Not going home was what saved you. It's what gave Charlotte and Martin a chance to be born. If you'd gone home with Raymond, you'd have been killed, too."

"Maybe ..."

"Not maybe. Definitely. You would have been shot. You would have died, Victor."

He doesn't answer.

"Would it help to talk about what happened? Just you and me?"

"I don't want to bother you."

"Don't be silly. You know I'm here for you. Besides, I have to admit that I've often felt guilty for not knowing more about your past. Mom told me a little about it before she died, but I really don't know much. She said it was better that way, water under the bridge. I remember hearing about a cop who really came through for you at the time. I forget his name."

Ted Rutherford. His former partner and mentor.

Dad was still breathing.

I was torn between hate and compassion.

He was my father, after all.

What young boy has no love for his father, even if the guy beats his wife and kids, even if he's a cowardly son of a bitch?

When he opened his eyes, I recoiled.

The rest of him didn't move. I don't know what went through his mind at that moment, as he looked at me. Was he aware of the horrors he'd just committed? Or was he disappointed? Was I living proof that he had failed in his attempt to wipe out our family?

Without thinking, without premeditation, I reached out and wrapped my hands around his throat. I was only twelve, but I was big for my age.

I strangled my father as he gazed at me — I squeezed until he turned purple, his tongue fluttered, and his eyes rolled back in his head.

I didn't do it out of empathy, but because I wanted him to die, because an irrational urge had seized me, because this was what he owed me after obliterating my dreams, my hopes, and my innocence at a single stroke.

Could he have been saved if medical help had arrived before I did?

. . .

For a long time afterward, I wondered whether the fact of having killed him made me a murderer. But I also realized that day that anger and revenge are rooted in the deepest part of ourselves. If I was capable of killing my father with my bare hands, then there was no doubt that I could take the lives of other human beings, too.

After discovering the bodies, I walked over to the telephone and called our neighbour, Mr. Duguay. I sat down beside Raymond and waited. The police arrived at almost the same moment as Mr. Duguay, who was running around in all directions. A cop aged about thirty came toward me. I was holding Raymond in my arms.

"Is that your little brother?"

"Yes."

"What's his name?"

"Raymond."

"And what's yours?"

"Victor."

"Listen, Victor. Ambulance attendants and doctors are on their way. They're going to look after Raymond. They're going to take good care of him."

"Okay."

"How about you come with me? We'll step outside and let the other police officers do their work."

"Okay."

I held his hand. We went outside. The sun was blinding.

"Want to see what the inside of a police car looks like, Victor? Come on."

"Okay."

He sat me down in the car. He explained how the radio worked. I was in another world, at the edge of a dream.

"What's your name, sir?"

"Oh, sorry. My name is Edward Rutherford. My friends call me Ted."

. . .

"You still there?"

"Yeah, sorry," Lessard says, emerging from his reverie.

"Oh, Victor, you've had a hell of a year. First the breakup with Véronique, now this. Of course you're depressed. Have you seen your doctor?"

"Not yet. I have an appointment with the police psychologist."

"You need to take care of yourself, honey. What are you doing Friday? Will Charlotte be with you?"

"I don't think so."

"How about we go have dinner on Monkland Avenue? Just the two of us."

"Okay. I don't know. Maybe ..."

"It's a date. I'll pick you up at six o'clock Friday. Does that work for you?"

"Sure. That works."

"You know you can call me anytime. You know that, right?"

"Yes. I know."

With Raymond following him, Lessard goes into the bedroom and takes out the shoebox from under the bed. He looks at the black-and-white photos of his adoptive parents — gentle, loving people who died too young — and a picture of himself with Raymond. The effect of a photograph is to freeze a moment in time, to immortalize its subject. He's always been fascinated by the fact that two people the same age appearing together in a photo can, though they're un-aware of it when the shutter captures their smiles, end up dying dec-ades apart. He thinks of a wife who might survive her husband by fifty years, though he's with her forever on film. Lessard can't stop his imagination from filling the blank space and imagining what his brother would look like today.

His cellphone rings again.

"Victor? It's Elaine Segato."

It takes Lessard a moment to make the connection ... Elaine Segato ...

The flies.

"I hadn't heard back from you, and I was curious. Did you find another dead body in the house?"

Lessard's first impulse is to tell her to call Fernandez, who's now handling the investigation. But he doesn't want to seem like a jerk.

"Sorry, I've been swamped with work. No dead body, but we did find a few animal carcasses in the neighbourhood. I took some pictures. I was going to show them to you, to get your opinion, but it slipped my mind."

"Do you want to drop by my office at the Insectarium?"

"Uh, well, it's just —"

"Around five o'clock?"

"Okay."

He memorizes the address and jumps in the shower.

Pasquale Moreno releases the air from the blood pressure gauge and loosens the cuff around his arm. Writing neatly in his notebook, he enters the reading from the gauge.

It's a ritual he's repeated every day since his mother died of an embolism when he was a teenager.

One-twenty over seventy. Pasquale smiles. His pressure is perfect, as usual.

Though the numbers never change, he can't break his habit of taking daily blood pressure readings.

Pasquale suffers from *Hysteria Googlosis*, an illness that first appeared in the early days of the twenty-first century. It's an obsessive-compulsive disorder that drives him, whenever he has the slightest ailment, to do an online search of his symptoms. Without fail, the resulting terror prompts him to go see his family doctor. Over the past year, he's been convinced that he was afflicted by a variety of cancers and incurable diseases. In his worst moments, he's had visions of his own funeral, with harrowing mental images of Maria and the children in all their grief.

What's the doctor's latest advice?

"Turn off your computer."

Despite the rain, Pasquale gets out of the car and takes a short stroll through the alley. He's sick of the stale air inside the vehicle. Not to mention the fact that spending his days on observation duty, never moving a muscle, opens him up to the risk of phlebitis or even graver illnesses.

He glances in the direction of the building on De la Gauchetière Street.

No activity. It's been like that since yesterday.

In a couple of hours, somebody will come to relieve him. Just a few more turns of the clock, and he'll be with his family again.

He's never so happy as when he's at home with his loved ones.

Having dressed and groomed himself with care, Lessard meets Elaine Segato at the entrance to the Insectarium's administrative offices, which, at this hour, are empty. Smiling, she kisses him on both cheeks.

Surprised by the greeting, he reacts stiffly.

He hopes he hasn't offended her with his apparent coldness, which reflects nothing more than shyness and lack of social skill. He follows her through a warren of corridors to her office.

He can't help watching her admiringly. Her hair is tied back and her lips are shining with gloss. She's wearing tight black jeans and an attractively unbuttoned blouse. Elaine is much more shapely than he would have guessed from the loose-fitting clothes that she wore when they met for breakfast.

"After you, Detective Lessard."

Stopping at a doorway, she ushers him into an office overflowing with papers.

Lessard sees a Mac on the desk and a microscope near the window.

The walls are lined with glass-covered frames containing insects and hideous little beasts pinned to cork rectangles. There must be dozens of them. Hundreds.

"Pretty impressive, huh?" Elaine says, seeing him gaze at the collection. "There are some rare specimens up there."

"How did you become an entomologist?" Lessard asks. It's a career choice that would never have occurred to him.

"Much to my mother's dismay, I was the kind of girl who kept little critters in baby-food jars. My father would poke air holes in the lid with a nail. I kept up the hobby in my teenage years, when a distant cousin gave me a butterfly collection. They were all over the house, driving my mother to distraction. She'd always wanted a daughter who loved dolls and pretty pictures."

"She must be proud of you now."

"Proud enough, though she still finds my lifestyle sort of weird. I guess it's a generational thing. How about you? How'd you end up becoming a cop? Did someone give you a pair of handcuffs when you were five years old?"

"Something like that," he says, making an effort to smile.

Lessard brings out the photos that he just printed up at a pharmacy and spreads them out on the desk. Elaine studies them closely, asking detailed questions about the distance between the animal carcasses and the house.

"I don't know what to tell you," she concludes. "You'd have to analyze each carcass to find out how long it's been lying there, then examine the eggs and larvae that were laid. But at a glance, I have to say, considering the number of flies that were found in the house, it doesn't seem very likely that these carcasses are the source. I was expecting you to find something inside the place. Something bigger, like, say, a dead dog."

"Which leads us back to my original hypothesis — that the flies were brought into the house."

"By whom? Wasn't it a domestic murder-suicide?"

Lessard tells Elaine about the note he found in the shed, and about Faizan's account. He isn't inclined to go into too much detail, but he suggests that at least one other person may have been involved.

"The priest seen by Faizan?"

"That's a possibility."

"But why bring in the flies?" Elaine asks. "What would be the point?"

"I don't know," Lessard says. "Is it hard to raise flies?"

"No, with some species, it's easy — particularly the ones you found at the crime scene. You buy a pork liver, lay it in a glassed-in space, like an aquarium, then put in a few male and female individuals. They'll mate, and the females will lay their eggs. You need to keep the temperature at the right level. The flies will go on laying eggs and reproducing as long as there's food."

"But what if you want to raise them in large numbers, like the swarm we found in the house?"

"All you have to do is scale up the process, with several aquariums. Or else you can create a long-term supply, by storing them."

"Didn't you tell me that once they become adults, the flies only survive for twenty to thirty days?"

"That's right."

"Then how can you store them?"

"You keep them in a cold room, to slow their development and their activity. But the temperature has to be monitored, or you risk killing them."

"I understand. Is there a men's room around here somewhere?"

"At the end of the hall. I'll show you."

After seeing to his urgent need, Lessard returns to Elaine's office and finds her poring over a large volume.

"What's that? A Bible?"

"I don't know why, but an idea came to me when you mentioned the priest. Do you remember the fourth plague?"

"The what?"

"The fourth plague. Didn't you go to Sunday school, Victor?"

"Not so you'd notice."

Elaine reads in her best biblical voice:

"Then the Lord said to Moses, 'Get up early in the morning, and when Pharaoh goes out to the water, stand before him and tell him that this is what the Lord says: let my people go, so that they may worship me. If you will not let my people go, I will send swarms of flies upon you and your officials and your people and your houses.'"

"Flies? I don't get it. What's the connection?"

Elaine chuckles.

"There isn't any. I just find it funny. When you think about what happened in the case you're working on, if you look at it from a biblical perspective, you'd think it was the fourth plague coming around again."

Lessard doesn't say a word. He doesn't want to seem silly. But fragments of Faizan's description echo in his memory.

A priest holding an axe in his hand.

They're on the sidewalk, across from the Insectarium, preparing to go their separate ways. Only this time, Lessard isn't going to let himself be taken by surprise. He's ready for a peck on each cheek.

"I don't know what you heard from Jacob," Elaine says, "but I'm an upfront kind of woman."

Lessard shrugs. He isn't sure what to make of this remark.

"He only talked about you in professional terms."

"Well, in that case, I'll just come right out and ask: Are you single, Victor?"

Despite Elaine's warning, the question catches Lessard off guard. An uncomfortable knot takes shape in his throat.

"No. I mean, yes."

"Which is it?"

"Yes! Yes. I'm single."

"Would you like to go out for a beer?"

Should I tell her about AA?

He opts for something less direct. "Unfortunately, I don't drink alcohol."

"No problem. I'll get straight to the point. I'm a trained biologist, Victor. Whatever some people may claim, we're all animals." Lessard frowns. *Where is she going with this?* "I'm ovulating at the moment, and consequently feeling a physiological need to copulate. I could cite studies showing that women at this stage of their menstrual cycle take greater care with their appearance. Really, it's just a matter of biology. You're male. I'm female. I find you attractive and sweet. We could go out for a bite to eat, talk for a while, then go back to my place. No strings attached, and the condoms are on me. Interested?"

"Yes," Lessard says instantly, his cheeks bright red.

Elaine gives him a joyful, sexy smile.

"Great. Do you mind if we put my bike in your car?"

"Not at all."

"One more thing. You'll have to go home afterward. I can't stand sleeping beside other people."

Lessard suppresses the urge to respond, "And I can't stand mornings after."

At the restaurant, they talk about the case without adding anything of interest.

They eat quickly and settle the bill in a hurry. Elaine and Lessard are both eager to move on to the main course.

During the drive, they're both perfectly silent, stealing sidelong glances at each other. Then Lessard puts his hand on Elaine's. The effect is electric. They turn and gaze at each other with unconcealed lust.

Lessard feels strangely calm.

Far from troubling him, the silence in the car feels like a protective bubble, isolating them from the rest of the world, as though nothing else exists beyond this shared moment.

Wanting to store her bicycle in the garage, Elaine asks Lessard to park behind her building, in a narrow alley that's plunged in near-total darkness. They're about to get out of the car when she places a hand on his leg.

Their eyes lock. Neither of them moves: it's as though they're trying to prolong the desire. Then he draws near. Their faces brush against each other, and Lessard softly kisses Elaine's silky skin.

Slowly, their mouths find each other, their lips mingle, their tongues entwine. The kisses become deeper, the hands more eager, as the intensity builds to a frenzy. Lessard's palms stroke Elaine's

small, round breasts. Zippers are opened in haste as articles of clothing fly across the car's interior. She grips his manhood as he fondles
her buttocks with both hands.

"Wait, the condoms are in my bag."

She helps him open the packet and he slips on the condom. With
some effort, they climb into the back seat. Turning her back to him,
Elaine lifts her slim hips, offering herself to him. He penetrates her
in a single stroke. A shudder runs along her spine, and she arches her
back to press him more deeply into herself.

With their clothes draped over their bodies, they've returned to the
front of the car. The seat backs are reclined. A few raindrops slide in
through the slightly lowered windows.

They've lit cigarettes. Elaine takes an enthusiastic drag.

"You're a smoker?" Lessard asks.

"Only after sex." They laugh. "Mmm … that was really nice. It's
been a while since I did it in a car."

"You've done this before?" he says candidly. "Not me."

"Then you can strike it off your bucket list. Car sex: check."

"Better yet, car sex with a doctor of entomology. You think anyone saw us?"

"In this rain?" Elaine says. "I doubt it."

"Anyway, we don't give a shit."

"Absolutely," she says, nodding. She turns to him. "Thank you for
a lovely evening, Victor."

"Thank *you*. After the day I've had, this was just what I needed."

"Would you like to come up for some herbal tea before you go
home?"

"I'd love to."

As it turns out, Lessard only gets back to his apartment, exhausted,
in the small hours of the morning.

Elaine Segato didn't have any herbal tea — just a voracious
appetite.

As he's settling into the La-Z-Boy, his cellphone rings.

Lessard reacts with a start.

He looks at the caller ID and reads a name he's seen before.

He remembers the note he found in the Cooks' shed.

"Hello?"

"Detective Lessard," a terrified voice says, "this is Viviane Gray."

18

Little by little, Laila emerges from a foggy stupor. Her eyelids are heavy, her mouth is dry, and a dull pain is radiating from the base of her neck.

Feeling queasy, she runs her fingers along the affected area and finds a swelling that hurts when she touches it. She knows she's been drugged. Though still disoriented, she's fully aware of what happened to her: she was kidnapped while on her way to the metro station.

Idiot!

She should have been on her guard when the van stopped in front of her. Instead, she turned her back on her aggressor, whose face she never saw.

How long has she been unconscious?

Where is she?

The darkness is dense, unrelieved, impenetrable.

Her heart is racing. She gets up, stumbles, regains her balance, and inches blindly forward, arms outstretched. Her fingers touch a wall. She gropes along its surface, then crouches down. The entire wall is uniformly padded.

I need to get out of here! I need to get out of here!

She spins around.

Did she hear something?

Her heart is pounding in her ears. It feels like it's going to explode in her chest. She's going to die here, without even knowing why. She rushes around desperately, bouncing off the padded walls, until her shins collide with something and she falls violently. Her elbows break the impact.

Her mind is whirling, assembling theories of all kinds. What did she just bump into? What is that thing on the floor?

A body?

She'll never get out of here. She's convinced of that. She starts to shower kicks and punches on the walls.

"I want to get out of here! I want to get out of here! Let me out! PLEASE! LET ME OOOUUUT!!!"

Laila shouts until she's exhausted, but the only result is to make herself hoarse. No one reacts. No one responds to her cries, not even to make her shut up.

Her mind continues to whirl.

Did anyone see her being abducted?

Will anyone notice that she's missing?

It all happened so fast.

I'm going to die here, alone.

I'm going to be like all the others who have disappeared and never been heard from again.

She sits down in a daze, drained of tears and shouts.

A song comes back to her: "Distinctive Sign" by Richard Desjardins. Mélanie used to play it over and over. Its lyrics, about a vanished woman who wears a necklace of stars, ring in Laila's memory.

She makes an effort to compose herself.

If I want to get out of this rathole alive, I need to think. I need to stay calm and keep my wits about me.

Crawling on all fours, she explores her cell.

The object she tripped over isn't a body. It's a stainless-steel toilet. When she lifts the lid, a blue light goes on for fifteen seconds. She takes advantage of its glow to look around the cell. The walls, floor, and ceiling are padded. There's a roll of toilet paper, a pillow, and a blanket.

At first glance, she estimates the total area to be about a hundred square feet.

There's no water in the toilet bowl, only a greenish liquid, the odour of which is reminiscent of the chemical toilets used on construction sites.

To her dismay, Laila discovers that the toilet is equipped with a mechanism that limits the blue light to two fifteen-second periods per hour.

Bolted to the floor, the toilet is unlike conventional models: it doesn't have a water tank for flushing. Instead, there's a button on the wall that activates the flush mechanism. This makes Laila's heart sink. She had briefly hoped to detach the metal rod holding the float and use it as a weapon.

She sits back against the wall, discouraged.

Who would be twisted enough to imagine a prison like this?

She decides there's no point in worrying.

The second that just went by is gone; the one to come doesn't exist yet. Only the present moment counts — and in the present moment, she's alive. Not under the best conditions, certainly, but alive none-theless, with her body and mind intact.

That's already a lot.

Did she just hear a noise? Or was it an auditory mirage, a figment of her imagination? Now she hears a second noise, closer this time: something sliding, followed by a metallic sound.

She jumps. Her heart starts to beat like a deranged metronome. A gap opens in the wall and recloses an instant later.

The noise of the hatch is hardly deafening, but after hours of absolute silence, even the scrape of a matchstick would sound like a bomb going off.

Laila falls to her knees and begins to yell:

"Hey! Hey! What do you want from me?!"

By way of answer, the room is suddenly bathed in a muted glow, bright enough for her to see that something has been placed on the floor.

She tries to figure out where the glow is coming from, but it's as though the light were slipping in through spaces in the padding. She goes to the location on the wall where the gap appeared and tries to insert her fingers into it, to find its outline, to pry it open — but all she manages to do is break her fingernails.

The aroma reaches her nostrils before her hands have even touched the steaming bowl and the hunk of bread.

Soup.

What if it's laced with drugs or poison?

In the absence of a spoon, she laps at the liquid, drinks it in small sips. She also dips in the bread, which is doughy and thick with whole grains. Her hunger isn't fully satisfied, but at least there's something in her stomach.

The glow fades and goes out. She repeats her mantra.

I'll die at a hundred, in Milan.

Total darkness has an eerily powerful effect on the senses.

Laila's been sitting in the inky stillness for hours. She's kept her mind busy trying to figure out why she's being held captive.

At first, she wondered what the kidnapper's intentions might be.

She found some consolation in the thought that if he'd wanted to rape, torture, or kill her, he could have done it a while ago.

Then she remembered *The Silence of the Lambs*, in which a young woman is kept in a hole in the ground, while the psychopath who abducted her sews a second skin for himself, using patches of flesh that he's cut off the bodies of his previous victims. She also recalled several recent high-profile kidnappings in Quebec, most of them involving little girls who were never seen again.

She cried when she realized that she might be the victim of such a crime.

As Laila continues to ponder, she decides that instead of trying to guess what the kidnapper wants, she should first figure out who he is. That will yield a clearer idea of his intentions. She remembers a *CSI* rerun that she watched one night at 4:00 a.m. — one of the many nights when no amount of sleeping pills would knock her out. Arriving at the scene of a murder, one of the CSI investigators (whose Botoxed features gave Laila the creeps) told the dead man's wife that 90 percent of the time, the killer is someone the victim knew.

That remark echoes in Laila's mind. Does it apply to abductions, too?

And if so, does she know her kidnapper?

She needs to come at this logically.

What information does she have about the person who abducted her?

The facts:

Fact number one: it's a man, she's sure of that. What's more, he has great physical strength. She was grabbed and pulled into the van in the space of an instant, before she could even react.

Fact number two: he was alone in the vehicle. For one thing, she heard no conversation of any kind before losing consciousness. For another, she only felt two hands on her body. She couldn't see, but she'd be ready to bet her life that only two powerful hands touched her. If someone else had been present, that someone would surely have helped out during the most critical phase of the operation.

Now that she thinks about it, although her perceptions were foggy, she remembers that the van didn't speed away immediately after the kidnapper closed the side door. The vehicle wasn't yet in motion when she passed out. Which means there was no driver apart from her assailant. If there had been, he would have hit the accelerator as soon as the door was shut.

Fact number three: the man has access to powerful narcotics or, at the very least, to some drug strong enough to debilitate her almost instantly.

Fact number four: the man owns, or rented, a white van. Not an old beater with a skull and crossbones on the side panels. No, a clean white van — a recent model, if she remembers correctly. She doesn't know whether that means anything. But it's a fact.

Fact number five: there is no fact number five.

What does it all add up to?

Do her deductions make sense, or does she watch too much TV?

. . .

A list of potential suspects takes shape in her mind.

Of course, she's just speculating.

But what else can she do, short of calling the toilet bowl Wilson and starting to talk to it? Although, under the circumstances, Crane might be a better choice of name.

Razor's ferret-like features appear in a corner of Laila's mind.

Would that scumbag try something like this?

He has the physical strength for the job, and he has access to every drug imaginable. Does he have a white van? Whenever she's seen Razor in the past, he was always on foot, so she doesn't know what to conclude. But any idiot would be able to get his hands on a white van, so Razor definitely qualifies as a candidate.

Now comes the million-dollar question.

Why?

He just threatened her, making her pay interest in the form of a blow job. How is she supposed to give him the money she owes if he's holding her prisoner? Unless his sole objective is to frighten her.

In which case, way to go! She's scared shitless.

Razor is definitely a serious candidate.

8 out of 10.

Then there's HORNY_PRIEST, the nutcase who sends her messages through the webcam service. Apart from that session with Mélanie, how often has he communicated with her? Twice, maybe three times.

And always the same kind of message.

A description of her clothes, to make it clear that he saw her that day. The tone is basically respectful, not aggressive or grossly obscene. At most, there are compliments about her beauty and timid expressions of love.

What did Mélanie say?

That it might be David, expressing his desires anonymously.

Laila thinks that over for a few seconds.

David is a 3 out of 10.

He's too slight to have pulled her into the van with a single yank, and probably too nervous to buy drugs. And now that she thinks about it, David was actually standing in the bedroom one time when she got a message from HORNY_PRIEST.

No, she needs to consider the people she has regular contact with.

One of Nigel's guys?

Someone she met in the trailer?

One of the musicians?

The sound engineer?

Damn it! She's getting nowhere.

As for HORNY_PRIEST's intentions, she prefers not to think about them. After all, what's a sicko likely to want, if not to keep her in captivity for the rest of her life, inflicting the full range of his fantasies on her body? She remembers seeing a news report about a young Austrian woman who was held against her will for eight years. It was only when her captor dropped his guard for a moment that she was finally able to escape.

HORNY_PRIEST is a 9 out of 10.

Still assuming that the kidnapper is someone she knows, one final possibility remains — a possibility she doesn't even want to consider.

The worst one of all.

That HE has tracked her down.

19

The truth is, there is no truth.

— Pablo Neruda

"I have important information regarding John Cook," Viviane Gray says in a distracted voice, as though her attention weren't entirely focused on the conversation that she herself has just initiated with Lessard.

"I'm listening."

"We can't do this over the phone," she says urgently. "We need to meet. We need to meet right away!"

"It's not even five in the morning, ma'am. How about we get together for breakfast? Say, nine o'clock?"

He considers mentioning that he's been removed from the case, but decides against it. He's not going to pass up a chance to meet this woman.

"I'll be dead by then."

Having spent his career hearing people make claims of every conceivable sort — ludicrous, wild, melodramatic, funny, mendacious — Lessard knows that in this case, the woman is stating a fact about which she has no doubt whatsoever.

"Why do you say that? Have you received threats?"

"In a manner of speaking."

"If you're in danger, you should go to the nearest police station."

"It won't do any good. They'll think I'm a crackpot."

"What do you mean? Explain."

"All I can tell you is that John Cook didn't kill his wife and children."

"Then who did?"

"Not over the phone! Meet me at Central Station. Thirty minutes."

Lessard goes on talking for a couple of seconds before he realizes that Viviane Gray has hung up.

Grumbling, he puts his clothes back on. He'll find out soon enough whether the woman's information is worth getting out of bed for. The trouble is, he never actually got *into* bed — and he's feeling it.

He turns on the coffee machine and roots through the freezer, looking for the regular coffee that he keeps for special occasions.

"It's a matter of necessity," he says to himself, sipping the nectar with his eyes closed and a satisfied smile playing on his lips.

He drives east along Sherbrooke Street.

Coming to a red light at the corner of Atwater, he pulls up next to a taxi. He exchanges glances with a pretty girl sitting in the back, while Karkwa's music fills the interior of the Corolla.

Questions run through his head.

Why did Viviane Gray call me, since I'm not even on the case?

Where did she get my number?

What is she afraid of?

Before leaving the apartment, he hesitated over whether to bring his Glock. Unlike movie cops, he only has one gun — his service weapon. After wrestling with the issue for some time, he slipped the pistol into his belt.

5:50 a.m.

De la Gauchetière Street is wet and deserted.

With plenty of open spots to choose from, Lessard parks near the station entrance, at the corner of University Street. It's a metered space, but he tells himself he'll be back long before 9:00 a.m. He enters the train station, passing the En Route medical clinic, which he occasionally visits when he has a health problem. It was a doctor at this clinic who diagnosed his reflux condition. Lessard advances into the main concourse. The middle of the space is dominated by VIA Rail Canada's large, illuminated board, on which upcoming departures and arrivals are posted. The station has been open five minutes, and the first travellers are already coming in. As Lessard was parking his car, he saw a group of Japanese tourists getting off a bus. When the commuter trains begin to arrive — with their throngs of suburbanites who gorge at Montreal's economic trough by day and scurry homeward at the stroke of 5:00 p.m. — the station will turn into a hive of activity.

Lessard scans the concourse and realizes that he doesn't know what Viviane Gray looks like. He spots a woman sitting on a plastic bench and walks up, excusing himself — but no, she's not Viviane.

Clasping his hands behind his back, he walks around.

At both ends of the concourse, there are large bas-reliefs depicting Canada's industry, commerce, and arts. Carved below these images are the lyrics to the national anthem, which Lessard reads distractedly. He looks up at the frosted windows built into the walls on either side of the space, and calculates idly: twenty windows in all, fifteen panes per window, making a total of three hundred panes, plus the ones at both ends …

For Christ's sake, where is she? Calling him in the middle of the night, making him wait in the train station at this ungodly hour … if she doesn't turn up in the next five minutes, he's going home to bed!

Lessard is loitering near the VIA Rail counter, where the day's news is appearing on a TV screen. He sees that an AMBER alert has been issued for somebody named Laila François.

Drifting toward the food court, he unfolds his arms and looks at his watch: 5:55 a.m.

A woman steps off the escalator that connects the train platforms to the station concourse. She's wearing sunglasses and a long black coat, with a wide-brimmed dark hat pulled low over her eyes.

Could this be Viviane Gray?

She approaches.

"Detective Lessard …? Yes, it's you!"

"Do we know each other?"

"I've seen you on television."

He suppresses the urge to ask her in what context. No doubt she saw a report on the events that led to his being relieved of his functions on the Major Crimes Unit.

"How did you get my name and number?"

"From the press release that was put out by the police. Your name and contact information were posted for people who might have information."

He should have realized.

He leads her to a café, where they're the day's first customers.

"Was I followed?" she asks fearfully, looking around in all directions.

"Followed?" Lessard repeats, frowning skeptically. "If you don't want to be noticed, take off the hat and sunglasses. You stick out like a sore thumb."

"You think so?" she asks, removing them.

She's in her early forties, attractive, with blond hair and decidedly sad eyes.

"Why are you worried about being followed?"

"For two days now, there's been a car parked in front of my house, with a man inside. A man who never moves."

"Always the same car?"

"No. There are two of them. I've been watching. When one drives away, the other turns up less than ten minutes later."

"Do they park in the same place?"

"No, but they're always positioned so that they have a view of my front door."

"Do you work in an office?"

"No. At home."

"What happens when you go out? Does the car follow you?"

"No, but the other one's on my tail by the time I go around the corner. My God, listen to me! You must think I'm paranoid."

"Not at all. But the cars may have entirely legitimate reasons for parking there. Stress can put all sorts of ideas in a person's head. Believe me, I know a thing or two about that."

"I do, too, Detective Lessard. I'm a psychologist."

She lowers her eyes.

Is she going to cry? He doesn't have the strength to deal with that.

"You're a psychologist?" he repeats, to break the silence.

"Yes. John Cook was my patient."

From time to time, Felix glances over at the two grown-ups in the back of the trailer.

Monsieur Antoine is talking to a fat lady named Jacinthe, who swears a lot. Swearing is a bad thing to do. If Felix swore, he'd get a red card from Monsieur Antoine. The conversation, about some grown-up subject, is about as interesting to Felix as the idea of getting kissed by Rachel Boutin, who's always running after him at school.

Ugh!

Felix is tired. And he's sick of drawing pictures.

Besides, half of his felt pens have dried out. So, following his old habit, he turns to his best friend, the only friend in whose company he can let his hair down and talk about his troubles.

Dear stupid diary,

Grown-ups always look like they just got squeezed out of a tooth-paste tube.

Like when Monsieur Antoine heard that Laila was kidnapped by a stranger, the look on his face was like somebody had just told him Jesus Christ didn't know how to walk on water after all.

His jaw dropped so far that I figured I'd have to fish his dentures out of his shoes.

I'm not kidding, stupid diary. Monsieur Antoine's whole body got stiff, and his eyes looked like someone was holding a mountain of freshly chopped onions right under his nose. He picked me up in his arms and squeezed so tight that I thought I might pass out.

And then, because of the Big Split and the guy's back, I started getting ideas.

Do you remember, stupid diary? Sure you do. I told you all about the Big Split. It happened before I met Monsieur Antoine. That was when I stopped talking.

Want to hear the story again?

It was back when I used to spend a lot of time in the park with the old misters, who would give me a few coins whenever I tootled their horns. One night, I guess I wasn't tootling right. The boss got mad and started pounding my head against the wall.

I thought my best-before date had arrived. When your best-before date arrives, that's it, you're done. So anyway, I was feeling bad for the wall, because my head was messing it up. But then the Big Split happened. An axe chopped the boss's head in two. Afterward, the guy who swung the axe took off his shirt and gave it to me so I could wipe the blood off my face.

I know it was rude of me, but I didn't say thank you to the guy right away, and afterward, when we looked at each other, it didn't feel like we needed to say anything.

Then the guy took his shirt and walked away, and I saw his back.

What do you think, stupid diary?

Do you think I'm making it all up?

If Laila had known about the Big Split, if she'd had a look at the guy's back, would she have gotten kidnapped just the same?

"Did John Cook consult you on a regular basis?"

"Once a week."

"Starting when?"

"A few months ago. We were supposed to get together the day you found the bodies."

Lessard sees tears gathering in the woman's eyes.

"What were you treating him for?"

"Patient confidentiality prevents me from going into all the details, but basically, he came for therapy because of a recurring dream that he wanted to stop having."

"What kind of dream?"

"A dream about a man watching him as he slept."

"That hardly sounds very disturbing."

"Only the dream seemed real, and the man was talking to him."

"The man was talking to him as he slept?"

"Yes."

"What was he saying?"

"He was speaking an unfamiliar language. John would wake up badly shaken, in a state of profound distress, his head filled with horrible images that he claimed the man had suggested to him."

"As though the man were murmuring some kind of subliminal message in his ear?"

"Exactly. But John went even further. He said that the man's words evoked scenes of such tangible clarity that John's mind perceived them as arising from reality, not dreams. In fact, he had come to believe that these dreams *were* reality."

"What sort of images are we talking about?"

"My God, if only you could have heard him! He described, in minute detail, visions of pure horror, apparitions of repugnant cruelty and sadism, unnatural couplings between children and animals, acts of cannibalism on dismembered bodies, necrophilia ... need I go on?"

"Were the dreams frequent?"

"Two or three times a month, at first. After the family moved, things calmed down for a while. Then, over the past two weeks, it started happening practically every night."

"What about his wife? If the visions were so powerful, she must have noticed something."

"They'd been sleeping in separate beds since the birth of their youngest child. Oddly, when they slept in the same bed, he didn't have the dreams."

"In that case, why didn't he sleep beside her every night?"

"John was a man of reason. The impulse was stronger than he was. He had to know what was happening to him — he was obsessed."

"So his wife didn't know what was going on?"

"He didn't dare mention it to Elizabeth. He didn't want to seem weak or ridiculous."

"I'm no expert, but aren't we talking about a case of mental illness? Without taking anything away from your skills, wouldn't he have been better off with a psychiatrist than a psychologist?"

"That's a fair question," Viviane Gray says. "I said the same thing more than once. But you need to understand that John was brilliant, a man of truly exceptional intelligence. Deciding to see a psychologist wasn't easy for him."

Lessard gets it.

He's faced similar feelings in the past — as though admitting that he needed help might make him think less of himself.

"John was so cerebral, so controlled, that I'm sure he never showed the slightest sign of distress to anyone."

"I spoke to his boss and one of his co-workers," Lessard says. "They both said they hadn't noticed any change in his behaviour, or hardly any."

"That was John, through and through! He was highly skilled at hiding his feelings. His other reason for wanting to see me rather than a psychiatrist was that, almost alone among local psychologists, I make frequent use of hypnosis in my practice. He hoped that hypnosis might enable him to overcome his problem."

"And what was the result?"

"A total disaster! The worst experience of my career. During our second-to-last meeting, I was able to hypnotize John with ease. When I began deprogramming him — if I may use that term — he started to rave, speaking a language I didn't know. I had a lot of trouble snapping him out of it."

"Was this the same language that the man spoke in his dreams?"

"There's no way to know."

Lessard lifts his head and looks the woman in the eye. "I'll be straight with you, Ms. Gray. You claim you're being followed. You give me this strange story about John Cook. But I'm a police officer, not a parapsychologist. What do you want me to do?"

"Help me prove that John didn't kill his wife, his children, or himself."

"I wish I could believe you. But you've told me nothing that backs up your claim."

"John was an extremely devout man. For him, the very idea of suicide or murder would have been an aberration. He had an immense respect for life."

"Unfortunately, human history is littered with accounts of deeply religious people who made a daily practice of committing terrible crimes."

Viviane Gray bites her lower lip. Her hands twist her napkin.

"I ..."

She hesitates.

"Let me tell you something," Lessard says. "I know when a person is hiding information from me. It's my job to know. And right now, I'm certain that you're concealing something."

His words strike home. Viviane Gray begins to sob in silence.

"John and I ... we ... had an affair. My marriage had just ended. I admired his intelligence, I ..." She wipes her eyes. "It violated every rule in the code of ethics. I could be expelled from the profession if it ever got out. But it happened. That's the truth. We both regretted it."

"Was he planning to leave his wife?"

"No! That was never a possibility. It was just a transient thing, one of those moments when time seems to stand still, and ... oh, I don't know. I didn't come here to make excuses. All I'm saying is, John could never have done what he's suspected of doing."

"Is this his psychologist or his lover talking? Because it turns out that you've just provided me with a compelling explanation for what he did. He was mentally disturbed, in the midst of an extramarital affair — exactly the kind of situation we often see in domestic murder-suicides."

Viviane Gray's face is wet with tears.

She seems to be on the verge of saying something. Then she changes her mind.

"Excuse me, I have to go to the bathroom."

. . .

After she leaves, Lessard wonders how he and the rest of the team could have failed to find Viviane Gray. He specifically instructed Pearson and Sirois to go over Cook's expenditures. The man had private health coverage through his employer, so the psychologist's name should have turned up. But then Lessard recalls the remark that Gray just made, and understands why her name wasn't found. Cook was probably afraid that someone in the workplace might learn he was seeing a psychologist — so he never made a claim for her fees.

Lessard reflects on Gray's story of dreams and horrifying visions. It makes no sense.

Then he considers his own encounters with Raymond. But that's different, he tells himself. He, at least, is lucid enough to understand that Raymond isn't really there.

After thinking things over, he makes up his mind to call Fernandez and bring Viviane Gray in for questioning.

She may know more than she's been letting on. It now seems clear that Cook, even if he managed to keep up appearances with friends and family, was mentally unbalanced and consumed by guilt over his marital infidelity. He eventually cracked, giving in to the murderous urges that were manifested in his dreams. But then, in a final, improbable farewell, he tried to whitewash his sullied name and restore his image in the eyes of the mistress he had abandoned, by leaving her the message that Lessard found in the shed.

Lessard asks the waiter for the bill and gets up to stretch his legs.

He looks at his watch: 6:35 a.m.

Viviane Gray has been in the bathroom for five minutes.

He looks around, but doesn't see her.

A sudden thought strikes him.

What if she's decided to slip away?

Lessard glances toward the exits.

He never even noticed which way she went. If she's decided to make a break for it, she's already long gone.

He hurries to the washrooms, which are near the food court.

He pushes the door open.

"Ms. Gray?"

Without waiting for an answer, he steps inside.

A single stall is occupied. He sees the hem of a black coat on the floor.

Whew! He was pretty anxious for a minute there. Clearly, he needs to finish up with this woman and get some rest.

"Ms. Gray?"

No answer. The stockinged legs don't move.

Puzzled, Lessard steps closer.

"Ms. Gray? Do you need help …? Ms. Gray?"

He pushes the door of the stall, then recoils. The walls are splattered with cerebral matter. Nothing remains of Viviane Gray's face but a shapeless mass of flesh, bone, and cartilage.

Hanging by the thread of the optic nerve, her left eye is dangling out of her cranial cavity.

20

Viviane Gray was killed instantly.

A single shot, point-blank.

Swaying, Lessard grips the sink and wonders whether to leave the bathroom right now, or vomit in the neighbouring stall. He reaches into his pocket for his cellphone and walks back up the corridor that leads to the food court, steadying himself against the wall. He's trembling as he keys in Fernandez's number.

He sees a movement to his right and hears two muffled pops.

Instinct takes over.

He dives to his left, executes a tuck-and-roll, and lands behind the refrigerated counter of a food stand. Ceramic tiles explode in the location he occupied an instant ago.

Two more pops: Lessard hears the bullets hitting the stainless-steel surface of the counter behind which he's taken refuge.

When a silenced pistol goes off, the sound is less deafening than regular gunfire, but it's not as quiet as movies suggest. After the first few shots, time seems to stand still for a few endless seconds, then it resumes its flow in a rush. Throughout the crowded area, people are shouting and diving under tables. They're running in all directions, seeking protection behind whatever furniture is at hand. In the blink of an eye, the food court has been transformed into a battlefield.

Lessard is holding his Glock, ready to return fire. A woman behind him spots his weapon and starts to scream.

"Police!" Lessard roars. "Everybody get down! Take cover!"

Another pair of pops. Two more bullets hit the metal.

Lessard knows he's the target.

He also knows the killer is advancing as he fires: the last two shots were louder. If the cop stays crouched behind the counter, the attacker will be on him in seconds, ready to put a hole between his eyes.

If Lessard has counted right, six rounds have been fired.

But he isn't about to wait until the killer empties his magazine. Depending on the kind of pistol he's using, the killer could have between five and twenty cartridges available. It only takes one to kill a man.

Lessard raises his head for a quick glance over the counter. A risky move, but necessary if he wants to get out of this jam alive.

Another pop.

A bullet whistles past his ear, so close that he feels the draft as it goes by. The killer didn't miss by much.

But Lessard, ducking back behind the counter, now has the information he needs.

As he suspected, there's only one shooter.

Wearing a balaclava, he's ten metres away, in the middle of the aisle. He's dressed entirely in black, firing calmly.

The killer is in the open. But Lessard can't return fire blindly; the risk of hitting someone else is too great. He's in the grey zone, that brief moment of indecision when he loses his bearings and things start to spin out of control.

The killer knows it. That's why he's not taking greater precautions.

Lessard visualizes the moves he wants to execute. He'll wait for the next salvo, then seize his chance. He hears no shouts, sees nothing beyond the objective he must reach.

Two more bullets ricochet off the stainless steel.

Now!

With a rapid movement, Lessard extends his arm and fires twice in the killer's direction. There's always a risk that if the bullets miss the target, they'll strike some other person in the vicinity, but by this point, he thinks, people have had time to find refuge out of the line of fire. At least he hopes so. Without hesitating, he throws himself into a roll, coming down behind a thick cement column. The landing is brutal, but now he has proper cover.

His two shots missed, but they forced the killer to dive behind a newsstand.

Lessard's gambit has succeeded. He's gotten himself out of a vulnerable position, and he now has a better angle of fire than he had behind the counter. Unless the killer is suicidal, he won't risk advancing in the open any longer.

Lessard hears half a dozen pops. Fragments of cement fly off the column, close to his head.

He hesitates to return fire.

He knows that several people have sought safety near the newsstand.

Suddenly, he hears a loud bang, followed by more pops, along with yelling and a great deal of commotion. He takes a quick look and sees the killer sprinting along a corridor that leads to the tunnels of the underground city.

Without a moment's thought, he emerges from his cover and sets off in pursuit.

Gripping his pistol, he passes the newsstand and runs through the station. All around him, he sees terrified faces, people lying on the floor, their hands over their heads.

A mother has thrown herself over her two children to shield them; two elderly men are clinging to each other, trembling; a man in a suit is sobbing.

Lessard is running as fast as he can, driven by pure instinct. An electric surge of adrenalin is coursing through his veins.

In front of the National Bank branch, he sees a group of people. Employees from the nearby office supply store are standing around the bank's security guard, who's seated on the floor, leaning against the wall, with a star-shaped bloodstain on his shoulder.

In an instant, Lessard realizes what's happened.

The armed guard drew his weapon and fired at the killer. Caught by surprise, the killer returned fire, striking the guard, then fled.

"Call 911!" Lessard shouts as he runs by. "And put pressure on the wound!"

Reaching the glass doors that open onto De la Gauchetière Street, he hesitates. Did the killer go out, or did he descend into the network of tunnels? The cop glances down the staircase and sees a woman pointing a finger toward the doors at the bottom of the stairs.

"He went that way?"

The woman nods. He goes down the stairs four at a time and pushes through the doors.

The city within a city.

Underground Montreal consists of more than thirty kilometres of tunnels: a labyrinth in which the killer could board a metro or dissolve into the mass of humanity, while Lessard searches in vain.

The detective sergeant steps into another corridor.

Alerted by cries of alarm, he veers to the right.

A crowd has formed at the top of the long escalator that descends to the metro station. Lessard elbows his way through. The killer is there, at the bottom, about to go through the doors that lead to the Bonaventure station. The killer pulls off his balaclava, but Lessard doesn't get a look at the man's face. He's going to lose him.

Despite the solid metal projections installed to prevent thrill-seekers from sliding down the metal ramp that separates the up and down escalators, Lessard slides down anyway. He makes it to the bottom in one piece, but his back is bruised and tingling from the repeated impacts.

He enters the metro station, holding his gun against his leg as inconspicuously as possible. But it's almost 7:00 a.m., and the crowd is dense.

Whatever happens, don't provoke a panic.

Lessard looks around the station, trying to spot a man dressed in black.

Standing on the mezzanine, he leans over the railing and scans the platforms.

A westbound train has just pulled in. A dense crowd disembarks and moves quickly toward the stairs.

Lessard watches expectantly, waiting to see a black-clad man dart into one of the cars.

The train leaves the station. He hasn't spotted the killer.

Now an eastbound train comes in. Lessard runs to the other mezzanine and watches once again.

The same routine unfolds. No sign of the man.

For a moment, Lessard considers setting off the emergency alarm to stop the train, but he decides against it. This guy isn't a deranged shooter like Marc Lépine or Kimveer Gill. He's a professional: he poses no immediate threat to the public. But if cornered, he won't hesitate to shoot his way out. Under the circumstances, Lessard doesn't want to do anything that might put innocent lives at risk.

In any case, he has no way of knowing whether the killer even boarded the metro.

The Bonaventure station is a hub for the Montreal underground. It provides access not only to the metro, but also to the Place Bonaventure office complex, to the Bell Centre, to Central Station, and to Windsor Station. Lessard gives up.

He's long gone by now.

Concealed behind a concrete pillar, Pasquale Moreno waits for the detective to walk away before escaping through the crowd.

Of the two targets identified by his employer, he's liquidated only one. Though disappointed, Moreno doesn't feel any personal animosity toward the individuals he's supposed to execute. His job is to pull the trigger. After that, funds are transferred into his bank account, and he can go home to Maria and the children.

For Moreno, killing people is just a job.

The detective's coolness has surprised and impressed him.

Victor Lessard is a tough opponent; Moreno feels admiration for him.

Cellphone in hand, Moreno sends a text to Noah to let him know what's happened, and to receive further instructions.

The work of *Propaganda Fide* is so important, and the territories it oversees so vast, that its cardinal prefect has been nicknamed "the Red Pope."

From his room in the archdiocesan residence, with the metal briefcase open on the bed, the SIV agent is in conversation with the cardinal prefect over a secure link.

"We're making progress," Noah says. "Despite his reluctance, Aldéric Dorion gave us some useful leads. We're closing in on our objective."

"Poor Aldéric," the cardinal prefect says. "Poor stubborn fool. I don't want him to suffer unnecessarily."

"No need to worry about that," Noah says, with a nasty little smirk.

"When do you think you'll be able to send us the latest video?"

"Soon. We've been delayed by some unexpected developments over the last few hours."

"What sort of developments?"

"One of our men was obliged to eliminate John Cook's mistress."

The cardinal prefect's sad voice comes through the phone as clearly as if he were sitting beside Noah. "What was her name?" he asks contritely.

"Viviane Gray."

"I will pray for her. I hope it wasn't too painful."

"No. Death was instantaneous. There's one more thing I'd like to discuss."

"What's that?"

"Viviane Gray spoke to a police detective. Our operative was unable to eliminate this detective before escaping. Having said that, I think it's highly unlikely that the detective will be able to trace any of this back to us."

"I have complete faith in you, Noah. I needn't remind you that the last thing we want is public attention. You've been given carte blanche in this matter. Still, you must not take action except in situations of absolute necessity."

"Of course."

"I know these deaths are as repugnant to you as they are to me, Noah. But this is war. We are Christ's sworn knights, and God has set us a single task: to fight the decline of the Catholic faith. Let us prove that we are worthy."

"The Soldiers of Christ are at your service."

. . .

The SIV agent puts the satellite phone back in the briefcase.

Then he opens his MacBook Pro and plugs in his headphones. Logging into the SIV server, he accesses the latest version of the video that he shot in the house on Bessborough Avenue on the night of the killings.

An SIV technician has done some rudimentary editing of the footage. The sequences that Noah wants the cardinal prefect to see — the ones that are most striking — have been spliced together.

Noah watches the video once again in silent fascination.

The images are horrifying. They show things that no human being would ever want to see. Yet they also contain seeds of hope for the Catholic faith.

Lessard reholsters his Glock and takes the underground passage to Place Bonaventure to get back to street level. He wants to avoid the area he just came from. It will soon be crawling with police officers.

He's eager to step out into the fresh air. He feels like a prisoner in the maggot-infested belly of some unclean beast. He needs to get out of this sordid environment before he goes crazy.

The human tide absorbs him. As he walks, Lessard can't help peering into every face. Every hand reaching too quickly into a pocket puts him on edge; every sudden movement makes his fingers tighten around the butt of his gun.

He steps outside through the Place Bonaventure entrance. From that vantage point, he watches the flow of pedestrians near the Corolla. Only after satisfying himself that nothing suspicious is going on does he run across the street, jump into the car, and start the motor.

As he drives off, the Corolla's wheels skid briefly on the wet asphalt.

While he's turning on his windshield wipers, the first patrol cars start to arrive behind him amidst a chorus of sirens.

They were slow in arriving because of the 7:00 a.m. shift change.

. . .

Lessard turns left onto University Street, then right on René-Lévesque Boulevard, heading east. He wants to put as much distance as possible between himself and the person, or persons, who tried to kill him. Continuing east along Notre-Dame Street, he drives past the large storage tanks of the oil refineries.

Little by little, the steady hiss of his tires on the wet pavement calms him down.

He glances in the rear-view mirror to make sure he isn't being followed. Sitting in the back seat, leaning against the window with his chin on his palms, Lessard's younger brother is scanning the horizon, as though there were danger out there, waiting for them.

"You gave me a scare, Victor. Who was that guy who tried to kill you?"

Lessard's expression brightens. A little company will do him good.

"Hi, Raymond."

When his hands have stopped shaking, he turns onto a quiet side street, parks the car, and gets out.

After considering his options in the wake of what just happened, and after weighing the pros and cons several times, Lessard lights a cigarette, takes several drags, and calls Fernandez. The conversation may get heated, but his mind is made up.

When she answers, he says, "Go someplace where you can talk freely."

"Just a minute."

He hears Fernandez walking. He imagines her stepping away from her desk and shutting herself in the conference room.

"Okay. I'm listening."

He wipes beads of rain from his eyebrows and gives her a detailed account of what happened, making it clear that he isn't injured.

"My God, that was you? We just heard the call over the radio. The tactical squad is heading there now. This is huge, Victor. Everyone is talking about it. Are you sure you're not hurt?"

"No, no, I'm fine. Just a little shaken up."

"And the woman — are you certain that she's dead?"

"Believe me, she's dead. Her face was shot off. Get the word out over the radio. Tell them they'll find her in the women's bathroom, next to the food court."

"What do you mean, 'they'? Where are you?"

"Someplace safe."

"Tell me where. I'll come and get you with Sirois. We'll be there in ten minutes."

Lessard knew Fernandez would react this way. He closes his eyes.

"That's out of the question."

"What are you talking about?"

"If you come and get me, I'll have to go to the station with you. I'll spend days filling out paperwork and talking to shrinks, with Tanguay riding my ass the whole time. I fired my service weapon, Nadja. I'm on forced medical leave. Get the picture? I don't have time to deal with any of that stuff. Viviane Gray's killing wasn't a coincidence. Someone decided that she knew too much and needed to be silenced — which means I was right about the Cook deaths. That was a quintuple murder, not a domestic rampage. When the people behind those deaths got scared that I might have learned something from Gray, they tried to kill me, too. They're not going to stop now."

"Don't tell me you want to keep investigating this thing by yourself!"

"I have no choice, Nadja. I've got to find them before they find me."

"Victor!" Fernandez exclaims, in a voice that combines anger and panic. "Have you lost your mind? Stay where you are, we'll come and help you."

"I've never been more lucid in my fucking life! I need to move fast, before they can get organized."

"Who's 'they'? You're making it sound like a conspiracy."

"Viviane Gray was followed. The killer was masked, Nadja. His gun was fitted with a silencer. He waited until she was in the bathroom, then eliminated her. The guy was a pro."

"What did Viviane Gray say to you that was so important?"

"Honestly, I don't know. But I'll find out."

"Headquarters is going to put out a search alert, Victor. You'll be a wanted man, and you won't be any closer to the truth."

"At the moment, you're the only person who knows I was involved in the shootout."

"Victor, I —"

"Did you look through those databases, like I asked?"

"No."

Silence.

"Okay, well …"

"Don't do this, Victor. I'm begging you … Victor?"

He's already hung up.

21

Jacinthe Taillon walks up and down both sides of Saint-Catherine Street between Berri and Amherst, waving a photograph of Laila François in the face of every person she sees with rings in body parts other than their ears; every person who's smoking a joint or a cigarette, or begging for either; and every person who has more than one dog on a leash.

She knows she's found her guy as soon as he looks at the picture of Laila — or, rather, as soon as he pretends not to recognize her.

Such details never escape her notice. Neither, for that matter, does the relentless expansion of her waistline, despite her constant dieting — a circumstance that drives her nuts. All she does is starve herself, while her partner, Gilles Lemaire, stuffs himself to the gills on a daily basis and never puts on a milligram.

There's no justice in this damn world!

Which is more or less what the pimply young goth is saying as she grips his arm and steers him roughly into a nearby alley:

"Owww! Get your hands off me! I know my rights …"

"Calm down, buddy. All you have to do is answer a few questions, and Auntie Jacinthe will let you go back to playgroup."

The goth looks at her in silence.

"You're the one who called 911 about the kidnapping, right?"

"I'm not talking to you. I don't know anything!"

With a sudden sharp motion, Taillon grabs the goth's scrotum through his pants, as though it were a doorknob.

And generally speaking, what does one do with a doorknob?

One turns.

The goth wants to cry out, but he can't. His attention is entirely focused on his private parts.

"I gotta tell you, buddy, it's been a while since Auntie Jacinthe cupped her hands around a guy's family jewels. She may have lost her gentle touch. We wouldn't want you to get hurt, now, would we?"

The goth shakes his head. His eyes are watering.

"Okay. I'm going to loosen my grip a little, to make things more comfortable. But if you cry out or try to bullshit me ... *squiiirk!*"

Taillon's tongue trills in the goth's ear, and he starts to tremble. This little encounter is giving her a pleasant buzz of sadistic satisfaction.

"Now, then. Why didn't you wait for the patrol car after you called 911?"

"Because I was high ..."

Taillon tightens her iron grip on the goth's testicles.

"Stop! Stop ...! I was waiting for a buyer. I had a deal going down."

"Heroin?"

"Crystal meth."

"Quite the little businessman, aren't you?"

Taillon loosens the pressure and breathes in the goth's ear:

"I don't give a shit about your drug deal. I'm trying to find the girl. Did you know her?"

"I saw her a couple of times in the trailer."

"She used to be a street kid?"

"I think so. A few years back."

"Do you know what she was doing for a living?"

"I heard rumours."

"What kind of rumours?"

"She was doing online porn."

Taillon instantly recalls the audiovisual equipment in the girl's apartment.

"Using a webcam?"

"Yeah, something like that."

"Who'd you hear the rumours from? I want names!"

"They were just rumours.... Aaaagh! Okay, ease up. I'll talk."

"Wise decision, buddy."

"Steve Côté told me about her."

"Côté? Who's he?"

"One of Nigel's guys. He's totally obsessed with her."

"You mean Nigel Williams? The pimp?"

"You didn't hear it from me."

"You worry too much, buddy. Anything else you want to tell Auntie Jacinthe? Details that may have come back to you about the van, the driver, stuff like that?"

"Like I told the 911 operator, I didn't see anything else."

"I believe you, buddy. I believe you."

She releases the goth's crotch, and he lets the air out of his lungs.

"Next time you diddle yourself, think of me," she says, giving him a sly wink before she walks out of the alley.

As Laila tries to guess her captor's identity, the nightmare she lived through with HIM replays before her eyes.

Pascal Pierre.

The mere thought of her stepfather's name is enough to make Laila sick to her stomach. In all of her short life, she's never encountered anyone more vile, more twisted, more repulsive than HIM. Though the scale may be smaller, Laila believes that for sheer cruelty, HE deserves to be ranked with the worst tyrants in the history of humanity.

Pascal Pierre is a verminous, filthy, crawling animal. In a better world, HE would have been strangled at birth.

She realizes that HE meets all the requirements she's been thinking about. HE has the necessary physical strength. HE has easy access to drugs and a van. On top of that, HE's a true psychopath.

As far as Laila's concerned, Pascal Pierre is a 10 out of 10.

If HE's behind this abduction, then she's as good as dead. But how could HE have tracked her down?

Laila puts her face in her hands and starts to weep. All the other scenarios she's imagined, even the ones in which her life is in danger, seem less awful than this one.

She's done everything in her power to forget, to banish the past from her consciousness; but now, amidst the solitude, the silence, and the darkness of her captivity, every barrier collapses, and a flood of memories rushes into her mind.

Jacinthe Taillon and Gilles Lemaire are watching intently as the Radio-Canada news anchor, Julie Roy, speaks to reporter Maxime Savoie.

"Maxime, you talked earlier with Pascal Pierre, whose stepdaughter Laila François was kidnapped last night."

"That's right, Julie. The fifty-four-year-old man delivered a poignant plea to the kidnapper, and to the people of Quebec. Mr. Pierre explained to us that Laila, whose mother is deceased, ran away from home three years ago. He's heard nothing from her since that time, and while the news of her abduction was, of course, very distressing, there was also a measure of relief in the knowledge that she was still alive. Let's listen."

Pascal Pierre appears on the screen.

"To whoever kidnapped Laila, I want you to know that I'm a great-grandson of slaves, a man of modest means. But I'm ready to give everything I have to get Laila back safely. I pray that the Lord helps you to make the right choice, and I ask everyone in Quebec to join me in that prayer. Choose love. Choose courage. Choose life. And to you, Laila, light of my life … if you can see this, don't give up hope. Stay strong. I want you to know that I'll always be there for you, whatever happens. May God help us all."

Taillon turns down the volume after the interview with Pierre Pascal is over. "I don't like the look of that guy," she says. "Something's not right about him."

"What?" Lemaire asks. "I found him impressive. Dignified. What didn't you like about him?"

"I don't know, the shifty eyes, the preachy way of answering questions. It's pretty obvious that he enjoys being in the spotlight."

"He's comfortable in front of the cameras. He looks good on TV. He's a pastor. Of course he's well-spoken. So what?"

"So nothing."

22

Sheets of rain sweep through the sky, piercing the dome of cloud that churns over the city.

An emaciated dog, yellow-haired, mud-stained, is shambling across Notre-Dame Street, seeming to carry the weight of some crushing misery, some immense, unendurable sadness on its bent back.

Lessard slows the car and touches the horn.

Instead of getting out of the way, the dog halts in the middle of the street and looks at the cop with a gaze that is at once arrogant and resigned, as though to say, "Come on, pal, let's put an end to this right now."

Lessard stops the car centimetres from the animal.

When it's clear that a collision has been averted, the dog looks away with an expression of silent reproach, and trudges to the sidewalk.

Another loner with nothing left to lose.

Lessard's cellphone buzzes just as he's about to turn it off, to prevent Tanguay and headquarters from locating him by triangulation.

"This makes no sense! Don't do it!"

"Stop, Nadja. I've made my decision."

"But —"

"Don't make this harder than it already is!" he barks.

He sighs and shakes his head. He lost his temper, despite himself.

"I'm sorry, Nadja. I'm on edge."

"I can't make you change your mind?" Fernandez persists. "Are you sure?"

"Positive," he murmurs.

There's a long silence.

"I lied to you earlier," Fernandez says at last. "I've got some information for you." She hesitates. "Do you have something to write with?"

"Hang on."

Lessard pulls the car over and pats his pockets, looking for his notebook.

"Okay," he mumbles, pulling the top off his ballpoint with his teeth. "Shoot."

"There was a murder-suicide in Sherbrooke, in June 2006. The Sandoval case."

"Doesn't ring a bell. What happened?"

"Richard Sandoval, aged sixty-one, killed his forty-six-year-old wife, then himself. The case got a fair amount of attention because Sandoval was involved in municipal politics, and they seemed to be an ideal couple."

"Any other similarities with our case?" Lessard asks.

"There was an unexplained swarm of flies in the house."

"Flies. That's ..." Lessard begins, then trails off, pondering.

"The lead detective was Sylvain Marchand of the Sherbrooke Police."

Lessard takes down Marchand's number.

"Thank you, Nadja. For everything."

"Don't mention it. I've thought it over, Victor. I'm going to take a couple of vacation days and come join you. You'll be needing some help."

Lessard closes his eyes and winces. He'd love to see her right now, but for all the wrong reasons. Even after the night he spent with Elaine Segato, Lessard has found himself longing for Fernandez ever since he saw her in Miguel's company.

"No way, Nadja. If you helped me openly and things went wrong, your career would be ruined. You're taking enough risks as it is."

"But Victor, I —"

"Forget it. The answer is no. Anyway, I'll still be needing your help with database searches."

If Lessard could only see Fernandez right now, if he could see the anguished worry on her face and the lost look in her beautiful eyes, he'd surely be touched. Perhaps he'd be affected enough to overcome his pathological timidity and make a first move.

The silence lengthens, becoming as eloquent as any number of useless words.

"I wa—"

"We'll talk later, Nadja."

Lessard turns off his phone and slips it into his pocket.

On the street, a teenager shuffles by, wearing a Canadiens jersey.

Seeing the red-white-and-blue jersey, Lessard thinks of Pat Burns, who, of all the team's former coaches, is his favourite. Lessard's preference may be connected to the fact that Burns is an ex-cop and, like Lessard himself, a good-hearted curmudgeon. And right now — to borrow an expression that Burns made famous — the detective sergeant has no intention of going bear hunting with a butter knife.

Before travelling to Sherbrooke to meet Sylvain Marchand, Lessard needs to make sure he's got the necessary tools: specifically, firearms and ammunition.

He doesn't have additional weapons at home, and going to a gun shop might attract attention — not a good idea. But Lessard knows where to find what he needs: the home of his former mentor, Ted Rutherford, who lives in Saint-Henri.

His nerves are near the breaking point. As he drives, he keeps scanning the rear-view mirror.

He stops at a red light.

"Are we going to see your friend? Your friend Ted?"

"Yes," Lessard says, without turning to look at the back seat.

"It's been a while since you last visited him."

"Yes, it's been a while."

"Almost three years."

"That long?"

"You know very well how long it's been, Victor. You've only been to see him four times since his stroke. Four times in seven years."

The cop hangs his head, overwhelmed by shame.

"When you see him, you don't know how to express your compassion. You're ashamed."

"No."

"Yes, you are, and you know it. You're ashamed. Worse than that, you're disgusted. Admit it, Victor. Ted disgusts you because he's in a wheelchair. He disgusts you because he drools. Because he wears a diaper. Because he's old and smells of shit."

"You're wrong!" Lessard exclaims, pointing angrily at his brother.

"Come on, Victor, stop lying to yourself. You'd rather see him as the cop you once admired, rather than the wreck he's become. You don't want him staining the ideal of invincible paternal authority that he used to represent."

"Shut up, Raymond! Shut the fuck up!"

The elderly lady crossing the street in front of the Corolla jumps when she hears the driver shouting obscenities. Seeing him alone in the vehicle, she has no doubt that he's just another phone addict, one of those people who spend their lives with a gizmo in their ears, talking to the empty air.

Once upon a time, only village idiots did that sort of thing.

He arrives at Sir George-Étienne Cartier Square.

He rings the ground-floor doorbell of a grey stone building facing the park. The door is opened by a handsome man in his sixties, elegantly attired in a collarless white shirt.

At the sight of Lessard, the man puts a hand to his mouth.

"Oh my god … Victor?!"

"Hello, Albert."

Albert Corneau and Victor Lessard have known each other for nearly thirty years. They exchange hearty pats on the back and kiss each other's cheeks, moved to tears.

"Goodness, Victor, it's been a while. Two, three years?"

"Yes, it's been a while," Lessard says, lowering his eyes sadly. "Too long a while." He looks up again. "How are you, Albert?"

Corneau's lips form a Mona Lisa half smile.

"Oh, you know …" Sadness flickers across his features. "I guess I'm like all the other caregivers in the world, sometimes exhausted, often despairing. But I keep putting one foot in front of the other, because I know it's the right thing to do. Life goes on."

"Ted's lucky to have you."

"Ah, well … but look at you!" Corneau says, leading Lessard into the front hall of the apartment. He gives the cop an appraising look. "You've lost weight. And updated your wardrobe."

"Yeah, I've dropped a few pounds," Lessard says, reddening.

"Not another dud romance, I hope."

"What you and Ted have just doesn't happen anymore, Albert."

"Thirty-five years. Can you believe it?"

"These days, thirty-five months is an accomplishment."

"Yes, but straight relationships can be a challenge — juggling careers, kids, and all the rest."

Without discussing it, by force of habit, the two men end up in the kitchen.

Lessard knows the place like the back of his hand.

If attitudes toward homosexuality hadn't been so intolerant in the late 1970s, he'd have come to live here after the massacre of his family. Instead, he ended up in a succession of foster homes, where he experienced rejection, violence, and humiliation. He ran away frequently, often ending up in this apartment, where Ted and Albert would shelter him in secret for as long as they could without drawing the attention of the authorities. When that ceased to be possible, Lessard lived on the streets and hung around the trailer where Monsieur Antoine was just starting to offer help to young people in need.

Things took a turn for the better when Ted convinced his secretary and her husband to take in sixteen-year-old Victor. Eventually, they became his adoptive parents.

"So," Corneau says, "does that mean you aren't seeing anyone at the moment?"

Images of Véronique and Fernandez flash before Lessard's eyes, but he shakes his head.

"Don't you try that with me, Victor Lessard! I know you too well. Is she married? In a relationship?"

"Something like that," he answers, unable to suppress a smile. "Now, what about Ted?"

"Physically, he's the same as ever. Mentally, he's had his ups and downs. More downs than ups, to be honest. But lately, he's been in a good frame of mind."

"Is he asleep?"

"No, he's in the den."

"Can I go say hi?"

"Of course." Corneau hesitates for an instant. "He'll be happy to see you, Victor. But you know how he is. Illness hasn't made him any more —"

"I know."

"Wait here. I'll tell him you've come."

Corneau could have explained that Ted Rutherford hates surprises, but the detective sergeant is well aware of that.

Lessard comes forward, watched intently by Rutherford, who's sitting wheelchair-bound in the midst of his books, his suffering, and his silence.

This man is the last living piece of a complex mosaic. He's the third and perhaps the most important part of the paternal triangle that shaped Lessard's personality, standing between his murderous biological father and the loving adoptive father who gave young Victor the privilege of a family life again.

Lessard composes his face, putting on an expression that's meant to convey joy at this happy reunion.

Frozen, with his arms hanging at his sides, unable to step across the small gap separating them, Lessard stands facing the man who encouraged him to enrol in police college — the man who subsequently became his mentor and partner during his early days on the force.

"It's good to see you, Ted."

Sorry I don't come around more often. It's too hard.

Rutherford's response is cold and abrupt, more of a statement than a question.

"You're in trouble."

Since Rutherford's second stroke, the right side of his mouth has been deformed by paralysis. His enunciation is laboured and muddy.

"What makes you say that?"

"I can see it on your face."

Lessard has never been able to hide anything from Rutherford, but he persists in the charade.

"You're looking well."

"Give it a rest, Victor. We both know you're not here to see how I'm doing."

Lowering his eyes, with a lump in his throat, Lessard struggles not to lose control and, above all, not to be overwhelmed by the surging emotions that are hammering his insides and smashing his heart to pieces.

"You're right," he whispers, and pulls up a chair.

"Talk to me."

Lessard opens up, omitting nothing: the investigation into the Cooks' deaths, his doubts, his hunches, the message he found in the shed, Faizan's account of what he saw, the flies, the murder of Viviane Gray, her eye dangling from her cranial cavity, the shootout at Central Station, and everything else.

It all comes out.

"Give me a cigarette," Rutherford commands in a tone that doesn't allow for contradiction.

Lessard wants to point out that Rutherford has been under orders not to smoke since his stroke. But why deprive a man in his condition of the guilty pleasure of nicotine? He lights two cigarettes and places one between his old friend's lips. Rutherford savours each puff with the greedy joy of a prospector who's just found the motherlode.

"What are you going to do?"

"Find the people who did this before they find me."

Rutherford closes his eyes and weighs his response as though the fate of the world depends on it. Which, in a way, it does. He knows that his opinion matters more than anything to Lessard — who, apart from Albert, is all Rutherford has left. He would never forgive himself if anything happened to Victor.

"It's dangerous," Rutherford says, looking the detective sergeant in the eye, "but there's nothing else you can do."

The tension that was gripping Lessard by the throat dissipates.

The man who taught him everything he knows about police work, the man he's trusted with his life countless times in the past, has just confirmed the wisdom of his decision.

Lessard puts a hand on Ted's arm. In the space of an instant, all the love and goodwill in the world is exchanged in the two men's gazes.

"You have everything you need?" Rutherford asks gruffly, not wanting to get sentimental.

"I was thinking I might borrow a couple of things from your basement."

"I had a feeling you weren't just here for my blessing."

As Lessard is about to go out the door, Rutherford calls after him.

"Victor, if I still had my legs, I …"

The detective sergeant stops, but doesn't turn.

"I know, Ted. I know."

The door closes behind him.

A tear runs down Rutherford's cheek. There are so many things he wishes he could say to the man he's always regarded as his own son.

Imprisoned by decades of silence, he doesn't know how.

After crossing the Champlain Bridge and getting onto the highway, Lessard calls Sylvain Marchand, the Sherbrooke police detective whose number Fernandez gave to him.

As he listens to the phone ring, he thinks about Albert Corneau and Ted Rutherford, to whom he said goodbye a few minutes ago.

How long will it be before he sees them again?

His call goes to voice mail. He leaves a message.

Having stored the metal briefcase under his bed, Noah kneels on the floor and prays fervently, as he does every morning. After that, he eats his only meal of the day: two hard-boiled eggs from the kitchen.

Then he takes a numbingly cold shower — a ritual he inflicts on himself as a penance — and puts on his cassock. This rigid lifestyle, which he's cultivated since he first entered the priesthood, enables him to subjugate his body and elevate his soul to a state of contemplation. Before his call to Christ and his ordination as a priest, Noah's gluttony had turned him into a fat young man, empty and tormented, a commonplace creature who was marked by life's vagaries and the jeering of other youths.

He comes out of the archdiocesan residence through the door on De la Cathédrale Street and walks north toward René-Lévesque Boulevard and downtown Montreal.

The SIV agent is familiar with the city, having served as Apostolic Nuncio to Canada from 1985 to 1990. He was a frequent visitor during those years. As Nuncio, he represented the Holy See in its dealings with the Canadian government, performing a role similar to that of an ambassador.

Looking straight ahead, Noah walks with a decisive gait, but without haste, paying no attention to the rain or the passersby. After his conversation with the cardinal prefect, his immediate objectives are clear, as are the methods by which he will achieve them.

At the corner of Drummond and Saint-Catherine Streets, Noah steps into an office building.

Before getting on the highway, Lessard withdrew a thousand dollars in cash at an ATM. Sooner or later, investigators will tie him to the shootout at the train station. Which means he can't use his credit card anymore. Doing so would make it easier to track him down. For the same reason, he stopped off at a phone store and bought a prepaid BlackBerry — which he paid for in cash — so as to avoid using his police-issue cellphone.

He tosses the BlackBerry onto the passenger seat, next to the hunting knife and pistol that he borrowed from Ted Rutherford. In his trunk, he's placed a twelve-gauge shotgun, a rifle mounted with a scope, and several boxes of ammunition.

He remembers the words of his former mentor:

"I had a feeling you weren't just here for my blessing."

Ted's blessing.

Isn't that what he really went for?

Driving along the wet asphalt of Highway 10 toward the Eastern Townships helps clear his head.

He thinks about the events of the last few hours: the senseless killing that took place under his nose and the subsequent attempt on his own life.

It all seems unreal.

During his entire career as a police officer, Lessard has never experienced anything so outlandish.

This is real life, not the movies. What kind of secret could possibly be so important that it justifies deciding to kill two people in broad daylight?

The SIV agent descends several flights of stairs into a subterranean environment, where Vincenzo has secured the disused cellar of a downtown office building. The location is soundproof, hidden away, inaccessible to prying eyes — all essential qualities, given what's being done here.

Noah wouldn't be so brazen as to carry out his operations within the precincts of the cathedral itself.

The cardinal's aversion to conflict has its limits.

Seeing Vincenzo Moreno's scowling features and puffy eyes, Noah knows that his henchman spent an uncomfortable night down here on a makeshift bed.

"Any news from your watcher in Chinatown?"

"Nothing so far, *Padre*," Moreno replies, brushing a lock of hair out of his eyes.

"Do you still have someone keeping an eye on the apartment?"

"The man we're looking for hasn't been home since the murders. But we're short of resources, *Padre*. I won't be able to post a watcher there indefinitely. We can't be everywhere at once."

"He's hiding out somewhere. It's just a matter of finding out where."

"Yes, but how? Time is working against us, *Padre*. And the detective is getting closer. I almost lost an operative at the train station this morning."

"I know, Vincenzo. Your brother texted me. I have someone going over every detail of the man's credit card transactions, his bank accounts, and all available information in the databases."

"That won't change anything if he stays hidden and doesn't use his credit card."

"Which is why, when you're done here, you're going to go search his apartment."

"I already went over every inch of the place, *Padre*."

"And you will do so again. All it takes is a single detail that you missed the first time around. If we keep searching, we'll eventually find something that leads us to him."

"You should have let me come with you to Bessborough Avenue. You never would have lost him."

"You needn't remind me, Vincenzo."

Noah's tone is harsh. He points an index finger at a closed steel door.

"Make him talk," he says. "Until we have proof to the contrary, he's our best bet."

A cruel smile appears on Vincenzo's face.

"You can count on me, *Padre*. If Dorion knows where your man is, he'll spit it out."

Despite Lessard's efforts to look at the matter from every angle and come up with useful hypotheses, he still can't seem to identify any solid leads.

What does he know?

Scribbling in his notebook while driving through the rain would be unwise, so he goes over the facts mentally, organizing them logically in his head.

One: five people died on Bessborough Avenue.

Two: in the shed, he found a note written by John Cook, suggesting that he was innocent.

Three: Faizan said he saw a cloud of flies through the kitchen window and a priest with an axe in his hand in the Cooks' yard.

Four: in his medical analysis, Jacob Berger concluded that Cook killed his wife and children with his own hands, then committed suicide. The only unexplained detail, in Berger's opinion, was the shoulder wound. Was it inflicted on Cook by his wife, whose fingerprints were found on the axe handle? Lessard pointed out to Berger that Elizabeth Munson was left-handed, while the blow seems to have been struck by someone right-handed. Berger invoked the theory of cross-dominance to justify his conclusion. His logic is unassailable, but Lessard's gut is telling him that something isn't right.

Five: Viviane Gray certainly thought something wasn't right. She arranged a meeting at Central Station, and confirmed that the message in the Cooks' shed wasn't simply a coincidence. Gray was then murdered before she could give the detective sergeant any additional information. Someone decided that she knew too much, and that Lessard himself needed to be eliminated, as well.

He turns on the windshield wipers.

The rain is falling harder.

As far as Lessard is concerned, Gray's murder doesn't invalidate Berger's conclusion that Cook killed his wife and children.

But he can't help thinking Cook might have had outside help, which would explain the things that Faizan saw. He wonders whether he put words in the little boy's mouth. If Faizan did, in fact, see something, rather than imagine the whole thing, was it a priest he saw in the yard that night, or was it simply someone dressed in black?

Lessard isn't ruling out the possibility that Cook acted under duress. Part of his conversation with Viviane Gray comes back to him. What did she say about the strange dreams Cook was having?

He dreamed that a man was talking to him in his sleep.

Lessard tries to make sense of that detail, but he can't.

Whatever else is true, one fact seems beyond dispute. The murder of Cook's mistress proves that the killings on Bessborough Avenue were more than a simple domestic murder-suicide.

The two events are definitely linked at the heart of some wider pattern. Wanting to conceal the truth, someone took the risk of ordering the execution of two people in a crowded railway station.

But who?

And, above all, why?

His ringing BlackBerry brings him back to reality.

"Lessard."

"This is Sylvain Marchand of the Sherbrooke Police," says a friendly voice. "You left me a message?"

"Yes, hello, Sylvain. Thanks for getting back to me so quickly. I'm on my way out to Sherbrooke to meet you."

"Oh? About what?"

"I'd like to look at the Sandoval file."

Dead silence greets this statement. No police officer likes to have another cop nosing around in his affairs. When Marchand speaks again, every trace of warmth is gone from his voice.

"May I ask why?"

"I'm not totally sure, but I think there may be a link with a case I'm investigating."

More silence.

"Is something wrong, Sylvain?"

"No, no. Nothing's wrong." There's a pause, then Marchand adds, in an ill-tempered voice, "It's just that the file has been archived. It'll take a hell of a lot of digging to find it."

"I won't be there for at least an hour," Lessard says. "That gives you plenty of time."

He hangs up before Marchand can protest.

. . .

Lessard is past Carignan when he notices the distress signals coming from his fuel gauge. The needle is on *E* and the warning light has been shining for several minutes now.

After executing a series of complicated manoeuvres to make sure he isn't being followed, Lessard gets off the highway.

Shit.

He sees a sign indicating that he'll have to spend ten minutes on a secondary road before coming to a gas station. He finally pulls up at an antiquated pump, beside which an attendant sits dozing in a hut with scratched Plexiglas windows. Muttering, his hands covered in grease, the attendant approaches the Corolla as Lessard cranks down the driver-side window.

"Fill 'er up."

Next to the gas station, there's a muddy parking area full of tractor-trailers, beyond which Lessard sees a building with metal siding. A sign in front reads Rest-O-Bar.

Though the name is hardly suggestive of gourmet fare, Lessard is hungry. He decides to have a bite to eat after the tank is filled.

While the attendant, his back bent by a lifetime of drudgery, stands over the gas nozzle, Lessard walks through the parking area to stretch his legs. Before getting out of the car, he took care to throw his jacket over the arsenal on the passenger seat.

He doesn't want to attract attention — not even in the middle of nowhere.

A light drizzle falls from the scudding clouds.

As he exhales smoke from his cigarette, Lessard thinks of Fernandez.

Will he ever find the courage to tell her how he feels? To take the first step?

Sitting among the truckers in the diner, he lingers over his cheeseburger and fries, washing the meal down with an occasional sip of lukewarm Coke.

The aging waitress in her polyester uniform smiles at the customers' off-colour comments, replying tartly to their lewd remarks. Lessard watches her for a moment. She seems to be enjoying the idle banter.

He doesn't speak to anyone, makes no effort to break into the circle of regulars. With a toothpick hanging from the corner of his mouth, he returns to the Corolla, patting his stomach a couple of times.

Maybe he shouldn't have ordered that sugar pie.

He tries to call Martin. No answer. He leaves a message, mentioning his new cell number.

His son's radio silence is starting to worry him.

Though he makes an effort to stay rational, he can't help thinking that the people who tried to eliminate him might go after his family.

He comes very close to calling his ex-wife, Marie, but decides against it. He doesn't want to worry her unnecessarily.

He tries to reassure himself with the thought that this isn't the first time Martin has dropped off the radar.

But the anxiety is stronger than he is. Suddenly, he's very afraid.

"They'll kill him, Victor," murmurs Raymond, who's been sitting in the car this whole time, watching the raindrops run down the windows. "That'll be one more person you've abandoned."

23

Criminal Investigation Division
City of Sherbrooke

Lessard gives his name and rank to the youthful female officer at the reception desk. For a moment, he fears that his description might already have been sent to police units province-wide after the events at Central Station, and that a dozen cops are about to rush out and overpower him. But no, the young officer leads him enthusiastically through the office hallways, unleashing a barrage of excited questions about working conditions on the Montreal force, and concluding with a whispered confession that she's been dreaming of a move to the big city for some time now.

Lessard wants to urge her to think twice before leaving Sherbrooke. He wants to explain that police work in Montreal is a nightmare. But he doesn't have the heart to dash such high hopes.

The conference room in which he waits for Marchand is subdued, but tastefully decorated.

He can't help taking note of the well-maintained premises and the cutting-edge technical equipment. Compared to the rundown office in which he and his colleagues work, this place is the height of luxury.

The door opens and a large woman enters, out of breath. She places a cardboard box on the table in front of him.

"Sylvain's in a meeting. He asked me to bring you this."

"Is that the Sandoval file?"

The woman gives him a furtive glance through her thick glasses. A few coarse black hairs are sprouting from her chin.

"I don't know if it's the Sandoval file, but I can definitely confirm that it weighs a lot."

"Thank you."

"No problem. Is there anything else you need? A cup of coffee, maybe?"

"No, thanks."

"Sylvain asked me to tell you that he'll be by after his meeting."

"Perfect."

The woman closes the door behind her.

Lessard contemplates the box for a moment, unsure of what he'll find inside and nervous about the scale of the task awaiting him. Each time he starts a new case, he feels this void, this sense that his efforts will be in vain, that he won't be able to scale the peaks that rise up before him.

He takes out a file folder, scans its contents, and sets it aside. He withdraws a second folder and does the same thing, continuing the process until he comes to a folder full of photographs.

When looking through the file of an investigation that he didn't conduct himself, Lessard always starts with the photos. They provide the only means of forming his own impression of the case, without external influence, without the inevitable slant that the lead detective will have imparted to the file, however inadvertently.

An initial series of shots shows the crime scene in its entirety.

The first detail that strikes Lessard is the same one that struck him in the house on Bessborough Avenue — the unusual number of flies.

Many of them have been caught by the camera in midflight. They're mostly concentrated in the kitchen.

After a moment, the detective sergeant sets this pile aside.

He wants to see the bodies. He wants to know what he's dealing with.

The first photograph in the second pile shows the naked body of a woman, stretched out on a bedroom floor.

She's lying face down in a pool of blood.

Her legs are slightly spread, her arms bent at strange angles under her torso.

Probably broken.

Her black hair, as far as Lessard can tell, is covering the sides of her face. No injuries or signs of violence are visible on the flesh of her back.

A second shot, taken from a different angle, shows the same victim. Lessard leafs feverishly through the photos until he finds one of the man.

The killer. The one who murdered his wife before taking his own life.

The detective sergeant looks away too late. The image is permanently engraved on his memory.

The corpse's eyes have been gouged out.

A nasty smile lights up Jacinthe Taillon's fleshy features.

The man she's looking for is seated in La Belle Province restaurant at the corner of Saint-Catherine and Amherst Streets. Four all-dressed hot dogs and a poutine are set out on the table in front of him.

He's a typical small-time hood, with his vaguely dim-witted expression, his thick, tattoo-covered arms, his skull-and-crossbones T-shirt, his tanning-booth complexion, his chains, his bracelets, and all the rest of his low-rent bling.

"Steve Côté?" Taillon demands in a loud voice.

A few customers glance over.

Côté looks up. "Who's asking?"

"Police, buddy-boy. We need to talk about Laila François."

"Fuck off. I got nothing to say."

Côté's cheeks and ears are red. Taillon grabs one of the hot dogs from the tray and takes a bite, cramming half the hot dog into her mouth.

"Come on, Stevie," she says, pulling out her handcuffs. "You and me are going for a ride."

Lessard takes a gulp of water from the glass that Marchand's assistant brought him. He's removed all the documents from the box and laid them out in neat stacks on the table before him.

He takes a deep breath and starts to read the final investigation report. It's a compendium of horrors.

MEMORANDUM

FROM: Sylvain Marchand
TO: File
DATE: July 27th, 2006
RE: Final investigation report on the deaths
         of Richard Sandoval and Sophie Landreville

Summary

On June 13th, 2006, at 9:24 p.m., a call came in to the
911 switchboard. The caller, Pierre Sandoval, had just
discovered the bodies of his son Richard, aged 61, and
his daughter-in-law, Sophie Landreville, 46, in their
home on Brooks Street.

The two individuals were pronounced dead at the
scene by ambulance attendants. The first responders,
patrol officers Guy Pelletier and François Corriveau,
immediately followed standard procedures, securing the
crime scene and establishing a perimeter around the
house.

I arrived at the house with my partner, Detective Pierre
Marion, at 11:22 p.m. The medical examiner, Dr. Yvon
Dufour, and crime scene technicians were already present.

Upon arrival, Detective Marion and I examined the
premises and the disposition of the bodies.

[...]

Sophie Landreville was lying on the floor in the master
bedroom. There were numerous signs of a struggle, as set
out in the technical analysis attached to this report at
Annex 1 ("Analysis").

[...]

Landreville's body bore multiple lacerations, as well
as severe fractures and contusions to the face, to an
extent that made her unrecognizable. It was as though
the killer had been intent on literally erasing her
features. [...] The medical examiner's findings, attached
to this report at Annex 2 ("Medical Findings"), show that
Landreville was struck in the face with a baseball bat
more than forty times, and that both her arms were broken
by bat blows.

Having looked at the horrifying autopsy photographs of Sophie
Landreville, Lessard skips some passages.

[...] Richard Sandoval was found in the home theatre. When
his body was discovered, the television set was on, tuned
to a 24-hour news channel. [...] The body was sprawled in
an armchair. [...] Sandoval had fired one shot into his
mouth with his hunting rifle, blowing out the back of his
skull. [...] On a coffee table beside the armchair, we found
a bowl that had been taken from the kitchen. It contained
Sandoval's eyes, which, according to the medical
examiner's findings, he had gouged out with a hunting
knife. [...] There were no other injuries to the body.

Lessard scribbles in his notebook.

*Sandoval gouged his eyes out. Cook cut out his tongue. Is there a
link? Some kind of symbolism?*

*Is it possible to gouge your own eyes out in a normal mental
state? Were drugs involved?*

Lessard continues to read through the report to get a clear understanding of the basic elements of the Sandoval case.

The couple had no children.

Sophie Landreville was five foot four and weighed a hundred and twenty pounds. From the photographs that Lessard saw, she was a pleasant-looking woman. She might even have been attractive if it hadn't been for her uninspired hairstyle and boring taste in clothes, dominated by shades of beige and brown. Lessard isn't surprised to read that she was employed as an accountant at a downtown Sherbrooke firm. Landreville also worked out at a local gym several times a week, and was enrolled in a painting class.

Unlike his wife, Richard Sandoval was tall and good-looking. Built like a weightlifter, with his open-necked shirt revealing a hairless chest, he seemed a decade younger than his age, and came across as a wild, charismatic playboy. Sandoval was a city councillor and the right-hand man of Mayor Jean-Guy Applebaum, who died some time afterward, following a long illness. The killings had been widely covered in the media, not just because of the horrific nature of the crime, but also because Richard Sandoval was well-known, widely liked, and active in the community.

Lessard opens the press file and skims the regional newspaper headlines that appeared in the days following the discovery of the bodies:

The Tribune:
CITY COUNCILLOR SANDOVAL DEAD: MURDER-SUICIDE?

The Sherbrooke News:
DOMESTIC RAMPAGE: RICHARD SANDOVAL KILLS WIFE, SELF

The Sherbrooke Daily:
THE BUTCHER OF CITY HALL

The most lurid details of the killings — the gouged-out eyes, the face beaten to a pulp — aren't mentioned in the reports that Lessard looks over, suggesting either that Marchand didn't divulge them out of consideration for the families, or that the media showed some restraint. Knowing nothing about the background of the case, Lessard is inclined by experience to the favour the first explanation.

In the absence of a suicide note, journalists speculated freely as to Sandoval's motive. Overwork, marital infidelity, financial problems, a fit of madness, depression — all the classic explanations were put forward, but no consensus emerged.

A columnist with the *Sherbrooke Daily*, Mario Desjardins, suggested that Sandoval might have cracked under the strains of a high-pressure project that he was overseeing: the construction of a new university hospital. Public meetings on the subject had been highly contentious, and Sandoval had been subjected to verbal attacks that Desjardins characterized as "mean-spirited, arbitrary, and partisan."

Some stories mentioned the reaction of Mayor Applebaum, who said he was "saddened by the loss of a man of the people, a tireless worker," and, above all, that he was "devastated by the death of a personal friend under inconceivable circumstances." Applebaum took care, however, to condemn Sandoval's crime, calling it "an unforgivable act," unworthy of the man he knew.

Another article referred to the personal friendship between Sandoval and Applebaum, who were roughly the same age. This friendship had been forged during their years as pupils at the Sherbrooke Seminary, a Catholic high school, and had deepened while they were both on the roster of the now-defunct Sherbrooke Beavers of the Quebec Major Junior Hockey League. Sandoval was an enforcer on the team, charged with protecting Applebaum, whose skills made him one of the top scorers in the league. Some commentators felt that Sandoval had played a similar role in politics, serving Applebaum in the same way that Jean Chrétien had once served the late prime minister Pierre Elliott Trudeau — as the guy who did the boss's dirty work.

The article also noted that the two men shared a passion for matchitecture, "an increasingly popular leisure activity that involves the construction of architectural models using microbeams, which are matchsticks minus the sulfur tips."

"Looks like fun," Raymond says, gazing at a photograph of a model over Lessard's shoulder, before he turns back to the window, where he's drawing pictures on the misty glass with his index finger.

After a little while, Lessard puts the press clippings back in the folder and gets up to stretch his legs. He goes and stands next to his brother at the window. Raindrops are pattering on the ground outside.

The downpour depresses him.

He's in the mood for a smoke, but decides to wait a bit before poisoning his system with another dose of nicotine.

He opens the interrogation file.

```
Interrogation of Claire Sandoval
[…]
Q:  Mrs. Sandoval, did you get the impression that your
    son was depressed lately?
A:  I … [Stenographer's note: The witness takes some
    time before answering.] Richard did seem a little
    different over the last few weeks.
Q:  What do you mean by "different"?
A:  I don't know. There were bags under his eyes. He said
    he wasn't sleeping well.
Q:  Was he under stress at work? Did he have financial
    problems?
A:  I don't think so. I think he was just going through a
    rough patch.
Q:  Did he ever talk about killing himself?
A:  [Stenographer's note: The witness takes some time
    before answering.] No.
Q:  Did he ever threaten Sophie Landreville?
A:  Never. He loved Sophie.
Q:  Can you explain why he killed her?
A:  [Stenographer's note: The witness takes some time
    before answering.] No.
```

Lessard reads between the lines.

Every word of the elderly woman's deposition reveals her distress and shock at the appalling actions of her son.

Even so, Lessard believes that Marchand conducted the interrogation competently.

The more time he spends reading the documents, the more convinced he becomes that Marchand's work on the case was impeccable.

The report is outstandingly clear and rigorous.

Sandoval's father and Landreville's mother were also questioned by Marchand and his partner. Lessard reads their depositions without learning anything new, except that all of Sandoval's loved ones were utterly unable to explain his actions, and that none of the usual explanations provided a satisfactory answer.

Marchand concludes his report by stating that, in light of the investigation and the autopsy report, "there is no doubt that Sandoval killed Sophie Landreville before taking his own life." The report adds that Marchand and his fellow investigators are unable to determine the precise motives that drove Sandoval to do what he did, but, according to a psychiatrist whom they consulted, "It's plausible to suppose that Sandoval was depressive, overworked, and profoundly hurt by the criticisms he had faced in recent months; that these emotional factors drove him to end his life; and that he decided to take Sophie Landreville with him, so as to spare her the suffering that would inevitably ensue from his death."

Before closing the report, Lessard notices a subject heading on the last page — a heading that only appears when the individual in question has a criminal record:

Antecedents
See the document attached to this report at Annex 19.

Lessard goes through the attached documents, but the annexes he finds in the file are numbered 1 to 18. There is no Annex 19. He concludes that Marchand must have used a previous report as a template for the one on Sandoval, and simply forgot to delete this heading. Lessard occasionally makes the same mistake himself.

The conference room door opens abruptly. Lessard looks up. Sylvain Marchand hurries in, his hair askew.

"Whoa, whoa! What do you think you're doing with that thing?"

"You'll find out, buddy-boy, if I don't get some answers."

"Okay, okay, I'll talk! Put away the knife!"

Despite Côté's protests, Taillon handcuffed him as soon as they were out of the restaurant, then put him in the back of her service vehicle. Without a word, she brought him to a vacant lot under the Jacques Cartier Bridge.

At that point, Côté didn't make things easy for himself. He wasted Taillon's precious time, putting her in a foul mood with transparently false claims that he doesn't work for Nigel Williams, that he's never heard of Laila François, etc.

Taillon doesn't beat around the bush when she wants information. That's especially true when the life of a young woman is at stake. She won't hesitate to step over the line if the situation is urgent and she's being lied to.

Which is the case here.

For starters, she pistol-whipped Côté, opening a cut over his right eye, which had the effect of loosening his tongue. Yes, he works for Williams. Yes, he knows the girl. No, he doesn't drive a white van. Yes, he has an alibi for the night of the abduction (he was having dinner with friends, whose names he's ready to give Taillon). And no, he had nothing to do with the disappearance of Laila François.

Having questioned Côté thoroughly, Taillon is satisfied that his answers are true. But she's dealt with plenty of scumbags in her time, and she knows Côté isn't telling her everything.

Faced with his persistent denials, she pulls out her knife. After each lie, she cuts the flesh under his eye, making a point of twisting the blade a few centimetres from the eyeball.

When it's all over, Côté's face is streaked with blood, but Taillon has the information she was looking for.

Marchand is a short, stout man whose protuberant belly seems too big for his delicate limbs. The hand he extends to Lessard is slender, damp, almost feminine.

"Sorry," he says, out of breath. "I had last-minute meeting."

"No problem. It gave me a chance to look over the file."

Marchand sinks into a chair.

"Good. So, I imagine you have a few questions, Victor."

"Yes, but not too many. The report's well written and very thorough."

Marchand looks pleased. His double chin jiggles. "Thanks. Before we get started, may I ask why you've come?"

Lessard gives him a rundown on the Cook case — neglecting, of course, to mention the shootout.

"I don't get it," Marchand says. "Apart from the fact that both incidents were domestic murder-suicides, what's the connection with the Sandoval case?"

"The flies."

"The flies?" Marchand repeats.

"We found an unusual number of them at the crime scene. You noted the same odd detail in your report."

Marchand's gaze goes blank for a moment as he scours his memory.

"Right. I remember, now. God, it seems like a lifetime ago."

"I went through the file," Lessard says, "but the flies are only mentioned briefly. Can you tell me a little more?"

Marchand picks up a document and leafs through it quickly.

"As I recall, the medical examiner, Dufour, looked into the matter, because the patrol officers arriving at the scene had noticed an abnormal number of flies, considering the time of death. The trouble is, one of the cops opened a window. By the time the forensic team got there, the number of insects had gone way down. Later, several dead rats were found in the basement. The forensics people and Dufour concluded that there must have been a high concentration of flies in the house before the crime was committed."

"Do you have the medical examiner's number?"

"Dufour? He died last year. Pancreas."

"Oh. Sorry." Lessard steers the conversation to a new subject. "Tell me about Sandoval. It looks like you never came up with anything that might explain his actions."

"That's right. We didn't have a lot of leads. He left nothing behind — no note or email to justify what he did. But as we questioned his colleagues and relatives, it became clear that he'd been overworked and probably depressive. The psychiatrist who helped us on the case thought he might have been psychotic."

"I saw in the press file that he had come under heavy criticism over the university hospital project," Lessard says, hoping to stimulate Marchand's memory.

"Yes, but I don't know how much that particular file affected him. Between us, Sandoval was such a key guy in the administration that it's easy to see how he might have crumbled under the pressure. Anyone else in his shoes would have burned out."

"He was Applebaum's right-hand man …"

"More than that. The two of them had been friends since their teens. The bond was stronger than blood."

"And Sandoval was Applebaum's protector on the hockey team."

"When a guy's ready to throw punches, and take them, to keep you safe, that creates a special kind of relationship. Applebaum had an unshakeable trust in Sandoval. We're talking about something that went beyond the workplace. Sandoval, Applebaum, and their wives used to see each other in their off-hours. The two men also shared a passion for matchitecture."

"I saw that. Weird hobby."

"Word has it that a fair number of major problems were sorted out over a tube of glue and a bunch of matchsticks."

"Applebaum's dead, right?"

"He died last spring."

"In cases like this, there's what's written in the report, and then there's the impression that stays with you afterward. Looking back, what do you think happened?"

"We have the medical examiner's confirmation. Sandoval killed his wife, then himself."

"I can understand the suicide, but why murder his wife?"

"We'll never know for sure what his motives were. When you looked through the file, did you see what the psychiatrist concluded?"

"Yes, that Sandoval killed his wife to save her from suffering. That's often the case for parents who murder their children. But for a spouse ..."

"You have to understand that Sophie Landreville was much younger than Sandoval. She was extremely fragile and dependent on him, psychologically and financially."

It's a plausible explanation. Lessard recalls the photos of the young woman, with her waxy features and her dull, bleary gaze.

"According to the toxicology report," Lessard says, "there were no drugs in Sandoval's system."

"As I recall, that's right."

"How can a person gouge his own eyes out when his mind is clear?"

Marchand makes a face. "I talked it over with Dufour at the time. It's horrible, but things like that have happened in the past. Dédé Fortin, who was the lead singer for the Colocs, committed *hara-kiri*."

"But he was high on drugs, wasn't he?"

"As I remember, no, he wasn't. In any case, the psychiatrist we consulted said that a psychotic episode can sometimes have a powerful anaesthetic effect."

"Did Sandoval have a criminal record?" Lessard asks, abruptly changing the subject. He holds up the report, pointing to the line that mentions Annex 19.

"No. That's a glitch."

Did Marchand just hesitate?

For a couple of seconds, Lessard is convinced that he did. Then the impression fades.

The conversation continues until Lessard has no more questions.

Before leaving the conference room, he obtains Sandoval's home address, as well as contact information for Mayor Applebaum's widow.

From the police station, he drives to Marquette Street.

He slows down and, looking to his left, contemplates the Sherbrooke Seminary, where Quebec Premier Jean Charest was once a student.

A few months ago, Lessard went for a long walk in Sherbrooke's old north ward. He was accompanied by Véronique, who grew up in the area. Apart from her love of painting, Véronique is also interested in history and architecture. And so, one fine autumn afternoon, she treated Lessard to a quick, fascinating lecture on the seminary.

As he drives past, he glances up at the high parapets of the old red-brick building, where statues of Lord Elgin, Frontenac, and St. Charles Borromeo look out over the city. Lessard isn't surprised to be recalling these details.

I have a great memory for useless stuff.

Lessard parks the Corolla near an imposing neo-Tudor house at the corner of Ball and Brooks Streets. This was the home of Richard Sandoval and Sophie Landreville. In front of the house, he sees a FOR SALE sign. On an impulse, he pulls out his phone and punches in the number of the real estate agent, whose dazzling white smile on the sign seems to have been Photoshopped to perfection.

"Christine Paint?"

"Speaking."

Lessard introduces himself simply as someone who'd like to visit the house.

"When are you available?" the agent asks, her tone becoming noticeably chillier when she hears the address.

"Could I see the place today?" Lessard asks, wincing and crossing his fingers. "I'm only in town for a few hours."

"You're in luck. I'm just wrapping up with a client in the same neighbourhood. I won't be finished for another few minutes, but I could meet you in, say, half an hour. Would that work for you?"

"That would be perfect," he says quickly. "I'll be in front of the house."

"You're going to get us in trouble, Jacinthe! Has it occurred to you that Côté might file a complaint for police brutality? Not to mention unlawful arrest."

Taillon rolls her eyes as she sits with Gilles Lemaire in the fluorescent-lit conference room of the Major Crimes Unit.

Lemaire is a good cop, but too by-the-book for her taste.

"Relax, Gilles. Côté knows that if he opens his yap, I'll tell his boss that he was harassing one of the girls. Believe me, Nigel Williams isn't somebody you want to piss off. All his guys are afraid of him."

"Okay, Jacinthe." Lemaire sighs. "I'll check out Côté's alibi and read all the messages he sent Laila François under that username he gave you ... Horny, uh ..."

"Priest."

"Right. Are you sure he had nothing to do with the kidnapping?"

"If I had the slightest doubt, do you really think I'd have let him go?"

Lemaire asked the question to be on the safe side. He knows that if Taillon actually suspected Steve Côté of being behind Laila François's abduction, Côté would be suffering right now. A lot.

24

"Mom died today. Or maybe yesterday, I don't know."

Those words aren't mine. They're taken from the opening of *The Stranger*, a classic novel by Nobel Prize–winning author Albert Camus, who died in a car crash a long, long time ago.

Famous though that sentence may be, no one ever wants to say the words "Mom died." Yet, sooner or later, everyone has to say them. And when your turn comes, that's when you're born for the second time.

To begin with, there's your first birth, the one in which you're expelled from your mother's uterus and land in her arms. Unless you're colossally unlucky, she'll be there to shower you with tender loving care.

That's how it was for me.

Then comes your second birth, the one that happens when your mother dies. This time, you're expelled into emptiness, and you land on your ass. No loving arms to catch you, no warm breast to lie against.

You're on your own.

To help you forget your solitude, there are all kinds of mother-substitutes, overflowing with trickery and deceit.

But in the end, nothing changes. You're still on your own.

The reason I'm talking about all this is that *The Stranger* was the first book I read after my own mom's death.

After everything went to hell.

I was eight years old when I was born for the second time. And landed on my ass.

. . .

Camus's narrator doesn't know what day his mom died. But I have a clear memory of the day my own mom left this world.

It was a Sunday in June. Precisely at midday.

I know, because someone had taught me to recognize the moment when the sun is at its zenith.

It was a glorious day. Birds were singing in the woods where we lived, and the sweet fragrance of spruce hung in the crystalline air.

Having eaten no breakfast, we'd been gathered around the altar since five in the morning. Two men, a dozen women, and six children. Only HE was sitting comfortably in a padded chair. Kneeling on the damp, bumpy earth, we were obliged to pray in silence, with our eyes closed, so that God might purify our souls.

The noise of Mom's coughing echoed through the forest and was cloaked in nature's abundance of consoling sounds, as though to restore the balance of things.

Sometimes, during our prayer sessions, someone would collapse from exhaustion.

Only at such times was it permissible to drink a little water. Then the other worshippers would help the fallen person to kneel again and resume praying.

That day, Mom didn't take a drink. Nor did she resume praying.

She was dead when she hit the ground.

She'd been coughing up blood for days.

HE said that she had nothing to fear. That God was testing her.

What would it take to restore her health?

The answer, HE said, was simple: she just needed to be purged of her sins.

To accomplish that, HE made her drink concoctions of HIS making — nasty, yellowish, foul-smelling potions whose only effect was to give her nauseous cramps that sent her running from our sleeping quarters to puke her guts out among the trees.

One day, when she came back inside with stains on her legs, HE gave her a beating in front of everyone, then forced her to scrub the floors and clean the straw mattresses in our quarters.

Stark naked, Mom obeyed without a word, wearing an angelic expression on her lovely features.

At the time, I knew nothing beyond my name, Laila François, and the hardships of our forest existence. But today, I can say without a shadow of doubt that Mom's death was caused by dehydration and pneumonia. If she'd received antibiotics and basic medical care, she would definitely have survived.

But — and this is something I only understood much later — more than the lack of medication, more than the insanity of the sadist she had embraced as her guru, it was her own unquenchable thirst for love, her boundless naïveté, her blind trust in the natural goodness of humanity, that had doomed her.

I never knew my true father.

When Mom arrived in the forest, she was already carrying me inside her.

She used to say my father was a heartless, violent man. I find it hard to accept that his blood is flowing in my veins.

HE welcomed Mom with open arms, despite the fact that she was pregnant.

How could she have ended up among HIS followers?

I've always wondered why no one offered to help her before she was reduced to that desperate measure. Yes, she had arrived by herself from a far-off country, without a single friend to turn to. Even so, I find it hard to believe that no one was willing to extend a helping hand.

But it's always easier to avert your eyes and mind your own business.

She said that HE had taken her in, that she owed HIM everything.

I think she truly loved HIM and reconciled herself to sharing HIM with other women. She said HE was her guiding light.

Was her unconditional attachment to HIM due to the fact that they were of the same race and came from the same country?

Mom, I believed you when you said that my biological father was malignant and cruel. But how could you have failed to see that Pascal Pierre was a vicious, bloody monster with an insatiable lust for flesh? The devil incarnate.

25

Opening the steel door, Vincenzo Moreno enters a windowless space, where he meets the gaze of Aldéric Dorion. Bound and gagged, the old man no longer has the strength to struggle, but his eyes are pleading for his tormentor's mercy.

Moreno closes the door and steps forward. The gauze pads that he placed on the old man's disfigured fingertips after ripping out his nails are now soaked in scarlet blood.

If the blood has coagulated properly, Noah's thug will be able to rip off the pads.

Standing in the background, the SIV agent lets his gaze stray over the room's raw concrete walls. Then he sits at a table that Moreno has placed in one corner.

From the bag slung over his shoulder, Noah extracts a thick file — part of the archival material that he found in Dorion's safe, whose combination Moreno extracted from the old man.

Although things aren't going according to plan, the SIV agent shows no signs of impatience or ill temper. He sees no bad omen in the disappearance of the man on whom the *Milites Christi* have founded all their hopes. At worst, this is a minor setback, a scheduling issue.

Though regrettable, the aggressive interrogations to which he's subjected Dorion, along with the death of that poor woman in the train station and the failed attempt on the police officer's life, have simply been auxiliary measures, subordinate to the noble goal pursued by the *Milites Christi* in the name of the highest authority there is: Jesus Christ.

The SIV agent takes Dorion's diary from the stack of documents.

As the elderly priest begins to scream, the SIV agent opens the little volume and resumes his perusal of the fascinating text that he started reading yesterday.

Emerging from a spotless Mercedes, wearing a designer outfit, bedecked with blood-red nail polish, gaudy rings, and bangles that tinkle at the slightest movement, Christine Paint looks every inch the fashion victim as she approaches the detective sergeant.

"Mr. Lessard?"

"Hello, Ms. Paint."

Lessard is surprised to discover that the smile on the sign wasn't Photoshopped. The agent's white teeth give her a slightly predatory look.

He also notes the disdainful glance that she casts in the direction of the Corolla.

"Luckily, I always keep a spare set of keys in my glove compartment," she says in a cheery tone that's as artificial as her bustline.

"Glad to hear it."

"How long have you been looking for a home in this area?"

"Here's the thing," Lessard says, having come up with a story while waiting for the agent to arrive. "My wife and I are living in Montreal at the moment, but I work in Sherbrooke. Our son will be starting high school in September. The only way to convince my wife to move is to find a house near the seminary. As I was driving around the neighbourhood, I came across this place."

"Mr. Lessard, I don't know what your needs or budget are, but I'd be happy to show you some other homes in the area."

"Sure. Let's have a look at this place, then we'll decide what to do next."

"Are you aware that it's been on the market for nearly two years?"

"Oh?" Lessard says, feigning surprise. "How come? Asking price too high?"

"The trouble isn't the price."

"What is it?"

"Well ..." She leans in and murmurs confidentially, "A horrible murder-suicide was committed here."

"I imagine the place has been cleaned up since it happened."

"That's not really the issue. I'm sure you'd prefer to —"

"Ms. Paint, I'm not a superstitious guy. If I like the house, I like the house. I don't care if Jack the Ripper lived in it."

A rictus — of horror, disgust? — appears on the woman's face.

"Who's the seller?" Lessard asks.

"It's an estate sale."

"Okay, let's check it out," Lessard says, seeming utterly unconcerned.

"I'll unlock the door, but if you don't mind, I'll wait in the car. The place creeps me out."

"No problem."

He doesn't mention that he actually prefers not to have her following him around. Now he can explore the place at his leisure.

Lessard is under no illusions. Crime scene technicians went over every inch of the house during the investigation, and he presumes that it's been emptied of its furnishings to facilitate a sale. Finding an undiscovered clue under these conditions is hardly a sure thing. At the same time, Lessard knows from experience that it's not impossible. And he has an advantage that the Sherbrooke Police didn't have at the time: if there's a link between the two cases, he'll be able to spot similarities that they missed.

But Lessard's principal motive is to get a sense of the house in which Sandoval lived, to move through the environment and get a clearer picture of the case.

The front door opens onto a large entrance hall. The space is entirely empty. The white plaster walls are framed by wood panelling. Lessard touches a switch, and a large chandelier over the staircase lights up. The windows are covered in custom stained glass. The waxed oak floor is spotless.

As Lessard steps forward and sees the living room with its mono-lithic fireplace, he whistles admiringly through his teeth.

Nice place.

An empty house is a body without a soul.

And yet, as he enters the dining room, the detective sergeant can imagine the life that once filled this home, the laughter that bubbled up, the intense conversations that went on until all hours, the quick-sand of routine into which the Sandoval-Landreville marriage grad-ually sank, the meals prepared in the kitchen, hastily, glass in hand, wanting only to get it over with. And, if he listens closely, he gets the impression that he can even hear the heartaches, the disappoint-ments, the quarrels to which these walls bore witness over the years.

He doesn't waste time tapping the panels to find a hollow spot, or scanning the floorboards for telltale irregularities that might reveal, as in a film, some hidden compartment which will yield up the key to the mystery.

He knows that won't get him anywhere.

Instead, as he moves through the house, he tries to empty his mind of all the stray notions that are bouncing around inside his head, clouding his thoughts.

From the ground floor, Lessard descends to the basement, where a humid odour greets him. He turns on the neon lights and sees a ce-ment floor, polystyrene-panelled walls, metal shelves.

He walks to the middle of the space and looks around. Clearly, this area of the house was only used for storage. Boards are stacked in a corner, with a rusty bicycle leaning against them.

He goes to an old, paint-stained acrylic sink and sees cracks and mould near the window that looks out onto the street.

The foundation is in need of repair — which hardly comes as a surprise, given the age of the house.

. . .

Lessard finishes up his exploration on the second floor, in the master bedroom, where no trace remains of the carnage that took place here, apart from a faint chemical smell, probably caused by the products that were used to disinfect the room after the bodies were taken out.

He's not surprised to see a few stray cardboard boxes.

Some people are so obsessively prone to hoarding that, after their deaths, their families have difficulty getting rid of all the stuff they accumulated over their lives. Lessard remembers that when his adoptive parents died, he and his sister started sifting through their father's possessions, only to get so discouraged that they finally decided to throw out whole containers full of objects and souvenirs that their father had painstakingly saved over the course of a lifetime.

In the end, exhausted, they left several pieces of furniture where they stood, instructing the real estate agent to offer them to the buyers, and, if the buyers didn't want them, to toss them in the garbage.

As Lessard looks through the boxes, he takes out a matchstick cathedral, wondering what possible pleasure Sandoval could have derived from gluing together all those thousands of tiny pieces of wood.

But then, Lessard has never shown much aptitude for detailed craftsmanship. He still remembers a high school art teacher appraising one of his efforts and declaring in a loud voice that on a scale of one to ten, Lessard's effort was a perfect zero.

The whole class, including Lessard himself, had a good laugh.

Also in the boxes are clothes, a few pairs of shoes, a cookbook, some magazines, an old TV antenna, clothes hangers, loose change, pencils, and some multicoloured paper clips. As he goes through these odds and ends, the detective sergeant feels a little like a voyeur.

Picking up the cathedral to put it back in its box, he sees something wedged into the base.

It's a piece of plastic. Using his thumb and forefinger, he pulls it free.

A keycard.

As he was searching the house, he didn't notice any card readers.

He pockets the card mechanically, thinking it may come in handy. *Sandoval or his wife probably had a keycard system at the office.*

Christine Paint has been on the phone the whole time Lessard was gone.

"There are still a few boxes in the master bedroom," he says, as he hands her back the house keys.

"For months now," the agent says, "I've been asking the family to come and get them. I have a feeling the buyer will end up throwing all that stuff in the garbage. Does the house interest you?"

"The kitchen could use an update, the basement is unfinished, there are traces of mould, and the foundation needs fixing. We're looking for something that doesn't need so much work."

The usual formalities are exchanged, and the agent promises to call Lessard soon to arrange another meeting.

The Mercedes's exhaust pipe coughs out a little white puff that hangs in the air as Lessard watches Christine Paint drive away.

He leaves the Corolla in front of the house and walks the short distance to Mayor Applebaum's residence, which is on the same street.

Seeing a glow behind the drawn curtains, he hopes Applebaum's widow is at home.

As he knocks on the door, he isn't even sure what his cover story will be. He has no authority outside his jurisdiction, nor any valid reason for an official interrogation. At the same time, he has to assume that if he identifies himself as a Montreal police detective, he risks upsetting the widow and causing problems for himself.

The door is opened by a woman in her midsixties who radiates goodness. The apron over her dress and the aroma of vanilla filling the house testify to the fact that she's been baking.

"Yes?"

"Hello, ma'am." The detective sergeant is holding his notebook. "My name is Victor Lessard. Do you have five minutes? We're updating the property assessment roll, and I have a few questions for you."

"Do you work for the city of Sherbrooke?"

"Yes, ma'am. Celebrating my tenth anniversary on the job this year."

"Please, come in."

"I should have called first, but I was in the neighbourhood, and I saw that your lights were on."

"I'm in the middle of baking pastries. Would you like a cup of coffee? I just made a fresh pot."

"No, thanks. I don't want to bother you any longer than I have to."

"You're not bothering me one bit. Now that my husband's gone, cooking is all I have left."

"Before starting in with my questions, I'd just like you to know that all of us at city hall miss your late husband. He was a fine mayor."

The woman smiles sadly.

"You're very kind. Did you know him?"

"Not personally. But I saw what a great team he and Mr. Sandoval were. It's a shame that we lost them both."

"Let's go sit in the living room. It'll do me good to have a little company."

This is working out better than Lessard expected.

He follows the woman into a luxurious room, tastefully decorated in shades of yellow and burgundy. In one corner, numerous framed photographs are arrayed on top of a grand piano.

Among a variety of what seem to be family portraits, Lessard sees a shot of Mayor Applebaum with his right-hand man.

"Mr. Sandoval and your husband were good friends, weren't they?" he ventures, stepping closer, with his hands clasped behind his back.

"Jean-Guy and Richard were enthusiastic hobbyists. They spent all their free time in my husband's workshop, out in the yard, building matchstick models while they solved the city's problems."

Lessard is only half listening.

He looks out the French doors at the backyard.

Through the pouring rain, he makes out the workshop, a rectangular structure with no distinguishing features apart from a chimney.

"Whenever they were in there, they weren't to be disturbed. They'd only come out for a quick bite before going back in. It was like that all year round. They were very hard workers."

"All year round? Is the workshop heated?"

"I guess so. The truth is, I don't know. No one was allowed in. Even I was forbidden to set foot in there."

"Why?"

"Jean-Guy used to say that it was his sacred space. He didn't like to mix his personal and work lives. The only time I ever strayed into the workshop, he got so angry that I never did it again. In fact, I haven't been in there since he died. I suppose I'll have to go in eventually."

There's a question that Lessard is burning to ask, but he resists the urge, not wanting to arouse the woman's suspicions regarding the real reason for his visit.

He turns his attention back to the photographs.

"Are those your grandchildren?"

"Adorable, aren't they? I have five in all. Which is lucky for me. If it weren't for them, I don't think I'd have gotten over Jean-Guy's death. Would you like to sit down?"

"Mmm?"

Once again, the detective sergeant's thoughts are elsewhere.

One of the photographs has caught his eye: it's a shot of Sandoval and Applebaum singing in a choir, in the midst of a dozen other people. Taken mid-song, the picture has a grotesque quality. Most of the choristers' mouths are open, and several have their eyes closed.

But that's not why Lessard has stopped short.

In the upper right-hand corner, a priest is standing behind the singers.

"They sang in a choir?"

"Every Sunday."

"Forgive me, but I'm drawing a blank. Who's the priest in the picture?"

"I don't remember his name. Are you sure you wouldn't like a cup of coffee?"

"Positive. Let's get to my questions, then I'll be on my way.

A priest ... simple coincidence?

He can't help recalling his conversation with Faizan.

Lessard is surprised at how easily the lies come to him as he invents serious-sounding questions relating to the property assessment roll. And unless the widow is a first-rate actress, she's completely taken in by the charade. He wraps up the questions as quickly as possible, because he's itching to follow up on the lead he's just discovered. As soon as he's back in the Corolla, he calls 411 and requests a number for the archdiocese of Sherbrooke.

Within seconds, he's on the line with someone at the archdiocese. Lessard cuts to the chase: he's trying to find a priest in the diocese whose name he doesn't know.

"That won't be easy. Which parish?"

He neglected to ask Applebaum's widow, but more than likely it's the parish in which the two men lived.

"Saint-Michel, I think. Why? Are there many?"

"Dozens. We're talking about over two hundred priests, if you include the ones who have retired."

"I have a picture," he says, looking at the photo he surreptitiously removed from the piano while the widow was in the kitchen turning off her oven. "Do you keep a register?"

"Well —"

"Could I come and see you?"

"What is this about, exactly?"

"I work for the police. It's in connection with a murder investigation."

There's a moment of dead silence.

"Your name is ...?"

"Victor Lessard. Yours?"

"Father Brunelle. I'll be waiting for you."

"Great. You can expect me within the hour."

The archdiocesan offices are only five minutes away.

But before he heads over, there's something he wants to check.

One of the widow's answers has been nagging at him.

"The only time I ever went into the workshop, he got so angry that I never did it again."

In the bowels of the building in downtown Montreal, the SIV agent, fascinated by what he's discovered, is eagerly reading the diary of the man he delivered into Moreno's hands:

June 1986

We had a choir rehearsal today. His voice is ethereal, the embodiment of bliss. Afterward, we went to the sacristy for a bite to eat, and he insisted on sharing his sandwich with another singer. [...] At every rehearsal, he seems to open up more fully to the others. [...] Perhaps my initial judgment was too harsh. I may have been overly quick to condemn him ...

The SIV agent is oblivious to the screams.

It's a good thing the cellar is soundproof, because Dorion's cries are deafening. Yet Noah lifts his head the second his cellphone rings.

Night has fallen as abruptly as if an axe had knocked the daylight from the sky. The rain hasn't stopped.

Lessard is crouching in the shadows, taking care to remain unseen as he picks the locks on the door of the late mayor's workshop. He has no reason to believe that Jean-Guy Applebaum had anything to hide. But if he did, this is the place to look — a structure shrouded in secrecy and mystery, where Applebaum and Sandoval spent time together regularly, and where even Applebaum's wife was forbidden to enter.

The second lock is stubborn. Lessard is dripping with sweat when he finally hears the click. The door opens noiselessly. He slips inside and closes it behind him. On his knees, he catches his breath for a moment in the darkness, his ears straining to catch the slightest suspicious noise.

When he's sure that he hasn't attracted any unwanted attention, he straightens up, shielding his flashlight beam with one hand, and looks around the room. He notices a black curtain over the only window, but hesitates to turn on the light.

Any escaping glow would be enough to give him away.

Lessard points his flashlight haphazardly around the space.

Two stools are tucked under a workbench equipped with a vise and an articulated lamp. Lying on the bench is the unfinished hull of a matchstick ship. Above the work surface, hanging from a pegboard, a wide selection of tools is within reach.

In a corner, Lessard sees two leather armchairs standing on a rug, facing a storage rack that holds a coffee maker, a telephone, and a fax machine. A few cups are stacked atop a metal file cabinet.

No doubt about it: this place matches the description he was given. With its plywood walls and cement floor, it's hardly luxurious, but Lessard has no trouble imagining Sandoval and the mayor in here, alternating between high-level discussions about Sherbrooke's municipal administration and the relaxing practice of their shared favourite pastime.

After unlocking the file cabinet, he pores over the documents he discovers inside.

He finds a file relating to the construction of the university hospital, but it contains no explosive material — none that he can see, anyway.

He puts the papers back and resumes his exploration.

Cautiously pulling the curtain aside, he sees metal bars over the window, which isn't surprising, given the fact that Applebaum kept confidential materials in here.

What is surprising, though, is the arrangement of long metal bars bolted to the back of the door, making it possible to barricade the place from the inside. Lessard can see why Applebaum might have wanted to keep intruders out, but why create the possibility of shutting himself in?

Clearly, there's something he's not getting.

Doing his best to make no noise, he moves the storage rack and looks behind it.

Nothing.

Then he pushes aside the file cabinet, which is on casters.

In the cleared area, he notices a fissure in the floor. It runs in a straight line under the rug. Hastily moving the armchairs out of the way, Lessard lifts the rug.

A jolt of adrenalin hits him.

Hidden by the rug and chairs, a rectangle has been cut into the floor.

A trap door.

26

Lessard spends ten minutes trying without success to open the trap door.

Not even a crowbar taken off the pegboard has any effect. Lessard begins to search the room. There must be a concealed button somewhere that controls an access mechanism.

He goes through the space, but fails to find anything. In desperation, he crouches over the trap door once more, trying to force it open with the crowbar.

No luck.

Then it hits him. The one place he hasn't looked is under the workbench.

At first he sees nothing. Then his flashlight beam reveals a black plastic rectangle about the size of an electrical outlet. He bends closer, examining the object, and realizes that it's a card reader.

With trembling hands, he pats his pockets in search of the keycard that he found in the Sandoval house.

He slides it over the reader.

A red light flashes. The trap door doesn't budge.

Flipping the card over, he tries again. The red light turns green.

The trap door swings open silently, exposing a cement staircase.

Without hesitating, Lessard unholsters his Glock and goes down the stairs.

I crane my neck and listen intently, senses alert.

Is my imagination playing tricks on me? No. I can hear footsteps in the hallway. Is my loving stepfather about to make an appearance in my cell?

Let HIM come. I'm ready.

I'm not scared anymore. I'm already dead. HE killed me.

That's when I was born a second time.

Pascal Pierre stole my mother's life and my childhood.

HE cradled our hearts in the hollow of HIS hand, then crushed them into a bitter powder that the wind carried away across the vast, black expanse of our existence.

But I'm no longer the little girl HE took sadistic pleasure in terrorizing. I liberated myself from the fears that swarmed through my nightly delirium, imprisoning me, preventing me from spreading my wings and leaving the death trap in which I was stranded.

I made a fresh start.

I lived on the streets with nothing more than the clothes on my back when I fled. I wrestled against despair; I never gave up; I fought tooth and nail.

And I survived.

Finally, after stumbling more than once into the pitfalls of an artificial paradise, I was lucky enough to meet exceptional people — people whose goodness transcended all the sorrow in the world.

After fleeing the demon, I met angels. They opened their arms to me.

I was dead. They gave me life.

The footsteps are coming closer …

If HE's coming to take my life again, I'll only have one regret.

That I didn't kill HIM when I had the chance.

He's barely taken three steps along the corridor when the trap door closes behind him.

After an initial moment of panic, Lessard is reassured to see, mounted on the wall, the same black box that he found under the workbench. A quick swipe of the keycard shows him that he has nothing to worry about if he wants to make a quick exit.

The naked concrete corridor angles to the right, leading to a pad-ded door that is locked by three bolts securely fastened to the wall. Lessard unlocks the bolts without difficulty and opens the door.

He touches a switch.

There's no reason to worry about turning on the lights. The room is underground — directly beneath the workshop, as far as he can tell.

The fluorescent lights come on, revealing a room whose total area is about a hundred square feet. He immediately notices ventilation pipes in the ceiling. Since the room has an electric baseboard heat-er, Lessard guesses that this subterranean space gets its air supply through the chimney he saw outside.

Intrigued, Lessard does a quick survey of the room: there's a bed with straps, a shower, a toilet, a small refrigerator, a microwave, a chair, a workbench with matchitecture pieces, and a pegboard laden with tools, as in the workshop. There's also a chest of drawers filled with sexy women's clothing and undergarments, a pair of steel man-acles chained to the wall, and, in a corner, a video camera on a tripod pointing at the bed.

Lessard turns his head. On a shelf, he finds a briefcase and a metal suitcase.

The contents of the suitcase startle him. There seems to be a wide selection of the most deviant erotic toys that one might hope to find in a sex shop. Lessard can't imagine the gentle woman he just met dressing up in latex and having wild sex with her husband in this room, especially not after her apparently sincere statement that she only ever set foot in the workshop a single time.

The mayor's rage when she stepped inside, combined with Sandoval's possession of a key card that opens the trap door, fills Lessard with foreboding.

The briefcase contains a laptop.

The detective sergeant turns it on.

. . .

He's initially surprised to discover that the computer has no password, but he tells himself that Applebaum must have believed his hideout would never be discovered. At first glance, the email folders, and indeed the entire hard disc, seem to be empty. Then Lessard clicks on the "My Videos" icon and opens an unlabelled folder containing more than a hundred video files.

Now the detective sergeant descends into a bottomless pit of horror. The shadow life of Richard Sandoval and Jean-Guy Applebaum comes to light.

Sickened, near tears, Lessard spends almost an hour grasping the implications of what he's found, assembling the puzzle pieces into a coherent picture. The videos cover a period of roughly five years, from 2000 to 2005. They show Sandoval and Applebaum, sometimes singly, sometimes together, perpetrating the worst imaginable sexual assaults on a young girl.

Sandoval and Applebaum were pedophiles. Monsters of the most horrifying kind.

Several times, Lessard has to stop watching, fists clenched, fighting back tears. From all appearances, the young victim was between ten and twelve years old when the first videos were shot.

The cruelty of the scenes is such that they'll follow Lessard to his grave. In all of them, the girl is crying, begging her tormentors for mercy. But the two men are impervious to her pleas.

How can anyone inflict such suffering with utter impunity?

Making connections between facts that he picks up from various clips, Lessard deduces that the two men abducted the girl — whose name was Sandrine — and abused her almost every day.

In several of the videos, Sandrine can be seen assembling matchstick structures, leading Lessard to believe that she was the one who created the finished pieces. The two predators not only took credit for the works; they also used them as a cover story for their ongoing atrocities. The scheme was as ingenious as it was malignant, a testimony to the twisted inventiveness of these two men, whose evil went to the very core.

Aldéric Dorion has fallen silent by the time the SIV agent ends the call on his cellphone and steps back into the room. The old priest's head is slumped on his chest. His hands have been reduced to shapeless, bloody masses.

"He's passed out, *Padre*," Moreno says, turning toward him, his shirt stained with blood.

"Did he talk?"

"No. And he won't last much longer."

"Leave him. We have more urgent matters to deal with."

"What's going on?"

"I've just received an electronic surveillance report. The police officer, the one Pasquale failed to eliminate at the train station ..."

"Lessard," Moreno says.

"He just got in touch with the archdiocese of Sherbrooke. He's on Dorion's trail."

Sandrine is dead.

Lessard discovers this fact when he sees a video clip that shows Sandoval, in a panic, trying to resuscitate her after Applebaum pulled too hard on the chain that was wrapped around her throat like a leash. The video cuts out abruptly. It's the last in the series.

The girl's bluish face and empty eyes are seared into Lessard's memory.

With a mouse click, he checks the date: December 24th, 2005.

Did Sandrine have any hopes left that day?

Did she know she wouldn't be alive for Christmas?

Did she even know what day it was, or how long the two men had been keeping her captive, when they finally took her life?

Did she hope for death?

Lessard has seen some terrible things over the course of his career, but never anything as monstrous, as despicable, as sordid as this.

The dam finally breaks.

His shoulders heave; bitter tears run down his cheeks.

Raymond puts an arm around his big brother's neck to console him. Lessard didn't hear him come in.

"Go ahead, Victor. Cry. It'll do you good. I have no tears left."

The detective sergeant tries to reach Marchand, but there's no cellphone signal. He's close to breaking down; the room seems to be folding in on itself. He's short of breath. He needs to get out of this death trap right now.

But first, there's something he has to check.

He's unable to connect the laptop to the internet, because the only available Wi-Fi is on a secure network. But when he checks the browsing history, he finds a single entry. Intrigued, he writes down the web address in his notebook.

After painstakingly wiping down the laptop with a cloth that he finds near the sink, Lessard puts the computer back in the briefcase, then returns the briefcase to where he found it.

Next, he carefully erases his fingerprints from all the objects he's touched — the light switch, the door handle, the bars. He does the same thing in Applebaum's workshop.

Having entered the place illegally, he wants to avoid contaminating the evidence, which would render it inadmissible in court.

Granted, Sandoval and Applebaum are dead, but it's possible that they had an accomplice, who may eventually face charges.

As soon as he's back in the Corolla, Lessard calls the number on Marchand's business card and leaves him a message.

He goes to an internet café, where it takes ten minutes to find what he's looking for on Google. Sandrine Pedneault-King, aged nine, was reported missing on March 5th, 2000, when she failed to come home after setting out by foot from her school in Sherbrooke's old north ward. Her parents called the police around 6:00 p.m., worried by the absence of their daughter, who should have gotten home around 4:30. Later that evening, one of her classmates said she'd seen Sandrine get into a black SUV.

Descriptions of the missing child and the vehicle were widely circulated by the media across Quebec. The case was in the headlines for several weeks. An unprecedented police search, assisted by a group of volunteers, turned up nothing.

As far as Lessard can tell from newspaper articles that he finds online, the investigation went nowhere during the month that followed the abduction. At one point, police questioned a mysterious witness in connection with the case — the owner of a black SUV answering the description provided by the victim's classmate. Certain media outlets suggested that the witness in question, a man, was a well-known personality in Sherbrooke, but they didn't reveal his name.

A well-known personality.

Lessard rereads the passage several times before his brain connects the dots.

He's filled with rage.

Those idiots!

Still burning with anger, he continues to search through the media coverage of young Sandrine's abduction, but he learns nothing of significance.

Having broken his resolution not to drink coffee, Lessard is installed in a booth, finishing his second cup, when Marchand walks into the café.

Marchand irritably orders a Coke and sits down facing the detective sergeant.

"We hardly know each other, Lessard, but you'd better have a damn good reason for making me rush over here."

Despite his dark mood, Lessard makes an effort to keep his voice neutral.

"I do. I was just at Jean-Guy Applebaum's house."

"So?"

"Sandrine Pedneault-King."

He watches Marchand's reaction. Either the man doesn't know what Lessard is getting at, or he's a first-rate actor.

"What's the connection with Applebaum?"

"Did you work on the girl's disappearance?"

"I helped the chief, yes."

"This afternoon, when I asked if Sandoval had a criminal record, you lied to me."

Marchand reddens.

"I don't know what this is about, Lessard, but you've got a hell of a nerve saying that to me. The search for that little girl was the hardest investigation of my career. I came out of it divorced, with a brutal alimony bill and a bad case of burnout. Every year, I take the file from the archives and put a week's vacation time into it. So how about you tell me where you're going with this?"

"I just did, Marchand. You lied to me."

"I didn't lie! Sandoval had no criminal record!"

"But you questioned him about the girl's disappearance, didn't you?"

"So that's what this is about! You fucking snake. You work for Internal Affairs?"

"No, I was straight with you. I'm investigating a domestic murder-suicide in Montreal."

"Then what do you want?"

"I'll get to that. But first, answer my question. Did you interrogate Sandoval in connection with the disappearance of Sandrine Pedneault-King?"

"I didn't. The chief did."

Bingo! Lessard celebrates his triumph by ordering a third cup of coffee.

"In the report you gave me this afternoon, that should have been mentioned under the 'Antecedents' heading, shouldn't it?"

"I didn't lie. You asked if he had a criminal record, and I said he didn't."

"Stop playing games, Marchand. You know antecedents aren't the same thing as a criminal record. Answer my question."

"Yes, it should have been mentioned."

"Why wasn't it?"

"You don't understand. Sandoval was an influential guy, and we had nothing on him. Just a witness who might have seen an SUV that looked like Sandoval's near the presumed site of the child's abduction. We looked into it and learned that Sandoval had been in a meeting with the mayor between the time the little girl left school and the time her parents called the police."

"What the fuck, Marchand? You're the one who signed the report. Why is there no mention of what you just told me?"

"Because that's how the mayor wanted it!" Marchand lowers his eyes, ashamed. "I had inserted an annex summarizing the testimony that Sandoval gave the chief on the subject of Sandrine's disappearance. But the chief asked me to take it out. When I asked why, he said the order had come from upstairs. Afterward, I checked the case file on the kidnapping."

"Let me guess. The transcript of Sandoval's interrogation was gone."

"That's right."

Applebaum had not only provided his henchman with an alibi; he had also arranged for the removal of any trace of the interrogation from both files. The two monsters must have had a good laugh when they saw how well their ploy had worked.

Lessard isn't judging Marchand.

He might have done the same thing in that situation. Nevertheless, having removed the Sandoval interrogation from the file, Marchand and his fellow investigators may now have blood on their hands.

Did they impede the solution of the case? Was Sandrine the two pedophiles' only victim? If the interrogation had remained in the file, is it possible that another investigator, working on a similar case, might have detected a pattern and enabled the police to stop the pair before they killed Sandrine?

The answer may never be known.

"Get a search warrant for Applebaum's workshop," Lessard says, placing the keycard on the table in front of Marchand. "This card will give you access to an underground space where Sandoval and Applebaum sequestered, raped, and killed the girl."

"What?"

Lessard watches Marchand's eyes fill with horror as he describes what he found a few hours ago. The Sherbrooke cop's cheeks are wet with tears as he stares at the wall behind Lessard.

He looks shattered.

"I can't believe it," he murmurs. "Are you sure she —"

"She's dead. It's all there, on the videos. Be gentle with Mrs. Applebaum. She's a good person who knows nothing about any of this."

Lessard reflects for a moment on the nightmare that awaits the widow. The edifice of falsehoods that protected her is about to collapse, leaving her defenceless against the horrific truth.

"I can't believe it," Marchand says, as though reciting a litany.

Lessard looks at his watch. He needs to get to the archdiocese before it closes. He starts to rise from his seat.

"I'll meet you at the Applebaum house in a few hours. It'll be simpler to discuss things after you've seen the videos."

Marchand emerges from his daze with a start. He grabs Lessard's arm, forcing him to sit back down.

"Stay where you are," he orders.

"We'll see each other later," the detective sergeant protests. "I've got to look into something."

"Hang on, Lessard. The last thing you want to do right now is leave."

"Why? What's wrong?"

"There's a patrol unit outside waiting to pick you up."

Incredulous at first, Lessard peers out the window and sees a police car parked across the street. The rain makes it impossible to distinguish faces in the vehicle's darkened interior, but the intermittent sweep of the windshield wipers confirms that someone's in there.

It only takes him a few seconds to figure out the reason for the patrol unit's presence and his possible arrest.

"The shootout at the train station!" he exclaims.

"I was on my way over here when the radio alert went out."

"Is it in the media?"

"Not yet. But we both know it's only a matter of time before reporters get wind of it."

"Just what I needed. I suppose you sounded the alarm."

"I advised the patrol cops across the street that I might need help apprehending a suspect. That's all they know. They're waiting for my signal before they move in."

"Why didn't you say anything?"

"Your message got me curious. I wanted to know what you'd found out. If I had arrested you right away, you might have refused to talk. By sitting down with you, I wasn't running any risks. I had backup ready and waiting."

"Did the radio alert say I'm dangerous?"

"Just psychologically unstable."

If they only knew about Raymond.

"Are you going to book me?"

"As I was coming over, there was no doubt in my mind. But now ..."

Lessard looks at Marchand, who continues: "I know you think I'm a scumbag for falsifying the report. But I'm not. I'm an honest cop who followed orders."

Lessard says nothing.

"This afternoon," Marchand says, "after you left, I talked to a Sherbrooke cop who knows you."

"Who?"

"Marc Bernard."

Lessard worked with Bernard on the Major Crimes team for several years. He's one of the finest cops Lessard has ever known.

"Marc's in Sherbrooke now?"

"He transferred here two years ago. He had only good things to say about you."

The detective sergeant can't help smiling. Bernard's favourable opinion comes as a consolation, even if it was expressed before Bernard knew that Lessard was a wanted man.

"So, this case you're working on," Marchand says, "do you think it's connected with what happened to Sandrine?"

Though it's all still murky in his mind, Lessard has some thoughts on the subject.

He's reluctant to open up to Marchand, whom he hardly knows. But on second thought, he has nothing to gain from keeping the

Sherbrooke cop in the dark. After all, Marchand holds Lessard's fate in his hands.

"I don't know exactly how or why, but I have a hunch the answer is yes."

Lessard tells Marchand about the so-called domestic murder-suicide on Bessborough Avenue. He describes the conversation he had with Viviane Gray before she was killed, and the shootout in which he was involved.

"I arrived in Sherbrooke convinced that John Cook and his family were murdered by people who are ready to do anything to guard a secret. I haven't changed my mind about that, but now I can't help wondering just how innocent Cook and his wife really were."

"What do you mean?"

"I found videocassettes of the Cooks playing some pretty wild sex games. On those same cassettes, there was also footage of their eldest daughter as a baby."

"Whoa! You think they might have produced child pornography using their own kids?"

"I'll admit that it doesn't fit with the rest of the information I've got on the couple," Lessard says. "And just thinking about it makes me sick. But this kind of thing has happened before."

"Which means Sandoval and Cook may have been killed by someone they abused. Someone who was out for revenge."

"Or possibly someone who wanted to silence them."

"Why?"

"I may be barking up the wrong tree, but when I started out, the only link between the Cook and Sandoval cases was the swarm of flies."

"Have you learned anything more about that?"

"No, but I think I have another connection."

"What?"

"A priest."

"A priest?"

Lessard recounts what he heard from Faizan, and describes the photograph that he discreetly lifted from the Applebaum house.

"I've got a priest at the scene of the Cook killings, and again in a photo with Applebaum and Sandoval. You see where I'm going?"

"Yes," Marchand says, "but it could also just be a coincidence. It isn't necessarily the same person."

"Maybe not," Lessard concedes, "but I have a feeling there's a connection. I'd be willing to bet on it. And if there's a link that ties the priest — or priests — to John Cook and the two pedophiles, I can't help wondering if their actions were coordinated."

"Why?"

"I found a single web address in the browsing history of Applebaum's computer. I tried to access it earlier, before you got here, but it's a private site. Members only. Password-protected. The only thing non-members see is an email address."

"Wait. Are you saying Sandoval and Applebaum were sharing videos of Sandrine on the site? Is that it? You think it's a ring?"

"That's what I believe, yes."

"A pedophile ring, priests …" Marchand murmurs, as though trying to grasp the implications. "You're not suggesting that this thing is as big as the child-abuse scandals involving priests in Ireland and the United States!"

"We tell ourselves that this stuff only happens in other countries, but there have been cases in Canada, too."

"No religious order would go so far as to commit murder to cover up its abuses!"

"Let's not get ahead of ourselves. The fact that a few priests may be mixed up in this thing doesn't mean the Church is directly implicated. And even if the Church *is* implicated, that doesn't prove that it hired the killers. All I know is that whoever's behind this will stop at nothing. They murdered Viviane Gray and tried to kill me in broad daylight at Central Station."

A sudden insight strikes Marchand.

"Wait a second. Is it possible that Cook and Sandoval were killed to prevent them from talking about the pedophile ring, and that their killings were made to look like domestic murder-suicides?"

"Why not?" Lessard says. "Suppose, for some reason, Cook and Sandoval threatened to reveal the existence of the pedophile network. The ringleaders may have taken drastic measures to shut them up."

"In that case," Marchand says with a rueful sigh, "my investigation of Sandoval's death was totally off the mark."

"It's unfortunate, but that possibility has to be considered."

"But then, why wasn't Applebaum killed, too?"

"Maybe because of his illness," Lessard says. "They knew he was already doomed."

"Or else he was part of the inner circle," Marchand suggests. "He was one of the people pulling the strings."

Lessard drinks the last of his coffee. Marchand gazes at the bottom of his soda can as though trying to read his future in its depths.

"There's something I don't get," he says. "Why would Cook and Sandoval have wanted to expose a criminal network that they were part of? Remorse?"

"Could be. Sandoval might have gone to pieces after the girl's death. A pedophile isn't necessarily a killer."

"What about Cook?"

Lessard reflects in silence for a few seconds. Suddenly, a flash hits him.

"We've been working from the hypothesis that Cook and Sandoval were both pedophiles. But we only have proof in Sandoval's case, right?"

"Yeah, so?" Marchand replies.

"Let's say Cook was abused by someone who was part of the network. Years later, he makes up his mind to denounce that person. In his efforts to track down the predator, Cook discovers the network and decides to reveal what he's found out."

"It's twisted, but possible," Marchand says. "Only you said earlier that Cook might not have been an innocent victim. Now you're saying the opposite."

Lessard's head is spinning. He's lost in a swirl of possibilities.

"I don't know anymore," he admits.

The seconds drift by, gradually accumulating into minutes, while neither cop speaks. At one point, the waitress approaches to refill Lessard's coffee cup, but when she sees the two men's grave expressions, she tiptoes away.

Lessard finally breaks the silence.

"Besides the search warrant for Applebaum's workshop, I'd like you to reopen the investigation into Sandoval's death. If there's any evidence that he and his wife were murdered, you need to find it. I'll go on digging on my side. We can stay in touch and keep each other posted." He pauses. "Assuming, of course, that you don't have me arrested."

Lessard doesn't need to explain the disastrous effects that his arrest would have on the investigation. Marchand knows that the detective sergeant would need to spend days explaining what happened, complying with the numerous disciplinary measures that would undoubtedly be imposed on him, and filling out mountains of paperwork. Getting another cop up to speed so that the investigation could resume would also take up precious time.

Marchand can't help smiling.

"An hour ago, Lessard, I wouldn't have bet that you'd be a free man much longer. But that's all changed." He looks the detective sergeant in the eye. "If there are other abused children out there, praying to be rescued, you need to find them."

27

I don't know how long I've been locked in this cell.

I can estimate the time that's gone by from the number of meals I've had. There have been three meals — so that means I've been here about a day. Or have there been four meals?

Whatever.

All I know is, I've been here long enough to have lost any sense of time. When that happens — to state the obvious — time doesn't matter anymore. It's just an abstraction created by the mind.

The hours that I spent on my knees praying in the woods have never been as valuable as they are right now. Those long fervent periods of enforced prayer taught me how to dive into myself, how to create a perfect void in my head, until nothing remains behind my eyelids but utter blackness.

After Mom's death, the other women in the community took care of me — especially Olga, a big blond girl with an eastern European accent. But the women had been indoctrinated. They all obeyed the rules that HE had laid down.

HE took care of me, too. Oh yes, HE did.

It was on the third night after Mom died that Pascal Pierre started coming to my bed, clamping a moist hand over my mouth, HIS breath reeking of alcohol as HE poured a mix of threats and bittersweet endearments in my ear and thrust HIS hard manhood into my guts.

When HE left, I cried in silence for the first time since Mom's passing. I don't know whether I was grieving for her death or for this second birth, which I cursed.

Little by little, my existence became a never-ending round of prayer sessions, unannounced visits from Pascal Pierre to my bed, and — when I dared to stand up to HIM or refuse HIS advances — periods of isolation without food or water.

That is, when HE wasn't beating me with the cold, clinical precision of a Gestapo torturer.

As the saying goes: give credit where credit is due. I learned the hard way that when it came to abuse, both physical and mental, HE was a true expert.

It all went on before the eyes of the terrified women, who remained silent. Olga once tried meekly to intercede on my behalf. The unhappy result for her was a broken arm — an open fracture that took months to heal because she never received proper treatment.

Obviously, seeking outside help was out of the question.

We were in HIS iron grip.

I was twelve years old when HE forced me to have sex with Monique, a member of the community who was in her midtwenties. Her pubic hair was thick and black. I'm a little ashamed to admit it, but I truly enjoyed those sessions. Not only did they keep me out of HIS clutches, but Monique, in her gentle, caring way, gave me my first orgasms. Most of the time, HE was content simply to watch and masturbate. When HE wasn't so drunk that HE fell asleep during the show, it was Monique who took matters in hand and "finished the job."

Those episodes provided the only agreeable interludes during the unhappy years of my captivity in the woods. Little by little, HE lost interest in me, and I stopped having to endure HIS assaults so regularly. The surprise visits to my bed became increasingly rare.

I don't know how HE has managed to track me down such a long time after my escape, nor by what miracle HE's still alive. And, to be honest, I don't much care.

What I do know is that I'd rather bash my head in than fall back into HIS hands. But it hasn't come to that yet.

I failed on my first try.

And yet, the night I got away, the night of my great escape, I was sure I'd killed HIM before I walked out of HIS little cottage.

Next time, I swear, I won't miss my chance.

In the darkness of my cell, I'm keeping busy.

In the next few hours, I swear on my own life, my teeth will have chewed through the leather of my belt. The prong of the buckle will have been sharpened to a point that can pierce HIS eyeballs or slash HIS windpipe.

Then, with the belt wrapped around HIS throat, I'll "finish the job."

28

The archdiocese of Sherbrooke is located in a castle-like grey stone building that houses a neo-Gothic chapel.

Lessard had no trouble getting here.

After Marchand left the café, Lessard watched him confer briefly with the patrol officers, who obediently drove away. In a wordless exchange of good-luck wishes, Marchand and Lessard waved to each other through the café window. Then Marchand disappeared into the rain.

The detective sergeant paid the tab and went to his car.

The front door of the building is locked, but it clicks open immediately after Lessard rings the bell.

He steps into a vast entrance hall whose muted lighting and marble counter create the impression — if one doesn't look too closely, or for too long — of being at the front desk of a high-end hotel.

"Mr. Lessard? I'm Father Brunelle. We spoke earlier."

A large individual, built like a longshoreman, gives the detective sergeant a bone-crushing handshake. Brunelle looks like the kind of guy you wouldn't want to meet in a dark alley. But his gentle voice dispels any fears that his appearance might provoke.

"Hello," Lessard says, rubbing his squashed knuckles. "Sorry to have kept you waiting. Did you get my message?"

"Yes. Actually, I'm glad you came later than expected. I had a chance to assemble the documents we'll be needing to identify the priest you're looking for. Come this way."

He leads Lessard along a corridor and steps through the first open door. They enter a sparsely furnished room containing a wooden desk with a few file folders on it, and two straight-backed chairs.

"Would you like a cup of coffee?"

"No, thanks. I just had three of them."

"Okay. Before you show me the photograph and we start our search, can you explain what this is about, exactly? You didn't say much over the phone, but you mentioned that it was in connection with a murder. Did the priest you're looking for commit a crime? If so, the archbishop is definitely going to want to be kept in the loop."

If Lessard is really on the trail of a pedophile ring in which priests are involved, the last thing he needs is to get the Church on his back.

"Don't worry, the priest I'm searching for hasn't done anything wrong. We're just trying to locate anyone who was acquainted with a particular crime victim, so as to verify some details of our investigation."

In a few sentences, Lessard outlines, in minimal detail, the murders on Bessborough Avenue — just enough to satisfy Father Brunelle's curiosity and keep him from getting suspicious.

Ten minutes later, Lessard is back in his car, having obtained the name and contact details of the priest who appears in the photo with Applebaum and Sándoval. Lessard caught a lucky break. After one glance at the picture, Father Brunelle instantly recognized the priest in question; it was someone with whom he had formerly shared parish duties. In a few moments, Lessard had all the information he was looking for.

As he starts his car, he tries to reach the man by phone, but he has to content himself with leaving a voice mail. Lessard's message doesn't get into specifics. He simply asks the priest to return his call.

Then he embarks on the drive back to Montreal.

His destination: Saint Joseph's Oratory, where Father Aldéric Dorion has served since his departure from the archdiocese of Sherbrooke, two years ago.

As he presses the accelerator, despite the horrible images of Sandrine that haunt his memory, Lessard makes an effort not to presume Dorion's guilt before he has actual proof. Perhaps Dorion isn't connected with the pedophiles. Perhaps he isn't the priest whom Faizan saw holding an axe. On the other hand, as Ted Rutherford always used to say:

"The only place where there's smoke without fire is in your dreams."

After giving Moreno the necessary instructions, the SIV agent needs to get out of the cellar's dank air, to take a break and clear his head.

Wearing a raincoat over his cassock, he walks along Saint-Catherine Street. The rain is falling so hard that the drops feel like projectiles hitting his face.

The priest walks aimlessly, wanting to empty his mind. His gaze moves over the multicoloured storefronts without really seeing them. As usual, traffic on the street is snarled. A long procession of cars is advancing slowly, bumper to bumper.

As he's crossing Peel Street, a young man emerges from a fast-food restaurant ahead of him, carelessly holding a takeout bag in one hand and an umbrella in the other. Noah adjusts his pace to follow him. Judging from the university crest embroidered on the young man's knapsack, he must be a McGill student.

Shortly afterward, they walk past a homeless man sitting cross-legged under an awning. The man's nails are grimy, his hair filthy, his clothing soiled. He asks the student for a handout.

The young man averts his gaze.

But then, after walking another ten metres, the student turns and retraces his steps.

Stopping in front of the beggar, without a word, he places his takeout bag before him.

Moved by what he sees as Christian charity, Noah watches with sympathy as the boy continues on his way, while the homeless man bites into a rubbery hamburger.

There is still hope for the faithful.

Lessard has been on the road back to Montreal for fifteen minutes and is starting to feel more relaxed when he realizes that he should have visited the bathroom before leaving the archdiocese. He's gotten as far as Saint-Élie-d'Orford when he sees a sign indicating a rest stop ahead. By now, his bladder is close to bursting.

He takes the exit and arrives at the rest stop, which turns out to be no more than a paved area where truckers can check their loads. There's no restroom.

Too bad. This can't wait.

He hops over to a bush, unzips his pants, and relieves himself into the foliage.

The area is deserted.

He lights a cigarette. Standing beside the open driver's door, paying no attention to the steady rain, he takes a few puffs and calls Fernandez.

She answers on the first ring.

"Victor? For God's sake, where are you?"

At this hour, she must be at home. What's she doing? Is he imagining things, or is there a man with her?

"Am I bothering you?"

"Not at all."

Did she just hesitate? Is she with that jerk Miguel? He feels sick thinking about it. Better to dwell on other things.

"I'm still in Sherbrooke."

"Did you switch phones? I've been trying to reach you for hours."

"Yeah. I didn't want you guys finding me by triangulation."

"That's what I figured." She's silent for a moment. "The word is out, Victor. You were caught on one of the surveillance cameras at the train station."

"I know."

"What? How?"

"I'll explain later."

"It gets worse, Victor ..."

"What?"

"They can't find Viviane Gray's body."

"What are you talking about?"

"The body's disappeared. Preliminary tests in the bathroom where you claim to have discovered the woman are inconclusive. No signs of violence, no blood, no human tissue, no fluids, no fibres, nada."

"I'm not *claiming* anything, Nadja. It happened! I know what I saw. This wasn't a hallucination. Just ask the people at the station whether they were imagining the bullets that whistled past their ears."

"Sorry. Poor choice of words. But finding a body would have made things easier with Tanguay and helped you get reinstated."

"I'm not so sure. I wouldn't put it past him to say I killed her."

"Oh, come on, Victor."

"Forget it, Nadja. I'm not coming back just to have him slow me down. I don't know what it'll take to make Tanguay understand that the Bessborough killings were more than a domestic crime — and I don't care. After what I've just found, I have no more doubts. I'm moving forward."

Lessard is blinded by the headlights of a vehicle entering the rest area. Caught up in the conversation, he pays no heed.

"Victor … is it possible that you're reading more into this than you should? If you came in, we'd be able to go over the whole thing together, calmly. Tanguay's not totally unreasonable."

"You think my mental state is affecting my judgment? Is that it?"

"I didn't say that."

"But it's what you're thinking! I can't believe it…. They managed to get the body out and clean the place up. Did the forensics team spray the room with Luminol?"

Luminol is a chemical marker used at crimes scenes. It produces a blue glow in the presence of blood.

"Not yet."

"Why not?"

"There's been a double murder in the north end. The forensics people are all up there."

"Who's working the station?"

"The team from Station 21."

"Roussel, the red-haired guy?"

"Yes."

"He's okay, but nowhere near as good as Adams."

"Victor, if there are any traces of blood, those guys will find them. It's just a question of time."

Lessard murmurs, almost to himself:

"While everyone was panicking after the shootout, they went in. They must have had at least one other operative at the scene. Fuck! They're even better organized than I thought."

The car that entered the area stops fifty metres away. In the glare of its headlights, he has to shield his eyes with one hand.

"Hang on a second, Nadja."

He calls out to the driver of the vehicle:

"Hey! What the hell's wrong with you?!"

A loud bang shatters the silence.

A lightning bolt of pain shoots through Lessard's right arm, just below the shoulder. The cellphone flies from his hand.

Instinctively, he dives to the ground and takes shelter behind the Corolla.

He knows he's just taken a bullet to the arm, but he doesn't understand how it came about. He didn't see anything suspicious in his rear-view mirror as he drove, nothing to suggest that he was being followed.

Yet here he is, in desperate trouble, with a torrent of fire coming straight at him.

He never had the least suspicion. Now he's got a bullet in his arm, fear in his belly, and his heart in his mouth.

Bullets ricochet off the car's metal surface, just above his head.

Lessard touches his arm, wincing. His fingers come away sticky with blood, which the rain quickly rinses off. He grabs his Glock, realizing how bad the situation is: he's never fired left-handed before.

He makes up his mind between two incoming rounds. Taking shelter in the woods at his back is his only chance. Escaping in the Corolla isn't an option. His right arm is useless, meaning he can't shift gears. He'd be a sitting duck if he tried to drive away. If he stays behind the car, which is lit up by the other vehicle's headlight beams, he's a dead man.

He squeezes off half his magazine in the direction of the head-lights and starts to run as though his life depends on it.

Which it does.

There's more incoming fire: three or four shots.

Lessard hears the bullets' high-pitched whistles over his head, and the sharp crack of branches being struck by the projectiles. Arriving at the edge of the woods, he dives forward and lands among the trees. Instantly, he jumps back on his feet and sprints between the trunks. Coming to a moss-covered tree, he sprawls behind it on a small promontory of earth. His heart is hammering wildly.

The forest has swallowed him. It's closed over him, holding its breath, wrapping him in its black veil — its cocoon of silence. The noises of the highway are suddenly distant, barely audible.

He curls his body, making himself as small as he can, listening for the slightest sound, trying to catch his breath as quietly as possible.

Within seconds of his violent intrusion, life resumes in the forest. The woods start to vibrate and whisper again. The insects and ani-mals hidden in the shadows gradually reclaim their rights and go about their business.

As the cop strains to hear his adversary's footsteps, the sound of the rain and the various little noises of the surrounding plants and animals are filling his ears.

Suddenly, fear grips him.

Down below, five metres away, the killer is moving forward cau-tiously, peering into the vegetation that separates them.

The man sees Lessard at the very instant that a streak of fire evis-cerates the darkness.

The trees shake. Time folds in on itself as the silhouette disappears from Lessard's field of vision.

Having finished his stroll, the SIV agent goes into Mary Queen of the World Cathedral. He walks up the nave, selects a quiet pew, and kneels down. With his eyes closed, Noah prays near the canopy that stands over the altar. It's a scaled-down replica of the canopy that is located in Saint Peter's Basilica in Rome.

The sound of footsteps rouses him from his contemplation. The place is empty. He knows someone is coming for him.

He raises his eyes and meets the menacing gaze of Bournival, the archdiocese's head of security.

When the imposing man leans down to murmur something in the SIV agent's ear, he makes sure that his jacket swings open to reveal the holstered pistol under his left arm.

"Follow me."

Bournival leads Noah to the sacristy, where Charles Millot is waiting. This is the first time the two men have met since the murder of the cardinal's lover.

Millot's eyes are sparkling with hatred.

"What can I do for Your Eminence?" the SIV agent asks.

"François's death was pointless and unnecessary. It could have been avoided."

Noah can't resist giving the cardinal a knowing smile.

"I sense that his professional skill isn't what you'll be missing most, Your Eminence."

Millot's hand shoots out.

With a quick gesture, Noah catches the cardinal's wrist before the slap reaches his face. Still smiling, he twists his grip, forcing Millot to his knees.

Bournival, who was standing back, places the barrel of his gun under the SIV agent's left eye. Noah holds his grip for another moment, then releases Millot.

Bournival is waiting for a word from the cardinal to pull the trigger, while Noah holds his gaze without any sign of fear.

"That's enough, Joseph," Millot says. "Put away your weapon."

Bournival obeys reluctantly.

The three men glare at each other in a tense standoff. Millot breaks the silence.

"I heard what happened at Central Station. How do you intend to rectify the situation?"

"One of my men is dealing with it as we speak, Your Eminence."

Millot glares at the SIV agent for what seems like an eternity.

"I'll be watching you," the cardinal promises. "You may have friends at the Vatican, but don't forget, I have friends, too."

Noah watches the fat cardinal and his thug walk away along the nave. He isn't afraid of Millot, but it's always preferable to avoid complications.

As he keys Vincenzo Moreno's number into his phone, he's hoping that Moreno has received good news, and that this time, the Victor Lessard problem has been dealt with.

Once and for all.

Lessard's legs are still shaky as he staggers to the body, which is lying face down at the foot of a spruce tree. A metallic taste fills the cop's mouth. He's just shot a man down.

Kill or be killed. Those words reduce life to its simplest expression. That time-worn phrase sums up a value system that has been dismissed by all civilized societies as a thing of the past.

And yet, too often over the course of his career, Lessard has seen that there are times when violence is the only option.

Using his good hand, he turns over the body.

Lessard looks at the stranger's face, then at his wound: a bullet in the heart.

He never had a chance.

Lessard searches the dead man's pockets.

As he expected, there's no identification, but he does find a cellphone and a balaclava.

The killer from the train station?

He leaves the gun next to the body.

As he reaches the edge of the woods, he falls to his knees and vomits onto a bed of twigs.

With the man's belt wrapped around his arm in a makeshift tourniquet, Lessard finds a tracking device under the Corolla's left front fender.

He pulls it out and crushes it under his heel.

It's clear, now, why he never noticed anyone tailing him. The killer was following at a distance, waiting for the opportunity to strike — an opportunity that Lessard inadvertently provided when he pulled into the empty, isolated rest area. The detective sergeant now sees that he's up against professionals, highly organized adversaries whose resources outstrip anything he's faced before.

He retrieves his cellphone, which seems to be intact, and calls Fernandez, hoping she isn't too worried.

No such luck.

Having heard the gunshots, she's beside herself.

Soaked, grimacing with pain, Lessard assures her that he's fine and that he'll call again in a few hours. He hears a stream of objections pouring out of the phone as he ends the call. Next, he dials Marchand's number. When the Sherbrooke cop doesn't pick up, Lessard leaves him a message, briefly outlining the situation and asking him to send a team of specialists to the crime scene, as well as someone to pick up his car — he'll leave the keys under the floor mat on the passenger side.

It's bad enough having the Montreal Police after him. Now the Sherbrooke force will be looking for him, too.

He has a lot to do, and he doesn't want to hang around too long, fearing that one of his attacker's confederates may show up. He transfers his weapons from the Corolla's trunk to that of the killer's sedan — the keys to which are still in the ignition. The car has an automatic transmission; driving won't be a problem.

The more Lessard thinks about the tracking device, the more convinced he becomes that it was placed on the Corolla in the archdiocese's parking lot, while he was talking to Father Brunelle. If it had been placed earlier, an attempt would have been made on his life before he searched the Sandoval house and Applebaum's workshop. He concludes that the two residences weren't under surveillance, which means his adversaries were caught off guard.

The only logical explanation is that someone in the archdiocese got in touch with the killer and let him know I was there.

Could it have been Father Brunelle?

For a few seconds, Lessard considers going back and confronting Brunelle, pistol in hand. Then he decides against it.

He has enough troubles as it is.

Besides, his intuition rarely steers him wrong when it comes to judging character. He doesn't believe that Brunelle is involved in any of this. Might the priest have mentioned their meeting to a colleague, who in turn alerted the killer?

Lessard puts that question on hold while he considers another one.

Was the man who just tried to kill him the same one who came after him in the train station?

If not, that implies that a second assassin was engaged to eliminate him — someone who lived near Sherbrooke.

If it was the same man, then it's reasonable to suppose that the killer from the station was still in Montreal when he learned that the detective sergeant was in Sherbrooke. But Lessard only spent twenty minutes with Brunelle. The killer couldn't have covered the distance between Montreal and Sherbrooke in so short a time. Which means it was Lessard's first call to Brunelle that set off a chain reaction. While he was examining the hideout in which Sandoval and Applebaum held Sandrine captive, the killer had a couple of hours to come to Sherbrooke and install the tracking device.

Lessard gives up trying to solve the puzzle, but the implications of his conjectures are dizzying. It's one thing to suppose that a group of priests may be involved in a network of pedophiles. But the idea that members of a religious order might have access to, and use, professional killers to get rid of troublesome witnesses is — literally and figuratively — heretical.

As Lessard starts the car, he can't suppress a shudder. He's up against something much bigger than he is, a beast with many tentacles, beyond his understanding. A beast that fills him with fear.

First things first: his arm requires immediate medical attention.

The temporary bandage that he created with a strip torn from his shirt seems to have stemmed the bleeding, but he's feeling weaker and weaker. The bullet needs to be taken out as soon as possible; the wound must be cleaned and dressed. That will be a challenge, because going to a hospital is out of the question. Hospital personnel are legally obliged to report gunshot wounds, which means Lessard would be under arrest before his medical treatment was even complete.

Under the circumstances, after considering the problem from every angle, he can only think of one solution.

"I'm sorry to have bothered you at this hour, but I had no choice."

You need to have been to hell and back, as Simone Fortin has, to understand that a person like Victor Lessard is going to press on no matter what. Nothing can slow him down, short of death or a badly lodged bullet.

"Shut up and roll over on your side, Victor," she says. "We'll talk later. That's it … perfect. Now hold still!"

Lessard was lucky. Simone answered on the first ring. By the time he pulled into the parking lot of the motel on Saint-Jacques Street where he had asked her to meet him, she was waiting with the keys to a room she'd just rented, following his instructions. She also had the foresight to bring along some clean clothes that she took from Laurent. Dizzy and weak from blood loss, Lessard barely made it to the room under his own power.

After watching over him through the night, Simone will ask a few questions when he wakes up. But not too many. She knows he won't tell her everything. She'll point out how lucky he was: the bullet didn't cause any serious damage, lodging in the biceps without touching any arteries or bones.

She'll advise him to rest for a few days and ask his colleagues for assistance. At dawn, she'll watch him go out into the rain, with his arm in a sling.

She won't give him a sermon. She won't try to convince him to change his mind. And she won't breathe a word to anyone.

But at the moment, the crumpled bullet is still stuck in his arm.

"The injections I gave you should be kicking in soon."

"My arm's dead from the elbow to the shoulder. I can't feel a thing."

"It's very important that you not move while I'm removing the bullet," she says, adjusting the strap on her surgical headlamp.

"No problem."

Lessard grits his teeth as Simone probes his flesh with a pair of pliers.

"It's almost over, Victor," Raymond says, stroking his hair. "It's almost over."

A black van is racing along Highway 10.

One of Moreno's men is at the wheel, while Moreno himself sits in the passenger seat, grieving in silence. Large tears are running down his smooth cheeks. In the back of the van, encased in a body bag, a corpse is rocking back and forth between an electronic listening post and a surveillance console.

"Take the next exit," Moreno says, wiping his eyes.

The van swerves onto the off-ramp without slowing down.

It takes an exceptionally skilled driver to manoeuvre the heavy vehicle in these wet conditions, with the risk of hydroplaning so great.

Moreno calls the SIV agent, who's been trying to reach him.

"Well, Vincenzo?" Noah asks. "What's the news from your brother?"

"Pasquale is dead. I just recovered his body from the woods beside a rest stop on the highway."

There's a moment of silence. Then: "I'm sorry, Vincenzo. It wasn't supposed to be this way."

Vincenzo doesn't respond.

"What about the police officer?" the SIV agent asks.

"He found the tracker and drove away in Pasquale's sedan. I think he's injured. There was blood near his car."

"Who took your brother's place at the observation post on De la Gauchetière Street?"

"I had to use the man who was watching the apartment. As I told you, we're short of personnel. And now that Pasquale is ..."

Moreno's voice breaks. He can't finish the sentence.

"I know it hurts, Vincenzo," Noah murmurs compassionately.

"We'd better find this guy you're looking for," Moreno says, in a voice filled with bitterness, "or my brother will have died for nothing!"

"Pasquale's sacrifice will not have been in vain. We'll find the man, Vincenzo, I promise you. After disposing of your brother's body, I want you to go back to the apartment and search it again."

Boundless hatred burns in Moreno's eyes.

Between him and the cop, it's a personal thing now.

Victor Lessard is a dead man walking.

29

May 10th

In the conference room where they've established their operations centre, Jacinthe Taillon tosses a stack of papers onto the table in front of Lemaire.

"I told you, Gilles. There's something wrong with the guy."

"Which guy?"

"Your pastor, Pascal Pierre. The one who looks so good on TV."

"What's wrong with him?" Lemaire asks, glancing at the papers.

"I'll tell you what's wrong. Your fine pastor leads a cult called the Solar Passage."

"You sure?"

"A hundred percent. I asked Vadnais to look into it. He hasn't finished digging, but he just sent me a report confirming it. Take a look."

"Hang on. Let's not jump to conclusions. Even if Pascal Pierre does lead a cult, that doesn't mean he's shady, or that he's mixed up in the abduction of Laila François."

"Jesus, Gilles," Taillon says, marching toward the exit, "you're so naïve!"

"Where are you going?"

"To pay a visit to your friend, Pascal Pierre."

Lemaire can see that she's planning to do something foolish. He jumps to his feet and grabs his coat on his way out the door.

"Wait! I'm coming with you!"

Lessard is at Chez Cora, Montreal's famous breakfast place, where he's just polished off a big meal to start the day.

He said goodbye to Simone an hour ago, promising to look after himself.

Then he called Fernandez and endured a lengthy tirade in which his young colleague expressed her fears for his well-being and her annoyance that it took him so long to get in touch: "You might have called sooner. I've been worried sick, thinking you'd bled out by the side of the highway!"

Lessard apologized sincerely: "I'm sorry, Nadja. It took all my strength to drive back to Montreal. After Simone took out the bullet, I fell asleep." Then he recounted yesterday's events, from his meeting with Sylvain Marchand to his lethal confrontation with the killer at the rest stop.

He also devoted a lot of time to explaining in detail why he thinks he's on the trail of a pedophile ring.

"A network of pedophiles, involving priests ..." Fernandez says, leaving the sentence unfinished.

"Marchand is searching Applebaum's workshop, and he's going to reopen the Sandoval case. He'll try to identify elements that might support the theory of a double murder, as opposed to the official finding of a domestic murder-suicide. We've agreed to keep each other posted if we find anything. In the meantime, I'd like you to focus on three things. First, go through the Cook file. Look for any leads that might connect Cook and his wife to the pedophiles. Don't forget, they could have been participants or victims."

"This may be irrelevant," Fernandez says, "but there's a detail that's been bugging me. Cook cut out his tongue. Sandoval gouged out his eyes. That could be significant, don't you think?"

"I did notice that, but I'm not sure what to make of it. I'll have to give it some more thought."

"Sorry. I cut you off."

It takes Lessard a moment to get back on track.

"Okay, yes ... second, try to get more information about Aldéric Dorion. Father Brunelle said he lived in Val-d'Or before moving to Sherbrooke. Look into that. And third, have one of the experts from

Digital Security try to crack that website I told you about. With a little luck, we'll be able to identify the people in charge."

"Sure," Fernandez says sarcastically. "Piece of cake."

"I know I'm asking a lot, Nadja. Maybe you can let Sirois in on this."

"I … I didn't want to mention it, but I already have. He's going to help us."

Lessard is simultaneously touched by Sirois's support and worried about the repercussions. He's well aware that Fernandez and Sirois could face disciplinary measures because of him.

"Really?" he says, embarrassed. "I … uh … thanks."

"No problem."

"Don't tell Pearson, though. He has a family to feed."

"I figured you'd say that. But he's never going to forgive you."

"I can live with it. Now that I know you've got someone helping you, can I ask you to look into a few more things?"

"Shoot."

"I'm going to text you the plate number of the killer's car, as well as a phone number I found in his call history. See what you can find out."

"He only made one call?"

"One outgoing, one incoming, both involving the same number. The guy was a pro. He must have deleted his history on a regular basis."

Lessard doesn't mention to Fernandez that the night before, while driving from Sherbrooke to Montreal, after weighing the pros and cons of the tactic, he typed a text message into the killer's cellphone and sent it to the number he just gave Fernandez.

It's done.

The person who received the text wasn't fooled. Less than ten minutes later, a reply came back.

Walk away while you still can.

"He also deleted his texts," Lessard continues. "But I found an unsent draft. It's the address of a building on De la Gauchetière Street in Chinatown. Take it down and see what you can find out about the owner, lessees, etc."

Lessard repeats the address twice, to make sure there's no error.

"Do you have the number of your assailant's cellphone?" Fernandez asks. "I'll try to find the name of the account holder."

Lessard gives her the number.

"Don't spend too much time on it," he says. "The phone is either stolen or a prepaid burner."

"I know. But even pros make mistakes."

"Not this guy. Not that kind of mistake. Just to give you an idea, the only things I found in the car were a blood pressure gauge and a notebook with daily readings from the gauge."

"Weird. Do you want to run a check for fingerprints and DNA?"

"No. He was wearing gloves when I went through his pockets. Besides, there isn't time."

"Anything else?"

"Yes. I'll need a list of children who've gone missing in Quebec during the past five years."

"How will you access it?"

"Send it to my Hotmail address. I'll download it to my BlackBerry."

"Okay."

"I've got to go. I'm going to pay a little visit to Father Dorion."

"Victor?"

"Yes?"

"Are you sure your arm's all right?"

Lessard does a couple of flexes. The pain is sharp, but bearable.

"Yeah. Simone gave me some painkillers and a prescription for something to prevent infection. I've got everything I need."

There's a hesitation at the other end of the line. "Be careful, Victor. I'm worried about you."

"I …"

He gropes for the right words to express his feelings: something, anything that might bring them closer together. But nothing comes.

"Thanks, Nadja."

When he gets up to pay the restaurant tab, he finds himself looking at his own features. On the flatscreen TV near the entrance, he sees a

close-up of his face on the Radio-Canada news channel. The volume
has been turned off, but the text running along the bottom of the
screen leaves no room for doubt:

> Montreal Police are looking for Detective Sergeant Victor
> Lessard, wanted in connection with the shootout at Central
> Station. Lessard, who was off-duty when the incident oc-
> curred, has gone missing, and senior officers on the force
> are concerned for his safety.

He lowers his gaze and hurries out of the restaurant, muttering:
"That's all I need."

Chronicle of a disaster foretold: Gilles Lemaire can already see Pascal
Pierre's sympathetic face on TV, indignantly denouncing investiga-
tors' strong-arm tactics and their failure to locate his stepdaughter.
Lemaire wants to avoid a scenario in which Taillon says something
offensive and leaves him having to deal with an impossible situation.
So, during the drive, he convinces her to let him question the pastor.

The door of the luxurious suite at the Ritz-Carlton is ajar.
Wearing an elegant charcoal suit, the pastor beckons them inside as
he wraps up a conversation on his cellphone. They'll learn later that
an anonymous benefactor has covered the cost of a week-long stay at
the hotel, allowing Pascal Pierre to participate in the search for his
missing stepdaughter.

"Thanks for agreeing to see us, Mr. Pierre," Lemaire says
respectfully.

"Not at all. I'm the one who should be thanking you. How is the
investigation coming along?"

Without going into too much detail, Lemaire tells the pastor
about the most recent developments in the case.

"Mr. Pierre, in an investigation like this one, it's standard procedure to —"

"I'm a suspect. Of course. That simply proves that you're doing
your job. Please continue, Detective."

Surprised by the man's openness, Lemaire takes a moment to recover his composure. He asks a number of preliminary questions, then comes to the heart of the matter:

"We've learned that you lead a … um … a …"

"A cult," Taillon barks.

"The Solar Passage," Lemaire says placatingly.

"We are an independent church, a community," the pastor says, offering them a thin smile. "I can assure you that all of our members are willing participants. We don't engage in any kind of indoctrination."

"Can you tell us about your property in the Eastern Townships?"

"The community owns a tract of land in the area. I spend most of my time out there. We lead a very simple existence in the forest, in harmony with nature."

"Your members also live on this property, don't they?"

"Indeed. We have members who are permanent residents on the community's estate, while others come out for occasional retreats. The situation is quite variable. It's all done on a voluntary basis."

The conversation continues for another quarter-hour, during which Lemaire asks all the questions on his list, while Taillon watches in silence, her mouth twisted in repressed anger.

"If you'd like to see the place," the pastor says, "you're welcome to come and visit. We have nothing to hide."

"That won't be necessary, Mr. Pierre. Right, Jacinthe?"

Taillon simply nods.

Lemaire is walking toward the door when Taillon bends toward Pascal Pierre and murmurs something in his ear that causes his eyes to widen.

The pills that Simone gave Lessard before he left have worn off. The wound in his arm is making him wince with pain. Adding to his discomfort is the burning sensation in his esophagus and trachea, reminding him that it's been over twenty-four hours since he last took his reflux medication.

Despite the risk that someone might recognize him, he goes into a pharmacy and renews his prescription for proton pump inhibitors.

He also fills the prescription that Simone has given him. In a nearby alley, he washes down the pills with several swigs from a jumbo bottle of Pepto-Bismol that he purchased at the same time. The pink liquid, which comforts him in the same way that coffee does, will provide temporary relief until the pills kick in. Wearing reading glasses and a Canadiens baseball cap that he saw on display near the drugstore's cash register, he hopes to avoid detection, despite the fact that all of Quebec has now seen his face on the news.

Since he's still getting no answer at what he presumes is Dorion's cellphone number, he decides to try the number for Saint Joseph's Oratory.

"Father Aldéric Dorion, please."

"Just a moment. I'll see if he's here."

Lessard hears elevator music. His fingers drum on the dashboard of the car.

As the wait lengthens, the detective sergeant's hopes rise. He expects to hear Dorion's voice.

Click. The call is cut off.

Shit.

He keys in the number a second time, grumbling as his fingers pound the phone.

"Saint Joseph's Oratory."

"Yes ... I was holding for Father Dorion, and I got cut off."

"Oh, sorry. I checked Father Dorion's schedule. He had a Mass earlier this week, but there's nothing on his agenda until next Wednesday."

"It's urgent, ma'am. I absolutely need to talk to him."

"Did you try his cell?"

Lessard tells her the number he's been calling.

"That's the right number."

"But he's not answering."

"Would you like to leave a message? Sometimes he stops by, even when he isn't celebrating Mass."

Annoyed that things aren't going as he'd planned, the detective sergeant gives the woman his name and contact details, then hangs up.

Dorion's presence in the photograph with Sandoval and Applebaum may be coincidental, but Lessard can't help thinking that the priest is on the run.

During the cop's visit to the archdiocese of Sherbrooke, Father Brunelle explained that priests often rent their own apartments. That's the case for Aldéric Dorion, who occupies an upper duplex at the corner of Stanley Weir Street and Cedar Crescent.

Lessard pulls the car over beside a park, a block from the duplex. Lowering the sun visor, he turns off the motor and looks around.

The wind is making the massed clouds play leapfrog through a mournful sky. A woman walks by, holding her umbrella at an angle so that it doesn't get blown inside out.

After assuring himself that there's no danger and that no one is watching the apartment, Lessard gets out of the car, walks to the building, and goes up the front stairs.

He knocks a few times and presses the doorbell repeatedly. Its ringing echoes through the empty dwelling.

He doesn't hesitate. After glancing around to make sure no one's watching, he starts to pick the lock. The sling encasing his arm slows him down, but the lock is rudimentary. After a few manoeuvres, he's inside.

From behind the curtain, he looks out at the rain-slick street.

Why is he worrying?

In this downpour, is anyone really going to pay attention to a guy who stands on a front stoop for a few extra seconds?

Dorion's three-room apartment consists of a kitchen that also serves as a living/dining room (furnished with a rusty stove, an ancient refrigerator, a rickety table against the wall, a weary kitchen chair, a holed velvet armchair, and an old TV set with a rabbit-ear antenna); a tiny bedroom containing a bed and a chest of drawers; and an office.

Clearly, Dorion makes do with minimal amenities.

The place is immaculate. Obsessively so.

Lessard only spends a few moments inspecting the kitchen and bedroom, which hold nothing of interest. He's rarely seen a living space that was so spare, so impersonal. The white walls are bare of pictures or other decorations.

The detective sergeant is a little taken aback: he was expecting to find at least a crucifix or a religious image somewhere.

Apart from an overstuffed bookshelf that takes up one whole wall, the office is furnished with a wooden table, a file cabinet, and a brand-new chair. The chair is the only luxury that Dorion has allowed himself, suggesting that he spends most of his time in here.

The work surface is bare. No pens, no papers, no computer.

Strange.

Looking closer, Lessard notices that the file cabinet is, in fact, a safe bolted to the floor. He immediately notices that something isn't right. The door is open and, apart from a few worthless papers, the safe is empty.

Why would Dorion, whose apartment is a model of simplicity, keep an empty safe? Lessard generally avoids jumping to conclusions, but he can't help thinking that the absence of the priest, combined with this empty safe, is troubling.

Has Dorion absconded, taking with him a computer that contains child pornography or compromising documents?

The detective sergeant examines the bookshelf, which contains literary classics and mystery novels, as well as books about philosophy and religion — including a leather-bound Qur'an — and numerous editions of the Bible and the Old and New Testaments.

He takes several volumes off the shelf and gives them a shake, hoping something will fall out. But he quickly notices that an entire section of the bookshelf has been given over to a single subject.

Exorcism.

There must be forty books on the topic.

His eye falls on a pamphlet: *Exorcism: A Practical Guide for Priests*, by Father Aldéric Dorion and Father René Trudeau, c.s.c., Church Press, Sherbrooke, 2002.

Lessard wears a skeptical half smile as he leafs through the document. He doesn't believe in this stuff. For him, exorcism is the subject matter of films, fakery, and folklore.

He lingers in the office for another few minutes, then leaves, after carefully putting everything back in its place. But he takes the pamphlet with him, because it's clear that Dorion and his co-author must have spent time together in Sherbrooke.

Father René Trudeau may be able to give Lessard some information about his former colleague.

His incursion into Dorion's home has taken less than thirty minutes.

On the drive back to his motel, Lessard stops at a phone booth and remotely checks the voice mail on his service cellphone. He deletes numerous messages from Fernandez, to whom he's spoken since she left them. His sister has also left several worried messages, as has his ex-wife, Marie, who offers her help, if he needs it — which touches him. Marie also asks about Martin, rekindling Lessard's anxieties. Controlled as ever, Véronique asks how he's doing. All of these callers mention that they learned about Lessard's troubles from TV news reports. The final message is from Elaine Segato. She asks Lessard to call her back as soon as possible — it's urgent. From the sound of her voice, Lessard can tell that she's genuinely worried.

After leaving Martin yet another voice mail, Lessard pulls into the motel parking lot and stops the car in front of his room. Then he dials Elaine's number.

She answers instantly:

"Victor, someone broke into my apartment."

30

It was the evening of my fifteenth birthday. HE had summoned me to his little cottage.

Things had been going well. HE hadn't touched me in several months.

I was convinced that HE and the other members of the community had organized a little birthday party. I thought I'd overheard some whispered conversations behind my back and seen knowing smiles being exchanged.

Not that our celebrations ever got wild. Far from it. They were always brief and meagre. But they allowed us to escape for a few hours from the misery of our daily existence.

So I had come to HIS quarters with a fairly light heart, considering the fact that HIS physical presence was still intolerable to me. But when I entered, I saw at a glance that I'd gotten it wrong. Totally wrong.

How nice it would have been if HE had handed me the keys to a beautiful pink Cadillac, setting me free to drive away from this place and never look back — but no, HE had something else in store.

HE was sitting in the middle of the room, HIS gaze already foggy from the large quantity of liquor that HE had obviously consumed.

Sitting on HIS knees was Anne, the daughter of one of the women in the community — HIS own daughter, in fact — a child of ten.

The little girl was crying silently.

I knew very well what HE had in mind.

HE wanted me to initiate Anne to "feminine pleasures."

I don't know why I reacted the way I did.

I saw red.

Was it because it was my birthday, and I'd been expecting some kind of celebration? Was it because I wanted to save Anne from the repeated rapes and barbaric abuse that I had endured before her?

I didn't ask myself those questions at the time. If I had, I might have behaved differently.

The truth was, the sexual relations that I'd had with Monique had been beneficial, saving me, to a large extent, from the physical attentions of my tormentor. At that moment, considering the psychological baggage that I was carrying, I might even have thought that it was a good thing for Anne to have sex with me, rather than to be raped and abused by HIM.

Even now, I have trouble understanding what went through my mind.

All those years of fear, of servitude, of tyranny, of humiliation and violence were annihilated in an instant.

Without being fully conscious of what was happening, I found myself gripping the knife that had been stuck in the counter.

I drove it into HIS back several times. HIS blood flowed out.

In remission of HIS sins.

Disoriented, panic-stricken, but also excited at the thought that I had shed a burden as heavy as a thousand worlds, I fled as fast as my legs would carry me, running through the forest toward freedom.

Since my birth, I had never lived anywhere but in the belly of the beast. I'd never left the confines of the community. I'd been given some semblance of an education — I could read, write, and count — but I hardly knew anything of the outside world, apart from a few fragments of information that the other women had managed to share with me over the years.

I won't talk about the things I went through between the moment a car picked me up on the road that ran past the property and the moment I finally landed, in desperate straits, on the streets of Montreal. It was in the city, after many painful false starts, that I met the two people who restored my faith in humanity: Antoine Chambord and Mélanie Fleury.

But I will say that nothing I endured in that period of fever and doubt could have been worse than what I had suffered at the hands of my stepfather.

As I lie here on my back, the darkness presses itself against my eyes. It envelops me.

For what seems like a lifetime, I've been cradling the prong of my belt buckle in my right palm, turning it over and over.

As I hold it in my hand, the cold, hard metal comes alive. It turns into a shining dagger, poised to fly through the air, to pierce flesh, to spill evil blood. I'm filled with a galactic power that lifts my soul and carries it beyond the lightless walls of my prison.

When HE comes in, I'll be ready. Every muscle in my body will launch me like a coiled spring. I'll fly forward and strike HIM down in silence — the absolute silence of all victims who rise up to face their executioners.

At that moment, either HE or I will leave this world.

Brutal images unfold in my mind.

I see Pascal Pierre's bloody face trembling in front of me. A foul liquid flows from HIS eyeless sockets, a poisoned stream that I want to suck up, to the very last drop, and spit back in HIS face.

HE explored every corner of my flesh. HE forced himself into all my orifices.

I remember every outrage committed by HIS bony fingers.

HE can imprison me for as long as HE likes. My hatred will burn until my very last breath.

Memories of my past life rise up to engulf me.

Mom's gentle face explodes into pieces that fly all over my cell. Mélanie's laughter bounces off the padded walls, and the smell of Monsieur Antoine's withered skin wafts into my nostrils.

My existence is reduced to these few things: recollections of the mother who abandoned me, and the pair of people whom I love more than anything — the pair who came to my aid.

I'm only seventeen, but I've already lived two lives.

I'm under no illusions. Even if I kill HIM, I won't get out of here in one piece. I've reached the end of the line.

On the walls of my memory, in letters of blood, I carve:

Laila François lived here.

Laila François lived here.

Laila François lived here.

31

Using his good hand, Lessard struggles with the knob on the motel room door while holding his cellphone between his head and shoulder.

"When was your place broken into, Elaine?"

"I noticed it when I got home from work last night."

The detective sergeant collapses onto the bed, then sits back up instantly, grimacing with pain. He placed his weight on his injured arm.

"Fuck!"

"You okay, Victor?"

"Yeah. Sorry. Was anything stolen?"

"No, that's what's so weird. They didn't take a thing. They didn't steal my computers or the jewelry that I inherited from my godmother. I had two hundred dollars in cash in an envelope on my desk, to pay for a second-hand chair I'm planning to buy. That wasn't touched, either."

"Did they take any files? Documents?"

"No."

"Was the door damaged? Did they jimmy the lock?"

"No."

Lessard frowns, puzzled.

"Hang on. Was your place broken into or not?"

"Okay, maybe I should have put it differently. What I'm trying to say is that someone visited my apartment while I was out. They went through my stuff, but they made sure to put everything back afterward."

Lessard's pulse accelerates.

"How do you know?"

"Little things. My work obliges me to be very meticulous, so I tend to notice small details. For instance, this may seem ridiculous to you, but when I get up in the morning, I always lay my pyjamas over my office chair in the same way. When I got home, the pyjamas were there, but in a different position. Same thing for my date book. It was in its usual place in the drawer, but upside down. And my laptop was closed. I always leave it open, even when it's off."

"Maybe your landlord came in."

"He's in Mexico for three months. I've been picking up his mail."

Lessard asks all the standard questions.

Though he tries to convince himself that the break-in at Elaine's place is a coincidence, he knows deep down that she's not imagining things. This intrusion into her home is linked to the fact that she helped with his investigation. Fear grips him. From the outset, people who have gotten too deeply involved in this thing have had short life expectancies.

"What's really strange," Elaine says, "is that I got the same impression when I arrived at the office this morning. And when I went out for lunch, I think I was followed on Pie-IX Boulevard."

A shudder runs up Lessard's spine. It takes a tremendous effort to stay calm and, above all, not to scare Elaine.

"Where are you right now?"

"At the office. Why?"

"Don't go home this evening."

"What? Victor, I —"

"Listen to me. Do you have relatives or friends who can put you up for a few days?"

"Why? What's going on?"

"Have you watched the news in the last twenty-four hours?"

"I never watch the news. Too depressing."

"I was involved in a shootout at Central Station yesterday morning. Someone tried to kill me, and they murdered a woman I was questioning. Turn on any of the news networks. The story is everywhere."

"Oh my god," Elaine says, suddenly terrified. "Were you hurt?"

"I'm fine. But I need to stay off the grid for a while."

"What do you mean? I don't understand."

"It's complicated. I'm investigating on my own, separately from the police. Meanwhile, they're trying to track me down."

"What are you talking about, Victor?"

"I'll explain when the time is right, but for now, Elaine, I need you to trust me. I have a feeling — more than a feeling, a conviction — that the break-ins you noticed at your home and office really did happen, and they're connected to the fact that you helped out with my investigation."

"Do you think —"

"No. If they'd wanted to kill you, you'd already be ..." He smacks his forehead. *Idiot!*

Don't terrorize her. "What I'm saying is, you shouldn't take chances. Can you find some place to stay for a few days? Avoiding the office would also be a good idea."

"Victor, I have a super busy week —"

"Elaine!"

Silence. Then: "My parents live in Champlain, overlooking the river."

"Perfect. I'm going to give you the number of a cop I work with. She's a friend. I'll tell her to expect your call in the next fifteen minutes. In the meantime, you're not to leave your office, understood? And I want you to promise that you'll do whatever she says."

"I —"

"Promise!"

"Okay, Victor. I promise."

His instructions to Fernandez are simple: Send someone to pick up Elaine Segato at the Insectarium. Don't let her go home to pick up her personal effects. Drive her straight to her parents' place, taking care not to be followed.

"I'll get Sirois to handle it," Fernandez says. "When that's taken care of, I'll call you back. I have news for you."

"Thanks, Nadja. Tell Sirois it's a top priority. I'd never forgive myself if something happened to her."

"Seems like you really care about her, Victor."

The hint is clear. Fernandez is fishing.

Lessard could put the whole thing to rest with a single sentence: "It's you I care about, Nadja. You're the one who's on my mind." It would be so easy.

In another life.

He calls home, hoping Martin will answer.

His son hasn't resurfaced, and Lessard can't shake the fear that his adversaries might target Martin, as they targeted Viviane Gray, and, to a lesser extent, Elaine Segato.

The voice he hears is his own, asking him to leave a message at the beep. He hates listening to himself. The sound of his voice irritates him.

"Martin, call me back right away. Something's happened. It's a matter of life and death."

In the shower, he has to contort himself to avoid wetting the bullet wound. As he rushes to answer the cellphone buzzing on his table, the towel around his waist unwraps and falls around his ankles. He picks up the phone just in time.

"You were right about your assailant's car and phone," Fernandez says. "The car's stolen, and the phone's a prepaid burner bought under a fake name and address. Same thing for the number in the call log: it's also a burner."

"I'd have been surprised to hear otherwise."

"The building on De la Gauchetière Street belongs to a provincially incorporated company, CLW Solutions Inc. They offer consulting services in digital document management. The company's sole shareholder and director is one Chan Lok Wan."

"Does he have a criminal record?"

"No. He's spotless. Same with the company."

"Even so, I think I'll pay him a visit. Any progress on that web address I found in the pedophiles' laptop?"

"One of the Digital Security guys has started working on it. I couldn't tell him it was a rush job. He'd have asked a bunch of questions, and I'd have had to explain. I'm trying to stay discreet."

"I get it, Nadja. But this is important. Cracking that website is the only way to find out for sure whether we're dealing with a pedophile ring. What about the Cooks? Did you find anything that might link them to Sandoval and Applebaum?"

"I haven't had time, but Sirois's working on it. And I emailed you a list of children who've gone missing in the past five years."

"Great. Is that everything?"

"No. I've found something that I think will interest you. Actually, I have good news and bad news."

Lessard is suddenly at the edge of his chair, muscles tensed, all his senses on high alert.

"Do you have a pen and paper?" Fernandez asks.

"Hang on."

He sets the phone on hands-free and retrieves his notebook and pen from his jacket.

"Go."

"You know that girl who was kidnapped yesterday? Laila François?"

The name is familiar. Did he see something about the abduction on the news?

"What about her?"

"The Major Crimes Unit sent out a report to all the local police stations, mentioning that she's done some volunteer work in Monsieur Antoine's trailer."

"I know Chambord. The man is a saint. But I don't see the connection —"

Shame and embarrassment prevent Lessard from telling Fernandez about his youthful years on the streets, when Chambord used to take him in.

"Let me finish. Laila François ran a support group for young drug addicts. And guess who was a resource person for the group."

"Nadja, I'm in no mood for guessing games —"

"Aldéric Dorion."

"Are you kidding me?"

"Nope. You asked for information about Dorion's time in Val-d'Or. I haven't come up with anything interesting on that score. But I found this information in a document that I got from the archdiocese. Dorion worked in the same support group as Laila. When I saw the Major Crimes report, I made the connection right away."

"Aldéric Dorion knew Laila François. Now she's been kidnapped, and he's gone missing. We have our link, Nadja! This should have been the first thing you said to me! I need to get in touch with whoever's heading up the investigation at Major Crimes."

"Calm down, Victor. That was the good news."

Lessard is silent for a moment. "What's the bad news?"

"You sure you want to hear this?"

"Nadja —"

"Jacinthe Taillon is in charge of the case."

32

Jacinthe Taillon.

Lessard has no problem with her. Unfortunately, she refuses to return the favour. She hates him with a single-mindedness that borders on obsession. Which complicates matters. If anyone else were heading up the investigation, Lessard wouldn't hesitate to emerge from the shadows and collaborate openly with the Major Crimes team. But Jacinthe Taillon would never stand for that. So he'll have to leave it up to Fernandez to get in touch with the other investigators and give them the information he's gathered so far.

Before leaving his apartment, Lessard pulls out his BlackBerry and reads the Major Crimes Unit's report on Laila François's abduction, which Fernandez sent him.

Shortly afterward he enters the trailer where Antoine Chambord has been welcoming street kids since time immemorial. The place has changed a lot since the days when Lessard used to come in as a teenager. Indeed, it's changed since the last time he dropped by to say hello to Chambord, a few years ago.

What hasn't changed, though, is the old man's gaze, the piercing yet benevolent eyes that seem to read your soul — eyes from which it's impossible to hide a thing.

Lessard notices a little boy sitting near Chambord.

"Victor Lessard! Is it really you?"

"Hey, Antoine."

The two men share a warm, heartfelt hug that elicits a wince of pain from the detective sergeant.

"It's been ages! What happened to your arm?"

"Oh, nothing, just a little accident. Who's the boy?" Lessard asks, lifting his chin in the direction of Felix, who buries his face in Monsieur Antoine's pants leg as soon as he realizes he's being talked about.

"This is my adopted son, Felix."

Chambord briefly describes the events that led him to adopt the boy. When Lessard kneels down to try to interact with the child, Chambord explains why Felix never talks.

The old man doesn't seem to have heard about the shootout, thus sparing Lessard the obligation of offering partial explanations, or worse, lying again.

"I wish I could tell you that I happened to be in the neighbourhood and dropped in to see how you're doing. But that wouldn't be true, Antoine."

"You're here about Laila's disappearance?"

Lessard nods.

"I figured as much. One of your colleagues has already been here — did you know?"

"Yes, I heard. Jacinthe Taillon."

"Not a very warm person," Chambord observes.

"But effective as hell," Lessard replies. "What kind of questions did she ask?"

"Mostly she wanted to know about some local hoodlums."

"Which ones?"

"She asked about a guy named Razor, who has ties to the Red Blood Spillers. She also wanted information about Nigel Williams, a local pimp and drug dealer, and about Steve Côté, who works for Williams. I told her everything I know, which isn't much."

"Did she give you any idea of where she's going with the investigation? What sort of leads her team is following up?"

"No, nothing. As I said, not very friendly. When she left, she didn't even thank me."

"That sounds like her. Did she ask about Aldéric Dorion?"

Chambord reacts with evident surprise.

"Aldéric Dorion? No. Why?"

"Laila François worked with him in a support group, didn't she?"

"Yes, that's right."

"How did that come about? Did you ask them to work together?"

"Not exactly. Laila used to have a serious drug problem. When she got clean, she wanted to share the lessons she'd learned with other young people who had similar problems."

"How did Dorion get involved? Is he an acquaintance of yours?"

"Not at all. I'd never met him. It was Laila who introduced us."

"Go on."

"One day, she told me that the group might benefit from having a spiritual adviser. She talked about Dorion, whom she'd met while she was in rehab ... or maybe she met him through a friend, I can't remember now. She asked if she could bring him onto the team as a resource person. I thought that was an excellent idea, so I contacted the archdiocese to ask for references."

"And?"

"Everyone praised him. Shortly after that, he started coming to group sessions. The kids really like him."

Lessard is surprised to learn that Dorion and Laila François knew each other. But what really maddens him is the thought that Chambord, whose judgment he respects enormously, was so taken in by a sexual predator that he inadvertently gave him the keys to the harem.

"Tell me about their relationship."

"Actually, Victor, I only saw Dorion once or twice. But as I recall, they got along well."

Lessard has always had trouble containing his temper. Today is no exception. He blows up.

"Damn it, Antoine! You let a pedophile insinuate himself into a group of young people. *Troubled* young people. And now he may have kidnapped Laila."

The old man's cheeks redden. But he answers in a calm voice.

"Dorion? A pedophile? Anything's possible, Victor, but that would really surprise me."

"Why?"

"For starters, Dorion is an old man. Very old. I doubt that he'd have the physical capacity to take on Laila. Especially considering what she's dealt with in the past. She knows how to defend herself. That girl is uncommonly strong and vigorous."

"He may have had one or more accomplices."

"Once again, anything is possible. But I'd be shocked if he was involved in her kidnapping. When you're in daily contact with people who live on the streets, you develop a sixth sense for judging character. I don't need to tell you that, Victor. When someone lies to you under questioning, you can usually tell. I may not have spent a lot of time in Dorion's company, but I saw enough to get a fair idea of what kind of person he is."

"And *I* don't need to tell *you*, Antoine, that there's no way to protect yourself against a gifted liar."

"That's true. And I'm going to look into this matter. I'll talk to the kids in the group who know the man. But I still have my doubts."

"I read the Major Crime Unit's report. It says Laila used to do webcam pornography. Were you aware of that?"

"Vaguely. If you want more information on the subject, you should talk to a friend of Laila's, Mélanie Fleury."

Lessard writes the name in his notebook.

"Dorion may have encouraged her to get into porn," the detective sergeant says.

Chambord frowns skeptically.

"I suspect Laila's disappearance has a lot more to with her past than with Dorion."

"What do you mean?"

"Something terrible happened in her life. She has a secret — a secret she's never talked about with anyone, not even me. I mentioned it to your colleague, Detective Taillon, when she questioned me."

Lessard's cellphone rings.

"Excuse me, Antoine. What's up, Fernandez?"

"Our expert cracked that website. He says it wasn't very difficult. You were right, Victor. It's a file-sharing site for pedophiles."

Lessard lifts his eyes heavenward. He was hoping he might be wrong, but this confirms his suspicions.

"Damn it! I'm with Antoine Chambord at the moment. I'll call you back as soon as I'm done."

"Okay."

"Is something wrong?" Chambord asks.

"Long story. Where were we? Oh, yeah. You were talking about Laila's past, and this secret that you think she's keeping."

"Yes. She's hiding something. I'm sure of it. I was considering the matter while you were on the phone. I wouldn't think she's the type that pedophiles go after. Have you seen her in person? She's seventeen, but she could easily pass for twenty-five. She has a generous bust and a womanly body. Nothing like a little girl, believe me." Chambord is silent for a moment. "I'm no expert, but as a rule, pedophiles have specific tastes, don't they? They're attracted to prepubescent children."

Lessard thinks about Sandrine Pedneault-King, who was nine years old when Sandoval abducted her. Suddenly, he feels like he's been barking up the wrong tree.

What he's hearing from Chambord bears no relation to the mental picture he had formed of Dorion. Still, Lessard isn't ready to remove the priest from his list of suspects. Not after what he heard from Faizan.

He feels the cloth of his pants pressing against his thigh.

He looks down and sees the little boy pulling on his pants leg to attract his attention.

The child makes what seems like a superhuman effort to produce a sound. Lessard watches his lips move. A hoarse, gravelly moan comes out, but the cop can't make any sense of it.

"What are you trying to say, little guy?"

The boy frowns reproachfully at Lessard, as though annoyed at him for not understanding. He tries again, doing his best to articulate. The words, his first in a long time, come out with painful slowness:

"Wa … watch out … fff … or the m … marks on … hhh … is back."

With tears in his eyes, Chambord sweeps the child into his arms and hugs him tight.

"Victor! It's a miracle! He spoke … he spoke!"

On the drive back to the office, Taillon and Lemaire are having a heated argument about Taillon's conviction that Pascal Pierre fed them a pack of falsehoods.

"You see conspiracies everywhere, Jacinthe. What else is new?"

"Open your eyes, Gilles. The guy's a fucking liar. He was hiding the truth about all kinds of stuff."

"And how do you know that?"

"I could see it in his eyes."

Uncharacteristically, Lemaire smacks the steering wheel with the palm of his hand.

"Listen to yourself, Jacinthe!"

"Let's have Vadnais do some more digging into your pastor's background. He'll turn up some prime shit, you wait and see."

"He's not *my* pastor! And we can't spare anyone at the moment. You know that better than anyone."

"Oh, get off your high horse! We're talking about a few hours."

Lemaire's cellphone rings. He listens, then says, "Okay. We'll be there in ten minutes."

"Who was that?"

"Vadnais. They've found Laila François's best friend."

"Mélanie Fleury?"

"Yes. She was visiting her grandmother in Trois-Rivières. She just got back. They've put her in the conference room."

The trailer door creaks on its hinges just as Lessard is about to open it.

He stops dead. His goofball son is standing there, opening and closing his mouth like a fish.

Martin is accompanied by a leather-clad young blond. She has Doc Martens on her feet and a multitude of rings through her ears and brows.

"What are you doing here, son?"

"Me and Mélodie came over for a cup of coffee. What happened to your arm?"

"Nothing. I fell in the shower. Where are you living, these days?"

"Uh ..."

"On the street?"

Martin looks down at the blond's boots.

"Kind of, yeah."

"That's fine, son," Lessard says, slipping five twenty-dollar bills into Martin's pocket. "You know you're welcome to come home, right? You can even bring Mélodie."

Though he's happy to see that Martin is safe and sound, he's still worried that the boy might get pulled into this deadly case.

"But if you do decide to come home, wait until next week, okay? There are some things I need to take care of, first."

Dumbstruck, Martin stares at his father, wondering if he's started drinking again. As for Lessard, he doesn't dare admit that his son is actually safer on the street than inside their own apartment.

"Did you know that Monsieur Antoine and I go back a long way?" the detective sergeant asks.

"Uh ... no."

"Tell him you're my son. That'll put a smile on his face. Well, gotta go. Call your mother. She's worried about you."

"You're not mad at me?"

"Mad? Not at all. So, we've got a deal, right? I'll see you back at home next week. Be sure to call before coming, okay? Oh, and while I've got you ... I left my new BlackBerry number on your voice mail, but take it down anyway."

"Whatever," Martin mutters as he keys the number into his phone, disappointed that his running away didn't produce the desired effect — pissing off his father.

"Wow," Mélodie says delightedly, as Lessard goes to the car, "your dad's totally awesome."

Dear stupid diary,

Grown-ups are mostly deaf and always dumb. When you try to tell them something, they almost never understand. I talked to Monsieur Antoine's friend. His name is Victor. He's a policeman.

I wanted to tell him about the Big Split. I used my chalkboard to spell out the name of Laila's friend, the guy who hit the boss with an axe, which stopped him from pounding my head against the wall, and also stopped him from sliding his fingers down my pants. I told Victor about the marks on the guy's back. I'm just guessing, but if Laila had known about the Big Split, if she'd seen the marks on the guy's back, maybe she wouldn't have been kidnapped. Anyhow, Victor's a nice policeman, but he isn't super quick. He looked at me like I was the dumb one. It took him a while to understand what I was talking about, but then it hit him like a lightning bolt, and his face got all excited, and he hurried away, saying thank you, Felix, thank you, thank you.

Mélanie Fleury blows her nose noisily.

The tears have been flowing without interruption since the interrogation began, leaving glistening trails on her cheeks.

In the surgical glow of the fluorescent lamps, she seems thin and pale in her ripped jeans and tight-fitting camisole.

Taillon sighs irritatedly. Compassion isn't her strong suit.

"Okay, Mélanie, let's see if I've got this straight. You haven't heard from Laila since the seventh. You were out of town, visiting your grandmother in Trois-Rivières. You got back this morning and tried to contact Laila, because you and she were supposed to do a webcam show this afternoon. But you haven't been able to reach her. Correct?"

The young woman nods and, with the back of her hand, wipes tears from the end of her nose.

"She never talked to you about Pascal Pierre, her stepfather. During your previous webcam sessions, she got weird messages from somebody calling himself 'Horny Priest.'" Taillon decides not to divulge that she's already questioned Steve Côté on the subject. "She was recently threatened by Razor, a scumbag who works for the Red Blood Spillers." Taillon pronounces the gang's name with disgust. "These threats were connected with an unpaid drug debt. Laila doesn't have a boyfriend, although there's a guy named ..." She looks through her notes. "… yeah, here we go, a guy named Cortiula. Laila likes him, but she's never had sex with him. Right?"

"Right."

Mélanie starts to cry again.

An evil gleam lights up Taillon's eyes.

She doesn't know Razor.

But whenever anyone mentions the Red Blood Spillers, her killer instinct comes alive.

"For what it's worth, Nadja," Lessard says as he walks to the car, "Antoine said the boy hadn't spoken since the attack. But Felix was hell-bent on writing down the guy's name."

"Does Chambord know this Cortiula guy?"

"No, he's never met him, and Laila never talked about him."

"But according to the boy, Cortiula is a friend of Laila's."

"Right. Felix also made a point of mentioning that Cortiula had numerous marks on his back. That may be useful for identification."

"And Cortiula killed a pimp who was attacking the child?"

"Yes. Felix was attacked while turning tricks in a park. From what I gathered, the guy was Felix's pimp and his client at the same time. He was in the midst of assaulting the boy when he was killed by an axe blow to the back of the head. Felix had always been unable to identify the killer, or even to speak, until today."

"He never spoke after the killing?"

"Never. With the information I've just given you, you should be able to track down the file. From what Antoine told me, the murder hasn't been solved. He also said that Felix was suffering from post-traumatic stress disorder, and that, according to the doctors, his memories might return at any time. I guess that's what happened just now."

"If I'm hearing you right, Felix thinks Cortiula is behind Laila's kidnapping. And because of the weapon that was used to kill the pimp, you believe Cortiula may have had something to do with the murders on Bessborough Avenue."

"Don't forget, Nadja, the Cooks were killed with an axe."

"And Cortiula's somehow mixed up in the abduction of his own friend?"

"You know as well as I do that in a lot of kidnapping cases, the victim is acquainted with the aggressor."

"I get it, but where does the pedophile ring fit into all this? What's the link with Sandoval and Applebaum?"

"Maybe they had some connection with the pimp who was murdered. Who knows? What did you find out about the website?"

"It's a file-sharing site for child pornography. It looks like there are about thirty members. It's going to take a little time to track down the individuals hiding behind the IP addresses. Everything is encrypted. But the Digital Security guy says it's doable."

"Which means, in the short term, that information won't be available to us."

"Right. But judging from how quickly he was able to crack the website, we won't have to wait for weeks."

"Tell the expert to get in touch with Marchand. This is directly related to his investigation. You and I need to keep a low profile, but Marchand can put everything he's got into the case. Ask him to keep us in the loop. And give him the names of Cortiula, Wan, and Dorion. Also the name of the pimp, when you get it. Have Marchand get in touch if he discovers that they're in the pedophile ring."

"Okay, but there's something we haven't figured out, Victor. Where does Dorion fit into all this? And what's with the marks on the guy's back?"

Fernandez's questions whirl through Lessard's synapses, twisting his neurons into knots and making his head spin.

"Honestly," he admits, "I don't know if Felix's account is reliable. But get me Cortiula's address. I want to question him as soon as possible. In the meantime, I'm going to Chinatown to have a talk with Chan ... Lok ..."

Lessard has written the name in his notebook, but, with only one functional hand, he'd rather not struggle to pull it out.

"Wan, Victor. Chan Lok Wan. Okay. I'll get back to you about Cortiula as soon as I can."

. . .

Chinatown

A world within a world. A city within the city.

With its origins historically linked to the construction of the Canadian Pacific Railway — a project that employed many Asian labourers — Montreal's Chinatown was first populated by Cantonese migrants from British Columbia and newcomers from southern China, starting in 1860. It's an eclectic, busy district in which the quest for parking is an adventure in itself.

To avoid having to hunt for a spot, Lessard parks the car on Saint-Antoine Street, near Steve's Music Store and the editorial offices of *La Presse*. Cutting through an alley near the Old Brewery Mission, he hands out a few cigarettes to the homeless men who are waiting for a bowl of soup, and fires one up for himself.

The light is red as he crosses Viger Avenue, weaving between cars whose progress has slowed to a crawl because of the interminable paving work around the convention centre. He turns left onto Saint-Laurent Boulevard and enters Chinatown through one of the two ceremonial gates donated by the Chinese government to the city of Montreal — a sort of Arc de Triomphe topped by a pagoda-style roof, decorated with Chinese lettering.

Lessard cuts across the parking lot of the Chinese Hospital.

A few steps to his left, he sees a restaurant where he and the kids sometimes go for Sunday dim sum, a brunch-style meal featuring Cantonese dishes steamed in bamboo containers. The place is usually packed, with waitresses slaloming among the crowded tables, pushing food trolleys.

Asian dining at its best, only fifteen minutes from home.

The office of CLW Solutions is located at the corner of De Bullion and De la Gauchetière Streets, next to a white ceramic-fronted building with shuttered windows that stands out among the surrounding structures.

The home of Chan Lok Wan's company has a brick façade, but it's just as unsightly as its neighbour — an ill-maintained building with a portcullis in the middle of its flaking wall.

Lessard scans the row of buzzers at the entrance and presses one marked by a simple label: CLW.

Several seconds go by. There's no response.

The detective sergeant presses again, repeatedly.

Suddenly, he hears a mechanical growl over his head. A surveillance camera that he hadn't noticed turns in his direction.

Strange. And not exactly welcoming.

Click.

The metal grate slides open without a sound.

Lessard advances toward the front door, which swings partially open before he reaches it.

He steps into a narrow space in which a woman is seated at a desk. In front of her is a computer so old that Lessard wonders whether it's actually functional. Hardly what one would expect in a firm that specializes in high technology. Behind the woman is a metal door with a combination lock.

Apart from a telephone on the desk, there are no papers, no file cabinet, no decorations.

Not a very homey environment.

The woman is a rebel without a clue — a redhead who should have figured out by now that she's too old to be dressing up like a goth. Lessard gives her his sweetest smile.

"I'd like to see Mr. Wan."

"About what?"

"It's personal."

"I'm sorry, Mr. Wan is in a meeting. If you leave your number, he'll call you back to make an appointment."

"Let me just show you my card."

He pulls out his badge and holds it in front of her.

"Is there a problem, Detective?"

"You tell me. Are you going to get Mr. Wan?"

"Just a minute."

The woman touches the keys on the combination lock and opens the door just wide enough to let her aging body slip through, then closes it quickly behind her.

A few moments later, Chan Lok Wan appears. He's an immense man with hard features.

"My name is Victor Lessard. I'm a detective with the Montreal Police."

"Yes?"

"I'd like to ask you a few questions concerning an investigation in progress."

Wan says nothing. The two men gaze at each other. Lessard is the first to lower his eyes.

"To begin with, can you confirm that this is the office of CLW Solutions?"

"It is."

"What exactly does your company do?"

"We provide consulting services in digital document management."

"Which means?"

"We develop software that helps our customers manage their archives."

"And who are your customers, mainly?"

"Businesses."

"In which sector?"

"In all sectors."

This is a sham. You're lying to my face and we both know it.

The hostility between the two men is palpable. The air is thick with tension.

"We found your address in the cellphone of a man who was involved in a murder and an attempted murder."

"Is that so? What's his name?"

"We haven't identified him yet. Do you have any idea who he might be?"

"Could be anyone. Is it a crime to have your address in a criminal's phone?"

"Not when you haven't done anything wrong."

"I haven't done anything wrong."

"Do you know a man named Aldéric Dorion?"

"No."

The answer comes out too fast, before Wan can think about it, and the sharp tone betrays what he's really feeling: surprise.

You're lying.

Lessard doesn't let himself be thrown off by Wan's attitude. He keeps asking questions.

"What about Laila François?"

"Don't know her."

"But you must have heard of her — the girl who was kidnapped. The story's been all over the news for the past few days."

"I never watch TV."

Lessard also mentions the name that Felix wrote on his chalkboard. Wan's eyes widen, but once again, he denies any knowledge.

"You're not being very co-operative, Mr. Wan."

"Oh, no?"

"May I have a look around your office?" Lessard asks, looking at the metal door.

"Do you have a warrant?"

The tension rises another notch.

"I can get one within the hour."

"That would surprise me. Come back when you have one."

"Are you hiding something, Mr. Wan?"

"Goodbye, Mr. Lessard."

The detective sergeant paces back and forth in the filthy alley that runs behind the CLW Solutions office. The area is littered with pieces of broken furniture, discarded syringes, lipstick-stained cigarette butts, and eviscerated garbage bags from which noxious fumes rise in revolting billows.

The rain creates a pattern of widening circles on the yellowish puddles nearby.

Leaning against a white van parked in the alley, Lessard lights a cigarette.

He's furious.

He knows that Chan Lok Wan is hiding something behind the combination lock on that metal door, but there's nothing Lessard can do without a warrant. And this isn't an ideal situation in which to get one.

For starters, his investigation has no official police status. But even if he managed to get around that problem by having Fernandez apply for the warrant, the lack of reasonable grounds would sink the application.

Frustrated, he punches Fernandez's number into his phone.

"Wan's refusing to collaborate. He's hiding something."

"Should we seek a warrant?"

"That crossed my mind, but we've got no evidence. The judge would want an explanation. If you admitted that the investigation was being led by a cop who's wanted by the Montreal Police, the application would be thrown out."

"Damn. You're right."

"Do you have Cortiula's address and phone number?"

Fernandez gives them to him.

"I also found the case file you asked for on the murdered pimp. It dates back to last year."

"And?"

"Luc Régimbald, fifty-four, a known pimp who specialized in underage boys. One blow to the head. Massive hemorrhaging. The murder weapon was probably a small axe. There were no witnesses, apart from Felix, who was unable to identify the killer. The psychological evaluation basically confirmed what you heard from Chambord: Felix's subconscious had suppressed the incident, insulating him from the trauma. The detective team considered hypnosis, but in the best interests of the boy, they decided to let time do its work."

"Nice work, Nadja. Make sure to pass along Régimbald's name to Marchand, just in case. Anything else?"

"No ... oh, yes. The killing happened in a park in Rosemont."

"Wait ... Cortiula lives in the Rosemont area, doesn't he?"

"That's right."

"Thanks, Nadja."

Lessard hangs up and dials Cortiula's number.

When the call goes to voice mail, he gets in the car and drives to the address on Masson Street that he wrote down under the name in his notebook:

David Cortiula.

"Has Lessard been in touch with you, Fernandez?"

Wearing a dark expression, Commander Tanguay is leaning against Fernandez's desk. Although a casual observer might think that Fernandez is entirely composed, she's finding it difficult to swallow.

Did Tanguay overhear her conversation?

"Me? Of course not, sir. Why do you ask?"

"I was under the impression that you and Lessard ..."

"That we what?" she asks when he doesn't finish.

"I ... you do realize that if you help him, even just incidentally, there will be repercussions. You understand that, don't you, Fernandez?"

"What are you insinuating?" Fernandez demands in an aggressive tone. "Are you accusing me of collaborating with Lessard behind your back?"

"Calm down, Nadja. Please. I just wanted to be sure we're on the same wavelength."

"I don't know what you're after, Commander, but the moment I hear from Lessard, you'll be the first to know."

"I'm counting on it, Fernandez. I'm counting on it."

She holds her breath until Tanguay goes around the corner at the end of the hallway. Then she puts her head in her hands.

Another few seconds' pressure, and she would have spilled her guts.

33

David Cortiula lives in an eighteen-unit apartment building on Rosemont Boulevard at the corner of Charlemagne Avenue.

Lessard presses the buzzer for the apartment. When no one answers, he starts pushing other buzzers, until a low hum signals that one of the other tenants — no doubt irritated by his repeated buzzing — has unlocked the front door remotely.

He goes up the stairs four at a time.

On the third-floor landing, he sees a woman in a nightgown, braless, heavily made up.

"Are you the one who buzzed, honey?"

"Yes," Lessard says, without stopping. "Police. Go back in your apartment, ma'am."

Cortiula's place is on the top floor.

Lessard bangs on the door. He hears a scraping noise and presses his ear to the wood. Something's moving inside. Without hesitating, he unholsters his gun and kicks the door hard.

The bolt is sturdier than he expected. It gives way on the second kick.

With his Glock drawn and his flashlight between his teeth, the detective sergeant sweeps the light beam across the darkened room.

He starts to breathe again when the beam strikes a parrot. Perched on its bar, the bird is pecking at a metal surface with its beak, producing the scraping noise that prompted Lessard to break down the door.

"Helloooo, Daaaavid," the parrot says. "Daaaavid!"

Unless Lessard is mistaken, the bird that retreats along its perch as he approaches is an African grey parrot. A few months ago, he helped his daughter Charlotte put together an oral presentation on the subject. One particular detail he recalls is that the species is known for its longevity. Indeed, legend has it that Charlie, the African grey that belonged to Sir Winston Churchill, is still alive. Charlie, who was taught to curse by the late British prime minister ("Fuck the Nazis!") is said to have reached the venerable age of 105.

The apartment is really just an ill-lit bedroom. There's a mattress on the floor. Beside the mattress, books and papers lie in a pile on a table, alongside a microwave oven. Lessard looks around the room slowly, taking in the cracked walls and patches of mould in the corners. Colourful clothes lie heaped on the floor. Next to the clothes are two milk cartons, from which an acrid, vinegary smell is rising. To his right, Lessard sees a television set sitting on a mini-fridge. On the balcony in the back, there's a rusty barbecue that Cortiula must use all year round. Opening what he thinks is a closet, the detective sergeant finds a shower, as well as a toilet that one would probably have to be a contortionist to sit on, given the narrowness of the space.

Lessard shakes his head. Desolation.

His attention is immediately caught by some photographs pinned to the wall.

Several of the shots are close-ups of a fair-haired young man, his eyes closed, his mouth open in an expression of beatific bliss. Looking over the photos, Lessard realizes instantly that they're of David Cortiula, at different stages of his life, singing in a choir.

Lessard examines the photographic mural. Cortiula has assembled it meticulously, spacing the shots at regular intervals with a rigour that seems almost maniacal, especially if the slovenly state of the bedroom can be taken as a reliable indicator of his usual mental organization.

Is Lessard altogether surprised when, looking at a group photo, he spots two faces that have been seared into his memory?

As soon as he realized, moments ago, that Cortiula sang in a choir, there was a corner of Lessard's mind that anticipated what he's now seeing: Sandoval's ruddy face and, to his left, the pasty features of

Mayor Applebaum, both singing in the choir. In the photo, Cortulia is standing to Sandoval's right, separated from him by a blond, curly-haired chorister.

Dressed in black, Sandoval, Applebaum, and Cortiula are gazing intently at their sheet music.

Though he isn't entirely taken aback by the photograph's revelation of a link between Cortiula and the two pedophiles, the detective sergeant is truly caught off guard — he's staggered, in fact — when he comes to another photograph, an older one, in black and white.

In it, standing in the midst of a group of choristers, David Cortiula, aged about ten, is singing beside an Asian boy of roughly the same age.

Cortiula is holding a music score on which the eyes of both boys are fixed.

The intervening years have hardened Chan Lok Wan's features, but his appearance hasn't changed all that much.

The same can't be said of the choir director, who looks considerably younger in this faded photo than in the one Lessard stole from the late Mayor Applebaum's house.

Even so, Aldéric Dorion is easily recognizable.

Not only do the two missing men, Cortiula and Dorion, know each other, but they've both spent time in the company of the three others.

For a moment, Lessard stands there in a blank-eyed daze, pondering the wide range of possibilities that he must now contend with.

"It's your fault, Vincenzo! You're the one who got him into this! I hate you!"

Moreno doesn't flinch as the young woman beats her fists against his chest until she finally breaks down and weeps in his arms.

Pasquale's wife, Maria, is right.

Vincenzo and Pasquale Moreno followed in the footsteps of their father Nico, once a lieutenant to the godfather of the Montreal mafia. Nico was eliminated in a purge that heralded a change of leadership.

After Nico's death, the two brothers went abroad for a few years to wait out the storm. When they got back, they kept their former contacts, but shifted their focus to security work. Apart from their legal activities, the Moreno brothers and their employees now provide a range of clandestine services — including witness intimidation, industrial espionage, and contract killing — while avoiding the internecine warfare that sometimes rocks the local underworld. They are, in short, an elite private militia. They offer their expertise to individuals and anonymous organizations that are ready to use any means necessary to achieve their ends, and can pay the stratospheric fees that such expertise commands.

A few weeks ago, on his son's fifth birthday, Pasquale told Vincenzo that he wanted to get out of the business. He was ready to go straight.

Vincenzo persuaded him to work on one last case before packing it in. Despite his reluctance, Pasquale said yes, only because he wanted to make his brother happy. Now he's dead.

"I promise you, Maria, I'll get revenge," Vincenzo says, his voice quavering.

"What's wrong, Mama?" a voice asks. It's Sofia, Pasquale's eldest daughter. Vincenzo is her godfather.

He closes his eyes, wanting the nightmare to end.

After the initial astonishment has passed, Lessard pockets the photo of Cortiula singing with Sandoval and Applebaum, as well as the picture that shows Cortiula in a choir with Chan Lok Wan, under Dorion's direction. The detective sergeant's mind is made up: he'll go back and confront Wan as soon as he's done here.

Feverishly, he starts looking through the papers and books stacked on the table.

Moving quickly, his head teeming with questions that he doesn't have time to dwell on, he sets aside a pile of musical scores and CDs whose jacket covers suggest that they're recordings of Gregorian chant.

He wasn't too surprised to find books on exorcism in Aldéric Dorion's apartment. But he's more troubled when his search of

Cortiula's papers turns up a thick file folder full of newspaper clippings about the devil.

Simple coincidence?

With the intense concentration of an archaeologist poring over ancient texts, Lessard starts to read the top clipping from the pile:

The Canadian Daily
Monday, November 25th, 1892

PARRICIDE ON SHERBROOKE STREET: THE DEVIL'S WORK?
by Flavien Vallerand

A ten-year-old boy was found Saturday in his family's apartment on Sherbrooke Street East. Covered in blood, the boy was holding a kitchen knife in his hand.

Neighbours responding to strange noises and suspicious smells broke down the door and discovered the boy's lifeless parents.

Robert and Lucille Petit, aged 32 and 28 respectively, were lying in a pool of their own blood. According to an autopsy report, they had been dead for several days when the neighbours made the macabre discovery.

One particularly gruesome fact emerging from the investigation is that the mother's heart had been cut out of her chest and boiled in a pot on the stove.

Behind Lessard, the parrot stirs and makes a cooing noise, followed by a call that sounds like an ambulance siren, but Lessard, absorbed in the morbid article, reads on:

While investigators are still struggling to understand his motives, the youngster appears to have confessed to police officers that he took his parents' lives.

A friend of the mother's, requesting anonymity, informed this newspaper that the boy had changed in recent months. He had grown violent and unpredictable, and was given to shouting abuse at his parents.

This same friend declares that she was present when the boy propelled objects through the air without touching them. She remarks that a priest had advised the parents to have their son exorcised, but, in their terror, they waited too long.

Because of the noise the parrot is making, Lessard doesn't hear any footsteps. But he definitely feels the cold metal of a gun barrel pressed to the back of his neck, making him jump.

"Well, well, Victor Lessard. Long time no see."

That voice ... he'd know it anywhere.

With Vincenzo Moreno stroking her hair, Maria finally falls asleep, clutching a frame that contains a recent photo of Pasquale and the children.

Moreno closes the bedroom door gently and descends the stairs without a sound. One of his sisters, Bianca, is in the basement, looking after the kids.

He retrieves his motorcycle helmet and jacket from the dining-room table and checks his messages. The SIV agent has sent him another text instructing him to search the apartment of the man they've been seeking in vain for days: David Cortiula. The SIV agent notes that no one has been watching Cortiula's apartment. They can't afford to let him get away.

Damn it! Vincenzo has already gone over every inch of the place without finding anything useful. What else can he do?

This contract was supposed to restore the family's finances after several difficult years. It was meant to be a simple surveillance operation, not to cost his brother his life.

He's haunted by the vision of Pasquale's corpse.

His employer can make all the demands he likes. As of now, every ounce of Vincenzo's energy will be devoted to a single purpose: putting Victor Lessard in the grave.

Jacinthe Taillon disarms the detective sergeant.

Though she's no longer aiming her gun at him, she's still holding it, her index finger poised over the trigger. Her eyes are gleaming with an unstable mix of disgust and hate.

Taillon wanted to go after Razor, but Gilles Lemaire insisted that she track down Cortiula. She relented when Lemaire threatened to take the matter to their superior officer. The last person she expected to find in Cortiula's apartment was Victor Lessard.

Taillon and the detective sergeant are now facing each other for the first time since Lessard was removed from the Major Crimes Unit. He starts off by trying to calm things down, suggesting to his ex-partner that they behave like adults and put an end to their hostilities. Taillon's response is dead silence, followed by a torrent of vicious insults. She still regards Lessard as her enemy. Though she doesn't mention it directly, his responsibility for the deaths of Picard and Gosselin is the unspoken source of all her bitter fury.

Lessard briefly absorbs the stream of invective without response, but his patience soon runs out.

"Fuck you, Jacinthe! Don't you think I've paid enough for what happened? I took the fall for everyone, but you and I both know I wasn't the only one to blame!"

The implication that Taillon bears some of the responsibility throws her into a rage. She rushes at him, eyes bulging, and waves her pistol in his face.

"You fucking slimeball! How dare you?!"

Lessard closes his eyes and sees Raymond walking on a wide, empty beach, as the sun sets into the ocean. The boy is smiling, radiant, unmarked by any trace of his wounds or the deathly greenish circles under his eyes.

Raymond holds out his arms, beckoning his brother to join him.

Lessard is suddenly brimming with a sense of fulfillment that he hasn't felt in a long time.

It's time to end this. He's ready.

Deliverance.

"Go on, Taillon. Do it."

How long do his eyes remain closed?

He doesn't know. When he opens them again, Taillon is weeping. Lessard pinches himself.

He never thought he'd live to see the day when she displayed the slightest emotion.

Her big fingers quickly wipe away her tears.

Sitting on the table, whose legs are precariously bent under her weight, Taillon puts her gun down on the microwave, where it's still within reach. For the moment, at least, she isn't a direct threat.

Lessard is sprawled on the mattress.

"Okay," she says, "let's cut the crap. You're in trouble. The whole police force is searching high and low for you. What are you doing here?"

The detective sergeant knows that he has nothing to gain from playing games with Taillon, who would be only too pleased to turn him in, thus putting an end to his investigation. He also knows that she may steal all the leads he's gathered so far. But at this point, he doesn't have a choice. He needs to earn her trust and hope that after an exchange of information, she'll be willing to let him go.

So he summarizes the progress he's made, starting with the Cooks' deaths and ending up here, in David Cortiula's apartment. Taillon is in a foul mood as his account begins, but she listens with increasing interest as Lessard tells his story. Even so, the detective sergeant isn't quite as forthright as he seems. He makes no mention of the photographs he found a few minutes ago, or of Chan Lok Wan.

Those details may have exchange value if Taillon becomes intransigent and decides to put obstacles in his path.

"Okay, so if I'm understanding you correctly, the investigation started out with a domestic murder-suicide. You followed the trail to Sherbrooke, where you believe you stumbled on a pedophile ring."

"That's right. Sandoval and the late mayor Applebaum."

"And somehow, mixed up in the killings and the pedophile ring, there's this priest, whom you've identified as Aldéric Dorion."

"I haven't yet established whether Dorion is the priest who was seen in the Cooks' backyard, but he did know the pedophiles. That much I'm sure of."

"This same Dorion was also involved in a youth support group with Laila François, is that right?"

"Yes. Antoine Chambord confirmed as much."

"Tell me again how that led you to Cortiula ..."

"Chambord's adopted son, Felix, gave me Cortiula's name. He said that Cortiula is a friend of Laila's, that his back is covered with scars, and that Laila should have stayed away from him. Felix also said that Cortiula killed a man with an axe. Since the Cooks were murdered with an axe ..."

Taillon's jaw works as she thinks.

"You believe this pedophile ring was behind the attempt to kill you at Central Station?"

Lessard nods.

"They were also behind the second murder attempt, at the rest stop," he says.

"Okay. So, if I follow your logic, Laila François was kidnapped by this network."

The detective sergeant hasn't forgotten what Antoine Chambord said to him about Laila being too physically mature to interest pedophiles, but he remains convinced that the girl's disappearance has some connection with the ring that Sandoval and Applebaum were part of.

"Yes, that's what I believe."

"A pedophile ring," Taillon murmurs, her gaze vacant. "So what's the link between the two guys in Sherbrooke, your priest, and Cortiula? They're all pedophiles?"

And they all sang in a choir, Lessard wants to add, though he realizes how ridiculous that would sound.

"I'm not sure yet. But I *am* sure they knew each other."

Taillon lapses into a near-catatonic silence.

Lessard knows she's weighing the pros and cons before deciding whether to tell him what she's come up with so far.

"This is where our investigations overlap, Jacinthe." He takes a chance: "How did you get Cortiula's name?"

His ex-partner looks at him. But what does she see?

A nightmarish scene seems to be playing out before her dilated pupils.

Then, suddenly, she snaps back to reality.

"Why the hell should I tell you?"

She stares intently at the wall behind Lessard, as though expecting her next words to appear there.

A yellow streak weaves among the cars and the sprays of water on the Ville-Marie Expressway.

Mounted on his Ducati 749, Vincenzo Moreno is on his way to David Cortiula's apartment.

Noah had to use all his powers of persuasion to make Vincenzo concentrate on the job at hand. Indeed, he had to promise a substantial raise to get Vincenzo to postpone his vendetta against Victor Lessard.

Moreno's cellphone buzzes against his thigh several times while he's on the road.

Someone is very anxious to talk to him.

He parks his motocycle in front of Cortiula's building and removes his helmet. When he looks at his phone, he sees that Civardi, the man he posted to watch the building on De la Gauchetière Street, has called three times.

He calls back.

"What is it, Marco?"

"Cortiula showed up."

"Is he still there?"

"No, he came back out almost right away. I'm following him now."

"In the car?"

"No, on foot. He's walking up Saint-Laurent Boulevard."

"Whatever you do, don't lose him. I'm on my way."

Eagerly, Moreno leaves a message on the SIV agent's voice mail.

"It's Vincenzo, *Padre*. Call me. We've found Cortiula."

Amidst a roar of pistons and cylinders, he steers the motorcycle into the street without a glance at the window of Cortiula's apartment, where, a second earlier, Lessard's face was clearly visible in the frame.

"I questioned Laila's best friend, Mélanie Fleury," Taillon finally says to Lessard. "She told me about Cortiula. She said Laila's been trying to seduce him for a while now, but he always refuses."

"Is he gay?" Lessard asks.

"Apparently not. Which is why your pedophile theory baffles me. If Cortiula wanted to have sex with Laila François, she was open to it. She gave him lots of opportunities."

"But that might not have been what interested him," Lessard says. "Being a pedophile, he wasn't attracted to her."

"In that case, why get involved in her kidnapping?"

"Maybe he had particular sexual tastes. Tastes he couldn't satisfy if she was a willing participant."

"Look, the chick does webcam porn. If Cortiula had kinky fantasies, I'm sure she would have accommodated him. Besides, we both know that pedophiles are drawn to kids who are prepubescent or just starting puberty. Laila François doesn't fit the profile."

"You're the second person who's said that to me today. The only thing I know for sure is that Sandoval and Applebaum were pedophiles, and they belonged to a ring. Following up on that fact led me to Dorion, then to Cortiula. How are those two involved? Are they mixed up in the pedophile ring? If so, how? At the moment, I don't know. What I do know is that they both had contact with the girl you're trying to find, and then she was kidnapped."

"I'm not ruling out the possibility that Cortiula or Dorion had a hand in Laila's abduction," Taillon says, "but I get the feeling something else is going on."

"Have you got suspects?" the detective sergeant asks.

Taillon looks at Lessard, unsure of where she wants the discussion to go from here.

"Come on, Jacinthe! You can't hold back now."

Taillon sighs. "Actually, I have two. The first is Steve Côté, a low-level gang member who works for Laila's pimp. He was stalking Laila online."

"But you don't believe he kidnapped her," Lessard says, observing Taillon's body language.

"No, I think Côté's just in love with her — in his own way."

"Who's the second suspect?"

"Laila's stepfather, Pascal Pierre. He's a pastor, a charismatic preacher. One of those touched-by-God types. I'm pretty sure he abused Laila during her childhood. She's been off his radar for a couple of years. I'm thinking she ran away, and now he's tracked her down."

"A pastor? Does he wear a cassock?"

"I know what you're thinking, but no. His ministry is a closed community with all the hallmarks of a religious cult. It's called the Solar Passage."

"Kind of like the group that Moïse Thériault led in the eighties?"

"Something like that."

On the table, beside her gun, Taillon's phone begins to skitter.

"What's up, Gilles? ... Are you sure? Is it solid? ... No, bring him in. I'm on my way ... Yeah. Put him in isolation. No contact with anyone, not even his lawyer, got it?"

She looks at Lessard.

"Was that Lemaire?" he asks.

"Yes. We have a statement from someone in the cult, confirming our suspicions. Laila was abused by her stepfather before she ran away. The witness also confirms that Pascal Pierre has been in Montreal for the last two months, trying to find her."

"Sounds like a real piece of work."

"Oh, yeah, but we've got him by the balls. The cult owns a white van."

Lessard remembers skimming the case report on his BlackBerry. At the time, he didn't pay much attention to the vehicle used in the abduction. So why does an alarm bell go off in his head when he hears Taillon mention the van?

"That was the vehicle used in the kidnapping? A white van?"

"Yes. Why?"

For an instant, he feels his mind gripped by contractions, struggling to give birth to something. But within seconds, the impression fades away. The thought is stillborn.

"No," he says pensively, "it's nothing. I was just asking."

Lessard's head is spinning. He's queasy, assailed by too many questions.

"You're going to interrogate the stepfather?" he asks.

"That's right. Gilles is on his way to arrest him."

Taillon punches a number into her phone.

"Put me through to Tanguay."

This is the moment Lessard has been dreading since Taillon showed up. This is where she knocks him out of the game for good.

"Jacinthe, don't do this."

The arrogant expression has returned to Taillon's fleshy features.

"Save your breath."

"Let me keep following up my leads," he says.

Taillon shakes her head.

"Wait!" he pleads. "Think for a minute. This'll help you as much as it helps me. Unless I'm totally wrong, there's a link between our two cases. We haven't figured out what it is, but you're as convinced as I am that it exists. I can see it in your eyes."

"You're wasting your time, Lessard."

"Jacinthe," he says, speaking fast, "we're up against people who'll do whatever it takes to get what they want. Let me try to locate Dorion and Cortiula and find out if they're mixed up in either of the two cases. If it turns out that you're mistaken about Pascal Pierre — if it turns out he didn't kidnap his stepdaughter — maybe I'll come up with something useful."

"And if you do, how can I be sure you'll share the information? I know you, Lessard. You're a loose cannon."

"You're going to have to trust me for once, Jacinthe."

"Last time I trusted you, Picard and Gosselin paid for it with their lives."

"They were my friends, too!"

Lessard looks his ex-partner in the eye. She gazes at him searchingly, as though trying to see into the depths of his soul.

Tanguay's voice can be heard at the other end of the line.

"Just a second, Commander," Taillon says.

She puts her hand over the mouthpiece. She's clearly wavering.

"We're at opposite ends of the tunnel, Jacinthe. If we both keep moving forward, we're bound to meet up."

Lessard holds Taillon's gaze, knowing his fate is in her hands. His arm is tormenting him. He pops two pills and washes them down with saliva.

Taillon speaks into her phone:

"Commander? Sorry to keep you waiting. I'm just calling to find out if you have anything new on the Laila François case."

As Taillon wraps up her conversation with Tanguay, she hands Lessard his pistol.

He closes his eyes with relief.

The image of a white van flashes through his mind.

At the corner of 6th Avenue and Masson Street, Vincenzo meets the SIV agent on the sidewalk facing the Church of the Holy Spirit. The two men waste no time on niceties.

"He stopped off at Schwartz's for a smoked meat sandwich. Then he took the metro and a bus to come up here. I've been tailing him in shifts with my watcher from De la Gauchetière Street. He hasn't noticed anything."

"Where is he now?"

"Inside."

"We can't lose him this time, Vincenzo."

"We won't, *Padre*. I have two men in position. With me here, we've got every exit covered."

"Good. No one is to move until I give the signal."

"Understood, *Padre*."

The SIV agent hurries toward one of the three main doors.

The church's Gothic tower rises into the cloud-filled sky, from which a dismal rain continues to pour down on Montreal.

As he makes his way back to CLW Solutions, Lessard isn't quite sure what he's doing anymore.

His encounter with Jacinthe Taillon has shaken him. Confused thoughts are fluttering through his head like moths, going in all directions at once. He can't quite grasp the solid branches of fact on which they occasionally alight.

Richard Sandoval. Jean-Guy Applebaum.

Aldéric Dorion. Chan Lok Wan. David Cortiula.

What connects these men?

For now, the only common denominator that Lessard can point to is the fact that they were all members of a choir at one point or another.

The photo of Sandoval and Applebaum with Dorion in Sherbrooke confirms as much. So does the second photo, taken at least twenty years ago, of Wan and Cortiula with Dorion.

Is Dorion the link — the fulcrum on which all this hinges?

What else does Lessard know?

Sandoval and Applebaum were pedophiles, rapists, kidnappers, and murderers. There's no doubt on that score. The images of Sandrine Pedneault-King haunting his memory are indisputable proof.

The two men were also part of an organized ring of pedophiles.

What about the three others?

For the moment, Lessard is assuming that they were part of the ring, or at least connected to it.

But were they?

He doesn't know. He just doesn't know anymore.

As Taillon and Chambord both pointed out, the kidnapping of Laila François doesn't fit with the expected pattern. She isn't a natural target for pedophiles.

He wishes the voices in his head would shut up!

He runs his fingers over his rough stubble, then touches the bags beneath his eyes. Sleep deprivation is starting to take its toll. Fatigue is numbing him, his mind is getting foggy, and the gaps in his memory are turning into chasms.

What about John Cook and his wife? How do they fit into all this?

Apart from the possible presence of a priest in their backyard the night they were killed — a priest Lessard assumes was Dorion, though he can't confirm it — he has nothing to connect the Cooks with the others.

He makes a mental note: have Fernandez find out whether John Cook sang in a choir. That's the only proven link between the Sherbrooke rapists, Dorion, Wan, and Cortiula.

Okay. What else?

David Cortiula. Who is he?

And what should Lessard make of the books and documents relating to exorcism that he found in Cortiula's apartment, as well as in Dorion's?

Is he dealing with pedophiles? A religious order trying to stifle a sex scandal? Satanists? None of the above? All of the above? Where's the truth in all this?

Dorion and Cortiula are nowhere to be found. The only remaining person he can focus on is Chan Lok Wan.

Lessard's stomach rumbles. He's hungry.

That, at least, is a fact.

He finds a parking space on De Bullion Street, a short distance north of the CLW Solutions office. He tries to avoid puddles as he walks, but water still seeps into his running shoes. It's as he's lighting a cigarette that — for no reason he can fathom — the realization hits him.

The nebulous image that had previously eluded him now appears clearly before his eyes.

Unless he's going senile, he spotted a white van a few hours ago. It was in the alley behind the building that houses Chan Lok Wan's office.

Out of breath, he arrives in the alley. The van hasn't moved.

After two failed attempts, he gets through to Fernandez.

"What kind of vehicle are we looking for in connection with the kidnapping of Laila François?"

"A white van."

"I'm leaning against a white van right now, in the alley behind Chan Lok Wan's building."

"Holy shit ..."

Lessard gives her the licence plate number.

"Is that number registered to CLW Solutions or to Wan personally?"

"Hang on. I'll run it through the system."

Lessard only has to wait a minute, but it's an interminable minute, during which the only sound he hears is the rapid-fire clicking of computer keys as Fernandez executes the search.

"It's registered to CLW Solutions," she says. "But that doesn't mean the van you just found is the same one that was seen on the night of the abduction."

Silence.

"What are you planning to do ...? Victor? Victor?"

34

In the storage area next to the interrogation room in which Pascal Pierre is being held, Gilles Lemaire and Jacinthe Taillon are in the midst of a discussion. A thick vein is standing out on Lemaire's forehead.

"Let me handle this, Gilles."

"What are you going to do?"

"What do you think? I'm gonna rough him up a little."

"Jacinthe! That's the last thing we need right now. His lawyer will be here soon."

"Listen, partner. Laila François may be dying somewhere. Vadnais's report and the witness account we've got are rock-solid."

"Exactly! We already have him. There's no reason to do something reckless."

"Oh, don't be such a fucking wimp. We need results. Now."

Lemaire looks at his shoes.

"I'm going for a walk. I'll be back in five minutes. But I'm warning you, Jacinthe, if this goes sideways, you're on your own. I won't be able to help you."

Taillon heads for the interrogation room door.

"And Jacinthe ... don't forget to turn off the camera."

Taillon bursts into the room. Looking wary, Pascal Pierre holds her gaze. Every trace of civility and false goodwill has vanished from his expression. Unobtrusively, Taillon turns off the video feed.

"How about we skip the unpleasantness? Just tell me where she is."

"I know my rights. I'm not saying a thing without my lawyer present."

"You watch too much TV, buddy. I'm allowed to keep asking questions until your lawyer gets here. That's true even if you invoke your right to silence."

"It makes no difference. I have nothing to say."

"Okay. If that's how you want to play it, fine by me." She approaches until their faces are centimetres apart. "I have a file an inch thick that sets out in detail the sexual abuses you inflicted on Laila François. She was eight years old the first time you touched her, you piece of shit."

Pascal Pierre rolls his eyes and shakes his head.

"Ridiculous. I never touched Laila, or any other children."

"That's not what some members of your congregation are saying."

"Which members?" he demands arrogantly. "I challenge you to find a single person in my community who's ready to back up your claims."

"Maybe not your present members. That's understandable — they're afraid of you, afraid of your revenge. But what about past members? A few of them may be ready to break their silence and tell the world what a monster you are."

"Who?" A ripple of doubt crosses the pastor's features. "Someone is obviously trying to sully my reputation."

"Not so cocky anymore, huh, buddy? I have enough to put you away for a long time. Sexual assault on a minor, indecent acts, aggravated assault — the list goes on."

"You're bluffing."

"Oh, yeah? Does the name Olga Svensson ring a bell? Do you think maybe she knows enough to fuck you over?"

The pastor's eyes widen with fear. He's seized by a sudden coughing fit.

Taillon grabs him by the throat and squeezes. The pain is so great that Pascal Pierre can't even struggle.

"Where's Laila? Talk!"

Taillon is beside herself. There are flecks of spittle at the corners of her mouth.

"I ... stop ..."

"Where is she?!"

Lemaire, whom Taillon didn't hear arriving, has to struggle with both hands to break her grip.

"Let him go, Jacinthe! You're going to kill him!"

The barrel of the Glock is hovering two metres from Chan Lok Wan's face.

Lessard didn't waste his breath negotiating.

He went through the same rigmarole as during his first visit, only this time, when Wan emerged into the tiny reception area, Lessard drew his gun.

Wan doesn't seem unduly concerned about the weapon that's threatening to drill a hole in his forehead.

"You said you didn't know Aldéric Dorion or David Cortiula."

"I don't."

The detective sergeant tosses the photograph he took from Cortiula's apartment onto the desk. It's the picture of a much younger Wan in the company of Dorion and Cortiula.

"That's not me."

"Listen up, asshole!" Lessard barks, flushing angrily. "We both know it's you! And we both know you kidnapped Laila François!"

"Who?" Wan purrs, smiling disdainfully.

Lessard's cellphone rings. He lowers his eyes for an instant — an instant too long.

With a sudden movement, Wan grabs Lessard's wrist and wrenches it. The gun falls from the cop's grip and lands on the floor. With his other arm useless, Lessard is on his knees within seconds. Wan wraps both hands around his throat.

A veil of darkness is already starting to fall across Lessard's field of vision. He looks up at his assailant. He doesn't want to die like this.

There's murder in Wan's eyes.

A mechanism that biologists know as survival instinct comes into play, blocking out the pain, focusing the cop's mind and magnifying his physical strength. With his left hand, he reaches down to the sheath around his ankle and retrieves the commando knife that he borrowed from Ted Rutherford.

The first thrust has no apparent effect on Wan, who merely raises one hand to his throat, while the other continues to crush Lessard's windpipe with overwhelming power.

Barely conscious, Lessard finds the strength for a second thrust.

Spent, he leaves the knife in the wound.

There will be no third.

Lemaire and Taillon are catching their breath in the alcove. Taillon's eyes are still bulging with rage.

"What were you up to just now, Jacinthe? Are you nuts? You could have killed him!"

"He didn't do it."

"What?" Lemaire asks, loosening his tie.

"The man is a rapist, a pedophile, and lots more besides. But he didn't kidnap Laila François."

"Whoa … where is this coming from? How do you know?"

"There was fear in his eyes when I described the witness account that we obtained. But when I started throttling him and demanding to know where Laila was, the fear turned into panic. The panic of a man who wants to give the answer that'll save his life, but who doesn't know what that answer is."

"You and your damn intuitions!" Lemaire says.

"This isn't intuition. He didn't do it." She's silent for a moment. "Have we located Razor?"

"Not yet."

As she parted company with Lessard, Taillon was convinced that she had identified Laila's kidnapper: Pascal Pierre. Now, realizing her error, she wonders what progress Lessard has made in his pursuit of David Cortiula.

He can't be in a worse place than the dead end she's arrived at.

The whole thing is over in seconds.

It takes Lessard a moment to regain his faculties and to understand the cause of his temporary blindness: blood has filled his eyes.

He wipes his face with his shirttail.

To his right, with still-blurred vision, he sees Chan Lok Wan's legs gripped by convulsions. Gathering his strength, Lessard rises to his feet. He staggers, leans against the desk, loses his footing, and falls to his knees, his face near Wan's.

That's when he sees the knife in his assailant's throat, and the two wounds from which blood is still pouring.

The man is done.

Wan emits a series of hiccups. A surge of blood, dark as petroleum, spills out through his nostrils and the corners of his mouth.

Lessard watches helplessly as Wan dies, open-mouthed.

"You had no choice, Victor. It was you or him."

Raymond is bent over Wan, peering at him as though he were a curious specimen.

Wan's secretary comes into the reception area and starts screaming. Covered in blood, Lessard leaves her where she is and rushes into the corridor, gun in hand.

A single thought is running through his head: Laila François is in this shithole, and he's going to find her.

When he sees a row of padded doors, he stops short.

There must be a dozen of them.

Cells! She isn't the only one!

He never would have guessed that the pedophile ring was this extensive.

The first two cells are empty.

In the third, instead of discovering Laila or some other imprisoned youngster, he finds himself face to face with an old man in chains, who gives him a doubtful look.

What the hell is going on?

The blood is pounding at his temples, threatening to burst his skull.

I hear a flurry of yells, followed by a tremendous uproar.

With my fist clenched, I'm holding the prong of the belt buckle firmly between my index and middle finger, while my other hand whips the leather strap through the air around me.

I'm on my feet, ready to fly at HIM.

The yellow light that streams through the half-open doorway dazzles my eyes, which have been in pitch-darkness for too long.

I leap backward, poised to lunge at my prey and tear HIM to shreds — but then a human form fills the door frame.

Instinctively, I lower my arms.

Though I can barely make out what's in front of me, I know it's not HIM.

And my brain has sensed the threat even before I become consciously aware that the silhouette is aiming a pistol at me.

A flashlight beam forces me to close my eyes.

A man's voice asks loudly:

"Laila?"

An indescribable chaos reigns.

"My name is Victor Lessard. I'm a police officer. Are you all right? You're not hurt?"

After Laila confirms that she's uninjured, Lessard rounds up the two men and one woman whom he found in three neighbouring cells and confines them, despite their vociferous protests, in a single enclosure. The scene is surreal: the thin, naked woman, her pubic area covered by a tuft of greying hair, had been shut up in a cage that was barely big enough to crouch in.

"Do you know who kidnapped you?" Lessard asks the girl as he leads her out into the corridor. "Did you see your attacker? Was it an Asian man?"

Laila doesn't seem to have suffered too much during her captivity.

"I don't know, I didn't see anything," she says calmly, shading her eyes from the light with one hand.

Lessard considers showing her Wan's body so that she can identify him, then thinks better of it. She's been through enough already.

"Were you mistreated? Abused?"

"Apart from you, no one's come into my cell since I woke up."

Lessard stares at her. None of this makes any sense.

"No one?"

"And I was fed."

The detective sergeant doesn't understand. When he saw the cells, he thought he'd achieved his goal. He was expecting, with some relief, to liberate several children from the clutches of the pedophile ring that he'd been tracking. But now, apart from Laila, he finds that he's rescued three adults who not only resent him for it, but claim they were imprisoned of their own free will.

"Do you have relatives? Anyone we can notify?"

Pascal Pierre's evil features sink back into the depths of her memory. She was wrong.

"I've got no relatives. Just my friend Mélanie."

Keeping the girl by his side, Lessard tries to question Wan's secretary to clear up the mystery, but it's useless. The goth is sunk in a corner, glassy-eyed, in a state of shock.

Lesssard is worn out. Emptied.

Was Chan Lok Wan the pedophiles' ringleader?

Did he give the order to have Lessard killed?

The detective sergeant can't say for sure, but someone else is going to have to figure it all out, because Lessard has decided to give up and face the music.

Taking out his phone to call for backup, he sighs as he thinks about the endless interrogations, the disciplinary sanctions, and all the paperwork lying in wait for him.

His 911 call has ended when Fernandez arrives, out of breath, pistol drawn.

"Nadja! What are you doing here?"

Fernandez didn't waste any time trying to guess his intentions. As soon as he hung up, she rushed over without a second thought.

"Is that her?" she asks, looking at Laila François.

Laila is hanging back, behind the detective sergeant, whose presence reassures her.

"That's her. Did you see the body out front?"

"Yes," Fernandez says. "Are you all right?" She raises a hand to his cheek and strokes it so gently that this time, for once, he feels strong enough to respond.

His heart stops pounding. The noises in the background cease. Fernandez's own words dissolve into the air. He leans toward her with a single intention: to press an eternal kiss to her lips and hold her in his arms forever.

Instead, he straightens up and hears himself say matter-of-factly: "I'm fine. But it's over, Nadja. I'm turning myself in, as you urged. I thought I was tracking a criminal network, but now I'm not sure. There were three adults in the cells, and they all claimed to be willing captives. I don't get it. I'm not sure of anything anymore. I thought I was after pedophiles, not sadomasochists."

Fernandez is barely listening. She seems to be caught up in an internal struggle.

"I ... did you call 911?"

"It's already done. What's wrong?"

"Something's happened, Victor," she says, almost reluctantly. "If you knew what it was, I think you'd leave before backup units arrive."

"What is it? What's happened?"

"Not now. You need to leave before they show up. I'll take over from here."

"Nadja, you'll catch hell if you let me leave. Tell me what's up."

"Later, Victor. Go!"

"For fuck's sake, what is this? You've been badgering me to throw in the towel, and now that I've decided to do just that, you're telling me to run away."

"Check your voice mail, then call me back. Get out of here! Now!"

Lessard turns to Laila. "Will you be all right?"

She blinks a yes.

"Get in touch with Jacinthe Taillon," Lessard calls over his shoulder to Fernandez as he runs up the corridor. "You can trust her."

The city's skyline illuminates the inky night.

Montreal is naked and wet. The streetlights' glow is streaked by the pouring rain.

He trudges miserably to the car. An approaching pedestrian crosses to the other side of the street after seeing the blood on his clothes.

Lessard sinks into the driver's seat and lights a cigarette. He's shaking. Nausea assails him.

For the second time in a matter of hours, I've killed a man.

Tears course down his cheeks.

In a zombielike state, he drives around aimlessly.

He pulls over at the corner of Rachel and De la Roche Streets, in front of a restaurant called Le Poisson Rouge, to check his voice mail, as Fernandez asked. In the rear-view mirror, beyond the rivulets of rain running down the back window, he can see the treetops of La Fontaine Park, their upraised limbs breaking the slate surface of the sky. In happier times, he used to come here on winter days to skate with Marie and the kids. The car's interior seems to be closing in on him.

He's struck by a fresh wave of despair. He needs to rouse himself and do something.

You have three messages.

First message.

Victor, we got cut off before I could finish. Sirois's been digging into Dorion's past, and he's found something on Cortiula. Call me back. It's important.

Second message.

Lessard, it's Marchand. We haven't finished our investigation, but I wanted you to know that none of the names Fernandez gave me appear among the users on the file-sharing site. Get back to me when you have a minute.

Third message.

Victor, I'm on my way. Call me as soon as you get this message! [There's panic in Fernandez's voice.] I ... Viviane Gray's body was just found in your apartment. There was a weapon nearby, with your fingerprints on it!

THE KISS OF
THE MAIMED

Montreal
May 18th

I'm the worst brother in the world.

Believe me, I'm an expert on the subject.

I just ended a phone conversation with my sister, Valérie.

The sister who's been worried sick about me.

The sister I was supposed to have dinner with; the sister who learned from the TV news that I was a wanted man; the sister I never got in touch with while I was on the case; the sister to whom I just lied so that she'd stay away from the hospital; the sister, overflowing with compassion, to whom I found it hard to say even a few sentences during the call. The sister to whom I lied about my condition.

I won't even talk about the fact that I didn't keep any of the promises I made to my little brother Raymond.

I may never understand myself, but one thing is for sure: none of this is a reflection on the love I feel.

I should have guessed that my career would end with a whimper. Beavis and Butt-Head from Internal Affairs came back. They've been in my room for half an hour now. They keep alternating between threats and sweet talk, hoping I'll tell them what they want to hear.

They're about as subtle as jackhammers.

They won't give up until my head is mounted on a wall.

Do I look like a moose?

"Okay, Lessard, let's start at the beginning," the rotund Masse brays.

"No problem, guys. I've got all the time in the world."

Lachaîne leans forward, bringing his fleshy, glistening features close to mine.

"Wipe that smirk off your face, Lessard. I don't think you realize how much trouble you're in. Tell us again how it went down between you and Chan Lok Wan."

Needless to say, I roll my eyes and let out a loud sigh.

"Whatever you want, Lachaîne. But do me a favour. Keep your distance. Your breath is disgusting."

"Why, you fucking son of a —"

Red-faced, he takes a step in my direction, but his partner holds him back.

"Just answer the question, Lessard," Masse says.

"I already told you. It was self-defence."

And I describe what happened. In detail. Again and again.

What's the matter with them? Are they stupid? Just plain rude? Out to get me?

All of the above.

In fact, when it comes to being dickheads, they make me think of Buzz Lightyear's famous motto.

To infinity, and beyond.

When Simone came by, she had a word with the surgeon who operated on me, after which she was able to calm my fears about a possible amputation. She said the surgeon had a lousy bedside manner. ("Most surgeons do.") He was just trying to help me understand that even if I did lose the leg, it wouldn't be the end of the world. Simone also pointed out that prosthetic limbs are really impressive these days.

And the bullet wound in my arm?

Coming along just fine, thanks.

. . .

Commander Tanguay also dropped in for a visit.

Contrary to my fears, our talk was quite cordial. I told him that I bore full responsibility for everything that happened. I wanted to downplay Fernandez's involvement, hoping to minimize the disciplinary fallout for her. But Tanguay raised a hand to shut me up, and made a comment about how predictable I was.

Then he said something that surprised me. He said he should have given me more support.

When he urged me to get well soon, he seemed sincere.

Kind of.

The two dickheads are really starting to bug me with their questions.

"If Chan Lok Wan wasn't armed, why did you draw your pistol, Lessard? Was he threatening you?"

"I've answered that question a dozen times!"

"It's not our fault your story keeps changing," Masse barks.

"When you make a guy describe the same event fifty times, there's a fair chance that he'll use different words."

"Okay. Seeing as you don't want to be helpful, let's change the subject. Tell us about Viviane Gray. How did her body turn up at your place if, as you claim, you're not the one who killed her?"

There's a flurry of activity in the hallway. The door opens.

Taillon walks in, leaning on crutches. Now, that's a hefty surprise. No pun intended.

"Time's up, you two," she says, looking like she means business. "Get the fuck out."

"This doesn't concern you, Taillon," snaps Lachaîne, who's the brains of the duo. "You've got no business being here."

A second visitor enters.

I freeze. My smirk evaporates. It's Paul Delaney, head of the Major Crimes Unit.

I don't know Delaney personally. I was kicked off the unit before he took over. But he's unquestionably one of the most powerful people on the Montreal police force. They say he's tight with the chief and the mayor.

What's he doing here?

"Masse, Lachaîne," he says in a peremptory tone, "come with me. I want a word with you."

The two dickheads glare at me. From my bed, I give them a scornful look.

"How's the leg?" Taillon asks.

"Fabulous," I say. I point at her cast. "How's yours?"

"Good as new!"

"What is this, Jacinthe? What are you and Delaney doing here?"

"We have an offer for you," she purrs, with an enigmatic smile on her fleshy features. "Paul will tell you all about it."

35

Montreal
Eight days earlier, May 10th

When he checks his call log, Lessard notes that Fernandez's two messages arrived ten minutes apart. After the initial shock and panic have passed, indignation and mute rage take hold of him. He keys Fernandez's number into his phone. This thing has now turned personal. He's more determined than ever to see it through.

Whatever the cost.

"You can't believe I'm the one who killed her! You know as well as I do that it would be child's play to put my fingerprints on a weapon I never touched."

"Yes? … Just a second, Commander, I can barely hear you …"

Fernandez is speaking to someone else. Lessard realizes that she's going someplace private so that she can speak freely. Half a minute passes.

"Victor? Sorry, there were other people around."

"I had nothing to do with Viviane Gray's death, Nadja."

"You think I'd have let you go if I had the slightest doubt?"

"What the hell happened?"

"Tanguay got an anonymous call an hour ago. He sent a team to your place to check it out."

"Who?"

"Garneau and Pearson found the body. Adams and his assistant are at the scene now. Pearson gave me the news just before I got to

De la Gauchetière Street. Tanguay suspects I'm collaborating with you, so he's kept me away from the case."

"It's a set-up, Nadja. Adams will instantly see that Viviane Gray wasn't killed in my apartment."

"Despite how things look, no one believes you did it."

"What about Tanguay?"

"You know him — everything's black or white. And the higher-ups are breathing down his neck."

"Does any of this goddamn madness make sense to you?"

"Not even slightly. I'm worried about you, Victor."

"I'll be okay. Thanks for getting me out of there."

"Don't thank me, thank Sirois. My first impulse was to bring you in. Sirois said if I did that, you'd never forgive me."

"He was right. How did you explain the situation to everyone else?"

"I said you'd called for backup without giving me any details, then slipped away while I was dealing with the three captives."

"You found them?"

"Yes."

"What were they doing there?"

"I'm not sure. The place is a madhouse right now. The commander from Station 21 is on his way over. I haven't been able to reach Taillon."

"What about Laila?"

"I talked to her before the others got here. She'll keep her mouth shut."

"Do you trust her?"

"Victor, you rescued her. I've got to go, they're signalling to me. Do you have a pen and paper?"

With the phone in hands-free mode, scribbling left-handed in his notebook, Lessard takes down the number that Fernandez gives him.

"The guy's name is Carol Langelier. He's a retired provincial police detective who used to work in Val-d'Or. Call him. He gave Sirois some interesting information about Wan, Dorion, and Cortiula."

"What did Sirois find out?"

"Yes, Commander. Will do. If anything comes up, I'll call you right away."

The line goes dead.

She's hung up.

While Lessard was in conversation with Fernandez, Sirois has left a message offering his assistance, and even proposing that they meet to discuss their next move.

The detective sergeant hesitates for a moment, then decides not to return the call.

Sirois's hotheaded temperament reminds Lessard of his own early years as a Montreal cop. Asking Sirois to do some discreet information gathering is one thing; having him out in the field is quite another. If Sirois gets directly involved in this thing, there will be no going back.

Lessard fears the consequences of getting the young cop mixed up in this deadly affair. If it becomes apparent that Sirois is involved in the ongoing game of cat and mouse, he's certain to be targeted for retaliation. Fernandez is already in it up to her neck — much to Lessard's dismay. If he'd known that the investigation would turn out the way it has, he would never have dragged her into it.

Having decided not to involve Sirois, Lessard considers walking north to Mont-Royal Avenue to make his phone call. The car windows are fogged, and the stale, humid air in the vehicle's interior is chilling him to the bone. He pulls the key from the ignition and buttons his coat ... then has second thoughts. The prospect of getting out and walking up De la Roche Street suddenly seems beyond him. Besides, he'll be more comfortable talking in the lugubrious silence of the car than among clamouring voices in one of the overcrowded cafés on Mont-Royal Avenue.

"You should get out, Victor," Raymond says, stretched out on the back seat, hands clasped behind his head. "Seeing people will do you good."

"Maybe," the cop says, lost in thought.

But socializing is the last thing he wants to do right now. He starts the ignition, turns on the heater, and calls the number that Fernandez gave him.

"Carol Langelier."

"This is Detective Sergeant Victor Lessard of the Montreal Police. My colleague, Detective Sirois, suggested that I get in touch — it's about David Cortiula and Aldéric Dorion."

"Yeah, no, Sirois told me you'd be calling, Detective. Can I call you Victor?"

"Of course."

"Seems like Cortiula's a hot topic, eh, Victor?" Langelier laughs.

Lessard has always made a point of being respectful when he questions older people. He can't bring himself to call the man by his first name.

"Could you tell me about him, Mr. Langelier? I wasn't able to speak to Sirois before calling you."

"Yeah, no, I'll tell you what I told your colleague. You've gotta start with Cortiula's childhood to get a sense of the guy's unique personality. And let me tell you, that is one hell of a unique personality."

Langelier has the slow, slurred speech rhythms of a man who takes his first drink when he gets out of bed in the morning. Lessard fears that the conversation may go on longer than he has patience for. On the bright side, at least he doesn't have to smell the man's breath, which, he suspects, is laced with the fetid reek of alcohol.

"Cortiula spent his childhood in Val-d'Or. His mother was a stripper in the local clubs. His father was a lumberjack. Worked in a camp north of the city. I can't remember what company he was with. Anyway, he didn't play much of a part in the boy's upbringing. He only came home for a couple of weeks a year, to drink his paycheque and wet his wick."

Langelier laughs, obviously pleased at his own wit.

"I hope that doesn't shock you."

"Not at all."

"Yeah, no, seriously. Whenever the father came to town, we'd start getting calls to go to the house. The guy was constantly getting drunk and beating on his wife. And the wife ... man, I remember her ..."

Langelier's account is interrupted by a violent fit of smoker's cough, which goes on for several seconds.

"That woman was fuckin' gorgeous. Take it from me, I saw her naked plenty of times. Her titties ... oh, man, she had great titties. What can I tell you? Back then, there wasn't a lot to do if you were fifty-five and divorced. So me and my partner, more often than not, we'd end up at the strip clubs. Those were some good times. The Native girls used to get in on it, too. They were fuckin' hot ... but I guess we're getting off topic."

Lessard nods to himself. *Way off topic.*

"So anyway, that woman was gorgeous, but she also had a fuckin' mean streak. I mean, she was one crazy bitch. Sometimes, we'd turn up at the house and find them both, her and the husband, covered in blood. Shit, I remember one time, she whacked him in the forehead with a clothes iron. By the time we got there, the poor bastard had a melon head." Langelier laughs. "Hah! That's good! Melon head ..."

"What about David?"

"Yeah, no, I'm getting to him. So every time we walked into the house, the kid would be sitting in a corner, playing quietly with his toys while all hell was breaking loose around him. I've gotta say, he didn't seem too upset about the whole thing. He didn't even notice that we were there. Hell of a way to bring up a kid, though, I'll tell you that for nothin'. And the boy had these piercing eyes. I swear, when he looked at you, it was like he could see all the way to the back of your fuckin' head. I'll tell ya, that kid scared me. Some people even said he had powers."

"Powers?"

"Yeah, no, it was just a lot of fuckin' old wives' tales, but still, that's what they said."

Lessard has noted Langelier's verbal tic of starting sentences with "Yeah, no," regardless of what he actually intends to say.

"Did he do well at school?"

"Yeah, no, see, that's what's so weird. The kid was a fuckin' genius. Straight As, right down the line. I'm telling you, Victor, that little boy was smart as hell. Which, considering the kind of parents he had, makes no sense at all — but that's how it was. The fuckin' priests noticed, though, and when his mother died, they took him under their skirts." Langelier laughs. "Hah! Under their skirts. Get it?"

Lessard is no history buff, but, having been through the youth protection system himself, he knows that the orphanages administered by Quebec's religious orders were abolished during the early 1960s. To replace them, the government created a network of youth centres. Cortiula is too young to have spent any time in an orphanage.

"Didn't he go into a youth centre when his mother died?"

"Yeah, no, see, that's the thing. His father didn't want him, and there were no other relatives. So the youth centre took the kid, and then they put him in a group home."

Group homes didn't exist when Lessard was young, but he knows they involve approximately ten children living together under the guidance and supervision of educators.

Above a certain age, though — is it ten or twelve? Lessard can't remember — youngsters go into foster homes.

"You just said the priests took care of him …"

"Yeah, no, it's like this. The priests at the seminary saw the kid's potential and realized they could do something with him. Priests are pretty sharp themselves, right? So the kid got a fuckin' top-notch education, courtesy of the priests. The Church had money in those days. I don't think they were grooming him for the priesthood. He wasn't just another piece of meat in the homo sausage factory! Ha-ha-ha!"

"So the priests let him study at the seminary for free, which meant he didn't have to go to public school. Is that what you're saying?"

"Yeah, no, exactly! They paid for everything, educated him, the whole nine yards. And the kid had a ton of musical talent. My partner called him 'Little Mozart.' He sang in the choir. Had a voice like a goddamn angel. Whenever I went to Mass and heard him sing, the hairs used to stand up on my arms."

"Tell me about his mother's death."

"Yeah, no, that's one hell of a story. We got a call, one evening. The kid hadn't been to school in three days, and the principal was worried. Me and my partner, we went to the house, rang the bell, knocked. Nothing. So my partner put the boot to the door and we went in. I remember like it was yesterday. A Wednesday evening. We found her in the bathroom. She was naked, but oh, man, she wasn't pretty to look at. She'd slit her wrists with a razor blade. By then, she'd been dead four or five days. The house was crawling with flies. Smelled like the end of the world."

The sight of his own mother's pale body rises up secretly before Lessard's eyes: she's pale in her flowery dress, her legs touched by a ray of sunshine coming through the curtains.

"You still there, young fella?"

"Yeah. Sorry. Where was David?"

"When me and my partner arrived, the kid looked up at us with those cat's eyes of his. He didn't seem to give a shit about his dead mother. It was almost like he found it funny. He stared at us for about ten seconds, then went back into his room, like nothing had happened."

"Was there an autopsy?"

"Yeah, no, the medical examiner came, they took her away, the whole thing was done by the book. The report came back three days later. She'd taken a bunch of pills before slitting her wrists."

"What about the father?"

"That low-life? He was out in the woods when it happened. Me and my partner took his statement and checked his alibi, just in case. But there was never any doubt. He'd been on the job with a dozen other guys. He came into town for the funeral, then went right back out into the woods. Never looked after his boy. That was when the kid went to live at the youth centre."

"What became of the father?"

"Died in a car accident a few years later. Hit a fuckin' moose."

Lessard realizes that he's misjudged Langelier. The man swears like a sailor, but he's still an ex-cop. What Lessard initially took for meandering has begun to take shape. Little by little, a clear picture is emerging.

"How old was David when his mother died?"

"This was in eighty-four, so he'd have been six or seven."

"And that was when he went to the youth centre?"

"Yeah, no, exactly. He moved in there."

"And started going to school at the seminary?"

"Not right away. That only happened after young Carbonneau tried to kill himself."

Lessard closes his eyes and lets Langelier talk. There's no point in trying to impose his own logic on the man's account. In any case, he senses that they're coming close to the heart of the matter.

"Young Carbonneau?"

"There were three of them. Three friends who sang in the choir. David, young Carbonneau, and an Asian kid."

"Chan Lok Wan?"

"Somethin' like that. So one night, young Carbonneau's mother organized a sleepover. The three of them were thick as thieves at school. This was during their week off."

"March break?"

"Yeah, no, that's it. So anyway, the three of 'em went to bed. Then, in the middle of the night, the mother gets woken up by her son, young Carbonneau ... what the fuck was his first name? Anyway, the kid's screaming blue murder. The mother goes into the bedroom and finds him with a bayonet stuck in his belly. A wartime souvenir from his grandfather, apparently. The mother flips out, calls the ambulance, the whole nine yards. Me and my partner get woken up and dispatched to the scene. When we arrive, we can't believe our fuckin' eyes. Young Carbonneau's in agony, covered in blood, being tended to by the ambulance guys, while his mother is screaming and pointing at David. I tell ya, it was crazy."

"The mother was pointing at David? What had happened? Cortiula stabbed the boy?"

"No. Young Carbonneau stabbed himself, but he told his mother that David and the Asian kid had talked him into it."

"Then what?"

"Me and my partner questioned the two of 'em. What the hell were we supposed to do? A couple of kids — it was ridiculous."

"Did they confess?"

"No, they said it wasn't true. They said they'd been playing with the bayonet, and it was an accident. They claimed the woman was a fuckin' loony-tune. Man, she was mad as hell. She hired a lawyer."

"To sue a couple of children?"

"Yeah, no, she wanted to sue the youth centre, because that was where David and the Asian kid were living."

"What happened at trial? Did the mother win?"

"Come on, young fella, you know cases like that never go to trial. The centre's lawyers talked to the mother's lawyer. Then the priest talked to her, and they made a deal. A week later, the woman was walkin' around town in a new fur coat, looking real pleased with herself."

"And the priest was Aldéric Dorion?"

"You could say he's the one who took David under his wig. Ha-ha-ha! Under his wig — get it? Yeah, no, Dorion thought pretty highly of himself. He figured he was smarter than everybody else."

Lessard closes his eyes. He visited Val-d'Or once, a lifetime ago. He remembers the toothless old codgers smoking cigarettes on 3rd Avenue; the cars parked diagonally on both sides of the street; the groups of kids hanging around the convenience stores ...

"Did young Carbonneau pull through?"

"Yeah, no, he came out just fine. He's a big shot now. Works in Africa, feeding the hungry, stuff like that."

"So the story ended there?"

"Oh, no, young fella. Those two kept on with their shenanigans."

"Cortiula and Wan?"

"Yeah, no, they kept on doing stuff, but the priest covered for them. Since he was their teacher, he could make sure they never got into trouble."

"Hang on. Wan was also a student at the seminary?"

"You got it, young fella."

So David Cortiula and Chan Lok Wan were childhood friends who had become Aldéric Dorion's protégés in the wake of young Carbonneau's suicide attempt.

Strange.

"You say that afterward, those two kept on with their shenanigans. What kind of shenanigans?"

"I don't know how else to say this — they were a couple of fuckin' weirdos. But David was the real troublemaker. I can't tell you how many calls we got about his breaking and entering."

"He was stealing?"

"No. He'd go into people's homes while they were asleep."

"And do what? Vandalize the places?"

"Nope. You gotta understand, young fella, everybody had a theory about what he was up to. People would wake up in the night, and he'd be sittin' there, in their bedrooms, staring at them with those spooky eyes."

"He was watching people as they slept?"

"You got it. And folks were scared as hell. It even got around that the kid had goaded his mother into killing herself. But the priest was always there to defend him. Dorion was constantly saying it wasn't the boy's fault, he hadn't had a normal upbringing, of course he was kinda strange … but I'll tell ya, as he grew up, he kept getting stranger and stranger."

"In what way?"

"Oh, there were plenty of rumours, young fella. A lot of terrible shit went down in a very short time. And whenever something bad happened, everybody just got into the habit of blaming the kid."

"Can you give me an example?"

"One night, a farmer had ten of his goats killed. Their heads were cut off. The next day, me and my partner had to go down to the church, because a bunch of men had showed up at the presbytery. They were demanding that the priests turn David over to them."

"What kind of weapon had been used to kill the goats?"

"Yeah, no, we never knew for sure, young fella. But if I had to guess, I'd say it was an axe or a machete."

"Did you ever find an axe in David's possession?"

"No. But don't forget, his father was a lumberjack. People put two and two together and thought they had it all figured out."

Lessard doesn't want to jump to conclusions, but he can't help remembering the murder weapon that was found amidst the carnage on Bessborough Avenue.

"Did you ever arrest Cortiula or Wan on criminal charges?"

"No, young fella. If they broke the law, they broke it in secret. Not only were the priests always there to get them out of trouble, but there was no evidence against them. We never caught them doing anything wrong. Even in the case of young Carbonneau, the stabbing was self-inflicted. No one did it to him."

"I understand. What happened to Cortiula and Wan afterward?"

"Nothing."

"What do you mean?"

"I mean nothing. A week after that lynch mob came looking for the two boys, they left town. Not that anyone actually saw them leave, but from one day to the next, they were gone."

"Gone?"

"That's right, young fella. I imagine it was because folks were all claiming that the kid was bad luck."

"Where did they go?"

"Good question. Me and my partner went to the youth protection office and to the centre where they'd been living. We were told that everything had been arranged. The boys were in a new city, which was being kept confidential, for their safety."

"And Dorion?"

"Yeah, no, he left, too."

"Where did he go?"

"If you ask me, not even the other priests knew that."

"Are you telling me that Aldéric Dorion left Val-d'Or at the same time as David Cortilua and Chan Lok Wan?"

"You got it. We never saw any of them again. And people started breathing easier around here. Everyone was happier, all of a sudden. It was fuckin' crazy, I mean, it practically felt like a public holiday. When things go wrong, everyone needs a scrapegoat."

"A scapegoat."

"That's what I said, young fella."

"And the two boys had sung in the choir with Dorion?"

"Yeah, no, that's right. I don't remember whether the Asian boy was any good, but Little Mozart, like my partner called him — that kid had the voice of a fuckin' angel."

"Would it be possible for me to speak to your partner?"

"Louis? Sorry, young fella, he blew his brains out after Margot left him for a railway engineer. He was in a coma for three years before he died. Tough son of a bitch."

Lessard racks his brain.

He can't think of any more questions, but he fears that they'll come flooding into his head as soon as he hangs up the phone.

The SIV agent glances toward the transept.

A few elderly worshippers are sitting on the hard wooden pews, heads bowed, praying in silence. The priest smiles. At last, he can carry out the remainder of his plan: to record one final video and complete the file that he's preparing for the cardinal prefect.

The pieces are laid out. Everything is ready.

The choir practice begins.

The luminous tones of a crystalline falsetto rise from the nave, soaring above the murky turbulence of the other voices, nestling in counterpoint against the deep notes of the organ's accompaniment.

Overcome by the power of the canticle, with the bass frequencies rumbling in his rib cage, Noah closes his eyes.

That voice …

It's a revelation. A flawless bloom among stinging nettles.

The SIV agent can't see the choristers in the balcony, but he doesn't need to. He would know that voice in a multitude.

It's the voice of the boy to whom he was introduced by Aldéric Dorion one April day in 1985.

The voice of David Cortiula.

36

Lessard desperately needs to escape from the car's oppressive atmosphere.

With his jacket collar turned up and his empty right sleeve flapping in the wind, he crosses Rachel Street and enters La Fontaine Park. The trees' ghostly silhouettes rise up into the night sky, swaying in the wind, their limbs extended to embrace and imbibe the rain that heaven pours down unceasingly upon them.

He wants to clear his head, but shreds of his conversation with Langelier are swirling through his mind, cracking, disintegrating, exploding.

As he walks, his gaze is unfocused. Images appear, transform, vanish before his eyes. Why can't he concentrate on one particular point? Why can't he stop the vortex into which his mind has fallen?

He sits down on a bench, despite the fact that it's soaked. The unpleasant sensation of water seeping into his pants brings him back to reality.

In an effort to clarify his thoughts, he takes out his notebook and makes himself go back to the beginning, to recall the main pieces of the puzzle. Though he writes with his left hand, the letters are more legible than he would have thought.

Murder of the Cook family
Sandoval and Applebaum — pedophile ring. File-sharing website.
Link between pedophiles and Dorion? Pedophile priests? Link
between pedophiles and Cortiula? Wan?
Organized structure: murder of Viviane Gray, attack at rest stop.

This is where he loses his way.

Wan and Cortiula met in childhood. Despite Dorion's protection, they were hounded out of Val-d'Or by residents who believed the boys were responsible for all the ills that afflicted the city. Lessard writes down two questions that are nagging at him:

Where did they go? Did Cortiula and Wan accompany Dorion to Sherbrooke?

The answer seems to be yes in Cortiula's case, judging from the photos that Lessard found in his apartment — photos that show him singing with Applebaum and Sandoval. But to get a clear sense of what happened, it would be necessary to reconstruct the three men's movements over the past twenty years.

And what about Cortiula, that enigmatic figure with the catlike eyes, who spent days beside his mother's corpse, seemingly amused by the situation?

What did Langelier say?

"The house was crawling with flies."

Flies — Cook murders and Sandoval??

"Are you okay, Victor?" a voice asks as the detective sergeant stops scribbling.

His brother is sitting on the guardrail next to the bicycle path. Lessard rubs his temples for a moment, then looks at the boy.

"I can't figure it out, Raymond."

The cigarette that he laid on the bench beside him is burning down. He ignores it, absorbed in his thoughts.

What does he know for sure?

I don't know anything anymore.

He gives himself a shake, tightens his grip on his pen, and tries to organize his thoughts.

Wan is dead. Wan kidnapped Laila François.

Why?

He hopes Fernandez and Taillon will find an answer to that question soon. His hand moves over the paper.

Where are Dorion and Cortiula? On the run? Vanished?

The two men may have done nothing wrong, but they need to be found and questioned. Unless they've been eliminated, too. Lessard's thoughts get bogged down. Suddenly, he remembers the detail he was trying to put his finger on. The documents that he found at Dorion's and Cortiula's apartments are worth studying more closely:

Cortiula — articles on the devil?
Dorion — pamphlet on exorcism?
Cortiula starts a Satanic cult in Val-d'Or?

Was Lessard dreaming, or did Langelier hint at the possibility that the boy had "powers"?

He frowns. This supernatural stuff isn't his strong suit.

But he knows from experience that some people are fascinated by such things, and that they'll occasionally go to great lengths in their pursuit of an alternative reality.

Too great, sometimes.

Finally, Lessard's thoughts turn to the strange dungeon in which Chan Lok Wan was holding Laila captive — a sort of hidden world, where the adults whom Lessard discovered claimed that they'd been locked up of their own free will.

Who were those people? What were they doing in the cells?

He scribbles a few guesses:

Pedophiles? Sadomasochists? Satanists? A cult?

A cult …

He considers the matter briefly. It's an intriguing possibility that crossed his mind at the very outset, as he and his team were starting to investigate the Cook killings. Didn't Taillon mention that Laila François's stepfather was the leader of a cult?

What was it called again?

"The Solar Crossing." Something like that.

Did Wan, Cortiula, and Dorion belong to this cult?

Were they devil-worshippers?

After making a huge scene in front of a stunned Gilles Lemaire, Jacinthe Taillon walks out of the conference room, slamming the door so hard that she gets startled reactions from several of the cops working nearby.

She doesn't give a damn about Lemaire's objections.

If the other team members are too incompetent to find Razor, she'll do it herself.

With a photograph of Razor lying on the car's passenger seat, she drives around the neighbourhood in which the Red Blood Spillers' headquarters are located, hoping to spot the young gangster.

In the early days of her career, she wouldn't have been so patient.

She'd have marched right into the building with her gun drawn. Leap first, look later. But she's learned the hard way that, unlike bikers and mobsters, the street gangs don't abide by any code. When you face those guys, you'd better be ready to go in guns blazing, because otherwise, there's a fair chance you'll be full of holes before your weapon is out of its holster.

This whole investigation is a mess.

Grumbling, in a foul mood, Taillon picks up her ringing cellphone.

"Hi, my name's Nadja Fernandez. Victor Lessard said I should get in touch."

"Can it wait?" Taillon says. "This really isn't a good time."

"Suit yourself. But just so you know, I'm with Laila François at the moment."

Other details come back to the surface as Lessard lets his mind drift freely on a tide of stray thoughts. What was it that Viviane Gray said about John Cook?

That he was convinced someone was entering his home while he slept.

And what about Langelier?

Didn't he say he'd gotten numerous calls in connection with David breaking into people's homes to watch them as they slept?

What does it all mean? One thing's for sure: Lessard hasn't yet found the common factor that can turn these disparate details into a coherent picture. A crucial piece of the puzzle is still missing.

For a moment, he wonders whether the connection between Applebaum, Sandoval, Wan, and Cortiula is that they were abused by priests while they were members of a choir.

In the case of Wan and Cortiula, this conjecture is plausible, since they were boys when they came under Dorion's supervision.

As for Applebaum and Sandoval, were they victims of abuse before becoming pedophiles themselves? In order to answer that question, one would need to know at what age they started singing in the choir.

Were they young enough to have been abused, or were they adults at the time?

Lessard knows from experience that many people join choirs later in life, simply for the pleasure of singing. His sister, Valérie, joined her parish choir after separating from her husband.

Another detail occurs to him, something he forgot to ask Fernandez to look into.

Of all the individuals he's come across in the course of his investigation — with the exception of Dorion, who directed a choir — only John Cook doesn't seem to have been a chorister.

Lessard doesn't want to talk to Fernandez or Sirois right now, for fear of interrupting the flow of ideas. Instead, he clumsily types a cryptic text, which he sends to them: Cook in a choir?/Applebaum, Sandoval in a choir as kids?/Where did Cortiula-Wan-Dorion go after V-d'Or?/ Were C-W-D in P. Pierre's cult?/Devil-worship?

"What is it that keeps you going, Victor?"

The detective sergeant watches a gust of wind bending the branches of a tree.

He's silent for a moment.

"It's your face, Raymond ... I see it superimposed over the faces of the victims I encounter. As long as you're there, I'll keep going."

"I'll always be there, Victor. You can't erase the past."

The boy lays his head on his brother's lap. Lessard strokes his hair.

"I'm tired, Raymond ... so tired," Lessard whispers, his eyes filling with tears.

"Why don't you give it all up? Come home with me. Mom will make us dinner."

The wind is blowing.

Lessard huddles on the bench, shivering with cold and fear. He's shivering because his son and daughter are out there somewhere, defenceless against the blood-soaked, unpitying monster that is the human heart. He's shivering because, in this unequal combat, he stands alone against an adversary whose power far exceeds his own. He's shivering because men are prowling in the shadows, men who will stop at nothing to protect a secret that he hasn't yet grasped. He's shivering because not even the sacrifice of numerous lives will slow those men down.

What kind of hellish maze has he wandered into?

Despite his shorts and his tank top, Raymond isn't cold.

No one shivers in the land of the dead.

Lessard returns to reality.

At this late hour, in this weather, the park is deserted. Not even an earthworm has ventured out to leave its slimy trail on the pavement.

Lessard flicks his extinguished butt into the wet underbrush.

As he raises his eyes and takes his head in his hands, an immense, blank scream lodges in his throat.

He's at the brink of a precipice.

A skeletal, yellow-haired dog advances toward him.

The gaunt-faced animal seems to embody misery. Affliction blooms in its muddy eyes. Lessard recognizes it as the yellow dog that crossed his path on Notre-Dame Street while he was driving to Ted's place. At this point, he isn't even particularly surprised to see that the animal has somehow managed to cross the city.

The mongrel comes close enough to sniff his fingers.

Lessard has had a panicky fear of dogs since he was bitten by one in childhood.

But now he pats the animal as though it were an old friend, a sharer of his misfortune. The dog lies down at his feet as he lights a cigarette.

"You smoke too much, Victor," Raymond says, sitting beside him on the bench, legs swinging in the air.

"Am I setting a bad example for you?" Lessard responds, with a sad smile.

The night suddenly becomes more opaque. As he sits here in the midst of the park, the lustful city that surrounds him, with its thousand lewd tentacles and its hives of debauchery, no longer exists. Apart from the raindrops bouncing off the leaves and the wind whispering in his ears, no other sound reaches him.

Anguish sweeps over him. Solitude presses him to her breast; dangles her flaccid, withered, whorish nipples above his mouth; offers him her putrid, curdled milk. His throat tightens. He's struck by the sudden impression that he's the last living thing on earth.

Although Raymond's presence comforts him and helps him to carry on, the longing to speak to someone other than this simulacrum of a brother gnaws at him until he gives in.

"Victor?"

"Hi, Elaine. I just wanted to be sure you're okay."

"Yes. Detective Sirois was very nice. He left about an hour ago. I told my parents he was a friend, so that they wouldn't worry. How about you? Are you all right?"

"I'm fine," he lies, without conviction.

"Listen, Victor, I don't know what's going on, but I'm scared."

"Don't worry, it will all be over soon." He pauses. "One way or another."

Before his eyes, the raindrops are turning into flies.

"What do you mean?"

"It doesn't matter. This won't go on much longer, I promise."

"Are you sure you're all right?" Elaine asks.

"Yes, yes."

A deluge of flies is tumbling past his gaze, and shreds of a previous conversation between them are whirling through the air.

"Do you have any leads?" she asks.

He doesn't want to admit that he has no idea what to look for, or where.

"Things are taking shape. Listen, I'd like to ask about something you mentioned, last time we talked …"

"Yes?"

"As I recall, you spoke about the fourth plague, something along those lines."

"I remember."

"Could this fourth plague somehow be relevant to a Satanic cult?"

"What do you mean?"

Lessard is trying to organize his thoughts, but they're strewn in confusion across the interior of his mind.

"How can I put this …? Would it make sense for a group of Satanists to stage murders in a way that evoked the plague of flies described in the Bible?"

"I think I understand your question. No, that wouldn't make sense. The fourth plague isn't about the devil. It's simply a curse from God that takes the form of a multitude of flies."

"Okay. I get it."

"But if we're talking about devil-worship, there's a much more obvious connection with flies."

"What's that?"

"Beelzebub. The King of Flies."

"Excuse me?"

"In Philistine and Phoenician culture, *Baal* or its variant *Beel* means 'master' or 'owner.' *Zebub* or *Zoubeb* is the word for 'fly.' In the gospels, the name Beelzebub is used to designate Satan, the prince of devils."

Beelzebub, the King of Flies.

As he ends the call, Lessard promises Elaine that he'll call again tomorrow. Then, besieged by his own dark thoughts, he puts the barrel of his pistol in his mouth.

Since becoming convinced that John Cook didn't kill his wife and children, Lessard has been struggling to suppress an idea that keeps rising from the depths of his mind.

What if his father wasn't the murderer Lessard has always supposed? What if someone else was responsible for the death of his family?

I ended his life without even giving him a chance to explain. If only …

"Stop torturing yourself, Victor. I was there. Dad killed us."

Silence.

"I don't know where I am, Raymond."

"Put the gun away. Come with me."

His finger stays on the trigger for a long time. Finally, he goes down to the pond, near the fountain. As he's seen homeless people do hundreds of times, he gives himself a rough wash to remove the lingering stains of Chan Lok Wan's blood.

Then he walks to the car, holding his brother's hand.

37

*The devil's greatest trick is to make you believe he
doesn't exist.*

— Charles Baudelaire

Montreal
May 11th

The sun is sinking fast beyond the desert dunes.

*He's running like a madman. His soiled tunic is impeding his prog-
ress; there are flecks of whitish spittle in his thick beard. Apart from a
single dense, black cloud, the sky is virginal, immaculate.*

That cloud is like no other.

*It's nearly a hundred metres long, moving at a height of three metres
off the ground. With its shape and density changing constantly, it
seems to be following him. He knows what it is: a swarm of millions of
flies, moving in formation, pursuing him. He's trying to outrun them,
but he has no illusions. He's already covered three kilometres, and the
distance between him and the insects hasn't changed.*

He knows that as soon as he stops moving, the cloud will catch him.

He's not going to make it.

*He's already getting weaker. Lactic acid is numbing his legs, the arid
air is parching his throat, and the hot wind is blowing sand into his eyes.*

Suddenly, he freezes.

An unfamiliar man has just appeared before him. Where did the stranger come from? He wasn't there a moment ago, and there's nothing else in sight — not a shack, not a tree, not even a pile of rocks — behind which the man could have hidden himself.

Surprised, he feels his strength suddenly disappear. He collapses to the ground. The stranger addresses him, but he doesn't understand the language the man is speaking.

Will the stranger help him?

The cloud engulfs him.

He sees the compact mass of flies wrapping itself around him, pressing against his body, turning him around, drawing him into its centre. He screams, his arms flail, his hands struggle to grab something, anything, as his ears drink in the sickening noise of beating wings.

The flies enter his nostrils, his ears, his mouth. They force their way through his larynx, past his trachea, and quickly invade his lungs and stomach.

He starts to run out of oxygen. Convulsions seize him. His face turns red, then takes on a bluish hue. Before choking to death, he casts a final glance at the stranger, whose forehead is now encircled by a ring of fire.

With his lips parted, the stranger watches him in silence.

Flies emerge from Beelzebub's mouth by the thousands and swarm over Lessard.

He wakes up with a start, coughing and spitting to expel the flies he's swallowed.

Then he realizes he hasn't swallowed anything.

What a hellish nightmare.

The pain in his arm and between his shoulder blades is so excruciating that he feels like a dagger is stabbing him. Fatigue overwhelmed him while he was sitting in the driver's seat, preparing to start the car and drive to the motel, where the relative comfort of his room awaited him.

When Morpheus wrapped him in his embrace, Lessard sank into a deep yet troubled slumber.

Despite the rain, it was a mild night. He wasn't cold.

He glances at his watch: 7:00 a.m.

This time, reflux or not, Lessard is going to have a cup of coffee.

With his legs feeling weak, he wrestles himself clumsily out of the car. Then he pops a handful of pills to deal with his pain, his infection, and his reflux, and washes them down with a long swig of Pepto-Bismol.

The blood on his clothes has dried, but it's still visible. He puts on the yellow raincoat that he previously took out of the Corolla and stowed in the killer's car.

He buttons the coat up to the collar and looks at his reflection in the car window.

Between the yellow coat, his red Canadiens cap, and the black frames of his glasses, he looks pretty nutty. Not to mention the sling around his arm and the bandage over his eyebrow. All of which, he tells himself, will help him blend in on the streets of the Plateau Mont-Royal, where crunchy-granola oddballs abound.

A few bloodstains are still visible on his jeans, but they'll easily be mistaken for ink or motor oil against the dark denim.

As he walks along the street in the falling rain, his head feels clearer than yesterday.

First of all, he needs to check his messages and get an update from Fernandez or Sirois concerning the questions he texted them. Then he'll put in a call to René Trudeau, the priest who co-authored the pamphlet that Lessard found at Dorion's apartment.

Still intrigued by his earlier conjecture that Pascal Pierre's cult might be linked to the Satanists, the detective sergeant wants to do some digging on that subject.

But first things first: he needs a shot of caffeine.

With her eyes stinging after a long, sleepless night, Jacinthe Taillon has lost count of the cups of coffee she's consumed over the past few hours.

Her interrogation of Laila François has yielded nothing.

The girl wasn't mistreated. She doesn't know who abducted her, or why. The truth is, she'd been convinced that Pascal Pierre was behind the crime. Taillon's interrogation of the pastor, combined with her initial examination of Chan Lok Wan's office, suggests that Wan was the kidnapper.

Laila left a few hours ago, accompanied by Gilles Lemaire and a case worker from youth protection, leaving the offices of CLW Solutions to Taillon and the crime scene technicians.

Laila may not know anything, but Nadja Fernandez does.

Taillon is convinced that the young detective has been helping the fugitive Lessard, and that she has information on the case. Even so, Taillon hasn't been overly aggressive with Fernandez. It's Lessard she wants to talk to, without intermediaries. Trouble is, the bastard hasn't called.

Which comes as no surprise. Taillon is sure that Fernandez passed along her message. But she also knows that Lessard's style is similar to her own: they both prefer to work solo. They don't like having to answer to others, and they hate to share information.

Nevertheless, despite the animosity she feels for the detective sergeant, Taillon wishes he'd get in touch. She's convinced that he has additional information on the case. For the hundredth time, she replays the tape of her interrogation of Josée Labrie, the goth secretary. Taillon questioned her shortly after arriving on the scene, while Gilles Lemaire was interviewing the three captives whom Lessard had found in the other cells.

Q: What kind of activities were you and Chan Lok Wan involved in? How long had you been working with him?

A: Seven years. Basically, people came to us — professionals, for the most part. Depending on their beliefs, they came for physical punishment, like whipping, or to get locked up for a while.

Q: Why?

A: To make up for their bad deeds, their sins, stuff like
    that.

Q: How did you fit in?

A: I'm a trained nurse. I made sure the wounds that Chan
    inflicted on our customers were properly treated,
    disinfected, et cetera. I also cooked meals for
    people who were locked up for extended periods, that
    kind of thing.

Q: So Wan was a torturer?

A: You could say so. Customers would ask him to adminis-
    ter whatever punishment they wanted to receive.

Q: Did he also specialize in abduction?

A: No. Laila François was a special case.

Q: Why did Wan kidnap her?

A: Because his friend asked him to.

Q: You're referring to David Cortiula?

A: Yes. Anyway, that's what Chan told me.

Q: Did Cortiula come here often?

A: It varied over time, but yes, he came several times a
    year.

Q: And received corporal punishment?

A: David got so many floggings that his back looked like
    a patchwork quilt.

Q: Why did he ask Wan to kidnap Laila?

A: Chan said it was to protect her.

Q: Protect her? From who? From what?

A: I don't know. Chan didn't say.

Q: You must have an idea, Ms. Labrie.

A: I don't know for sure, but I think David wanted to
    protect her from a priest who was after him.

Despite the caffeine she's ingested, Taillon's fatigue is affecting
her, slowing down her body and her mind. With an effort, she
lifts her gaze. On the surveillance screens, she can see images of
the empty cells.

The three people whom Lessard shut up in a single cell include a lawyer who specializes in information technology law. All three have confirmed what the goth secretary told Taillon: that they came here willingly to undergo prearranged punishments, which they paid Chan Lok Wan to inflict.

Taillon is too exhausted to have an opinion on the subject, but this isn't the first time she's remarked to herself in a general way that the world is full of whack jobs.

The chair groans as she rises from it. Two file cabinets stand against the wall. She fully intends to examine their contents, and, if necessary, to ransack the entire office, room by room. There's something she's not getting about this whole situation, something that prevents her from understanding why Cortiula instructed Wan to abduct Laila François.

"David wanted to protect her from a priest …"

Lessard also talked about a priest, didn't he?

Has he found Cortiula?

Lessard has always seen Mont-Royal Avenue, with its succession of bars, cafés, and trendy clothing boutiques, as an imaginary passage linking the mountain to the Olympic Stadium.

He walks into the St-Viateur Bagel café.

He can hear Miles Davis's "So What" coming through the speakers on the wall.

Lessard goes to a table in the back and orders two bagels with cream cheese and a cup of coffee. He's one of the first customers of the day.

As he sits down, the burning pain in his arm makes him wince. He takes out the pamphlet on exorcism and skims through it:

INTRODUCTION

This booklet is intended as a practical guide for priests who face actual or presumed cases of possession.

[…]

The entity ostensibly causing the possession is the spirit of Evil, generally known as "the devil" or, depending on the belief system in which it occurs, "Satan," "Beelzebub," or "Lucifer."

[...]

While great caution is always called for, the Church cannot rule out the possibility of demonic control over certain individuals.

[...]

In its primary form, exorcism is practised during the celebration of baptism. The canonical rite of solemn exorcism, or "major exorcism," can only be performed by an exorcist priest with the bishop's permission.

Absorbed in his reading, Lessard takes a gulp of black coffee, burning his tongue.

"Oww!" he says out loud, bringing a hand to his mouth.

A woman seated at a nearby table glances over with amusement. He gives her a contrite smile and continues to leaf randomly through the pamphlet.

RITE

The new rite incorporates developments in medicine and psychiatry. This seventy-page document, prepared in accordance with the decrees set forth by the Second Vatican Council, replaces the formulas and prayers contained in Chapter XII of the Roman Ritual.

[...]

The rite includes, among other procedures, sprinkling with holy water, various prayers, the display of a crucifix to the possessed individual, and an imperative formulation (*"Vade retro, Satana"*) which is directly addressed to the devil, commanding him to depart.

MENTAL ILLNESS AS OPPOSED TO TRUE POSSESSION

[...]

Exorcism may only be undertaken following diligent inquiry — while respecting the secrecy of the confessional — and consultation with psychiatric specialists. This is required to protect individuals whose personality disorders might prompt them to believe that they have fallen prey to the devil. It is necessary to distinguish paranoia, schizophrenia, and other psychotic disorders from true diabolical attacks. [...] This does not mean refusing spiritual assistance to those who need it. But we must bear in mind that exorcism is always a last resort, not to be used as an initial response, and certainly not at any cost.

[...]

As we have seen above, the rite of exorcism applies only to cases of true diabolical possession, in which the demon seizes power, not over a soul, but over a body, which the demon can manipulate as it wishes. In such cases, exorcism will only be performed if the affected individual displays the typical signs of possession: the manifestation of strength exceeding normal capacities, the comprehension of an unknown language, the revelation of distant or hidden facts, and a violent aversion to religious symbols and the name of Jesus.

Lessard finds the authors' contact information on the last page of the pamphlet. The number listed for Dorion is the one at which Lessard has been trying vainly to reach him. He hopes he'll do better with Trudeau's number, though he isn't overly optimistic. The pamphlet was printed in 2002; it's possible that he'll simply get a recorded message: "The number you have dialed is no longer in service."

But this seems to be his lucky day. His call goes to voice mail.

He leaves a message.

The moment he puts down his BlackBerry, it starts to buzz.

Father Trudeau doesn't waste time.

"Dad?"

"Oh, hi, Martin."

"I just went by the apartment," Lessard's son says, his voice tight with anxiety. "The place is full of cops. They wouldn't let me in. There's a dead woman inside."

"Jesus Christ, Martin! I told you to stay away until next week!"

Heads turn. Lessard lowers his voice.

"What were you doing there?"

"I was out of clean clothes."

"Are you still at the apartment?"

"No, I'm in a café on Sherbrooke Street."

"Did anyone ask if you'd seen me, lately?"

"Yeah, Pearson did."

"What did you tell him?"

"That we had an argument, and I haven't seen you in a few days."

"Did you give him the number for my new BlackBerry?"

"I'm not an idiot, Dad. I didn't say anything."

Lessard lets out his breath. For once, he's glad that his son's an experienced liar.

"What's going on, Dad? I just saw in the paper that you're wanted. Do you need help?"

"The less you know, the better, Martin. Don't stay in the neighbourhood. Go to your mother's place." Lessard's tone allows for no contradiction. "And don't give out my number to anyone, you hear me? Not to anyone!"

"I promise, Dad," Martin says, taken aback by his father's firmness.

Lessard ends the call. Shaking his head, he pinches the bridge of his nose between his thumb and forefinger.

Ever since he was born, Martin has had a knack for showing up where he's least expected.

The waitress, a petite blond in a tight-fitting skirt, comes by to warm up his coffee. Barely a minute later, as Lessard is about to ask for the bill, his phone buzzes in his pocket.

"Lessard."

"Hello. This is René Trudeau."

"Father René Trudeau?"

"Uh … yes."

"Hello, Father. As I mentioned in my message, my name is Victor Lessard. I'm a detective with the Montreal Police."

"That's why I called back so fast. I don't often get calls from the police."

"I understand. Thanks for the quick response."

"Don't mention it. Are you the same detective I saw on the news? The one who's gone missing?"

Damn. This was bound to happen sooner or later.

"Yes, I … that's right." Lessard's mind is racing, trying to come up with a credible explanation. "It's kind of complicated. All I can tell you is that I've gone undercover, and to make my cover story believable, I've had to give certain people the impression that I'm on the run. If you like, you can check with my liaison officer, Nadja Fernandez, then call me back. Her number is —"

"No need for that, Detective. I believe you. I was just curious. What can I do for you?"

The detective sergeant doesn't have time for long explanations. He cuts to the chase. "I found your name and number in a pamphlet on exorcism that you co-wrote with another priest. Does that ring a bell?"

"Good heavens," the priest says, surprised. "That was quite a few years ago. Did you read the pamphlet?"

"I'm looking at it as we speak."

"Is that what you're calling about?"

"Partly, yes. You may find this odd, but I'm investigating a series of murders and a kidnapping, and certain details have got me wondering whether I'm on the trail of a Satanic cult."

"I don't find it odd at all. It's what I do. As an exorcist priest, I'm required to be an expert on the devil."

Unsure of how to ask his next question without insulting Trudeau, Lessard stammers a few unconnected words, then makes a fresh start. "I'm sorry, Father, but I thought all this exorcism stuff was ancient history, the kind of thing you only hear about in the movies. Do exorcist priests still exist, nowadays?"

A gust of frank, good-humoured laughter greets his question.

"I understand your skepticism, Detective, but you'd be surprised at how often we're called upon to intervene."

"You mean you regularly perform exorcisms?"

"We don't get up every morning and go to war with the Evil One. We don't have weekly confrontations with people whose heads do three-hundred-and-sixty-degree rotations in front of a crucifix. Genuine possessions are rare. Still, there's a lot of interest in the occult, these days, especially among young people. We've had a rising number of requests for exorcism. In fact, two years ago, on the Pope's instructions, three thousand new exorcist priests were trained."

"I'm not much of a churchgoer," the detective sergeant says, astonished. "But I've got to admit, that surprises me. We have exorcist priests in Quebec?"

"Very much so. The object of exorcism, Detective, is to expel demons or to release individuals from demonic control, through the spiritual authority that Jesus conferred on his Church. In canonical terms, it's the bishops who, as successors to the apostles, are authorized by the Church to perform exorcisms. As a rule, they delegate this authority to subordinates like me — exorcist priests. In any case, if you think you're dealing with a group of Satanists, they wouldn't be seeking liberation from the powers of darkness, like those who come to us for exorcism. Quite the contrary."

"What do you mean?"

"Generally speaking, there are two kinds of Satanists. First, there are those who worship Satan and practise rituals in organized settings. Most of the time, the members of such groups aren't identifiable in their private lives. They practise their 'religion' in secret."

Lessard thinks of Pascal Pierre and his cult. He's eager to find out if Fernandez has learned anything about them.

"The second kind of Satanism," Trudeau goes on, "is what we call the syncretic Satanism of the young."

"Which means?"

"Basically, it's a combination of doctrines and religions that don't have much to do with each other. Many people get involved in Satanism because they're going through a crisis of identity. Unable to make a life for themselves, they turn to 'higher powers.' They're looking for security, identity, adventure. The result is a kind of homemade Satanism, blending together a wide variety of magical and esoteric practices. In both varieties of Satanism, worshippers invoke the Evil One. They seek to be immersed in his power — not to be freed from it, like the people who come to us to be exorcised."

"I understand. And what about the exorcisms you perform? Do they look like what we see in movies?"

"No," Trudeau says, laughing. "Among other things, the rite involves sprinkling with holy water, a number of different prayers, the laying on of hands, the showing of a crucifix to the possessed person, and an order addressed directly to the devil, commanding him to depart. The rite is rarely used. In thirty years, I've performed it fewer than a dozen times. Generally speaking, our struggle is more often against anxiety than against Satan. You see, Detective, the aim of my ministry is to listen. Most people who come to me are troubled, weighed down by suffering. In a majority of cases, talking to me helps them to shed their burden. Church authorities prefer to create structures that offer active listening and psychological support to individuals in trouble. The rite of exorcism is only appropriate in cases of true diabolical possession."

"But how can you be sure you're not dealing with schizophrenia?"

"That's the hard part, obviously, distinguishing between mental illness and true possession. I'd say it comes with experience. Exorcist priests gather at annual conventions, and they're backed up by multidisciplinary teams, with which they discuss cases of suspected possession. My own team, which meets every six weeks, is made up of other exorcist priests, a layman who specializes in active listening, and two psychiatrists."

Trudeau's mention of regular meetings to discuss suspected cases gives Lessard an idea.

"I know you're bound by the secrecy of the confessional. But without revealing any specifics, can you tell me if someone named David Cortiula ever came up among the cases you treated or examined? I'm asking because, in Cortiula's apartment, I found a lot of newspaper clippings and documents relating to the devil. He seems to be very interested in the subject — if not fascinated."

"Cortiula … let me think…. No, sorry, I've never heard the name. You know, requests for exorcism have to be submitted to the diocese where the person lives. An exorcist priest is then designated by the diocesan authorities. For the archdiocese of Quebec City, it's me. If a request had been submitted, I'd have been notified, because a file is automatically created for every request."

Confidentiality doesn't seem to be a concern for Trudeau, who gives the same answer when Lessard asks about Chan Lok Wan.

"There's something else you should keep in mind, Detective," the priest says. "Collecting articles about the devil doesn't in itself make someone a Satanist. Trust me, lots of healthy, sensible people are interested in the subject simply because it's fascinating."

The detective sergeant has a sudden thought. "You said you're the exorcist priest for the archdiocese of Quebec City, right?"

"Right."

"Cortiula lives in Montreal."

"Then he would have been referred to the exorcist priest for the archdiocese of Montreal."

"Who's that?"

"A former teacher of mine, and one of the top people in the field. Aldéric Dorion."

38

As she searches the room that was Chan Lok Wan's personal office, Taillon finds a DVD in the wastebasket. This wouldn't be of particular interest if it weren't for the fact that Aldéric Dorion's name is written on the disc in indelible ink.

Without thinking, she inserts the disc into a DVD player that's connected to one of the monitors. After pushing several buttons, she manages to get a picture and sound.

An elderly man's face comes up on the screen. He's wearing a cassock. Above him, the date appears. The video was shot a few days ago.

My name is Aldéric Dorion. I'm a priest in the parish of Côte-des-Neiges and the exorcist priest for the archdiocese of Montreal. I have asked Chan Lok Wan to give this recording to the authorities if something should happen to me.

I'll get right to the point. On December twenty-fourth, 1983, the Pope issued a confidential directive to all members of the clergy — cardinals, archbishops, bishops, priests, deacons, monks, and nuns — ordering them to inform their local exorcist priest if they witnessed any activity that was related, or might be related, to cases of diabolical bewitchment or possession. Thereafter, secret files began to be assembled in numerous parishes, without parishioners' knowledge. Every case of presumed demonic bewitchment, and every completed exorcism, was catalogued and reported to Rome.

When the directive was issued, I had recently taken up my post as a parish priest in Val-d'Or.

In the aftermath of a violent incident in March 1985, I was asked to take an interest in two boys who had been implicated in the matter. These boys, David Cortiula and Chan Lok Wan, had lived together in a youth centre before being placed in the same group home.

Suffice it to say that the boys had persuaded a schoolmate to try to kill himself with a bayonet.

Following this incident, I was asked to start meeting the boys in my capacity as a resource person. The underlying facts, combined with certain suggestive signs and the boys' answers to my questions, led me to suspect demonic possession. The suspicion was strong in David's case, less so in Chan's. Over the course of our meetings, I discovered that David had, since early childhood, developed a skill for reading people and guessing their innermost thoughts — a skill that bordered on telepathy.

In keeping with the papal directive, I reported the two cases to the exorcist priest of the diocese. A few weeks went by, during which there was no follow-up to my report.

I soon forgot about the whole thing. This was made easier by the fact that I liked the boys. During the previous few years, they'd been members of a choir that I directed with the help of a singing teacher.

In April 1985, I received a surprise visit from a man then serving as Apostolic Nuncio to Canada, Alessandro Bartolozzi, who called himself Noah.

He questioned me at length about David and insisted on meeting him. He also examined my notes. Before leaving, he instructed me to keep him posted about noteworthy developments, and suggested that I offer the boys free enrollment at the seminary, where they could finish their education. With the boys' best interests in mind, the youth centre where they were living accepted my offer. I also had the seminary administration name me as the boys' tutor for the duration of their schooling.

From 1985 until early 1989, apart from a few minor scrapes, the boys' progress was uneventful. David was a brilliant student. Chan was above average.

At that time, I was convinced that the boys had benefitted from a timely intervention, and that I had been too hasty in suspecting possession. But in early 1989, the city was shaken by a series of violent acts and strange phenomena.

Initially taken aback by the contents of the DVD, Taillon regains her composure, presses the PAUSE button, and takes out her notebook. She jots down a few sentences summarizing what she's just heard, then hits PLAY:

There were several cases of animal sacrifice, as well as a series of strange accidents that might have been deliberate acts. Two of the accidents nearly resulted in fatalities. I documented these events at length in my files.

During this period, David repeatedly broke into nearby homes. Though he caused no damage — all he was doing was watching people as they slept — this bizarre behaviour quickly spread fear throughout the city.

One thing led to another, and the boys began to be blamed for every misfortune in the area, including the series of accidents and animal sacrifices.

The situation quickly got out of hand, to a point where the boys' safety was at risk. In collaboration with local youth protection authorities and the administrators at the centre, we moved the boys to the city of Sherbrooke. In light of their close friendship, they were placed in the same group home.

Wanting to monitor the boys' development, I asked the archdiocese for a transfer to Sherbrooke. Shortly after my arrival there, having completed the required training, I became the exorcist priest for the diocese of Sherbrooke. In that capacity, I was fascinated by David's case.

I continued to see the boys regularly, because they were choir members at the church to which I was assigned. Within a short time, I became the choir director.

The café is jammed.

The air is filled with the clamour of conversation. A groundswell of voices bounces off the walls, and Lessard's ears are assaulted by the jangling noise of glassware. Nameless faces twist into terrifying shapes, then melt away like waxen masks.

He closes his eyes.

For a moment, he seems to see a nightmarish, filth-covered face in the crowd, wreathed in a ring of fire.

On the verge of fainting, he pays his bill and escapes the pandemonium.

With the cold rain stinging his cheeks, the detective sergeant slowly comes back to himself.

The conversation with Father Trudeau has left him puzzled.

On the one hand, Trudeau told him that Aldéric Dorion is the exorcist priest for the archdiocese of Montreal. But Trudeau has no contact information for Dorion, apart from the numbers that Lessard has already tried.

On the other hand, Trudeau explained that the articles and documents found in Cortiula's apartment don't prove anything in themselves. Lots of people are interested, even fascinated, by all things connected with the devil — but that doesn't make them Satanists.

Lessard has asked Trudeau to find out whether Cortiula recently sought an exorcism from the archdiocese of Montreal, but the detective sergeant isn't getting his hopes up. Cortiula has known Dorion for over twenty years. He could have requested an exorcism a long time ago.

As Lessard sees it, the question remains unanswered: Why has Cortiula amassed his impressive collection of documents relating to the devil? Could it be simple personal interest, unconnected with the case at hand?

If, however, Cortiula's collection *is* connected with the case, then Lessard comes back to his original hypothesis. The only logical explanation is that Cortiula belongs to a Satanic cult.

Which leads to another question: Does Dorion belong to the same cult?

When Lessard suggested that Dorion might be a Satanist, Trudeau laughed and said the chances of Aldéric Dorion being a Satanist were about as great as the chances of Queen Elizabeth being an exotic dancer.

Lessard has come to a dead end. He knows it, yet he continues to rack his brain.

After locking his bedroom door, the SIV agent pulls the metal briefcase out from under the bed, extracts his MacBook Pro, and starts to type an email. As the text appears in the window of the secure interface that he uses to communicate with Rome, thoughts come crowding into his head. He's obliged to stop typing for a moment to jot some notes onto a sheet of paper.

Is he forgetting anything?

One of Moreno's men has been tasked with disposing of Dorion's body. The old priest's heart gave out. Which simplifies matters. Vincenzo and two of his henchmen are now following David, making sure they don't lose him again.

The camera and audiovisual equipment are waiting in the van.

His fingers start moving over the keyboard again.

Before encrypting the file and sending it along, he reads the closing lines of his message to the cardinal prefect.

As of tonight, we will have gathered all the evidence we need. Our work will be complete.

The Soldiers of Christ are at your service.

Lessard walks along Mont-Royal Avenue, his eyes straying over the colourful shop windows.

Fernandez has left several messages on his voice mail since last night, but until now, he hasn't felt strong enough to call her back.

"Hey, Nadja. Did you run into trouble because of me?"

"No. You were right. Taillon came through. She made sure nobody asked questions about what I was doing at the scene. I have to say, though, she doesn't think very highly of you."

"Yeah. Long story. Did you manage to find out what those three people were doing in the cells? Were they sadomasochists?"

"I don't know. Taillon had me fill her in on everything I knew about the situation, then told me I should get out of there if I wanted to avoid problems."

"What did she ask?"

"All the standard questions. By the way, I didn't say anything, but she knows I'm helping you behind the scenes. As I mentioned in one of my messages, she really wants you to call her. I can give you her number ..."

"I have it. Did you get my text?"

"Yeah. Taillon's staying tight-lipped about Pascal Pierre and his cult. I know she questioned him, and he's still in custody, but nothing has leaked out, so I don't have anything else for the moment. Tell me, why do you think the trio in Val-d'Or are involved in the cult?"

"It's just one of several hypotheses. The truth is, I'm lost, Nadja. I've got the two pedophiles in one corner, the three amigos from Val-d'Or in another, and Laila François and Pascal Pierre in a third. Not to mention the pedophile ring and the three people who were locked away with Laila — the sado-masochists, or whatever they are. I'm trying to find the common thread that connects all these people, but I'm getting nowhere, and it's driving me crazy."

"You're putting too much pressure on yourself, Victor. An army of detectives would have trouble solving this thing. And you're all by yourself."

Solitude is eating away at him. The desire to ask her to join him is so great that he has to bite his lower lip until it bleeds. The desire subsides.

"I may be wrong," he says after a moment's silence, "but my instinct is telling me that the first thing I need to figure out is how Wan, Dorion, and Cortiula are linked to Laila François. At Dorion's place, I found a bookshelf full of documents relating to exorcism. At Cortiula's, there were writings on the devil. And I learned that Dorion is the exorcist priest for the archdiocese of Montreal. I figured if they all belonged to Pascal Pierre's group, it might be some kind of Satanist cult. But a source has just given me confirmation that Dorion almost certainly isn't a Satanist."

"I can help you on that score. I made a few calls and talked to a contact at the Info-Cult Resource Centre. From what he told me, the Solar Passage has nothing to do with devil-worship. It's just a variant on the polygamous groups that you find across Canada and the U.S. — basically an excuse for Pascal Pierre to create a harem of more than ten women."

Lessard stores that information in a corner of his brain for future reference. Meanwhile, his hypothesis about Satanism seems to be wrong.

"There's something else," Fernandez continues. "Sirois is still looking into the histories of the three amigos. For now, all I can tell you is that Cortiula lived in Sherbrooke at the same time as Dorion. I don't know about Wan yet. Sirois is also trying to establish when Sandoval and Applebaum started singing in a choir."

"Nadja, starting now, I'd like you to keep Sirois's involvement in all this to a strict minimum. I don't want him getting in trouble because of me. I already regret having mixed you up in the whole thing —"

"Hang on. I made my own choices. No one twisted my arm. I hear what you're saying about Sirois, and I'll be careful. But you know him. He's a mini-Lessard."

"Don't say that. I feel guilty enough already."

Lessard has been working closely with Sirois for the past year. As he reflects on his own unorthodox methods and occasional rule-bending, the detective sergeant hopes he hasn't been a bad influence on his young colleague.

"Anything else?" he asks, wanting to change the subject.

"I also checked to see whether Cook ever sang in a choir."

"And?"

"You were right. He sang in the choir at the Church of the Holy Spirit."

"Is that in Notre-Dame-de-Grâce?"

"No, in Rosemont, the family's former neighbourhood."

Lessard remembers that the Cooks moved to Notre-Dame-de-Grâce a few months before the killings.

"Am I wrong, or did they live in the same area as Cortiula before moving?"

"In Rosemont? I hadn't thought about it, but you're right."

An electric jolt runs through him. He hadn't paid much attention to the question, but if Cortiula sang in the same choir as Applebaum and Sandoval in Sherbrooke, is it conceivable that …?

"Jesus, Nadja! Were Cook and Cortiula in the same choir?"

"Why? Does it matter?"

"Possibly."

"I'll check and call you back."

Sandoval and Cortiula sang in the same choir. If the same was true of Cook and Cortiula, what does that mean? What conclusions can be drawn?

That Cortiula knew both men, certainly.

What else?

Lessard senses that this goes deeper. The pounding of his heart confirms that something is eluding him. His instinct tells him that he's getting close, that the solution is within reach.

Having gotten back into the car, he lights a cigarette. Tendrils of blue smoke curl through the vehicle's interior.

He closes his eyes and lets his brain process the information. He replays Viviane Gray's account in his memory: John Cook had told the psychologist that he felt like someone was watching him in his sleep. Cook was so shaken that he wasn't sure whether it was just a dream.

Fast-forward to the conversation with Carol Langelier.

According to the retired cop, Cortiula was repeatedly found in the homes of Val-d'Or residents, watching them while they slept.

Is it possible that Cortiula kept up this strange practice in adulthood? Is it possible that he slipped into John Cook's home at night and watched him sleep? Might he have done the same thing to Sandoval?

And if so, why?

Lessard is convinced that Cook and Sandoval were murdered, which leaves only one possibility. If Cortiula was slipping into the men's homes, it was as reconnaissance in preparation for returning to kill the occupants.

The detective sergeant is persuaded that his deductions are sound, but he has nothing tangible to back them up. What's worse, he doesn't yet understand Cortiula's motives for killing the two men, nor why a powerful organization seems bent on preventing the police from solving the mystery. But while Lessard hasn't yet found answers to these questions, he remains convinced that he's on the right track.

He opens the car window. As the cigarette smoke dissipates, so does the fog of bafflement clouding his mind. A sudden insight strikes him — a conjecture as simple as it is blindingly obvious.

Cortiula chose his victims from among the members of the choir.

Fascinated, Taillon can't take her eyes off the screen, where the old man is gazing directly at the camera through his thick glasses as he pursues his calm narrative.

I continued to send occasional reports to Noah, who came back to see David in early 1990. I realized then that David, not Chan, was the subject of Noah's interest.

The boys were separated at age twelve and placed in foster homes. Despite their separation, and despite the fact that they attended different schools, they managed to stay in touch.

When the Pope revoked his directive in late 1992, I stopped submitting my reports, but I kept up my interest in the boys. David and Chan remained in the choir during their teenage years. Neither of them was very outgoing, but we were on friendly terms, and I was happy to see that they seemed to be straightening out.

At the same time, I had new responsibilities to keep me busy. Apart from our choir practices, my contact with them became more and more sporadic over the years.

Chan left school in 2000 and went to live in Montreal. I had lost track of him the previous year, when he quit the choir.

Two years after Chan's departure, I could see that something wasn't right with David. He was living alone at the time, having cut ties with his foster family.

Everything went to pieces in the space of a few weeks. David dropped out of university, where he had been studying philosophy. He began to behave strangely, and to make threatening, offensive statements.

After several years in which things had seemed to be progressing normally, the dark side of his soul — the side that I had glimpsed when he was a child — revealed itself once again, and my old fears returned.

At first, I hoped he was having a breakdown, or even that he was schizophrenic. I sent him to see the psychiatrists with whom I worked when I was evaluating cases of demonic bewitchment. But his problems didn't seem to be psychological in nature.

To be an exorcist, one must believe in the devil. But in David's case, it was as though I refused to acknowledge reality, perhaps because I knew there was something good in him.

For several years, periods of crisis alternated with cycles of relative calm. David did odd jobs here and there to pay the rent, and he even registered as a student at the Quebec School of Professional Hypnotism. He was expelled for bad behaviour after a few weeks.

Taillon hasn't moved a muscle: she's riveted by the video. But even as she watches, her mind is assailed by a nagging question: What was the DVD doing in the wastebasket?

The downward spiral continued, until one day David was arrested for breaking into the home of an antique dealer in Sherbrooke. No charges were laid, but a week later, the antique dealer attempted suicide, lapsing into a neurovegetative state from which he never recovered. Although I still had great affection for David, I remembered what had happened in March of 1985, and I began to suspect that David had, in some way, influenced the dealer's actions. My suspicion was intensified by the fact that we both knew this man, who was a member of our choir and hadn't previously seemed depressed.

As suddenly as the situation had deteriorated, it returned to normal after this incident. David became his old self. He resumed his former activities and even went back to university.

Everything seemed to be on track until 2006, when he had another breakdown. This one coincided with a horrific murder-suicide in which Richard Sandoval killed his wife, and then himself. I couldn't help being struck by the strange coincidence that Sandoval, too, had been a member of our choir.

But sometimes we only see what we want to see. Looking back, I realize that I should have confronted David. I should have asked if he was responsible for the antique dealer's suicide attempt, and for the deaths of Sandoval and his wife. But that's not what I did.

Instead, like a sorcerer's apprentice, I believed that I could fix everything myself. I proposed to David that I exorcise him. Although I had the necessary experience and qualifications, I was neglecting the most elementary precautions. I was intervening in a case in which I was emotionally involved, a case for which I was inadequately prepared, and for which I should have requested the assistance of a colleague. In short, my effort failed. For the first time in my career, I was afraid. This was my first failure as an exorcist. I had been unable to repel the force that had taken control of David's body. And by then, I was indeed convinced that David was possessed by a demon.

After that, our relationship began to go downhill. David eventually broke off all contact between us. Even so, when I learned that he had moved to Montreal, I immediately secured a transfer to Côte-des-Neiges. I couldn't bring myself to give up on him. His case had become an obsession.

One thing led to another, and I got back in touch with Chan Lok Wan. Through him, I was able to stay informed about

David, who seemed to have settled back into a normal life. He had found a job as a delivery man for a convenience store, and he sang in a choir in the Rosemont district. I kept tabs on him from a distance, respecting his desire not to see me.

Eager to return to his motel room, Lessard zigzags between the puddles on Saint-Jacques Street. In a state of excitement, he pulls over to take a call from Fernandez.

"I don't know how you guessed it," she says, "but you were right. Cortiula and Cook were both choir members at the Church of the Holy Spirit."

"Bingo!"

"Why is that so important, Victor?"

"I may be wrong, but I think Cortiula killed the Cooks and the Sandovals. And I think he chose his victims from among the people he sang with."

"My God. What makes you believe that?"

"I don't have time to explain, Nadja. We need to find that son of a bitch in a hurry."

"Sure. But how?"

"Do you have a list of choir members at the Church of the Holy Spirit?"

"I'm looking at it. Why?"

"Just a hunch. Run all the names through the database and check to see if any of them recently filed a complaint for home invasion, anything along those lines."

"Okay, but wh—"

"Nadja, do what I ask, okay? We'll discuss it later."

"Okay. Give me an hour or so. I'll get back to you."

Lessard pulls into the motel lot.

He's cold, hungry, and exhausted. The pain in his arm is so severe that he can barely move.

"You should take the pills Simone prescribed," Raymond suggests.

The detective sergeant parks the car and, following his brother's advice, swallows two anti-inflammatories.

A long, hot shower will wash away the day's grime. Then he'll put on some clean clothes from the supply that Simone was kind enough to bring him, and he'll go get something to eat at one of the fast-food places in the neighbourhood.

With an effort, he extricates himself from the car and walks painfully to the door of his room. He has trouble sliding the key into the lock, which is refusing to co-operate.

He knows it's the right key.

As he bends down to check the lock, his skull explodes.

While the old man continues to talk, Jacinthe Taillon watches with rapt fascination, impressed by his phenomenal memory. Aldéric Dorion isn't reading from a text. He's delivering a detailed account straight to the camera, as though he were reliving the events he's describing:

During the mid 2000s, I learned that the *Milites Christi*, a secret, radical arm of the *Propaganda Fide* — the organization that spreads Catholicism throughout the non-Catholic world — had decided to revive the papal directive of 1983. This decision, which came in response to dwindling faith in Catholic countries, was made without consulting the Holy Father. The new directive also authorized the *Propaganda Fide* to extend its activities to Catholic lands where religion was in decline, and to have agents of the Vatican intelligence service — the SIV — investigate possible cases of demonic possession. I learned at the same time that Noah was an SIV agent, and that he belonged to the *Milites Christi*.

I didn't understand why the *Propaganda Fide* had taken an interest in cases of possession. It was Noah who gave me the answer a few months later, when he came and asked for help in approaching David. The aim, this time, was not to exorcise individuals who were thought to be possessed. Rather, it was to observe them, to film them, to assemble files on them.

"For what purpose?"

"To prove that the devil exists. And, therefore, that God does, too."

When I asked Noah to explain, he told me that Rome had fallen into a state of apostasy. It had lost its faith. Numerous prominent members of the Curia were questioning their beliefs, or worse, leaving the Church outright. Any evidence that could help consolidate their faith by demonstrating God's existence would be welcome. For example, new analyses of the Shroud of Turin had been undertaken. Noah declared that those who experienced doubt were longing for a sign. He said they would be ready to accept a negative proof of God's existence — that is, a proof that established the existence of God's most ancient adversary: Satan. Because, for a Catholic believer, if the devil exists, then there is only one force that can counterbalance him: God.

At that point, Noah revealed something that astounded me. For several years now, it had been suspected that David Cortiula was one of the rare cases of true possession in the world. David was their chosen one.

They had watched him, leaving him alone for all these years so that he could ripen. Noah, who was under orders to investigate and gather evidence, had continued to visit Canada in secret during that time, for the purpose of observing David at a distance.

According to Noah, David was governed by irresistible urges that seized control of his body and compelled him to act. His modus operandi was simple: He selected his victims from among his fellow choristers. Over a period of weeks, or even months, he would slip into his victims' homes, bewitching them and eventually prevailing on them to commit suicide.

Noah said that David didn't kill with his own hands, except on one occasion when, to protect a child who was being abused by a procurer, he had split the aggressor's head open with an axe.

Taillon hits the PAUSE button and scribbles down what she's just heard.

Wanting to be sure that she hasn't missed anything, she goes back several times to replay the section in which Dorion declares that Cortiula is a killer. Then she resumes the playback.

I expressed vehement opposition to the whole scheme. It was unthinkable that we would knowingly allow David to kill innocent people. I wanted to terminate the project, but I was unable to. I had forgotten that Noah belonged to a small but powerful group of men who would stop at nothing to achieve their aims. In medieval times, a crusader was considered to be a soldier of Christ, a *miles Christi*. Those who joined the Crusades believed that God had given them a unique task: to liberate the Holy Land and purify the world in preparation for the Second Coming.

The members of the small group I'm talking about are fundamentalists. They see themselves as modern-day soldiers of Christ, a label they've chosen as the name of their organization. Only their objective distinguishes them from their medieval predecessors. They have sworn to restore faith among Catholics by any means necessary. Like crusaders, they will not hesitate to spill blood, because when they kill, they do so in Christ's name. They see their cause as just. Nothing matters but achieving their ultimate aim. In that respect, they are no different from Islamic fundamentalists who commit acts of terrorism.

Noah needed my help to gain David's trust, to get close to him, to gather the evidence necessary to assemble a convincing file. Noah made it abundantly clear that if I refused to help him, he would exact retribution.

And so, with Chan's help, I got back in touch with David a few months ago. David seemed happy to see me again. He even introduced me to a friend of his, Laila François, whom I agreed to work with in a support group for drug-addicted street youth.

Recently, Noah's demands have grown more and more insistent. Yet I can see that David has been making a new life for himself. He seems to be in a positive phase.

Above all, I know what Noah has in mind. I don't excuse the things David may have done, but I don't want him to become a circus freak.

That's why I've decided to stop collaborating with Noah.

Even if David has committed all these crimes, I can't deny him one last chance. I've decided to have him re-evaluated by the psychiatrists and resource people on my team. Except that this time, if another exorcism is called for, I'll have a colleague do it.

I know my decision will have consequences. Noah and the *Milites Christi* are prepared to do whatever it takes to prevail. This recording is therefore a necessary precaution.

A few days ago, David was involved in a domestic murder-suicide in Notre-Dame-de-Grâce. Chan and I haven't heard from him since. Noah was on hand to film the incident and gather evidence, but David disappeared afterward.

Chan has agreed to help me convince David to accept treatment, on condition that the police be kept out of it. But if something happens to me in the meantime, Chan has promised to hand this recording over to the authorities.

I realize, as I say these things, that I'm taking an insane risk. By rights, David should answer for his crimes. I make no excuses for what he's done, but he's a slave to impulses that he can't resist. I also know that I've passively abetted his crimes for years. I'm not asking the families of his victims to understand my motives — only to forgive me. I'm an old man. I'm ashamed of my weakness.

Taillon suddenly stops the DVD, jots down the name and address spoken by Dorion in the video, and runs out.

Fernandez freezes. Lessard was right.

When she runs the choristers' names from the Church of the Holy Spirit through the Police Information Centre database, she discovers that on March 7th, at 2:43 a.m., one Jerome Baetz called the provincial police detachment in the Laurentian municipality of Saint-Sauveur.

From the information on the database, Fernandez learns that Baetz, aged fifty-two, told the patrol officers who came to his home that he had been suddenly roused from his sleep around 2:30 a.m. when he became aware of a presence in his bedroom.

Terrified, he started yelling.

He said the intruder had fled, going out the back door.

The patrol officers found no sign of forced entry, but they did notice footprints in the snow near the door. Their report also mentions that Baetz, who had an injured back, had taken powerful anti-inflammatories and sleeping pills to cope with his pain. If the officers thought this detail worth noting, it's fair to conclude that they doubted Baetz's story.

Fernandez does some more digging and discovers that Baetz, who sings in the church choir, has addresses in Saint-Sauveur and on Bourbonnière Avenue in Rosemont. The house in Saint-Sauveur must be a country home.

She leaves a message on Lessard's voice mail, asking him to call her back.

Taillon is racing along the highway toward the Laurentians.

As she weaves through traffic, she knows there can only be one reason why the DVD ended up in the wastebasket: Chan Lok Wan never intended to give Dorion's video to the authorities.

She calls the goth secretary, whom she ordered to stay available in case Taillon had further questions.

Josée Labrie's voice is hoarse with sleep.

Taillon tells her about the video and summarizes its contents, then asks Labrie if she was aware of its existence.

"No, I didn't know anything about it."

"What kind of relationship did Wan have with Father Dorion?"

"It was hard to tell with Chan, but I think he liked him."

"So why would he have thrown Dorion's DVD in the wastebasket?"

There's a long silence.

"Chan hated cops. I may be wrong, but I think handing over the video and letting David get arrested might have felt like a betrayal. One thing's for sure: Chan would never have betrayed David. The guy was like a brother to him."

Taillon ponders. Could Wan have taken the DVD from Dorion simply to avoid hurting his feelings, while knowing that he would never keep his promise if what the old man feared came to pass?

"You'd need to know Chan," Labrie adds, "and the life he chose, to understand what kind of person he was. He heard confessions from a lot of people who'd done terrible things. Even if David was a murderer, as you claim, Chan wouldn't have judged him."

"And they'd been friends since childhood, so Chan had probably already known the truth for years."

"Probably," Labrie says.

"Do you think Chan might have been an accomplice to David's murders?"

"He could have known about them, definitely. Besides whipping David whenever he was asked, Chan served as a kind of confessor to him. But an accomplice? Honestly, I doubt it."

Taillon floors the accelerator, praying that she gets there in time. The final thirty seconds of the video keep replaying in her head:

If this recording is now in the hands of the authorities, you should know that unless I'm mistaken, David Cortiula's next intended victim is another member of the choir at the Church of the Holy Spirit.

His murder will take place on May eleventh, at sixty-four forty-five Lac Millette Road in Saint-Sauveur.

His name is Jerome Baetz.

666

He who does not believe in the devil does not believe in the gospel.

— John Paul II

Lessard wakes up in darkness, lying on his side, his hands tied behind his back and his legs bound. There's a metallic taste in his mouth. Excruciating pinpoints are spinning inside his battered head, and his skull feels like an iron band is compressing it mercilessly. He's nauseated, his eyes feel too big for their sockets, and the pain in his arm is driving him crazy.

After a few minutes, his mind is clear enough to realize not only that there's a hood over his head, but that he's in the trunk of a moving car.

The tires are squealing on the wet asphalt as a cold wind blows through the gaps in the trunk and whistles in his ears. He knows he needs to fight down the panic that's threatening to overwhelm him. He needs to hold his own against the sickening sensation of being buried alive. He needs to keep his wits about him as the car's movements bounce his body against the sides of the trunk, knocking the breath out of him. He needs to resist the terror of suffocation that's clutching at his throat, and, with each century-long second that passes, he needs to keep hoping that light will touch his eyes again.

What will he see by that light?

The barrel of a gun, aimed at his forehead?

Whatever happens, he intends to look death in the face, unflinchingly.

The car stops. The trunk creaks open.

A weak glow seeps through the cloth of the hood. Hands seize him roughly.

His legs are untied. He's pulled upright and forced to walk at a rapid pace.

He collides with unseen obstacles, stumbles into unsuspected barriers, and falls to his knees. He hears laughter behind him, to his right. He's set back on his feet. He resists, stops moving, tries to orient himself — but he can't see a thing.

He's shoved from behind, and a gun barrel is jammed into his ribs.

A harsh flow of bile rises in his throat.

He's completely lost control of the situation. Images from his worst nightmares crowd into his mind: the bloody faces of Picard and Gosselin appear before him. He doesn't want to perish as they did, tortured to death by bloodthirsty animals.

No. Not like that.

He wants to die well, fighting to the last. He wants to feel the blood pumping through his struggling limbs one last time before his heart is stilled forever.

He hopes he gets the chance.

Is this the end?

His mind is racing. There are so many things he hasn't done, so many experiences he hasn't had.

He thinks of his kids, Martin and Charlotte.

Will they miss him? He's not sure. At this moment, with death looming, with the final reckoning upon him, it would be a solace to know that his passage through life had left some mark on his loved ones, if not on the world.

Will Marie and Véronique come to his funeral?

What about Nadja Fernandez? Does she have feelings for him?

If she does, will his death hit her hard? Never until this moment has he been so sure that he's missed out on something with her.

Tears of rage fill his eyes.

Not here. Not now. Not like this.

He isn't ready.

"Sit," a voice says sharply.

"Go fuck yourself."

Something hits him crushingly in the ribs. A pistol butt.

He's shoved down onto a chair.

"That's enough, Vincenzo. You will have your chance. Remove the hood."

His eyes are dazzled by the sudden brightness.

When they get used to the light, he recoils at what he sees. In the raw glow of a ceiling lamp, a priest and an immense man are standing in front of him. The immense man is giving him a stony look as he points a gun at his head.

Lessard sees that the two men are wearing latex gloves. Not a good sign.

He also sees that the priest isn't Aldéric Dorion.

As he struggles to subdue the trembling in his legs, Lessard barely registers the nondescript space in which he's sitting: a windowless room painted in chocolate tones, a wide leather couch, and, against one wall, a plasma TV and home cinema system.

With his hands still tied behind him, he's seated on a straight-backed chair in the middle of the room. His arm hurts like hell.

Where is he?

No idea. The room could be in any of the thousands of anonymous bungalows that fill the suburbs of Montreal.

"Thank you for accepting my invitation, Detective Lessard."

The priest looks him up and down, as though appraising the adversary who's spent the past few days poisoning his existence and impeding his progress. From the dark expression and clenched jaw of the priest's imposing, more youthful companion, Lessard knows he's doomed. But he can't help himself: when he's afraid, he strikes a careless pose.

"Sorry, but I have other obligations."

"I'm afraid they'll have to wait," the priest says.

"How about we cut to the chase?" Lessard says. "Where's Cortiula?"

"Don't worry about David. He's close by."

"Butchering his next victim?"

"You're an excellent police officer, the kind of man I like to work with. But this time you've gotten in over your head. You should have walked away when I gave you the chance."

Lessard's mind races, connecting the dots. Is this priest the person with whom he exchanged text messages after the attempt on his life at the rest stop?

"How did you find me?" he asks.

"One of my men has been following you since you left Chan Lok Wan's place. Nice work, incidentally. He never had a chance."

Lessard shakes his head scornfully. "You can't seriously think you'll get away with this. You may have left Viviane Gray's body at my place, but the forensics people will eventually confirm that she was killed at the train station."

"That hardly matters," Noah says with a dismissive wave of the hand. "Coming after your suspension, and given your depressive state, your suicide will add yet another confusing element to a case that already makes no sense. Besides, by the time your body is finally found, none of it will make any difference anymore."

A wave of fury washes over Lessard. He struggles against his restraints. He needs to play for time, to keep the man in the cassock talking until he can think of a way to free himself.

"Why the fuss over Cortiula? Why are you protecting a common killer?"

"That's where you're mistaken, Detective. David is anything but common."

Lessard has nothing to lose. He baits his hook with every sordid, slimy morsel at his disposal, and throws out his line.

"Let me put it more clearly. He's a murderous animal who also happens to be a pedophile and devil-worshipper."

"Perhaps," Noah says musingly, "I've overestimated you, after all. I thought I needed to get you out of the way before you interfered with our plans yet again. I believed you were closing in on the truth. But you've understood nothing."

"Great," Lessard says, starting to rise from the chair. "In that case, I'm sure you won't mind if I run along."

Moreno shoves him back down.

"Sorry," the SIV agent says, his voice filled with false compassion.

Lessard stops playing games. He looks into Noah's eyes. "I don't want to die like this, without understanding."

He sees Noah hesitate. The priest is wondering whether he can safely reveal his secrets to the detective sergeant. Seeming to decide that there's no risk in doing so, Noah nods, confirming to Lessard that he won't get out of this alive.

"I've had my eye on David since he was seven years old. He is definitely not a pedophile or a devil-worshipper. David is inhabited by a power that controls him without his knowledge. He has a gift."

Lessard remembers his conversation with Father Trudeau, the exorcist priest for the archdiocese of Quebec City. He also recalls the documents that he found in Cortiula's apartment.

"Is this a case of possession? Are you going to exorcise him?"

"Once again, you're mistaken. Over the years, I've watched the power grow in him. I have no intention of exorcising him now that it's finally reaching maturity."

"You think he's possessed by the devil, is that it?"

"Your conception is so reductive. Good versus evil. God versus Satan. These dichotomies are a recent development in the history of religious faith. Did you know that the earliest belief systems conceived of God and Satan as a single being? Satan was nothing more than God's anger, his dark side. It was the Judeo-Christian tradition that set up Satan as an entity distinct from God — an entity that was the source of evil in the world. This vision may have been necessary to persuade the masses, but if you ask me, it's a caricature."

Lessard isn't sure what to make of all this speechifying. For him, the question is simpler:

"Why have you allowed Cortiula to kill as he pleases?"

"You're so focused on the tree that you've lost sight of the forest. David has the potential to restore faith among Catholics."

"If a psychopathic murderer has that potential, then the Church is in worse trouble than I thought."

"Faith is on the wane. Even the most fervent believers are demanding evidence that God exists. Whatever name you choose to give that entity, it inhabits David. Good or evil, it's the closest we've come to tangible proof of God's existence since the death of Christ."

"And this justifies letting him kill with impunity? It justifies your own murder of anyone who stands in your way?"

"You know, Detective, in the eyes of a Catholic believer, death is a deliverance. It's the doorway to eternal life. You must never lose sight of that fact. Death is worth living through."

"Is that how you rationalize the slaughter of innocent human beings?"

"I won't try to convince you. If you saw him at work, you'd understand."

"Did Aldéric Dorion understand?"

If Noah is surprised at the number of clues Lessard has been able to gather in so short a time, his expression doesn't betray it.

"He was the first person to witness the gift, while David was still just a child. In a way, it was Father Dorion who discovered him."

"Where is Dorion now?" Lessard asks.

"He's where he can no longer cause problems," the priest says, in a voice that offers little hope for the old man's well-being.

"Why?"

"Let's just say we had some differences of opinion." There's a brief silence. The priest looks at his watch. "David went missing after the Cooks died. I asked Dorion, among other things, to help me find him. He refused."

Questions are rushing into Lessard's head. First and foremost, he knows he needs to keep his captor talking, to buy time, hoping for a miracle.

"Were you the one standing in the Cooks' backyard, holding an axe?"

Noah smiles. Lessard has surprised him once again.

"Did someone see me? Cook broke the spell for a moment and ran into the shed with the axe. I brought him back into the house after David re-asserted his control over him."

The scene plays out in front of Lessard's eyes in fast motion: after taking refuge in the shed, knowing he's finished, Cook hastily scribbles a message to his mistress.

It's not me, Viviane.

"Why did you kill Viviane Gray?"

"I couldn't run the risk that she might provide you with a lead."

"Were you the one who struck Cook in the shoulder?"

"No. That was David. He panicked momentarily after Cook broke free of his power."

It takes Lessard a few seconds to grasp the significance of what Noah has just told him.

"You mentioned a spell. Does David hypnotize his victims? Is that why he was slipping into people's homes at night?"

"Well done, Detective. Yes, David has a gift. It's in his eyes. He can look at you and read thoughts that you refuse to admit even to yourself. That's the power that enables him to incite his victims to violence, without ever raising a hand against them. As I said earlier, you would understand if you had seen him at work."

"Was that how he killed Sandoval?"

"Yes."

"Did he kill Sandoval because he was a pedophile?"

Glancing at his watch once more, Noah seems surprised by Lessard's question, but he shows no inclination to explore the matter.

"I don't know what you're talking about, but it's beside the point. David is impelled by urges he can't resist, not by moral considerations. The only reason Sandoval died was that he sang in the same choir as David. That's how all the victims were chosen." Noah claps his hands. "Now, if you'll excuse me, I must be off. But before I go, I do have one question for you."

"If you insist," Lessard says, still playing for time.

"Are you a believer, Detective Lessard? Do you have faith?"

Lessard thinks for a moment. "I had faith as a boy. It was in my teens, when I started taking philosophy courses in college, that I became an atheist. But I still abide by the Christian value system, which is the foundation that society stands on."

"You know, Quebec is hardly the only place on earth where religion has been tossed onto the trash heap. Throughout the Western world, people have stopped placing faith in anything beyond themselves. We've killed God and replaced him with millions of foolish, narcissistic, imperious little self-worshippers who can't see past their own navels. What, I'd like to know, have we gotten in return? And one final question, Detective. When the fateful moment comes — when, a few minutes from now, Vincenzo pulls the trigger, will there really be no lingering doubt in your mind? Can you declare with certainty that as you draw your final breath, you won't put your fate in God's hands?"

At this point, Lessard is out of tricks. Only honesty remains.

"I don't know," he says truthfully.

"Then you see what I'm fighting for. If I could offer you proof that God exists, would the prospect of death not seem more bearable?"

"The end justifies the means, is that it?" Lessard says.

"But what will justify the end, Detective?" Noah is silent for a moment. "As Camus told us: it is the means."

The priest heads for the door.

Lessard considers asking him to leave Elaine Segato out of all this, but realizes before opening his mouth that there's no need. Elaine was simply an instrument for getting at Lessard and forcing him to abandon his efforts. As soon as he fell into the hands of his enemies, she stopped being in danger.

"And now, Detective, I'll leave you in the hands of Mr. Moreno. I'm sorry it has to end this way."

Lessard knows that the last grain of sand has fallen through the neck of the hourglass. He's reached the end. His life is as good as over. There's only time for one last desperate ploy: provocation.

"About that man I killed in the woods ..."

Noah turns around. A vicious gleam appears in Moreno's eyes.

"… he squealed like a pig before he died."

Moreno pistol-whips Lessard, reopening the cut on his brow that the detective sergeant sustained while chasing Cook's co-worker, Pierre Deschênes.

Moreno lifts the weapon to strike again, but Noah's calm voice stops him.

"Vincenzo. This has to look like a suicide. It won't work if he's covered in bruises."

Tears of rage run down the killer's cheeks.

"He killed my brother, *Padre*."

"I know." There's a brief silence. "Don't disappoint me, Vincenzo."

From his office window, looking south along De la Cathédrale Street, Cardinal Charles Millot watches the headlight beams of a car sweep past the office tower at the corner of De la Gauchetière. Through the gathering gloom, he sees a yellow umbrella approaching the Marriott Chateau Champlain.

Bournival, the archdiocese's head of security, has just left. Lying on the desk is a file that Bournival gave the cardinal. It contains a report on the secret activities that the SIV agent has engaged in.

Millot's eyes are brimming with tears. His jaw has been clenched for hours.

For the first time, he realizes the full extent of Noah's scheme. For the first time, he understands that he had only seen the tip of the iceberg before this moment. The situation is far graver than he could have imagined, even in his worst nightmares.

His conscience is stained. His soul is irretrievably desecrated.

How can he forgive himself for having given free rein to this barbarism?

Holding the report, he goes to an armchair near the fireplace, in which a few logs are crackling. The papers ignite, forming a ball of flame in the hearth.

Lessard is led out of the room where he was being held.

Moreno pushes him into a dingy corridor whose walls must once have been white.

They go through a door.

With the thug's gun pressed to his back, Lessard comes to a basement staircase. The smell of piss assaults his nostrils.

They're in a house: that much is plain.

As he places his foot on the first stair, with death only seconds away, he can't stop his mind from continuing to race, assembling theories, trying to understand. Having once hired a hypnotist during an investigation, he knows they're capable of remarkable things.

But can they make someone kill?

He remembers the time he took his kids to see a hypnotist. Lessard was skeptical until his daughter climbed up on the stage and fell utterly under the man's power, obeying his every word, laughing and crying on command, spellbound by his powers of suggestion. What most impressed Lessard was the surprise and incomprehension that Charlotte — normally so rational — manifested when she returned to her seat.

By the time the show was over, he was convinced.

As Lessard descends the stairs, the dark fragments of the mystery finally come together to form a clear picture.

Initially, the Cook case seemed like a straightforward murder-suicide.

But as Lessard proceeded with his investigation, he uncovered certain elements that led him to suspect the involvement of a third person. There was the note in the shed that seemed to exonerate John Cook; there was Faizan's account of seeing a priest at the crime scene; and finally, there was the inexplicable multitude of flies, which — as Elaine helped him to understand — might have been placed in the house.

The murder of Viviane Gray under his very nose strengthened his conviction that someone outside the Cook family was involved.

Following up on the flies, Lessard went to Sherbrooke, where he discovered the atrocities of Sandoval and Applebaum. Learning that those two men were connected to Aldéric Dorion, Lessard mistakenly assumed that Dorion was the priest whom Faizan had spotted in the Cooks' backyard. The detective sergeant's error on that subject was corrected moments ago by the man in the cassock.

As his search continued, Lessard began to suspect that the two men had been sharing child pornography online. Simple deduction led him to conclude that he had discovered a ring of pedophiles.

What followed was a surreal sequence of events, as Lessard's investigation advanced at a dizzying pace: the murder attempt at the rest stop; the finding of documents related to exorcism in Dorion's apartment; Fernandez's revelation that Dorion knew Laila through a support group for drug-addicted street kids; Felix's statements about Cortiula murdering a pimp; the discovery in Cortiula's home of articles about the devil, along with choir photos of Cortiula with Wan, Dorion, Applebaum, and Sandoval; Taillon's information about Pascal Pierre and his cult; the identification of the white van and the death of Chan Lok Wan; the liberation of Laila François; the explanation by Langelier, the ex-cop from Val-d'Or, of the link between Cortiula, Wan, and Dorion, and of their move to Sherbrooke; the phone conversation with Father René Trudeau, from whom Lessard learned that Aldéric Dorion was the exorcist priest for the archdiocese of Montreal.

And finally, the blow to the head, followed by his conversation with the priest.

All of it leading here, to this confrontation with the inevitable end. This culminating moment in the drama of Lessard's life.

The truth is, he's been dead since 1976. He should have gone with Raymond.

His one remaining wish, as death looms before him, is to look it in the face.

If only Raymond were here to hold his hand at the final instant.

As he goes down the stairs, Lessard squints, trying to make out the shadowy details of the basement. It's no use: the naked bulb lighting the room blinds him with its glare.

He doesn't mind. For the first time since this investigation began, the entire case is illuminated in his mind's eye.

David Cortiula was the black soul concealed in the deathly gloom of the Cook and Sandoval cases.

Yet, if Lessard has understood the priest correctly, apart from inflicting the wound to Cook's shoulder, Cortiula never touched the weapons that were used to commit the crimes. Hard as it is to conceive, Cook and Sandoval committed those horrific acts themselves, under Cortiula's hypnotic power. This helps explain the conclusions that were reached in the autopsy reports. Lessard's conversation with Langelier lends further credence to the priest's claims. In 1985, Cortiula convinced young Carbonneau to stab himself with a bayonet. It was by luck that the boy survived. If the priest is to be believed, the victims owed their terrible fates to the simple fact that they sang in the same choir as Cortiula.

Only one stair remains before Lessard sets foot on the basement floor, where death's infinite stillness awaits. His head is spinning. His thoughts are tumbling and colliding with each other, merging into a shapeless, oily, indistinguishable muck. Stubbornly, he tries to remember the unanswered questions that remain.

Seconds from now, it will be too late.

Suddenly, the fog lifts. If Cortiula really did murder the pimp who assaulted Felix, then that killing doesn't fit the pattern. Why would David have changed his modus operandi? The only explanation Lessard can think of is that the killing of the pimp wasn't planned. Cortiula acted on the spur of the moment.

Another lingering mystery: Lessard still doesn't understand the motives behind the abduction of Laila François. But he's resigned to the idea that he'll die without solving that part of the puzzle.

As his right foot drops down onto the basement floor, he smiles. He feels like all the pieces have finally fallen into place.

Suddenly, it all seems so simple.

Cortiula chose his victims at random among the choir members with whom he sang.

Lessard had sought to establish connections that didn't actually exist. David couldn't have known about the pedophile ring that Sandoval and Applebaum belonged to. Nor could Dorion have had any inkling that the two men preyed on children. He simply knew them because he directed the choir. By the same token, John Cook never committed any acts of pedophilia. While investigating the death of one of Cortiula's victims — Sandoval — Lessard had stumbled across an unrelated crime and set off in pursuit of the pedophiles. Even so, the irony is striking: after participating in the murder of Sandrine Pedneault-King, Sandoval was murdered himself.

For Lessard, the rest of the situation is clear.

The priest. His murderous henchmen. His mad scheme to restore the Catholic faith.

What else remains?

As he steps onto the concrete floor of the basement, Lessard launches himself backward in an effort to knock Moreno off his feet and make him drop his gun.

The cop knows it's a lost cause, but he refuses to go down without a fight.

His head strikes Moreno in the chest, staggering him briefly, but the thug recovers his balance. In two steps, he's on Lessard, seizing him by the hair and pulling him back with all his strength.

Moreno's features, distorted by hatred, fill Lessard's field of vision, centimetres above his face.

The detective sergeant is bent over backward. He cries out in agony.

"Who's squealing like a pig now?" Moreno bellows.

Energized by the white-hot pain coursing through his scalp, Lessard roars back, "Your chickenshit brother was begging for his life when I killed him!"

A howl of rage and grief erupts from Moreno.

The blows rain down on Lessard's face.

Through stalks of wheat swaying in the breeze, he sees Raymond running toward him. The boy's arms are outstretched. His face is bathed in sunlight.

"Come on, Victor! Let's go home!"

Though it hardly seems possible, the smile on Lessard's bloody lips drives Moreno to new heights of fury.

Spent, Lessard offers no resistance as Moreno drags him to a far corner of the basement and dumps him there. Despite the agony in every fibre of the cop's body, there's a delicious goodness in feeling so alive with death so close at hand. But then, through the thick rivulet of blood running into his eyes, he sees something that makes him freeze.

A large woman is sprawled in the corner. Her face is bruised, her eyes are bulging, her hands are tied behind her back, and her mouth is covered with duct tape.

"Jacinthe! What the fuck are you doing here?"

The rain-slick cobblestones are glistening as Cardinal Charles Millot walks along Saint-Paul Street. He slows down, shades his eyes with one hand, and looks up at the silvery dome of Bonsecours Market. Then he turns south on Bonsecours Street and makes his way down to the waterfront.

Millot stops in front of the clock tower. Its white walls contrast starkly with the blackness of the night. He looks to his left and sees the greenish metal structure of the Jacques Cartier Bridge. Greedily, his eyes take in every detail of the vista before him.

Millot looks up at the clock: it's 11:00 p.m. Breathlessly, he clambers over the parapet in front of the tower and, unseen by anyone, plunges into the cold waters of the Saint Lawrence River.

Cardinal Charles Millot doesn't know how to swim.

For a moment, the skirts of his black robe flutter at the surface.

Then they sink beneath a swirl of concentric ripples.

Moreno has placed them facing each other.

Like Taillon, Lessard has been gagged with duct tape.

As Moreno begins to free Lessard's right arm, the detective sergeant realizes what the thug is planning. First, Moreno will put the gun in his hand and force him to shoot Taillon. Then he'll make him put a bullet in his own head.

Other police officers will eventually find the bodies and struggle to understand. Murder. Suicide. They'll wonder whether there was some link with the investigation in progress. Lessard had been depressive. Commander Tanguay had placed him on sick leave. And Viviane Gray's body had been discovered in his apartment.

A hopeless tangle of clues that even Fernandez would have trouble sorting out.

Lessard will struggle until the bitter end, but when Moreno applies maximum pressure and the pain becomes unbearable ...

Taillon is staring at him. She understands what's in store.

With a simple look, she makes it plain that her hatred is gone.

Lessard now knows the answer to the priest's question. At the threshold of death, he feels no need to put his fate in God's hands.

An explosion of pain rips through him: Moreno has torn open Simone's sutures and is driving his fingers into Lessard's bullet wound. The torment is so excruciating that he can't even cry out.

Then everything happens very fast. He hears a familiar voice.

"Police! Drop your weapon!"

Moreno turns quickly toward the staircase.

Two detonations shatter the air; two streaks of flame light up the darkness.

Fernandez and Moreno go down in perfect synchronization.

Fortunately, Moreno loosened the rope that was binding Lessard's injured arm.

Despite the atrocious pain that slices through him with every movement he makes, Lessard manages arduously, knot by knot, to untie himself. As soon as his left arm is free, he pulls the tape off his mouth. On shaky legs, with one eye closed and his face covered in cuts and bruises, he makes his way painfully to Fernandez.

Leaning against the cement wall, her face contorted, she looks at him with wide eyes.

A red flower is blooming on her shoulder.

"Talk to me, Nadja," Lessard murmurs, tearing a strip of fabric from his shirt and pressing it to Fernandez's wound.

"It hurts, Victor. God, it hurts …"

"You're going to be all right. Stay with me."

"When you didn't answer your phone, I took a chance. I figured you might be here." She's silent for a moment. "How did you learn about Jerome Baetz?"

"Save your strength. We'll talk later."

She catches her breath.

"Backup is on the way. I knew there was trouble when I saw blood in Taillon's car."

Lessard hears a low hum that he hadn't noticed before. It fills the air, growing, spreading, until it's all around them.

A fly skims past him through the air. Then another.

Within seconds, a swarm fills the room.

The detective sergeant knows exactly what's going on. A man's life is in jeopardy upstairs. He needs to get up there.

"Hold this," he says to Fernandez, pressing her hand to the make-shift dressing.

He straightens up and staggers over to Taillon, then unties her and removes the tape from her mouth.

"My leg is broken," she says.

Reaching under her armpits, Lessard strains to drag her across the room. But his right arm is useless: he can hardly budge her. He grabs the lapel of her jacket with his left hand. Planting his feet firmly, bending his knees, he pulls her along the floor.

Centimetre by centimetre, Lessard patiently drags Taillon across the concrete surface. Sweaty-faced, with the veins standing out on his neck, he turns Moreno over. The man is lying in a pool of his own blood. His eyes have rolled back in his head.

The bullet pierced his throat.

Moreno raises his head. Through misty eyes, he sees Lessard a short distance away, bent over Taillon. At the sight of the two cops, Moreno can't help thinking that Noah made a mistake in ordering the other members of the team to leave. The priest didn't want David to be disturbed. As a compromise, Noah allowed Moreno himself to stay, to prevent Cortiula from disappearing the way he did after the Bessborough killings — but that precaution wasn't enough. His men would have watched the road, making sure no one sneaked up on him. A bitter smile plays on the dying man's lips. Where he's going, at least, Maria won't be able to reproach him for Pasquale's death.

Lessard distinctly hears Moreno's dying sigh as Taillon's feet slide past the thug's head.

The detective sergeant strains, heaves, falls, pauses, catches his breath. Little by little, expending precious seconds and vast amounts of energy, he manages to get Taillon to the other side of the room.

The three cops look at each other. No words are necessary.

Lessard wrestles Taillon into a sitting position so that she can reach Fernandez's shoulder and apply pressure to the wound.

He rises to his feet and picks up Fernandez's pistol, which has fallen to the floor by her side. He leans over the young cop and strokes her pale cheek.

"Get going, Lessard," Taillon barks. "We'll be okay. Move it, big guy. Go!"

Fernandez gives him a nod.

Raymond is ahead of him on the staircase, leading the way.

Lessard emerges onto the ground floor and stops.

The sight that confronts him is magnificent and horrifying. Thousands of flies are whirling chaotically through the room, bouncing off the walls, colliding with the furniture, spinning and diving in every direction. He has to wave his hands ceaselessly in front of his face to keep the insects out of his eyes and ears. The hum of their wings seems to resonate and amplify into a deafening roar.

Lessard remembers Elaine Segato's words.

Beelzebub. The King of Flies.

Raymond has reached the end of the hall and is signalling to him. "This way, Victor. Hurry!"

Lessard pushes open the door where his brother is standing. He walks through, gun drawn.

And finds the apocalypse.

Is it his imagination, or is the air colder inside the room? He looks around, registering the details of the scene. The priest is standing in a corner, behind a video camera.

In the middle of the room, a naked man is sitting on a chair while a second man, younger, with flaxen hair and angelic features, is speaking in his ear. The naked man is holding a knife in his right hand, cutting into his left thigh at regular intervals.

A large puddle of blood has accumulated under the chair.

Lessard instantly recognizes David Cortiula. The naked victim in his thrall must be the man Fernandez referred to: Jerome Baetz. Neither of them seems to have noticed the cop's arrival.

Lessard's injured arm is hanging by his side. The bullet wound that Moreno reopened is bleeding heavily. He's weak from blood loss — black dots are dancing in front of his eyes.

The walls of the room are closing in, turning opaque and blurry, shrinking into a thirty-centimetre halo that frames the face of David Cortiula.

At that moment, Cortiula looks up at Lessard and unleashes a blinding smile.

His eyes, blue as an autumn sky, show no surprise; they're strangely empty. Lessard suddenly feels himself falling into them. His head is filled with oppressive, unfamiliar words, as a vision of squalid degradation and filth appears in his mind, gripping him, refusing to be shaken off. He sees his mother sitting on the couch where she died. She's pulled the hem of her flowery dress back over her thighs to reveal her parted labia, through which a steady stream of blood is flowing. Crouched in front of her, Raymond is eagerly lapping at the red liquid as it sloshes over her bare legs.

"Victor! Look out!"

His brother's warning cry brings Lessard back to reality. Cortiula straightens up and walks toward him. His eyes transform into red, glowing coals from which Lessard is unable to look away. The pistol in his trembling left hand becomes heavier and heavier, until it hangs uselessly by his side.

An axe appears in Cortiula's rubber-gloved hand. A sadistic grin contorts his face.

Lessard knows he's in danger. Yet he's petrified, unable to move. "Shoot him, Victor. Do it for Mom."

Cortiula is less than a metre away, his gaze drunk with cruelty. He drives the axe into Lessard's leg. As the blade slices through his thigh, Lessard sees the young man's face dissolve. A familiar image take its place — a vision that releases his arm from its paralysis. The Glock rises through the air. His finger strokes the trigger.

The blast seems distant, muted, as though swaddled in cotton.

A perfect red circle appears on Cortiula's forehead.

The King of Flies collapses, his body sucked downward to the floor.

Lessard is already lying there. His leg has given out.

The walls are trembling around him.

Before losing consciousness, he notices that there are only a few flies left in the room.

Raymond approaches. Smiles at him.

"You did it, Victor. You got him this time."

Lessard tries to explain to his brother that Cortiula's power disappeared when his twisted features were replaced by their father's face.

The face of the devil.

Lessard sinks down, down, into unconsciousness ...

POST-MORTEM

When Lessard wakes up, he's lying on a gurney, with a tangle of wires and tubes snaking around his arm. Through the ethereal fog, the world seems to be moving in slow motion.

For the first time in a long while, he feels a sense of communion with everything around him. To his right, he sees the massive outline of Mont Saint-Sauveur bathed in the glow of the emergency lights.

He raises his eyes. Clouds are racing through the sky.

Directly above him, a gust of wind ruffles the foliage of an over-hanging tree. Oblong raindrops slide across the leaves' tender surfaces and cascade onto his face, purifying him.

He lifts his head: ambulance attendants are working feverishly on him, and an army of police officers has arrived at the scene.

That's when he sees her.

With her arm in a sling, she's seated in the back of an ambulance, talking to Sirois and Pearson, wincing occasionally as her shoulder is bandaged.

Lessard feels the gurney move. The distance between them starts to widen. He wants to call out to her, he wants to catch her attention, but his mouth is dry and his tongue is thick. The best he can manage is a raspy growl.

She looks up. Their eyes lock.

From that moment, he knows.

Fernandez says "Excuse me" to her colleagues.

She frees herself from the grasp of the EMT who's putting the final touches on her bandage.

As she walks away, the EMT follows.

She approaches Lessard at a walking pace. Then, seeing that the gurney is about to be loaded into the ambulance, she speeds up, ignoring the pain that's burning through her.

He opens his eyes as she leans down.

She presses her sweet mouth to his and gently parts his lips with her tongue.

A shiver runs up his spine.

The kiss of the maimed.

The EMT catches up to Fernandez and leads her back to the vehicle where his medical equipment is waiting. Before she turns, she and Lessard gaze at each other, their eyes filled with desire. Neither of them says a word.

As Lessard watches her walk away, he knows he's the luckiest man in the world. He's managed to look death in the face and send it packing with a hearty "Better luck next time." And now a love goddess has descended from the sky to plant a sensual kiss on his lips.

The attendants are about to close the ambulance door when Raymond appears in the open space.

"Hey, Victor." An electric smile is shining on the boy's face.

"Hey, Raymond," Lessard murmurs gravely.

"I just came to say goodbye. I'm going to miss you."

"You're leaving?"

"Yes. I have to get back to Mom and Guy."

Tears moisten the cop's rough cheeks.

"Take care, Raymond. I love you."

"I love you, too, Victor. I'm proud of you. Dad won't bother you anymore."

The little boy skips away, and the night enfolds him in its arms.

The two ambulance attendants exchange looks as their patient converses with an invisible friend, then passes out.

CANTATA IN B-HAPPY

MEMBERS OF THE CHOIR

Laila François

The night I was set free, Jacinthe Taillon's partner Gilles Lemaire brought me to his home, where I had dinner with his wife and seven children.

In the days that followed, everyone was very nice to me — police officers, social workers, even Nigel Williams, who, at Mélanie's request, paid off my debt to Razor without asking anything in return.

I owe a lot to the cop who found me, Victor Lessard.

I stopped by the hospital the other day, to say thanks. While we were talking, we discovered that I've met his son Martin, who works as a sound engineer with some musicians I know.

I'll probably work with Martin myself in a few weeks, when I record demos of my songs.

I'm not walking away from the webcam thing just yet. I need the money, and it'll keep me going until I can find something else. I have no problem getting naked in front of the camera.

Mélanie's coming over later.

We're going to do a session together. Then we'll go for a walk, hang out on Mont-Royal Avenue, step into a few boutiques. I want to get a pair of shoes. Afterward, we'll go say hi to Monsieur Antoine and Felix.

I don't know what to make of everything that happened to me — the way I was abducted and then set free. I've refused to do any interviews on the subject.

Why did David ask Chan Lok Wan to kidnap me? They're not around to explain. But Jacinthe Taillon says David wanted to protect me. There were people around who might have hurt me, the way they hurt Aldéric Dorion, wanting me to lead them to David.

It hardly matters.

All I know is, according to Jacinthe, neither David nor Chan ever meant me any harm.

It breaks my heart to think of all those deaths, especially Father Dorion's. David was the one who introduced me to him. He was a sweet old man.

As for David, I have mixed feelings about his death.

Despite the evidence, I had trouble getting my head around the idea that he was behind all those murders. How could the guy who knew the secrets of my past, the guy who listened as I talked about Pascal Pierre's repeated abuses — how could that guy have managed to hide his true self from me?

Even now, I find myself thinking that it's not all black or white.

I know David had a good side. I saw it. He wasn't just the horrible serial killer that people have been reading about in the papers.

At the same time, I can't pretend that his death is an unbearable loss.

I liked David. I found him attractive. But I'll get over it. I learned a long time ago that I can't let myself be defeated.

I guess that's the one positive thing that came out of being abused by that human filth, my stepfather. I learned the value of hanging on, of never giving up.

Speaking of Pascal Pierre, Jacinthe Taillon tells me HE's been arrested for HIS crimes. She says there's going to be a trial, and it's important that I testify.

It'll be a pleasure.

The world needs to know. And HE needs to be stopped from ever committing crimes again.

. . . .

Whatever happens, I'll keep holding my head high. I'll keep moving forward until my very last breath. All the Pascal Pierres in the world can't stop me.

I'll die at a hundred, in Milan.

Jacinthe Taillon

As I lay in Jerome Baetz's basement, I was scared I was going to die. Baetz was scared, too.

It was a lucky thing that Lessard showed up when he did and put a bullet between Cortiula's eyes.

I'll admit that after everything that happened, I had to rethink my attitude toward Lessard. I'd been unfair to him.

For a long time.

It wasn't easy, but I apologized.

Between Lessard and me, I'd say we pretty much solved the whole case.

I can't deny that Lessard was the one who did most of the heavy lifting. In the space of a few days, he rescued Laila François and stopped David Cortiula, one of the most sadistic killers I've run across in my whole career.

Paul Delaney made Lessard an offer in his hospital room. It's a good offer. I hope he accepts. Of course, that'll depend on his leg.

I should have called for backup before rushing to Baetz's place.

I have a bad habit of believing I can handle everything on my own. When I arrived, Moreno got the jump on me. He'd been watching the access road from the house. Under torture, I told him what I knew.

The sledgehammer did some serious damage to my left leg, but it's healing nicely. The cast will be off in another couple of weeks.

Gilles Lemaire is supposed to pick me up in the next few minutes.

He's the one who wrapped up the Laila François case. Now we're going to a meeting with Church officials at the archdiocese. I don't imagine that very many details of the story will ever come out in the media. Especially now that Cardinal Charles Millot has killed himself.

Pascal Pierre is out on bail.

I've built an airtight case against him.

That son of a bitch is going down.

Victor Lessard

In a few minutes, I'll go outside for the first time since the events that led to David Cortiula's death. Beavis and Butt-Head from Internal Affairs haven't been back since Delaney and Taillon visited my hospital room. These few days of peace have helped my recovery.

As an added bonus, Taillon and I are back on speaking terms.

It's about time.

Marie and the kids came by a few days ago. At one point, I was watching Marie as she typed a text into her phone, and I had a sudden urge to say, "God, you're beautiful."

Not that I have any lingering romantic feelings for her — we're still as divorced as ever — but simply because it's true. When she isn't wearing her serious-businesswoman face (which she does too often), I sometimes see the light in Marie's eyes that made me fall madly in love with her while we were both still children.

That love saved me, by preventing me from going home to be murdered with my mother and brothers. And so, when I look at Marie, I occasionally recall the pivotal role that she's played in my life.

True to form, Martin and Charlotte didn't stop bickering the whole time they were in the hospital room. Martin has moved back into my apartment. After the forensics people were done with the place, it got a thorough cleaning from a company that specializes in that sort of thing. I also asked Martin to throw out my old La-Z-Boy. I've made a promise to myself: when I get home, I'm finally going to sleep in my bed.

Martin mentioned his plans to do some recordings with Laila François. They used to run into each other at the trailer, though they weren't really acquainted. Of course, Martin never watches the news, or he'd have known about Laila's kidnapping long before I found her. Not that he could have helped with the investigation, but it still pisses me off that at eighteen years old, he's too much of a goofball to watch the news and stay abreast of what's going on in the world.

In any case, Laila's clearly a good person. I was glad to be able to talk to her for a few minutes.

Apart from Laila, Marie, and the kids, I've had plenty of other visitors.

Simone Fortin came by with Laurent and little Mathilde; Antoine Chambord stopped in with young Felix. When Elaine Segato showed up, she brought an armful of magazines. Even Albert Corneau made an appearance, carrying an enormous bouquet of flowers. Ted wasn't well enough to join him, but we made a pact to get together for dinner as soon as my strength returns.

And then there's my sister, my sweet Valérie, who's ignored my orders and spent several afternoons at my bedside. She's brightened my days and made me laugh out loud. And she's been there to comfort me when I couldn't hold back the tears.

It's been an enormous blessing to have all these shining people around me.

After I discovered that Faizan was being treated at this hospital, I got one of the villainous nurses to push my wheelchair to the ICU so I could pay the boy a visit. His condition was touch-and-go for a while, but he's expected to make a full recovery.

His courage has given me the strength to continue.

. . .

On the career front, I'm not sure what the future holds.

I'll be sitting down with Tanguay next week. The forensics people have concluded beyond any doubt that I had nothing to do with Viviane Gray's murder. Not that anyone ever thought otherwise. But a lot of people got killed while I was on the run, and things like that tend to affect a cop's career file. On the other hand, there are plenty of mitigating factors working in my favour. Also, knowing that senior members of the clergy were implicated in the case, the top brass at police headquarters are doing whatever they can to keep the matter quiet.

Besides, I saved Jerome Baetz from a gruesome death, didn't I?

The priest has disappeared.

What can I say?

After the axe hit my leg, I lost consciousness. I don't remember anything else until the moment I woke up outside the house, lying on a gurney. I've since learned that the backup units found no trace of the priest or his video equipment. Since I'm the only person who actually saw his face, I helped the police artist draw up a composite sketch that's been transmitted to Interpol.

But I'm not getting my hopes up.

He's the kind of person who knows how to land on his feet.

He'll lie low for a while, then resurface under a new identity.

Bastards like him almost always get away.

I've had a few conversations with Sylvain Marchand about the murder of Sandrine Pedneault-King and the pedophile ring that Richard Sandoval and Jean-Guy Applebaum were part of. Investigators searched the room in which the two monsters imprisoned, raped, and killed the young girl. The evidence that was gathered has led Marchand and his team to conclude with certainty that no one else participated in the atrocities that were committed against the child.

But that same evidence has led to seventeen arrests, and to the dismantling of the pedophile ring that was sharing files through an encrypted website — the website that I discovered when I descended into the chamber of horrors created by Sandoval and Applebaum.

Sandrine's family is still living in anguish. Her body hasn't been found. But I don't think they'll have to wait much longer. Needless to say, the media are all over the story. The twenty-four-hour news channels have been covering it continuously for days now.

As far as I'm concerned, that case is closed.

Marchand and his team will see it through.

Pascal Pierre was released on bail.

I heard that a few hours after his release, he was assaulted in the parking lot of a shopping centre. Two masked men attacked and drugged him. When he woke up, he had no visible injuries, but he was in excruciating pain. He went to a hospital emergency room, where it took doctors several hours to extract the cucumber that had been jammed up his rectum.

The assault is similar to an incident that Robert Kennedy described during the years when he was battling the American mafia in the 1950s. A union organizer who had defied the mob was punished with the forcible insertion of a cucumber into his posterior.

The man was warned that if he didn't back down, it would be a watermelon next time.

I don't know if Pascal Pierre received the same kind of warning, but I can't help suspecting that Jacinthe Taillon had something to do with the attack.

And what about David Cortiula?

Although he's not available for questioning, I've done my best to put the pieces together. Father Dorion's DVD, which Taillon played for me, has been very helpful in that regard.

As far as I'm concerned, Cortiula was nothing more than a serial killer. According to the priest, Cortiula had a gift. But I don't buy that for a second.

The most I'm prepared to concede is that the young son of a bitch had a talent for hypnosis — the power of suggestion. But I'm not even sure about that. Not after talking to a professional hypnotist with whom I've worked in the past.

While this professional didn't absolutely rule out the possibility, he made it clear to me that using hypnosis to make someone commit suicide or murder would be very unlikely.

We're all free to draw our own conclusions. Personally, if I have to choose between (A) the devil, and (B) hypnosis, to explain the deaths caused by David Cortiula, I'm definitely going with (B). The human brain is a complex, fascinating mechanism that most of us use at only 10 percent of its capacity. Maybe Cortiula found a way to surpass that limit and tap into abilities that most of us don't have access to.

For that matter, I find myself wondering whether we even need to go down that road.

Since Cortiula wore gloves, who's to say he didn't wield the murder weapon himself? Wasn't he the one who used an axe to kill the pimp, and to wound John Cook's shoulder? Maybe the priest and his powerful allies helped Cortiula to falsify the crime scenes. Those same allies had impressive tools at their disposal — tools that enabled them to plant Viviane Gray's body in my apartment, and to put my fingerprints on a weapon that I never touched in my life. Elizabeth Munson's prints were found on the axe handle, but did she actually hold the weapon? Or were her prints simply placed there to create the impression that she had struck her husband in the shoulder?

The only way to answer these questions would be to get our hands on the priest's video recordings. But those have vanished, along with the priest himself.

One thing we do know from the autopsy results is that Cortiula regularly submitted himself to floggings administered by his friend Chan Lok Wan. As Felix and the goth secretary both noted, Cortiula's back was criss-crossed with welts and scars resulting from numerous strokes of the whip.

Some aspects of the case still puzzle me. Is it significant, for instance, that under Cortiula's influence, John Cook cut out his tongue and Richard Sandoval gouged out his eyes? As far as I can tell, there's no way to answer that question conclusively.

Another secret that David Cortiula carried to the grave.

. . .

And what about the flies?

I've had plenty of time to mull that one over as I lay in my hospital bed. Two factors have convinced me that the flies were brought in.

First, during Elaine Segato's hospital visit, she repeated what she'd told me before — that it would be easy and inexpensive to raise a large number of flies using simple methods.

Second, while going through Cortiula's apartment in the wake of his death, Pearson and the forensics team found a deed to a woodlot in the Laurentians that Cortiula purchased five years ago. There was no house on the property, but at the end of a dirt path, in a secluded corner of the lot, police searchers came across a shack teeming with flies. Inside the shack, plastic bins contained half-consumed pieces of meat, and living flies were found in a propane-fuelled refrigerator.

An on-site analysis revealed that Cortiula had been raising flies in the shack. With ample food, the insects had multiplied in abundance. Tire tracks on the dirt path matched the treads from an old pickup truck registered in Cortiula's name. The truck itself was found near Jerome Baetz's house. Large sacks made of mosquito netting were found inside the house and in the truck. From all appearances, Cortiula had used these sacks to transport flies to the scenes of his crimes.

Then there's the information that I got from Carol Langelier, the retired cop in Val-d'Or.

While still a boy, Cortiula had spent several days locked in a house with his mother's corpse. When the police showed up, the place was swarming with flies. I'm no shrink, but it seems obvious to me that a childhood experience like that would leave deep scars.

Seen in that context, releasing flies into his victims' homes might have created a psychological resonance for Cortiula, a link with the days he spent watching over his mother's dead body.

. . .

One of the doctors has given me a prescription for antidepressants.

I have to admit that the last few days have done me a lot of good. I feel better today than I did in the heat of the action.

Above all, I'm feeling positively giddy about getting discharged from the hospital.

A nurse comes in and helps me get dressed.

I haven't told anyone about my hallucinations. There haven't been any more of them since the evening I killed Cortiula. I suppose that's a good sign.

Still, I miss Raymond.

I thank the nurse. As we leave, she's preparing the room for the next patient.

We move along the corridors in silence.

We burst out into the opalescent air, like two splatters on the pavement.

The sun's rays are bouncing off buildings and passing cars.

The birds are serenading us with their cantata in B-happy.

As she pushes my wheelchair, Nadja Fernandez murmurs something in my ear.

My heart skips a beat. I promise myself that as soon as my leg is strong enough, I'll take her for a moonlit stroll on Mount Royal.

A carpet of stars is stretching out before my eyes.

Felix

Dear stupid diary,

It's more fun to say "see ya later" than "goodbye." So that's what I'm going to say to you, the way hockey players do when they leave the ice at the end of the season. Not goodbye. See ya later. The truth is, now that I can talk again, writing has gotten kind of boring. I'm tired of carrying my chalkboard around. Also, Monsieur Antoine smiles when he hears me talk, and I like to see him smile. He may not have many years of smiling left before he goes to the big trailer in the sky.

I just want to say one thing before I go. I know the guy who saved me with the Big Split, the guy who kidnapped Laila — that guy is dead. I keep calling him "the guy," but his name is David. That's what Laila used to call him whenever she talked about him with the old priest.

Right after the Big Split, there was a policeman — not Monsieur Antoine's friend Victor, another policeman — who showed me a bunch of pictures of men I didn't know, and asked if any of them were the guy who hit the boss with the axe. I didn't say a word about David, even though the scars on his back made him look weird and scary. I didn't want to get him in trouble after he had saved my skin.

And I didn't say anything to Laila when I saw her hanging around the trailer with David. By then, the Big Split had happened a while ago, but I remembered that David had saved me when the boss was messing up the wall with my head.

I know what you're thinking, stupid diary. You're thinking that the Big Split and those weird scars should have made me realize that David had some loose screws between his ears, and I should have said something.

Well, here's what I'm thinking, stupid diary. I'm thinking that when a guy saves you, even if he does it with an axe, ratting him out isn't very nice. I'm also thinking that if you take a minute to look around this messed-up world, you'll see that there are more loose screws between more ears than you could ever count. So maybe pointing fingers isn't such a great idea.

Okay, stupid diary. I've said everything I wanted to say. End of story.

But don't be sad. Before you know it, there'll more stories. There always are.

So. Not goodbye. See ya later.

AUTHOR'S NOTE

Dear Readers,

In the author's note that accompanied *Without Blood*, I invited you to send along your impressions of the book. Thank you for the very, very numerous emails you've sent. Your messages of affection and encouragement have touched me, and helped me to persevere in moments of doubt. I made a promise to answer all your emails. As of the moment you're reading these words, I've kept my promise, though in some cases it's taken several months. Please don't hold back. Keep getting in touch! You'll find an email address where you can reach me, as well as a link to my Facebook page, on my website: www.michaudmartin.com.

   See you soon!

   And thank you for doing me the honour of reading my books.

THANKS

To my editor, Ingrid Remazeilles, for imposing strict delivery deadlines while giving me absolute creative freedom, and never looking over my shoulder. It's an ever-renewed pleasure to work with you, EHP!

To Alain Delorme, president of Goélette, and the whole team, for your trust, your support, and your devotion. A particular shout-out to Émilie and Katia, who stayed the course even in the darkest hours, when the devil was corrupting files ...

To my publicist, Judith Landry, for the superb promotional campaign on *Il ne faut pas parler dans l'ascenseur*.

To Patricia Juste and Geneviève Rouleau, for generously lending me their proofreading skills.

To Constable Geneviève Gonthier of the Montreal Police, for her invaluable advice on "police stuff," and likewise to Marjolaine Giroux, entomologist at the Insectarium, for her information about flies. Like any novel, this one takes some liberties with the facts in the service of the story. I won't enumerate those liberties here. Suffice it to say that any errors or imprecisions in the book are not attributable to Geneviève or Marjolaine, but to myself alone.

To my daughter, Gabrielle, who, at the table one day, while playing word games, spontaneously came up with an extraordinary sentence, which she was good enough to lend me: "I'll die at a hundred, in Milan." I hope it comes true, sweetheart.

To my son, Antoine, who occasionally lets me beat him at hockey on the PS3 (even though I keep telling him he plays like a wimp).

To my friend Marc Bernard, who, one summer evening, listened to my ravings, and even pressed me for more details, as I set out the broad strokes of this novel.

To my family, for always being there.

To my friends, for the same reason.

To Geneviève, my love, for your patience, your empathy, your encouragement, your attentiveness ... for all of that and much more, but also for nothing. For being you ...

To the city of Montreal for being at once so ugly and so beautiful, so perfectly imperfect.

To Sigur Rós, Alexandre Désilets, Vitalic, Karkwa, Arcade Fire, Jeff Buckley (the Master), David Guetta, Charlie Winston, Hôtel Morphée, Death Cab for Cutie, Portishead, Indochine, Jérôme Minière, TV on the Radio, Malajube, and Kate Havnevik, for the moods and the inspiration.

To the Montreal Canadiens, for making my heart beat faster (now and then) and for giving me the chance to razz my friends on Facebook (I'm looking at you, evil Élise!).

To the Second Cup on Monkland Avenue, which became my hangout for much of the time I spent writing this novel.

To the young Martin Michaud, who, almost fifteen years ago, had the slightly crazy dream of becoming a writer.

To Victor Lessard for the sleepless nights.

ABOUT THE AUTHOR

Martin Michaud is a bestselling author, screenwriter, musician, and former lawyer. His critically acclaimed Victor Lessard series has won numerous awards, including the CWC Award of Excellence and the Prix Saint-Pacôme for Crime Fiction, and is the basis for the award-winning French-language TV series Victor Lessard. He lives in Montreal.